ABOUT THE AUTHOR

When *USA Today* bestselling author Alissa Callen isn't writing, she plays traffic controller to four children, three dogs, two horses and one renegade cow who believes the grass is greener on the other side of the fence. After a childhood spent chasing sheep on the family farm, Alissa has always been drawn to remote areas and small towns, even when residing overseas. She is partial to autumn colours, snowy peaks and historic homesteads and will drive hours to see an open garden. Once a teacher and a counsellor, she remains interested in the life journeys that people take. She draws inspiration from the countryside around her, whether it be the brown snake at her back door or the resilience of bush communities in times of drought or flood. Her books are characteristically heartwarming, authentic and character driven. Alissa lives on a small slice of rural Australia in central western NSW.

Also by Alissa Callen

The Bundilla Series
Snowy Mountains Daughter

The Woodlea Series
The Long Paddock
The Red Dirt Road
The Round Yard
The Boundary Fence

Snowy Mountains Cattleman

Snowy Mountains Cattleman

ALISSA CALLEN

mira

First Published 2022
First Australian Paperback Edition 2022
ISBN 9781867215837

SNOWY MOUNTAINS CATTLEMAN
© 2022 by Alissa Callen
Australian Copyright 2022
New Zealand Copyright 2022

Published by
Mira
An imprint of Harlequin Enterprises (Australia) Pty Limited (ABN 47 001 180 918),
a subsidiary of HarperCollins Publishers Australia Pty Limited (ABN 36 009 913 517)
Level 13, 201 Elizabeth St
SYDNEY NSW 2000
AUSTRALIA

® and TM (apart from those relating to FSC®) are trademarks of Harlequin
Enterprises (Australia) Pty Limited or its corporate affiliates. Trademarks indicated
with ® are registered in Australia, New Zealand and in other countries.

A catalogue record for this book is available from the National Library of Australia
www.librariesaustralia.nla.gov.au

Printed and bound in Australia by McPherson's Printing Group

FSC
www.fsc.org

MIX
Paper from
responsible sources
FSC® C001695

To Luke

CHAPTER
1

Grace Davenport had two choices, but she wasn't ready to choose either.

She eased her foot off the accelerator to buy time as the road she'd been on since dawn climbed the sharp incline of a hill. When her car reached the spot where the black bitumen curved over the crest, there could be no turning back.

In her rear-view mirror she caught a last glimpse of the rural town she'd driven through nestled on the edge of the treeless Monaro plain. It didn't matter if her car held some of her most precious possessions, that her Sydney apartment was rented or that a colleague was running her interior stylist business, a single U-turn would send her back through Cooma's wide main street, then on to Canberra and finally home.

Her hand left the steering wheel to hover over the indicator so she could pull over. *Home.* The pitch in her stomach reminded her she no longer had such a place. The parents she'd loved were gone. Her every dream had been blown away by the wind that had scattered their ashes over the pale sand of their favourite beach. First kidney cancer had stolen her mother, and then her father's grief had triggered a heart attack. All it had taken was seven days to dismantle a close-knit family and a lifetime of happiness.

Grace secured her hand back around the steering wheel. She'd driven this road on purpose and the hill crest she'd been waiting for was seconds away. It was time. She had to make a decision: return to the world she knew or drive forwards into the unknown.

Chest tight, she held her breath as her car topped the rise. Everything seemed to still. There was no grief, no loss, just the first look at a distant vista of rugged peaks. Last winter when she'd made this drive with her parents the Snowy Mountains had worn a mantle of pristine snow. Now they were bathed in golden sunlight. Serene, rugged and immovable, they called to her.

Without thought, she pressed her foot on the accelerator and sped down the hill. It was impossible to reclaim what she'd lost, but she could do all that she could to live the life that had been cut short for her parents. As much as her mother and father had enjoyed the beach house she'd bought for them, they'd planned to spend their twilight years in a small town that reminded them of their English village childhoods. She scanned the mountains that now appeared a hazy blue green. On the far-off western slopes, they'd found the perfect place—a little book town called Bundilla.

She settled deeper into her seat and, keeping her eyes on the peaks, readied herself for a long and winding drive. Turning back was no longer an option.

Hours later, with only a brief stop for fuel, Grace passed the WELCOME TO BUNDILLA sign. Despite the ache in her lower back and a non-negotiable need for solitude, her journey wasn't over. She had keys, food and wine to collect, in that order.

A dust-covered white ute approached, the grey-haired male driver lifting a hand in greeting. Grace hesitated and the car passed before she could do the same. On her last visit she'd discovered that the locals waved to everyone, even out-of-towners. While her parents had returned such gestures with enthusiasm, she hadn't been as comfortable. Even when she wasn't preoccupied with work, social skills weren't exactly her forte.

She had no problem conversing about fabric textures and what rugs might suit what hardwood floor, but when it came to casual chitchat, or answering questions about herself, she always felt uneasy. She took the first turn right and banished the schoolyard memories of her English accent being mocked and the taunts about being a whingeing Pom.

A graceful historic building with columns appeared on her left. The old post office was a landmark she remembered along with the red brick clock tower that she could see at the end of the street. Last winter the branches of the Manchurian pears that ran along the footpaths had been bare. Now their summer-green leaves waved in the breeze as if in welcome.

She slowed as she passed the vintage charity shop that she'd spent hours rummaging through. Bundilla also had a regular charity shop with clothes and toys but this one specialised in collectibles and bric-a-brac with all proceeds going to the local hospital. Tucked away in a corner she'd found a perfect duck-egg blue lamp for a living room she'd been styling. Not that she'd been decorating anything of late. It was an effort to even match her socks.

The GPS indicated that she'd soon arrive at the real estate office and she stopped to let two girls cross the road. The younger sister wore a white dress with pink-and-brown cowgirl boots, and she skipped as she pointed towards the park that formed a cool oasis beside the library. The spring in the child's step only magnified Grace's bone-deep weariness. She ignored the uncertainty that would cause her to second-guess her decision to leave the city and instead focused on finding a parking space.

While the street had plenty of empty car spots, the ones directly in front of the real estate office were occupied. A group of three men and one woman chatting outside the building were most likely the owners of the row of utes and four-wheel drives. A tan-and-black kelpie wearing a blue collar with gold lettering sat beside a farmer who wore a wide-brimmed hat. She'd learnt the name of the working dog breed on her previous trip.

Grace parked and left her car to the sound of deep masculine laughter as the local wearing a blue shirt hugged the brunette beside him. While Grace couldn't see their faces, the way the woman embraced him and then kept her arm around his waist spoke of affection and familiarity. Grace looked away, blanking out the long-buried yearning to mean something to someone.

Her lacklustre small talk wasn't the only reason why she was single. Her English parents had sacrificed everything to give her a better life in Australia. She'd worked late nights, weekends and holidays to build her career so she could provide them with everything they'd gone without. Loneliness had been a small price to pay for making the people she loved happy.

She glanced at the man whose easy laughter had made her long to do something spontaneous and out of character like take a day off or dance in the rain. His hair was a sun-streaked tawny brown and his broad shoulders stretched the cotton of his blue shirt that hung loose over faded jeans. He half turned and she caught a glimpse of a tanned, chiselled profile. She again looked away.

Just as well she'd come to Bundilla to rebuild her life and not to socialise. She was far from an expert, but men who looked as good as he did usually had an ego to match. Her best friend, Aubrey, was always telling her she'd catch more bees with honey than vinegar. Not that she was ever rude, but flattery, let alone flirting, wasn't something she'd ever fully understood or seen the point of. She'd once spent two hours of her life that she'd never get back listening to an investment banker run her through his share portfolio over dinner. She didn't have time to waste on shallow conversations, no matter how gorgeous a guy might be.

The local with the felt hat grinned as he slapped the back of the man she'd heard laugh before striding away. The woman and her remaining two companions walked along the street before stopping outside a double-storey pub trimmed in grey wrought iron. The man in the blue shirt held the door open for the others to enter. Instead of following, he waited as if giving the kelpie who had accompanied them time to decide if he would too head inside. As she drew closer, a waft of beer and an air-conditioned breeze washed over her. For a second, she thought the local stared in her direction, but then the dog and the man disappeared into The Bushranger.

Thankful that she now had the footpath to herself, Grace lowered her tight shoulders. *Keys, food, wine,* she reminded herself as her steps dragged. The air pressing against her skin was again warm and she lifted her heavy hair from her nape. If this was a taste of a mountain summer, she'd need a haircut, something that hadn't been a priority for the year she'd been caring for her mother. She'd also need a cooler outfit than the black long-sleeved top and skinny jeans that had become her go-to clothes.

To her relief, the visit to the real estate office to collect her cottage keys took less than five minutes. The helpful and chatty receptionist didn't expect Grace to reply much in return and she was soon back in the sunshine. She breathed in the aroma of coffee coming from somewhere along the main street and added caffeine to the top of her to-do list. But instead of turning to go in search of the café, she suddenly stopped. Was that a kelpie sitting near her car?

The dog wagged his tail. His blue and gold collar looked familiar and she glanced towards the pub to check whether the locals she'd seen him with earlier were around. But apart from two women strolling towards her with sleek grey bobs wearing similar outfits of black trousers and white shirts, there were no other pedestrians.

Grace stared at the kelpie but didn't move closer. She'd had a sweet chocolate labrador called Cocoa growing up but as an adult her dog-whispering skills were a little rusty.

The kelpie's tail again thumped. The gold letters on his collar spelled out the name Bundy. One thing that had changed in the small town was that the water tower now sported a mural. While she hadn't paid the painting more than a fleeting glance as she'd driven past—she'd been too tired—she had a feeling that a kelpie with a collar like this one had been part of the design.

An impression confirmed when a quiet voice said beside her, 'You might recognise Bundy from the mural.'

Grace turned to the two women who she could now see had to be identical twins. Neither wore a smile but their eyes were clear and kind. As for the seriousness of their stony faces, she wasn't intimidated. She saw a similar expression in the mirror every morning.

She nodded.

The sister whose sleek grey bob was a little longer in length studied her before she spoke. 'Staying in Bundilla long?'

Grace took her time to answer. She wasn't used to strangers being interested in her business, but there was something about the elderly woman's steady stare that reassured her the question had only been asked with the best of intentions. 'How did you know I wasn't passing through?'

A brief smile tilted the other twin's lips. 'Just like how Bundy here knows you're staying at least two nights.' She glanced at the keys Grace held. 'All of the holiday rentals have a minimum two-night stay.'

Grace didn't immediately answer. Her mother had always said nothing much was missed in a small town. It was this sense of community and kinship that her parents had wished to return to.

She glanced at the kelpie who continued to watch her. 'Why would Bundy be interested in how long I'm staying?'

The sisters swapped a quick look before the sibling with the shorter bob replied. 'Bundy's a local legend. He calls the town home and spends his time with whoever he pleases.'

The second sister gestured towards the kelpie. 'By the way he's sitting next to your car, you're the one he wants to tag along with next.'

Grace fought a frown. She had no proper home to take the kelpie to, let alone any food for either of them. Not to mention what would the dog do with her when she wasn't intending to leave her cottage?

The older woman continued. 'I'm Millicent and this is my sister, Beatrice. Bundy's stayed with us many times and we can assure you he's no trouble.'

'He was with a group of locals earlier …'

Beatrice nodded. 'Now he's with you.'

Grace met her gaze. 'He'll be much happier with someone else.'

They all looked across at the kelpie, who had his amber stare fixed on Grace.

Millicent said softly, 'He doesn't want to go with anyone else.'

'If you call into the grocery or rural store,' added Beatrice, her tone gentle, 'they'll give you a bag of the dogfood he likes.'

As if Bundy coming with her was a foregone conclusion, each sister gave her a nod and continued on their way.

Grace narrowed her eyes at the kelpie. 'Really?'

Bundy's doggy grin didn't waver.

'I don't even know if the cottage has power. There's also bound to be rats.'

The kelpie left the footpath to stand beside her passenger-side door.

Grace shook her head at her poor word choice. No doubt Bundy would consider vermin in the roof a good thing.

Surely someone would come over to say what a bad idea this was? But there was no one else in sight.

She rubbed her tight forehead before moving to clear room on the cluttered back seat for the dog to sit. He jumped straight into the car. She slowly closed the door.

That morning, she might have had two choices. Now she had none. In under three minutes she'd become the temporary custodian of Bundilla's living kelpie treasure.

∝

Rowan Parker had been waiting all his life to become a third wheel.

He looked across the pub table in the outdoor beer garden to where his younger sister and best mate sat close together and didn't try to hide his grin. Clancy and Heath might have just come off a long-haul flight from Paris but neither looked jet-lagged.

Clancy, with her red-brown hair and sweet smile, had always drawn stares. But now it was as though she was lit from within. A table to their left filled with tradies in their fluoro work gear had been sneaking frequent glances. He didn't blame them. His sister radiated joy and happiness.

He kept his smile in place even though the contentment within him faded. When they'd lost their parents four years ago after their cruise boat capsized in a flooded Budapest river, Clancy hadn't appeared so radiant. He lifted his beer and took a long swallow. The knowledge that he hadn't been there for her hadn't lost any of its power. He'd been such a fool.

He realised too late that Heath's blue gaze was examining his face. Even before Heath had left to paint a mural on a German skyscraper six weeks ago, he'd been giving him concerned looks.

Rowan forced a smile and made sure his tension didn't show in his voice. 'You have no idea how glad I am you're both home. Every work boot I own is either buried or in pieces.'

Clancy laughed. 'I thought the hug you gave me outside was because you were happy to see me. You just want me to take you shopping.'

Rowan grimaced. He'd rather get bucked off his cantankerous stockhorse than step inside a store.

Clancy patted his arm. 'Monet will soon calm down and stop stealing your shoes. Look at Primrose.'

Rowan raised both brows. There was no hope for Heath's hyperactive kelpie puppy if Primrose was Clancy's measure of a quiet dog. The young golden retriever might technically be out of the puppy phase, but he had no doubt she was the instigator behind the seek-and-destroy mission waged on his wardrobe the second his sister had left.

It wasn't only new boots he needed; his untucked shirt was hiding a rip across the backside of his now only pair of jeans. Just as well Clancy had only been gone three weeks.

Heath chuckled. 'Sorry, Clance, I'm with Rowan on that one.'

Clancy's eyes grew dreamy. 'I can't wait to see all their doggy faces. I loved walking in the Swiss Alps but I've missed them so much.'

Clancy had always been a small-town girl. There was no place she'd rather be than running her peony flower farm and riding in the high country she loved. Now she and Heath were finally together she was discovering a world outside of Bundilla, but their family farm of Ashcroft would always be her, and now Heath's, home. Rowan's grip tightened on his beer. A home he'd left his sister to run alone when she'd been vulnerable, all because he'd allowed a woman's sensual beauty to blind him to who she really was. He avoided Heath's gaze as his best mate again studied him.

The buzzer at the centre of their table beeped and flashed red to indicate that their lunch was ready.

Heath clasped his shoulder as they went to collect their counter meals. 'Let me know when you're heading out on Goliath. I'll come too.'

Rowan nodded. A ride into the granite ridges where the wind carried away all regret sounded pretty good right now. He glanced at the front door as they passed. He wasn't usually so on edge but earlier his testosterone had had a moment that he'd vowed to never have again.

When he'd held the door open for Bundy, a woman on the street dressed in black had caught his attention. All he'd glimpsed was a cloud of long dark hair, pale skin, large eyes and an unsmiling mouth, but that had been enough. The woman had made his blood quicken and his lungs still.

He took his time to reach for his plate of chicken schnitzel that sat on the counter. No longer did he have any appetite. After he'd lost his head over Eloise he'd vowed to never react on a purely physical level to anyone again.

This time when he passed the pub door on the way to his table, he looked straight ahead. Acting on impulse and not taking the time to think through consequences were things he refused to do anymore. He owed it to Clancy, Heath, and all the others he'd let down when consumed with Eloise and then again when he'd fled overseas to get himself together.

Even though he'd dodged a bullet when Eloise had run off with a cashed-up newcomer to town, it had taken time to work through his self-loathing at being so easily fooled. He'd also needed to admit that since his parents had died, chasing an adrenaline rush had been less about the thrill and more about escaping his grief.

He returned to his seat. The only thing he could be grateful for was that the woman he'd seen would be a tourist travelling through town. He wouldn't have forgotten if their paths had crossed before. His reaction and lapse in control was simply a warning that he had more work to do on becoming a new and improved version of himself. He concentrated on listening to Clancy and Heath's travel anecdotes.

When they'd finished their meals, Clancy glanced around the beer garden. 'Where did Bundy go?'

Rowan looked past her shoulder to where he'd last seen the kelpie. 'He was over at the corner table with Ned so he probably followed him out.'

Ned was a family friend who helped Heath's mother run the family property of Hawks Ridge whenever Heath was away painting murals.

Heath's attention didn't leave Rowan. 'Ned said Bundy's spent some time with you?'

'He did but was waiting on the back of my ute this morning to come to town.'

Clancy smiled as she came to her feet. 'He must have known you were meeting us for lunch.'

Rowan also left his seat. Heath's stare was a little too intent as he finished his beer. Many locals believed that Bundy had a sixth sense. It wasn't unusual for him to turn up wherever he was needed. Over the years he'd kept widows company, sat by the beds of ill children and accompanied a bride who'd lost her father down the aisle. 'No doubt.'

In his case he was sure Bundy only stayed to help him with the cattle work that he'd been doing this past week to get ready for when he'd be working on his next stonemason project. Ashcroft no longer had any working dogs. It had been on Rowan's mind to get a pup to train but after babysitting Monet and Primrose maybe it was an adult dog he needed.

After more hugs were exchanged, Rowan left Clancy and Heath and headed for the grocery store. Now that they were home they'd live in the main farmhouse while he'd move back into the renovated coach house at the end of the garden. He'd left the homestead fridge fully stocked but the fridge over at his place was empty.

The sun warm on his shoulders, Rowan strolled along the main street, his tension ebbing. A white sedan honked its horn as it drove past. He waved at the identical occupants. The sisters were on their way out of town. As he walked by a bright green car his steps quickened.

The colourful vehicle belonged to Cynthia Herbert, the town's equally flamboyant and notorious matchmaker. Except ever since her teenage daughter had turned the tables on her and set her up with the town's longest-serving bachelor, Dan, Cynthia had less time for meddling. But that didn't mean he could relax whenever he came to town.

Conscious of someone watching him through the front window of the nearby gift shop, Rowan crossed the street. He needed to ask Clancy for a list of who was in the quilting club so he'd know who to be wary of. The rumours of the quilting group taking over Cynthia's matchmaking mantle were most likely true. There were only a handful of unattached men in town, and it wasn't his imagination that since he'd returned from overseas, not only did more people smile at him, they were also more interested in his private life. It wouldn't be concerning if almost every person who waylaid him for a chat wasn't female.

He'd almost reached the grocery store when his mobile rang. The name of a local deer farmer who had a talent for turning rusted metal into lifelike sculptures filled the screen. Taite too was single and determined to remain that way.

'Hi,' Rowan said, jogging the last few paces to the grocery store so he could duck inside the sliding door. Mrs Wright had exited the gift shop and now stood on the footpath looking up and down the street.

'You sound out of breath,' Taite said, tone hopeful.

Taite loved his rugby and was always trying to recruit Rowan for a gym session or run even though it was the off-season. Thanks to a stress fracture of his left leg last spring while skiing in France, he had a legitimate excuse to not put his body on the line. No one could keep up with Taite's agility or strength. A *simple* jog would probably lead to heart failure.

'Don't get too excited. Desperate times call for desperate measures.' Rowan rubbed at the dull ache in his leg. 'I'm not out of breath. I'm as fit as a mallee bull.'

'That would be a lame mallee bull.' Taite chuckled. 'The only thing to get you past a walk is either being chased by Mrs Moore's goose or Mrs Moore herself.'

Rowan peered through the glass door. 'It's Mrs Wright.'

'You wonder why I run. It's impossible to ask a moving target to dinner.'

'I might join you.'

'Anytime. I've been going out on Overflow Road.'

Rowan silenced his groan as the doors opened for two teenage girls to walk through. Overflow Road was gravel and all uphill. 'Actually, I'll take my chances with the quilting ladies.'

'You always were a risk-taker.'

When the teenagers shot him flirty looks as they passed, he turned to study the community noticeboard on the back wall that advertised the upcoming Bundilla summer book festival. He was far too old for either of them.

'Trust me, not anymore.'

'I can't tempt you into going mountain biking this weekend at Thredbo?'

Rowan went to say yes and then reconsidered. His leg wasn't up to it plus he was supposed to have retired from thrill-seeking. 'Thanks, but I've got farm work to do before I start on the old Russell mansion next week.'

'Good luck. That place will be a big job. Let me know if you change your mind about the run or mountain biking.'

'Will do.'

Rowan ended the call and, not bothering with a basket, strode along the grocery store aisles. With his arms full of items, he made a beeline for an empty checkout. Heels had clicked on the floor behind him as he'd collected a bottle of milk and he wasn't hanging around to see who it was.

Once outside, he didn't slow his pace as he strode along to where he'd left his dark merlot-red Land Cruiser parked outside the real estate office. That would teach him not to buy a white vehicle so that he blended in with just about every other Bundilla car. Everyone knew when he was in town.

After he'd loaded his grocery bag into the passenger seat he scanned the street for any glimpse of Bundy. As chaotic as it had been having him to stay the past week—the kelpie, Monet and Primrose had wrestled continuously—he now missed having Bundy by his side. Wherever he had moved on to next he hoped it wouldn't be long until he saw him again.

Instead of driving the regular way home, Rowan took the road that carried him over one of the wooden bridges that crisscrossed the flood plain. He'd do a drive by the Russell place. A heavy chain and padlock would secure the front gate shut but he'd be able to see from the driveway if the left-side wall had crumbled any further since his last inspection.

Not that he knew exactly when he'd be starting the restoration. The new owner hadn't replied to his last email, which wasn't out of the ordinary. She'd simply be busy. From the woman's succinct messages he knew nothing more about her except she'd purchased the derelict mansion sight unseen. Her plan was to focus on the stonework first before she brought in a builder. She obviously wasn't in any rush to make the place liveable.

The ute indicator sounded as he took the next turn left to where the valley floor had given way to the gentle undulation of foothills that stretched into granite peaks. A buzz of anticipation filled him. While he was foremost a cattleman, there was no doubt the DNA of a distant Scottish stonemason ran through his veins.

For years the mysterious mansion had fascinated him. Not because it was built of bluestone quarried from a nearby hillside, or because it was said to be both haunted and cursed as none of the last generation had married. His interest had been piqued because whenever he'd been inside something about the layout had felt off and had niggled at him.

Through the trees he made out the angular shapes of chimneys and the rusted planes of a vast roofline. When he reached the usually locked entryway, the gate was open and the chain missing. Without slowing, he continued towards the house to follow the tyre tracks imprinted in the dust. Not only had someone disregarded the large NO TRESPASSING sign that the new owner had organised to be put on the fence, but they'd cut the padlock and stolen the chain. He'd make sure whoever the culprit was, they weren't intent on doing any harm. The old house had already been damaged enough.

When black flashed in his peripheral vison, he didn't think anything of it. Crows liked the abandoned building as much as teenagers did at Halloween or whenever there was a full moon. But no sooner did he register that the shape had legs, he noted an unfamiliar car over near a jacaranda tree to his left.

He parked beside the vehicle. He had no doubt the dog he'd seen was Bundy. He also had no doubt the car beside him wasn't local. The sticker on the back windscreen displayed the name of a Sydney car dealership. He left his driver's seat and walked around to the front of the mansion to meet Bundy as he bounded through the overgrown garden towards him.

'Hi, mate.' Rowan ruffled the kelpie's neck. 'I'm happy to see you too.'

He glanced at the corner of the house where he'd first glimpsed Bundy. He wasn't superstitious but he had a bad feeling about who the kelpie had accompanied here. Bundy turned to look in the same direction, his wagging tail thumping Rowan's leg.

Even before his brain fully catalogued the details of the figure who rounded the house corner, his gut knew it was the woman he'd seen earlier. If Bundy was with her, she also wasn't passing through; she'd have a holiday rental nearby.

He locked his shoulders and his resolve. This time he wasn't reacting to her with anything but mild and curious interest. No matter if every step that brought her closer reinforced how stunning she was.

The stranger wore no makeup and in the full daylight her flawless skin was pale and smooth. In contrast, her windblown hair was a messy and rich brown that spilled over her shoulders. But it was her mouth that he had trouble looking away from. The longer he stared at the sombre curve the more he wanted to make her smile.

The woman stopped a body length away. While her expression was unreadable, just like with the high-country brumbies he sensed an ingrained caution and wariness. But when her chin tilted and her cool hazel gaze met his, any impression of vulnerability vanished.

'Afternoon,' she said, her voice as chilly as the snow that capped the winter mountain peaks.

Rowan grinned. 'Afternoon.' He couldn't have asked for a more perfect reaction. Whatever attraction he felt towards her was one-sided. The reminder he wasn't irresistible would do his male ego good. 'Can I help you?'

She shook her head as she lifted a hand to brush her tousled hair away from her cheek.

When the silence lengthened, he dipped his head towards the mansion, not hiding his reaction to the graffiti or broken windows. He hated seeing the once stately house in such disrepair. 'This is private property. You can understand why the owner isn't keen on people trespassing.'

When his attention returned to the woman, her eyes had widened. But when she turned to study the vandalised front facade all he could view was her profile.

The seconds stretched before she replied. 'It is a shame there's been so much damage.' The subtle lilt of an English accent softened her voice and her tone was now more weary than frosty. 'I know this is private property ... you see, it's my private property.'

CHAPTER
2

She'd been wrong. Grace gave in to her uncertainty and shifted on her feet while she waited for the man before her to respond to the news that she was Crookwell Park's owner.

As a child she'd learned to read people so she'd never be caught off guard. Bullies had come in many forms. But instead of the arrogance and ego that she usually found went hand in hand with good looks, this man standing still and silent in front of her had been open and unaffected. His dismay at the derelict state of the homestead also appeared genuine.

She searched for something more to say. If she hadn't seen shock temper the good humour in his gaze, she'd have thought he hadn't yet answered simply because he hadn't heard her properly.

Bundy sidled against the man's legs and as he bent to pat the kelpie, he finally spoke. 'Your private property?'

A half thought formed and then fled. His delayed reaction to her being the owner wasn't significant. People often thought she was younger than she really was. While she might share her father's hair colour, she hadn't inherited his height.

'Yes.' She moved forwards and offered him her hand. 'Grace Davenport.'

He slowly straightened. She'd made a career out of sourcing and appreciating gorgeous things. Up close, this man with his high cheekbones and the cleft in his stubbled chin was the embodiment of masculine beauty. His eyes appeared a blue grey, but when he wasn't wearing a blue shirt she imagined they'd be a soft pewter hue. As his calloused palm slid against hers she reminded herself now wasn't the time to think about how the shade was her favourite.

Just as if he were a prospective client, she squeezed his hand with the right amount of pressure. Not too much to signal she would be difficult to work with but just enough to say she also wouldn't be a pushover. Over the years she'd experienced every possible response, from bone-crushing grips to others that resembled limp lettuce, but never had someone matched their strength to hers with such care.

Whoever this man was, he returned her exact pressure before simply letting her hand rest in his. She knew she should slip her fingers free, but the warmth of his touch anchored her. Just like when she'd first glimpsed the mountains earlier that day, for a brief moment her grief lifted. Then an indefinable emotion darkened his eyes and she realised how close her hard-won composure was to unravelling.

She pulled her hand free and took a step back. This man with his quick smile and unexpected depths was someone she had to stay away from. Just like how the house beside her would be rebuilt stone by stone, she needed to put her life back together piece by piece. Until she did so she was in no position to deal with anything, or anyone, who surprised her.

Head high, she waited for him to introduce himself. Despite the relaxed way he stood, there was an intensity about him that triggered further warning bells. She knew all about having to conceal who you really were and she already had a sense that there was more to this man than what he allowed people to see.

A half thought again formed and this time it didn't slip away. There had to be more behind his protectiveness towards Crookwell Park other than him simply being a local. He'd come out of his way to make sure she wasn't causing trouble. She glanced at his large hands resting casually by his sides ... calloused hands that had felt rough against her skin.

Her gaze flew to his. 'You're Rowan Parker, the stonemason.'

'Guilty as charged.'

The smile that accompanied his words didn't quite reach his eyes.

Conscious of Bundy looking back and forth between them, she fought to hide her apprehension. This couldn't be the man she'd be having almost daily contact with. Even this short amount of time with him had left her feeling rattled.

'You're not ... quite what I was expecting.'

'I could say the same thing.' This time his smile was an easy grin.

'Sorry I haven't replied to your last email. I've been a little ... busy.'

'No worries. Shoot me a message when you want me to start.'

She nodded before turning to lead the way to where he'd parked beside her car. Now would be a good time to wrap up their impromptu meeting. She'd soon run out of small talk and any minute now her stomach would rumble. It would take at least two cups of tea to process that the stonemason she'd thought would be nudging forty because of his extensive resume was at least a decade younger.

Rowan fell into step beside her.

'Where are you staying?' His relaxed tone indicated he had no trouble making conversation. 'Do you need directions?'

'I'm staying here.'

He frowned at the small bluestone cottage ahead that stood at the end of an overgrown path in a garden of tangled weeds. 'Has anyone checked it out for you?'

She focused on the uneven ground to distract herself from his concern. Rowan's worry wasn't personal. One of the things her parents had appreciated about small-town life was how people were more inclined to look out for each other.

'The real estate agency. They also organised for the utilities to be put on.'

Rowan's attention lingered on the cottage before he nodded at the kelpie ambling between them. 'So, how did you end up with Bundy?'

'He was sitting by my car in town.'

Rowan chuckled. 'I bet you didn't quite know what to make of having a random dog wanting to come with you.'

Her lips curved before she realised she was smiling. Rowan's deep and ready laughter had the power to loosen the wedge of emotion lodged in her chest. 'I didn't but Millicent and Beatrice reassured me it was okay. I didn't want some irate owner thinking I was dognapping him.'

They stopped in the pool of shade thrown over their cars by the leafy jacaranda tree.

'Trust me, no one could dognap Bundy. He never does anything he doesn't want to.'

The kelpie cocked his head and Rowan tickled behind his ears. 'Yes, mate, we're talking about you.'

When Grace caught herself staring at Rowan's smile, she gave herself a mental shake. Exhaustion was no excuse for not having sent him on his way and for not already having the kettle on in her cottage. She opened the boot of her small car that the young employee at the rural store had managed to cram a massive bag of dog food into. He'd been insistent that this was the size she'd need.

She went to grab Bundy's food but then opted for a lighter duffle bag. Before she carried the twenty kilos of the kelpie's dinner she'd need something to eat herself. 'Thanks again for your help.'

Rowan's only reaction to her shall-we-wrap-this-up tone, which usually ensured her day ran to a tight schedule, was a quick grin.

'Trying to get rid of me already?'

Despite her fatigue and the day's heat sapping the last of her energy, she couldn't hide a brief smile. She'd never had anyone but Aubrey call her out on trying to move things along before. 'Yes.'

'Give me five minutes and I'll be out of your hair.'

Before she could stop him, he reached into the boot and hefted the heavy sack of dog food onto his shoulder as if it weighed little more than a bag of flour. He set off over to the cottage.

'Thank you,' she said, her voice slightly breathless as she caught up to his long strides, 'but I'm fine to unload everything.'

'It's no problem. It just seemed a waste to walk over here empty-handed.' He threw her a sideways look. 'When you meet my sister you'll understand why she'd have my hide if I didn't make sure your cottage was habitable.' It was only subtle but the lean line of his jaw tensed. 'You're not here for just the weekend, are you?'

'No … plan A is for the summer.'

Rowan opened the cottage door and stepped aside for her to enter first. 'Plan B's not the summer?'

'Something like that.'

The truth was she had no idea how long she'd be staying. She walked into the cottage, Bundy close behind her. She wasn't confessing that for once in her life she didn't have any other plan.

'Where would you like the dog food?' Rowan ducked his head to avoid the low doorway. 'Laundry?'

'Thanks.'

She went to unlock the kitchen window beside the fridge. She'd already opened the ones in the living room before she and Bundy had left to explore but a musty smell remained.

Rowan joined her in the kitchen. Between his height and broad shoulders, he filled the small space. In contrast to the stuffy cottage he smelled of fresh sun-dried cotton. He turned to study the living room through the narrow doorway. While she had paid for the cottage to be cleaned and the real estate had organised the furniture basics, she was the first to admit the place didn't look homey. But she hadn't come for its comfort or decor.

Rowan rubbed at his chin. 'Do you have my mobile number?'

'I do.' He'd provided it in his first email but she'd always preferred to communicate online. 'Why?'

He examined the ceiling. 'Bundy's going to have the best time.'

'Rats?'

Rowan shook his head. 'Possums.'

'How do you know?'

She followed him to the laundry where he waved a hand towards where it appeared rain from a roof leak had run down the corner of the wall. 'That's not a water stain.'

Without a word she swung around to check her bedroom for any further signs of possum urine. All the walls were clean. She then gave the living room a once-over. A possum making itself at home in her roof wasn't going to alter her plans but it would change where she ate, sat or slept.

'The possums could be long gone,' Rowan said as he came to stand beside her. 'But if you need a temporary plan B my sister has plenty of room and would love to have you stay.'

'That's very kind but I'll be fine.'

'Well, my five minutes is up.' He went to pat Bundy. 'See you later, mate.' Rowan's eyes met hers. 'Sleep tight.'

Even before his footsteps had faded on the gravel path outside, a sense of loss held Grace immobile. The cottage suddenly felt empty and even more drab. She'd always been self-sufficient and she'd come to Bundilla for solitude; it just didn't make sense she didn't feel anything but relief now Rowan was gone.

Bundy's soft whine had her bending to stroke his neck. 'You sure you want to stay? It's not too late to catch a ride back to town.'

The kelpie wagged his tail and pressed against her legs, making her smile.

'Okay then, let's get the kettle on and this cottage shipshape.'

Once the car was unloaded and she'd closed the windows to switch on the antiquated air conditioner—which had a rattle that would wake any sleeping possum—Grace flicked the kettle on. One of the precious possessions she'd brought from Sydney was a mauve floral tea cosy her mother had knitted and she slipped it over a chipped white teapot. Already the cottage felt a little more like home.

After finding a large bowl and filling it with water for Bundy, she made them both a cheese sandwich. Her mobile vibrated where it sat on the table before Aubrey's picture and name filled the screen.

Thanks to them both having dark hair and being of a similar height, they were often mistaken for sisters. The reality was they were opposites in every other way. Strategic and analytical, Aubrey hated all things creative and was only happy working with numbers—the higher the better. It had been her investment expertise that had provided Grace with the means to buy Crookwell Park.

'Hi,' Grace said, giving Bundy the last of her sandwich.

'Hi yourself. I haven't heard from you all afternoon.'

'Sorry, I went for a walk to stretch my legs and then had a visitor.'

'Already?'

'Two actually. This one ...' Grace angled her phone towards Bundy and sent Aubrey a picture.

'A *dog*. You don't even have time for a plant.'

'He's not mine. He hangs out with anyone apparently.'

'Please tell me your second one was human?'

'Yes. Rowan Parker, my stonemason.' She paused. Ever since she and Aubrey had sat next to each other in a high school library and talked the whole way through lunch there had never been any secrets between them. 'He's not what I expected.'

'In what way?' The interest in Aubrey's tone said that Grace now had her full attention. When Aubrey talked on the phone it wasn't unusual for her to be on her laptop multitasking. Grace wasn't the only workaholic.

'Younger.'

'Younger as in wearing braces or fan-your-face younger? No, don't answer. You're the queen of understatements. If he's hot you'll just tell me he's nice. I'll look him up.'

Grace groaned. 'No—'

The sound of computer keys tapping told her she hadn't answered quickly enough. Aubrey knew her too well; she *had* been about to say Rowan was nice.

'If this is him, *nice* doesn't come close to describing him.'

Aubrey switched their call to a video chat and Grace found herself looking at a picture on Aubrey's laptop screen of Rowan in front of what appeared to be a local horse-racing track. Dressed in a crisp blue-and-white checked shirt, navy tie and chinos, he had his arm around the brunette she'd seen him with in town earlier.

She slowly nodded, taking note of the way the smiling woman was tucked close to his side.

Aubrey fanned her face. 'You know I'm going to have to come and stay.'

'You don't do country or rustic.' Aubrey was a born and bred city girl. 'Besides, I might have another visitor ... a possum.'

'A possum.' Aubrey's fine brows lifted.

'There's one or two in the roof apparently. Then I've also got bees but they're at the back of the house.'

Aubrey's expression grew serious. 'Possums, bees, drop bears ... I'll stay if you need me to.'

'I really am okay. It feels right being here.'

On her visit to Bundilla with her parents, they'd glimpsed the bluestone mansion from the road and had driven up to the locked gate to take a closer look. There had been something about the way the derelict house stood tall and proud against the rugged mountain backdrop that had kept them all quiet. The wistfulness on her parents' faces when they'd said that the mansion reminded them of England and that they'd have loved to give it a second chance was why she was now Crookwell Park's new owner.

'I'm so glad. I want an update on your stonemason pronto. Remember, more bees, no pun intended, with honey.'

Grace shook her head with a smile. 'Rowan's actually a cattleman. I'll talk to you tomorrow.'

The screen went black but still Grace gazed at her phone. Aubrey didn't mean anything by her teasing words. They both knew a relationship wasn't anywhere on Grace's radar, even when her parents had been alive. And if one had been, Rowan wouldn't have been a contender. Not only did he appear to be involved with the pretty brunette, she'd felt so off balance when around him her normal defence mechanisms had struggled to cope.

She sat the phone on the worn wood of the wonky table and pushed back her chair. At least the next time she met him she'd feel more like herself. A full night's sleep would go a long way towards making sure she'd have her wits about her. Today had been the first step in reshaping the landscape of her new life. When the days shortened and the mountain weather cooled, she needed to have found a way through her grief for she had nowhere left to go.

⚬

'This never gets old,' Rowan said as he halted Goliath beside Heath's chestnut gelding to admire the high-country view. Timbered ridges rolled in a haze of blue waves until they disappeared into the horizon. It felt as though they were on top of the world.

A brisk breeze lifted the horses' manes and cooled Rowan's skin, providing a respite from the mid-morning heat of the now distant valley. Beside them the leaves of a twisted snow gum danced. Once winter drew close the caramel-hued swirls on its trunk would deepen to a striking reddish orange.

'Tell me about it.' Heath pushed the brim of his felt hat higher to watch an eagle soar.

Rowan too looked skywards as the eagle turned to fly in slow graceful circles. He rolled his shoulders and let his strain drift away. Clancy wasn't the only one to love the mountains that they'd spent their childhood exploring. A mint-like fragrance had him glancing over to the delicate white flowers interspersed amongst the granite. Where there was alpine mint bush there were also summer grasshoppers and he could just make out the tiny yellow-and-brown spotted bodies amongst the leaves.

'What time did you tell Clance you'd be back?' he asked.

'I didn't. If you're thinking what I'm thinking … I'm in.'

He and Heath swapped grins before turning to their left. Going home via O'Donnell's spur would add an hour to their ride but neither of them were in any rush to leave.

Rowan smoothed Goliath's warm neck as the gelding sidestepped. The blood bay was notoriously difficult but so far he'd only tried to unseat him once after they'd walked through the top paddock gate. Just as well he'd stayed in the saddle. He'd never hear the end of it from Heath if he hadn't.

While the gait of the young chestnut that Heath rode was now an even swing, Rowan knew it would only take a rustle in the grass for the green broke gelding to turn into a rodeo bronco. As if on cue, the chestnut shied.

Heath shot Rowan a look. 'You can stop smirking. I have no intention of ending up on the ground.'

'A little dirt never hurt anyone, especially me.'

'That's because you like jumping off things when they're moving. I still can't believe you leaped off your pony to catch that lamb.'

'In my defence I was six, my pony was at a walk and Clancy was thrilled to have another orphan to care for.'

'You forget the part where a rock knocked out your front tooth and you had a fat lip for a week.'

'Those were the days.' Rowan's laughter faded. 'I do things strictly by the book now. It took me long enough, but after Eloise I've learned my lesson.'

Heath slowed so he could meet Rowan's gaze. 'Not all women are like Eloise.'

Rowan shrugged. 'I'll never know if they are or aren't if I'm impulsive and jump into any relationship. And don't get me started on trusting my testosterone to be a good judge of character.'

Heath didn't immediately reply as the chestnut baulked at a tussock of swaying grass. 'Any news on the baby?'

'I know Eloise's baby isn't mine but I think her mother's still hoping it is. Janice gives me an update every time I see her.'

It was common knowledge that Janice had seen her daughter's relationship with the son of an established Bundilla family as an upwardly mobile move. He'd never believed Eloise had shared her mother's social ambitions until the day he'd discovered his ex-fiancée measuring the living room at Ashcroft. Eloise's explanation had been that she wanted to be ready to give the house a makeover once she moved in.

He'd sensed Clancy standing in the doorway and the hurt and sadness on his sister's face were things he'd never forget. The historic house was as much her home as his and Eloise had known this. So he'd slowed things down to make sure she was who he thought she was, only for her to replace him. He hoped for Eloise's and her unborn child's sake that this time her feelings were genuine.

Conscious of Heath's stare, Rowan sighed. 'I know what you're thinking … and I'm fine.' He pushed aside yesterday's unsettling reaction to Grace. 'Yes, I still have things to work through but I'm in a good place being Captain Serious.'

'Captain *Serious*?'

Rowan was the first to admit that the side of him that had chased an adrenaline rush and never sat still long enough to fully think things through hadn't always been associated with such a word. 'Sure.'

'So Brenna doesn't need to keep watching her back?'

Years ago at pony camp Taite's twin sister had shortsheeted his swag whenever she could and now they were adults he was always promising retribution. It was his way of easing the loneliness that at times dimmed the sass in her smile. 'Nope.'

'And Clancy doesn't have to double-check her boots?'

'No ... but come to think of it, it's been a while since I put anything in them.'

Heath didn't laugh like Rowan expected him to. 'Rowan ... you don't need to change or be anyone but yourself. We're all human; look at what I put Clancy through.'

Rowan glanced away. Not to hide how much Heath's sincerity moved him but to mask how much he didn't believe his words.

Heath spoke again, tone quiet. 'Go easy on yourself, mate.'

He nodded but they both knew he wouldn't. He'd never been one for doing things by halves.

The track narrowed as it wound its way through the boulders strewn across the hillside and Rowan allowed Goliath to take the lead. Heath's chestnut's nervous snorts had already caused the currawongs perched on a fallen tree to take flight. The click of the gelding's hooves quietened, and Rowan didn't need to look back to confirm that Heath was taking his time to follow.

Despite the tranquillity and beauty around him, now he was alone, his tension returned. While his surprise had faded that not only had the Crookwell Park trespasser turned out to be the woman he'd seen on the street but also who he'd be working for, the aftershocks of his reaction to Grace hadn't stopped.

This time he hadn't only felt physical attraction, an attraction that had already hit him harder than it had with Eloise. Grace's quiet strength had spoken to something within him. He recognised grief when he saw it and he knew the courage it took to function when within its grasp. But no good would come from remembering how when she'd sent him a brief smile, he would have given anything to see her smile again. Last night there'd been a legitimate reason to check his phone in case she'd messaged about the possums. Now there were no more excuses to keep thinking about her.

The track levelled out and Heath again rode alongside him. On a ridge to their right, first one horse and then another appeared in a grassed clearing as a herd of brumbies came into view. The grey stallion swung around to glare at them before tossing his head and following his mares and foals into the trees.

The conversation turned from brumbies to the latest cattle prices and then to how the summer was shaping up to be a wet one thanks to La Nina. The sun was almost directly overhead by the time they descended to the green foothills and crossed the lush lucerne flats. Cockatoos squawked as they flew overhead to land in the tops of the trees lining the Tumut River. The young chestnut, sensing he was almost home, didn't react to their raucous calls.

As they neared the homestead and rode past the paddock in which two highland cattle grazed, Rowan kept a close eye on Goliath. The gelding and the highland bull, Fergus, had a love–hate relationship. Fergus and Goliath shared a fence and whenever Rowan gave the highland cattle calcium blocks, Goliath would have white lick marks from Fergus over his coat. But at other times they went out of their way to rile each other.

He'd once ended up on his backside at this exact spot because he'd taken his attention off Goliath. Clancy must have told Heath the story as he looked across at him and grinned. Rowan went to speak and then stopped when Goliath's muscles bunched. All Fergus had done was lift his shaggy head and eyeball the gelding. Fergus went back to grazing and Goliath's stride again evened out.

Rowan shook his head, keeping a firm hold on the reins. 'They're as bad as Bundy and Orien.'

Whenever Bundy stayed, Clancy's silver tabby cat went from having a hissy fit at the kelpie to curling up on the mat beside him within five minutes.

Once at the stables, he and Heath unsaddled the horses before Heath headed off to his art studio near the cattle yards. What felt like a lifetime ago his parents had set up the old shed for Heath to use when his father had refused to allow him to paint. Even though Heath had left Bundilla for almost a decade, the art studio had remained untouched. Rowan's mother had always said, with a gentle smile at Clancy, that one day he would return.

The sound of dogs play-growling came from behind the drystone garden wall, causing Rowan to take the long way round to the 150-year-old coach house. The summer after they'd lost their parents, he and Clancy had renovated the red brick building as a way to work through their grief. When the growling stopped, he quickened his pace. Before he faced Primrose and Monet's puppy exuberance, he needed caffeine.

Thanks to stealth and luck, he managed to reach the coach house undetected. He opened the front door and walked into a kitchen filled with the aroma of banana and cinnamon. Clancy had baked his favourite morning smoko. Through the living room window he could see his sister hanging out washing on the Hills hoist. Even now the old clothesline had a tilt thanks to him swinging on it as a kid. He grabbed two muffins and went out into the back garden to help her.

He arrived in time to rescue a tea towel that Primrose and Monet were playing tug of war with. Clancy gave him a thankful smile as he picked up the washing basket so it was now out of reach of the cream golden retriever and chocolate-brown kelpie who gazed at him with innocent eyes.

'Butter wouldn't melt,' Clancy said with a laugh as she reached for a hand towel.

'Still glad to be home?'

Clancy's smile was sunrise bright. 'You have no idea.'

'Thanks for the muffins.'

'Anytime. Mabel called. Your Grace has already caused quite a stir. She was in the grocery store late yesterday with Bundy and had half a trolley of cleaning items. According to Cynthia she doesn't say much but is stunning.'

'She's not my Grace … she's my boss.'

'You like being your own boss.'

'I do.' He handed Clancy the last of the washing. This conversation couldn't end fast enough. He couldn't have his sister sense that Grace had already made an impact without him even having started work at Crookwell Park.

'How was her night with the possums?'

'I'm not sure. I didn't hear from her so everything must have been okay.'

Clancy stopped hanging out a pink shirt with her peony flower farm logo on the front pocket. 'Why haven't you called to check?'

'I only have her email.' He thought back to Grace's independence and reserve. 'I also get the impression she wants to be left alone.'

Clancy's hands rested on her hips. 'Possum shrieks can make a horror film sound like a Disney movie. If she had a bad night, she very well could have packed her car and left.'

He frowned. He hadn't picked Grace for a quitter but she was dealing with far more than possums in her roof, and the cottage wasn't the most comfortable place to live. For some reason the idea of Grace being gone sparked a sense of alarm.

Clancy's brow arched. 'Exactly.'

'You're right.' He handed the empty basket to her. Instead of reaching for his phone to check his emails, he turned to leave. His restless energy was too impatient to wait for a typed reply. He needed to physically confirm whether or not Grace was at Crookwell Park. 'Need anything in town?'

'Tell Grace she's welcome for dinner.'

Rowan hoped Primrose and Monet's new bout of wrestling covered his groan. He didn't need to see Clancy's face to know what she was thinking. A smile had been in her voice. A smile he wasn't so sure solely stemmed from him admitting that she had been right.

CHAPTER

3

Grace cleared her throat as the young male assistant in the Bundilla rural store waited for her to answer his query as to how he could help her.

'Where do I find the possum nesting boxes?'

At the first bang of the roof last night she'd stirred. By the time the thumps had turned into the scrape of claws running a marathon above her head she was fully awake. Then the screeches and hissing started. She'd welcomed the dawn by searching on her laptop for the best way to handle sharing her life with the local wildlife. While she knew her plan to give her possums a better place to nest was an approved relocation practice, she still felt guilty at wanting to evict her furry tenants.

'This way.'

The assistant, who had recognised her from when she'd picked up Bundy's dog food the night before, led her past shelves of unfamiliar rural items. When he stopped at a section filled with varnished and

unvarnished wooden boxes she knew she wasn't the only customer
to have come inside the store sleep-deprived.

'Any suggestions?' she asked.

'This one. It's ready to be installed.' When he gave her an
encouraging smile she figured other customers more awake than
her had asked for the quickest solution.

She took hold of the varnished nesting box he passed her and
then reached for two more. 'One possum couldn't possibly have
made so much noise.' She glanced hopefully around the store. 'I
don't suppose you have a ladder and anything else I'll need?'

It was only once the nesting boxes, ladder, tool set and wire were
paid for that she realised she wouldn't have a hope of fitting everything
into her sedan. She took in the ladder's length. Last night she'd stood
on a chair to reclean the cottage walls, but such an improvisation
wouldn't work for the nesting boxes. According to what she'd read
they had to be installed at a height of around four metres.

'Just do a mainy,' the assistant said with a grin. 'There'll be
someone there with a ute who'll help, especially if Bundy's with
you.'

'Mainy?'

'Walk along the main street.'

'Ahh … right.'

Small towns might be relaxed and sociable but big city habits
were hard to break. There was no way she was getting in a random
stranger's ute even if Bundy was with her.

'Or I can make some calls?'

The idea didn't fill her with enthusiasm. She was having trouble
keeping her eyes open. Making chitchat with someone, even if the
assistant knew them, was hard enough when she was awake. But
there was someone who had a ute and who she'd already covered

all the getting-to-know-you basics with. Even if Rowan was the last person she should be calling.

At the pinnacle of the possum celebrations, she'd twice reached for her phone to text him only to put her mobile back on her bedside table. Technically the possums weren't an emergency. She was also supposed to be self-sufficient. As for now asking him for help with the ladder, the truth was that after her poor night's sleep she'd need more time before she saw him. There could be no repeat of how she'd felt so out of her depth when around him yesterday.

'Thank you but I'll think of a way to get the ladder home. Can it stay here while I do some more shopping?'

'No problem.' The assistant moved the ladder to behind the counter.

She collected her smaller purchases and made her way outside. At first glance Bundy didn't seem to be where she'd left him sleeping in the shade of a gum tree. Then she saw the kelpie having his photo taken with two small children. A dark-haired girl and a little boy had their tiny arms around him. Grace's steps slowed as she watched the mother snap a photo of their beaming smiles.

Guilt merged with her exhaustion. There was one thing she'd run out of time to give to her parents. Grandchildren. It wasn't that she didn't want a family, she did, she'd just thought she'd have longer to find someone to grow old with. Her attention stayed on the children as the sister took hold of her brother's hand to steady him as they walked over to their mother. Grace swallowed past the lump in her throat when the mother drew them in close for a hug.

All she could now do to honour her parents' memory was to restore Crookwell Park, and to do this she needed sleep. She loaded the items into the boot of her car and with a sigh took her phone from out of her tote bag. And to sleep she needed her cottage possum-free. Now wasn't the time for her vulnerability when around Rowan to become a liability.

She opened her emails to find where Rowan had listed his number. She tapped off a message before she could change her mind.

Hi. Grace here. If you have a minute, I'd appreciate a hand with something that won't fit in my car.

She hesitated, debating whether she should add more, and then typed a hasty *Thanks* before hitting send.

A kelpie nose pushed into her hand and she smiled as she looked at Bundy. His steady presence last night had brought an unexpected comfort. It had also been a welcome distraction to think about someone else's needs. She'd made a place for him to sleep in her room out of a spare blanket even though he'd ended up on the foot of her bed. Then that morning she'd discovered he too liked peanut butter toast for breakfast.

She ruffled behind his ears. 'Let's find you a water bowl. I'm sure I saw one outside the café.'

The main street was only a short stroll away so she left her car where it was. With Bundy by her side, she crossed the road. Every shop they ambled past featured a strip of book covers along the bottom of each window. Her mother had been told that they'd been put up to celebrate the very first summer reading festival.

Grace stopped to peer through the window of a bookshop. Beside the door stood an old-fashioned bike on which a display of books was strapped on the back. Stories had been her solace when she was a child and she still loved the smell of a bookshop. Next visit she'd browse the full shelves she could see through the glass. Right now, she had a possum problem to handle.

When they arrived at The Book Nook Café, Grace waited beneath the awning of the newsagency next door while Bundy went to take a drink from the nearby water bowl. She checked her phone but there was no reply from Rowan.

Heels clicked on the cement behind her before a slender figure dressed in a black pencil skirt and cream blouse approached. The woman took off her sunglasses with a smile. 'You must be Grace. I'm Mabel.'

For a moment Grace thought she was back in the city. Not only was this local dressed in stylish clothes but her shoulder-length brown hair was perfectly straight. Grace resisted the urge to check her tousled hair had stayed in its ponytail.

Grace shook the hand she was offered. 'Hi.'

Mabel's smile widened. 'I'm the local journo and I run Bundy's social media page.' She took a card holder from out of her tan leather bag. 'Feel free to send me any photos.'

Grace cast Bundy a sideways glance to where he sat watching them as she accepted Mabel's business card. It was no surprise the photogenic kelpie's celebrity status extended far beyond Bundilla.

At sunrise she'd taken Bundy for a walk and as she'd forgotten her phone she'd missed a shot of him silhouetted against the early morning sky. She had everything crossed they would sleep through tomorrow's apricot sunrise but if they didn't, she'd remember her mobile.

'I'd love to show you around,' Mabel continued, her tone warm. 'There's a local book club, except it's on hold until after the reading festival, a walking group, or if craft is more your thing, a quilting club.'

'Thank you, they all sound great, but the restoration is going to keep me pretty busy.'

She didn't elaborate. The real estate office knew she'd bought Crookwell Park and news would travel fast.

'Hopefully you'll have time for a coffee?'

There was something about the sincerity of Mabel's words that silenced the automatic no on her lips. She'd come to the mountains for solitude and the space to heal, but once Bundy was no longer with her the prospect of being alone in her cottage wasn't as appealing as it should have been.

'I will.' She glanced at the elegant print on the business card. 'I'll give you a call.'

When Mabel smiled, Grace found herself smiling in return.

After a farewell pat to Bundy, the journalist continued on her way, waving to people as she passed the café tables overlooking the footpath.

'I'll just get a quick takeaway coffee,' Grace said to Bundy as she hitched her bag higher on her shoulder. She felt strangely reluctant to leave him. Maybe he'd be gone when she returned. The kelpie wagged his tail.

Except when she walked away, instead of staying where he was, Bundy came with her. Once through the café gate, the kelpie made a detour to the left. In the far corner of the outdoor eating area Grace caught sight of a dog bed. Bundy flopped onto the stretched canvas and with a sigh closed his eyes.

An elderly gentleman with polished brown boots held the door open for Grace and she thanked him with a nod. Once inside, the aroma of fresh coffee and the walls full of books had her reconsidering her takeaway order. With Bundy asleep outside, there was no need to rush. She spied an empty table at the back of the room and after making her order took a seat.

Engrossed in a book, she didn't initially hear the ring of her mobile. She fumbled through her bag to find her phone and answered before she realised it was Rowan's number on the screen.

'Hi.' She kept her greeting low so as to not disturb the table next to her but also to hide her uncertainty. She'd been expecting him to text not call.

'Sorry I didn't ring earlier. I'm on the road and was in a reception black spot.'

'It's all good.'

She kept her reply short to hide how much the deep timbre of his tone made her wish he'd keep talking. She'd never noticed before how good a man's voice could sound. Sleep deprivation had a lot to answer for.

'You need help loading something into your car?'

While his words were light, she didn't miss the underlying tension. Just like yesterday she was aware of a suppressed energy beneath his easygoing surface.

'It's more like I need something picked up. I bought a ladder so my possums can have somewhere else to party.'

She thought the phone signal had dropped out but then Rowan replied. 'Too easy. Is it at the rural store?'

'Yes, but it's okay if you're busy.'

'Definitely not busy.' His tone had relaxed. 'Where are you in town?'

'At the café.'

It was only after she'd answered that she questioned how he knew she wasn't at Crookwell Park. What sounded like a nearby conversation murmured in the background before Rowan said, 'Make sure you try the death-by-chocolate brownie.'

Still trying to work out where Rowan might be, she didn't pay attention to the café door opening until broad shoulders in an emerald green shirt blocked the doorway. The distance between them didn't dilute the potency of Rowan's smile as he looked straight at her.

She slowly lowered her phone. So much for believing the next time she saw Rowan she'd have her wits about her. If the flurry of nerves in her stomach was anything to go by, not even her double caffeine hit was going to help her get through the next five minutes.

Rowan slipped his mobile into his front shirt pocket and slowed his pace as he wove his way through the café tables. The relief that Grace was in town and not halfway to Sydney coursed through him like an adrenaline rush. When he'd gone to the cottage and found it locked and her car gone he'd acted on impulse, despite his best intentions, and headed to town to discover if anyone in the real estate office knew anything.

He risked a glance at Grace, knowing he only had seconds to turn into Captain Serious. Today she again wore all black and her long hair was pulled into a high ponytail, though wisps escaped to frame her pale face. Yesterday's smudges of exhaustion were now purple shadows beneath her eyes. Guilt had his jaw tighten. He should have contacted her last night.

A slim blonde gave him a smile from where she stood behind the coffee machine frothing milk. 'The usual?'

'That would be great, Beck. And one of your brownies.'

Her smile grew. He knew how early she would have been up that morning baking and he always bought something to go with his coffee. His sweet tooth was a running joke around town.

By now he'd almost reached Grace. He'd have a quick chat and then sit at a nearby table. She hadn't yet smiled, even though when they'd spoken on the phone her voice had been less reserved than when they'd met. As he drew near she moved the stack of books on the tabletop to make room for him. He hoped his expression didn't convey his surprise or his hesitation.

As much as the thought of her leaving had set him on edge, the prospect of sitting across from her proved just as unsettling. Yesterday whenever near her he'd breathed in a subtle floral scent that reminded him of the honeysuckle that rambled over the Ashcroft stone garden wall. He might now be standing a body length away but he still could catch a delicate flower fragrance amongst the other coffee shop aromas.

In his peripheral vision he saw a pair of grey nomad tourists seat themselves at the empty table he'd been planning to use. Even though this must have been why Grace had moved her books, his gaze met hers to double-check it was okay to join her.

After she'd gestured towards the seat opposite her, he sat, making sure his knee didn't bump hers in the tight space.

When she didn't break the silence, he initiated the small talk. 'Bundy's out for the count.'

'I'm sure he is.'

'I owe you an apology. I should have messaged last night to check how you were going and given you directions to my sister's.'

Grace shook her head, the tip of her ponytail swinging over her shoulder. 'No apology needed. I wasn't expecting you to and I wouldn't have wanted to impose.'

'I'll pick the ladder up as soon as I leave here.'

'Thank you.'

He smiled at Beck as she delivered his coffee and brownie.

Once he and Grace were alone he slid the plate into the centre of the table. He didn't classify the action as impulsive; he was used to sharing his food with Clancy and her best friend Brenna. For some reason they always thought what he ordered looked better than what they'd chosen. 'You're welcome to have some.'

'Thanks.' Instead of looking at the brownie, she straightened her already tidy stack of books. 'It's yours.'

'I'm happy to share.' He studied her, trying to work out what line he'd crossed to again make her feel wary. 'My sister thinks that as part of her sibling entitlements what is mine is always hers.'

As he'd hoped, the corners of Grace's mouth tilted. 'I'm an only child. You eat your brownie.'

He slid the plate back over to his side of the table. 'Any food-hogging cousins?'

'No.'

'So every Easter, Christmas and birthday you didn't have to hand over half of your chocolate?'

'Not at all.' The smile in her eyes made her irises appear more green than brown, but then the light ebbed. 'My father liked anything with mint while my mother preferred dark chocolate.'

Rowan noted the use of the past tense. His own grief surfaced and he worked hard to keep his expression from changing. 'My father was a chocolate and nut fan while my mum only ate white chocolate.'

When Grace didn't immediately reply, he knew she'd also noted his word choice. Her gaze searched his. Whatever she was looking for, she found, as the tense line of her shoulders lowered. 'Was there anything you didn't have to share?'

'Salty liquorice.'

She grimaced. 'No wonder you had that all to yourself.'

Rowan started on his brownie. While Grace had appeared to have relaxed, he was under no illusion she was truly at ease. Her wary stillness from yesterday remained.

'So,' he said, keeping his tone casual, 'anything I can help you with besides the ladder?'

'Actually, there might be.' She spoke slowly as if carefully choosing her words. 'I need a chest of drawers.'

'Tumut would be your best bet. I could pick you up one next time I'm there?'

'Thank you but I was hoping for one sooner rather than later.' She paused. 'The cottage won't really feel like home while I'm living out of a suitcase.'

He reached for his mobile in his front shirt pocket. There was something about the way she said home that reminded him about how displaced he'd felt when overseas away from Clancy and the high country. 'Maybe there's something on the online marketplace?'

He placed his phone on the table and angled it so Grace could see the screen filled with local items for sale. Before he could enter 'drawer' into the search bar, she leaned forwards and lifted her hand as if to stop him.

Pink washed across her cheekbones before she sat back and took her mobile from out of her bag. She typed on the screen and after a moment held it up to reveal the identical marketplace page.

She swiped at the picture of a large green and cream floral floor rug. 'This can't be genuine.'

Rowan could only stare. A tired and travel-weary Grace had made his blood rush; an animated Grace with colour in her face and her gaze bright left him dumbstruck. This was the woman Grace had been before life had thrown whatever curve ball it had at her.

Realising he hadn't replied, he scooped up his phone to examine the rug listing. From the glossy magazines Clancy had made him read when they'd renovated the coach house, he guessed Grace was asking if the item was an authentic Aubusson rug. 'It would be. It's a post from Millicent and Beatrice and they only buy the best.'

Grace's eyes widened, her smile so beautiful Rowan was thankful it wasn't directed at him. Curious glances were being aimed in their direction and he didn't now need whispers to circulate that he was seen looking dazed when with her. The news that he'd be working at Crookwell Park would have already spread around town with the speed of a summer grassfire.

'This is ridiculous.' Grace continued to stare at her phone screen. 'This rug is an antique. It's worth four times what it's listed for.'

'Millicent and Beatrice only live across town. I could go and get it after the ladder.'

Even before he'd finished, Grace was rummaging in her bag to take out her wallet. While she did so Rowan messaged Millicent. Her reply saying that it suited to collect the rug today was almost instant.

He arched a brow at the wad of cash Grace placed on the table. 'You have zero chance of the sisters accepting that much money. They are sticklers for the rules and that's not what the rug was listed for.'

Grace smiled again, and this time it was as sweet as it was determined. He made a mental note. His new boss not only didn't like needing help, she had a spine of steel. 'I also play by the rules. That's what it's worth. Isn't there a hospital fundraiser for a physio touch machine?'

She was also clever and far too observant. The only reason why the sisters might accept more than the asking price was if the extra amount was donated to charity. 'There is. The flyer's on the community noticeboard at the grocery store.'

Without breaking eye contact she pushed the money towards him.

He didn't move. 'I take it my ute's going to be well used this summer.'

'When it comes to possums and Aubusson rugs it will be.'

Her wry tone made him grin. But as he tucked the pile of notes into his wallet, the last thing he felt was amusement.

The longer he spent in Grace's company the more it became obvious that it wasn't only his attraction he had to worry about. Grace possessed an integrity and a dignity that on their own were enough to draw him to her. He didn't know if it was because they were qualities he'd never seen in Eloise or if it was relief that perhaps Heath was right and not all women were like her. But, whatever the reason, he'd be a fool to spend any more time than necessary with the beautiful woman across from him.

He flicked through more marketplace listings and held up his phone to show her a white tallboy with what looked like an oak top. He wasn't sure why he'd thought the style would be to her taste but her reaction to the classic rug said he might be in the ballpark.

Grace looked between him and the picture before her lips curved. 'That's perfect. I don't suppose ...'

He nodded as he lowered his phone to message the seller. It shouldn't make him feel so light inside that she'd appeared to have relaxed around him.

While he waited for a reply, he polished off his brownie. More and more heads were turning in their direction. Elderly Mrs Hudson sat over in the far corner and he was pretty sure Clancy had mentioned her name after a quilting meeting. While Vernette was hard of hearing, there was nothing wrong with her eyesight or her lip-reading skills.

He'd just finished his coffee when a reply came through from the tallboy owner saying that the item too could be collected now.

'We're all good to go,' he said in answer to Grace's unspoken question.

'I really appreciate your help.'

She reached for her wallet again.

He accepted the money, careful to make sure their fingers didn't brush. He didn't need a reminder of how when he'd clasped her hand yesterday the feel of her smooth skin had shot through him. He still wasn't sure why he'd kept hold of her hand other than an instinctive need to provide reassurance and to erase the caution in her eyes.

'I shouldn't be more than an hour,' he said, coming to his feet.

The rumour mill had already enough fuel for gossip and would only go into overdrive should they be seen leaving together.

She picked up her pile of books but didn't stand. 'I'll see you then.'

It wasn't his imagination that conversations paused as he strode to the door.

Once outside, he took his sunglasses from out of his shirt pocket and slipped them on. He had less than an hour to get himself under control. It was going to be a long summer if he couldn't spend ten minutes in Grace's company without his heart pounding as though he'd run up Overflow Road with Taite.

∞

A little over an hour later, Rowan drove through the front gate of Crookwell Park, feeling no more composed than he had when he'd left the café. The reality was he was as restless and wired as if he was about to leap out of a helicopter to ski down a Canadian mountain. He stopped tapping his thumb on the steering wheel to roll his tight shoulders.

Bundy bounded over to greet him and while there was no sign of Grace, beside her car sat possum nesting boxes and a toolbox. When he'd collected the ladder he'd also picked up chicken wire and wood to block any gaps in the roof eaves. It wasn't enough to put up new homes; the possums had to be prevented from returning to the cottage. In case they did he'd bought a portable light for the roof cavity that could be left on overnight. Hopefully it wouldn't be long until Grace's possums were happily settled in their new dens.

When Bundy barked and dashed past his ute, Rowan realised he wasn't Grace's only visitor. He checked the rear-view mirror and saw a familiar dual cab making its way along the driveway. Clancy hadn't mentioned she'd be coming to town today. The pale gleam of blonde hair in the passenger seat confirmed Clancy's best friend and Taite's twin, Brenna, was with her. She must be back from running her weeklong trek into the high country.

'Just great,' he muttered.

As much as he loved Clancy and knew Brenna had a heart of gold beneath her straight-talking, no-nonsense attitude, he did not need to be a psychic to know they were up to something. Their grins were a little too delighted as they parked alongside him.

An impression confirmed when he left his ute and Clancy came over to brush dirt from his shoulder. 'What have you been doing? Wrestling a wombat?'

He narrowed his eyes at her. It wasn't anything unusual for his work shirts to be covered in dust from the cattle yards or grease from the farm workshop.

Brenna smiled as she walked over carrying a container filled with a passionfruit sponge cake. 'Fancy seeing you here.'

'I could say the same thing about you.'

Brenna laughed and whatever she was going to say remained unsaid as footsteps sounded on the path to their left. Both girls whirled around as Grace approached. When Bundy ran over, Grace slowed to tickle behind his ears.

From where Clancy stood close beside him, he had no trouble hearing her murmur, 'Bundy adores her. I like Grace already.'

'The reason behind your sudden trip to town is …?'

Clancy's reply was a quick jab of her elbow into his ribs.

He wasn't sure what he expected when Grace stopped in front of them. Yesterday when they'd met she'd been frosty and cool but today her expression was a little more open and friendly. Except when her gaze flicked between him and Clancy her face became unreadable.

'Grace,' he said, wanting to put her at ease. 'This is Clancy.' He waved over to Brenna. 'And Brenna.'

'Hi. Nice to meet you both.'

Clancy went to clasp Grace's hand. 'It's so lovely to meet you too. I was worried you might have had a bad night. There's a reason why your place is known as Possum Cottage.'

'In case you did,' Brenna said, offering Grace the cake container, 'we thought you might like a little housewarming gift. Nothing makes things better like cake and a cuppa.'

A small smile broke through Grace's reserve as she accepted the passionfruit sponge. 'Thank you both so much.' Her hesitation was only brief. 'Would you like to come inside? I've just put the kettle on.'

Brenna and Grace nodded in unison.

Rowan made the most of his sister's distraction to move away to untie the straps on the back of his ute. There was no way he'd be joining their tea party. He needed to get out of there before Clancy and Brenna hatched any matchmaking ideas and especially before Clancy saw how much Grace affected him. He'd unload the rug and tallboy and install the nesting boxes before making himself scarce.

He glanced up to find Grace standing nearby. Clancy, Brenna and Bundy were already halfway along the overgrown path.

'Would you like coffee and some cake too?' Grace asked, her words too polite.

It was as though he'd imagined her warmth when they'd spoken in the café.

'Thanks but I'm still recovering from my death-by-chocolate experience.' When she didn't smile, he grinned to ease the strange tension between them. 'Can you see why I said I'd be in trouble with my sister if I hadn't made sure your cottage was liveable?'

Grace's forehead furrowed before she turned to look over to where Clancy and Brenna watched them from the cottage front door. 'Brenna's your sister?'

He was so used to small-town life and people knowing that he and Clancy were related he hadn't thought to introduce her as family.

He slowly shook his head. 'Clancy is.'

CHAPTER
4

For the first time in what felt like forever Grace slept through the night. She awoke to silence and an unfamiliar feeling of peace.

Eyes closed, she allowed her senses to slowly come awake. The warm weight against her foot was Bundy. Somehow the kelpie had known that by sleeping on the end of her bed he'd stop her tossing and turning through the dismal hours until dawn.

The croak of a frog outside in the water tank let her know that there'd be more rain today. It was no wonder the grass that the kangaroos and wallabies kept mown around the mansion was green and that the garden weeds were running rampant. At least her possums would be snug and dry in their nesting boxes. Last night at dusk she'd caught a flash of grey as one had vacated its custom-made living quarters.

Eyes still shut, she relished the quiet. There were no car engines, sirens or the clamour of city life beyond her dusty window. She hadn't been in Bundilla a week but she already felt something shifting within her.

She didn't know if it was Bundy's company, the serenity of the mountain scenery or having things like possums to distract her, but inside where there'd only been darkness there was now a flicker of light. The rich colours of the antique Aubusson rug had also given her creativity a gentle nudge. Although for months her mind had been nothing but a blank canvas, she now found herself running through interior design concepts on how to best use the rug once the mansion was restored.

Her eyes snapped open and her sense of calm fled. Today was the start of the restoration. She rolled over to check her phone on the bedside table and froze when she saw how late it was. Rowan would already be here. The knowledge didn't galvanise her into action; if anything it made her want to pull the covers over her head.

Yet again she'd been wrong. She hadn't realised she groaned until Bundy looked at her. Not only had she mistakenly thought Rowan was going out with Clancy but also that Brenna was his sister. She couldn't have gotten things more jumbled if she tried.

She slipped out of bed. Her bare feet made no sound on the smooth floorboards as she went to make a coffee. One thing she hoped she hadn't been completely wrong about was Rowan being in a relationship with someone. She needed him to be attached and unavailable. It didn't matter that she'd been around him several times now, he continued to throw her off balance. When he'd slid his brownie across the café table two days ago, she'd experienced a deep pang of longing at the familiarity of the gesture.

She took down a mug from the shelf and then reached for another. Day one of Rowan working at Crookwell Park was the perfect chance to set some ground rules between them. They had to stick to talking about the restoration; there could be no more personal disclosures like what had happened at the café.

While she hadn't said outright that her parents were no longer with her, she'd shared way too much information. Empathy had turned Rowan's eyes a soft and smoky grey that had made it impossible for her to look away. When he'd also spoken about his parents in the past tense, she'd felt a connection so strong she'd forgotten how uncomfortable she was with making small talk.

She dropped a slice of bread into the toaster. But while their shared grief had given them something in common, it had been foolish to lower her guard. She hadn't come to the mountains to burden anyone with her anguish or to trigger their own grief. The other afternoon, once Clancy and Brenna had left, she'd gone to help Rowan with the final nesting box. He'd been at the top of the ladder and hadn't noticed her. Even with the distance between them she'd recognised the grim bleakness of his expression. Rowan had his own demons to deal with.

After a quick breakfast and a shower, she left the cottage, two mugs of steaming coffee in her hands. Bundy walked alongside her. When a raindrop wet her cheek, she increased her pace. The sky had turned from a serene blue to a moody grey and heavy clouds shrouded the mountain peaks. She rounded the house corner to where the worst of the structural damage could be found. Rowan had been busy. Tall scaffolding ran parallel to the side wall and the fallen stones that had littered the ground were now sorted into neat groups.

He looked up from where he was placing a rock on the closest pile and with a smile tugged off his leather gloves. When coffee spilled to scald her left hand, she told herself her unsteady grip was a result of walking too fast and not because Rowan appeared happy to see her.

Thunder rumbled as he approached. The dark splashes on the blue cotton of his work shirt multiplied as the raindrops intensified.

'Perfect timing,' he said as he accepted the coffee she passed him before leading the way over to the side veranda.

Seconds after their boots clattered on the worn floorboards, the rain became an urgent drum on the tin overhead. Bundy raced up the steps and gave a vigorous shake, covering them in cold water.

Rowan's chuckle had her take a quick sip of coffee. Even though she'd heard him laugh several times now, the deep and easy sound touched a place inside her that she'd always ignored. In her workaholic world there had been little room for her own laughter.

'Thanks for the coffee,' Rowan said before taking a mouthful.

'It seemed like a caffeine type of morning.'

Needing something to do other than stare at the way his damp shirt clung to the width of his shoulders, she gazed out at the rain that had closed around them like a curtain. Water streamed from the loose gutter like a waterfall, further blurring the landscape beyond the veranda. For a second she thought she saw a bulky figure near the back garden corner, but it had to be her imagination. Except Bundy was staring in the same direction, his ears pricked forwards. She brushed hair out of her eyes to take a second look.

'What is it?' Rowan asked, his voice low as he took a step towards her and peered into the rain.

Grace shivered, not from the chill but from the way Rowan had sensed something was amiss. She was right to be wary of him. Since she was a child she'd always masked her thoughts and emotions and here Rowan was reading her like a book.

She wrapped both hands around the warmth of her mug. 'I thought I saw something.'

'It could have been a wombat. It's not just possums and bees who think Crookwell Park's their idea of paradise.'

She gave a half smile. Rowan would already think she was ditzy enough after she'd mistaken Brenna for his sister to now say what she'd seen had definitely been human.

Conscious of him watching her as if privy to her thoughts, the narrow veranda space suddenly felt too small. With the rain showing no sign of easing she had to put some physical space between them.

She bent to place her coffee mug beside a veranda post. 'Why don't we take a grand tour while we wait for the storm to pass?'

'I'd like that. It's been years since I've been inside.' At her curious look, he grinned as he placed his gloves and mug beside hers. 'No, it wasn't at Halloween. Kathy, the local studies officer at the library, gave a talk and tour.'

Grace took a set of keys from out of her jeans pocket and moved towards the side door. 'I can guarantee it hasn't changed.'

They stepped into what once would have been a grand reception room featuring a high decorative ceiling and ornate cornices. No longer weatherproof, the wind rattled through the sash windows darkened by mould and in which every pane had been smashed. Wallpaper that had loosened with time now lay ripped and trampled amongst the broken bottles and blown-in leaves strewn across the floorboards. Spray-painted graffiti tags in bold colours or brash black covered the walls and vied with each other for attention.

When Rowan stopped to look around and sigh, Grace didn't glance at him. Just like on the day they met, she shared his dismay at the state of the house. But this morning was not about connecting any further with the man beside her but about keeping a professional distance between them.

They crossed the room, Bundy picking his way through the debris. Once in the hallway, a musty and pervasive odour thickened the air.

Even though she'd worked with both a heritage consultant and the local council to gain approval for the restoration, one thing she didn't have were formal house plans. Now she was finally here, she'd have a draughtsman draw up a set for when the builder commenced phase two. But even without plans it was obvious that the labyrinth of rooms had been designed around an internal courtyard. Sunlight did its best to shine through the grimy windows to their left that overlooked a large weed-choked space.

Grace continued along the hallway. She'd take Rowan to see the rooms that weren't so damaged. The vandals had either been disturbed or grown bored with finding their way through all of the locked doors as the back of the mansion appeared to have escaped the brunt of their destruction.

At the first door, Grace took out her phone to turn on the torchlight. Until she had the house rewired she'd be doing things old school. She also wouldn't be moving in until the mansion had been replumbed. As it was now, wood had to be burning in the slow-combustion kitchen stove for there to be any hot water.

She walked through the doorway and shone her phone around the huge, empty space. 'I've been wondering what this was for. Those brackets on the far wall look like they would hold billiard cues.'

Rowan joined her, using his mobile light to inspect the twin rows of small cement squares inserted into the middle of the dusty floor. 'It's definitely the old billiards room. These are the eight supports for the table legs.'

They went into the next room.

'If only these walls could talk,' she said. The more she explored the more she had the inexplicable sense that while the mansion might have once been a happy home, it had spent a long time being an unhappy one. 'There's so many things I'd want to know.'

Rowan's torchlight illuminated the dark timber of a wooden fireplace. 'What do you know?'

'Not much.' She didn't add that she'd spent so long engulfed by a mental fog that her brain had trouble storing anything beyond the most basic information.

'Well, the short story is that Crookwell Park had been owned by the Russell family until Lawrence Junior, who was a bachelor and an eccentric recluse, passed away in his nineties. As a child I remember seeing him in old-fashioned clothes and riding a bicycle. My parents said he was a friendly man, but he was injured in the war and it was common knowledge he lived in a different world. He didn't make use of his land or appear to have a job and it's believed that as the family money ran out he simply shut off more and more rooms.'

'Did he have any siblings?'

'There were two spinster sisters, and rumour has it there was some sort of falling out as they would walk past each other in the street without any acknowledgement. Kathy, who hosted my Crookwell Park tour, will be able to fill you in.'

'When Lawrence died was there anyone to inherit Crookwell Park?'

'There was some distant cousin in Tasmania who planned to turn it into a bed and breakfast. That's why your cottage was modernised, so he and his wife could visit once the work started. But apparently the wife hated the place; she said the house didn't want her there. I think it also proved too much of a money pit. It's since been on the market for years.'

Grace nodded as they left to walk along to another room. Rowan had confirmed what little details she'd remembered from the real estate agent.

She opened the door to reveal walls of shelves. 'No guesses as to what this was.'

Rowan followed her into what had been the old library. Bundy went to sniff along the bottom of a bookcase where either the rat who had run over her foot yesterday or one of his many friends was hiding.

Grace ran her hand over the dust dulling the pale marble of the fireplace. On a winter's day, with snow on the peaks and the fire roaring, this space would be a cosy haven. She couldn't wait to fill the shelves with books.

Rowan moved his phone light slowly over the walls as though looking for something. 'Every time I come into this part of the house I get a feeling something is off. Maybe it's just me wanting symmetry. This room feels smaller than it should be, but it would just be the thick bookcases taking up space.'

Grace too looked around but after a cursory glance her attention returned to Rowan. She was having trouble resisting the interest and curiosity in his face. Rowan was as fascinated with old places as she was. She bit the inside of her cheek. Such a realisation didn't reassure her that her house was in safe hands; it was yet another thing they had in common.

When they returned to the hallway, rain no longer hammered on the roof.

'That was great.' Even in the dim light Grace could see the smile warming Rowan's eyes. 'I'd better get back to work but maybe we could see more of the rooms another time?'

She settled for a nod. Now they were no longer discussing the house, it was harder to keep their conversation flowing.

Together they headed outside to where the day seemed extra bright after the gloominess inside. Rowan plucked his sunglasses from where they sat on his cap and slipped them on. Thinking he'd collect his gloves and follow Bundy down the veranda steps, Grace bent to pick up their two coffee mugs.

She straightened only to find that Rowan had remained where he was. Even with his dark glasses concealing his eyes, she had no trouble reading his serious expression. 'Grace … why did you think Brenna was my sister and not Clancy?'

Grace made sure her grip on the mugs didn't become white-knuckled. She should have known the perceptiveness beneath Rowan's easygoing charm would have had him wonder about her mistake.

She lifted her chin. She couldn't lie even if the truth would make her feel more than awkward. 'On the day I arrived I saw you and Clancy hugging outside the pub. I assumed you were a couple.'

Rowan rubbed at his chin. 'I can understand why you would have thought that—we don't look all that similar. Clance had been overseas with Heath so I was happy to see her. I'd missed her.'

Grace swallowed as the grief that had ebbed now crashed over her like a wave. She had no one left in her family to miss. 'Sorry for getting things wrong. It won't happen again. Your private life is your own business.'

Worried that her composure would crumple, she fixed her gaze on where raindrops glistened upon the cobwebs strung amongst the weeds. If she wasn't careful the hot press against her eyelids would turn into the tears that she refused to again let fall.

She felt rather than saw Rowan search her face. 'Grace,' he said softly, 'everything will be okay. I give you my word there will be no distractions stopping me from getting my work here done. Trust me …' Despite her best intentions, she looked at him as bitterness rasped in his words. 'The only things in my private life are my cattle. I don't even have a dog. I'm as single as a stonemason can be.'

$$\infty$$

'Don't even think about it,' Rowan said to the chocolate-coloured kelpie puppy who was about to latch onto the hem of his jeans as he neared the back door of the Ashcroft farmhouse.

For once it was only Monet intent on waging another war on his wardrobe. Primrose was preoccupied over near the drystone wall with Orien, Clancy's silver tabby cat, searching for tiny lizards. Nearby, Iris, Primrose's mother, slept in the early morning sun. Unlike yesterday's storm that had interrupted his first day at Crookwell Park, today so far had delivered clear and sunny skies.

He made it to the homestead just as Primrose decided that chasing him would be more fun than waiting for antisocial lizards. He closed the screen door within seconds of her and Monet leaping all over him. They stared through the gauze, their expressions crestfallen.

'Both of you are too cute for your own good,' he said, shaking his head and opening the door to pat each of their silky heads.

Then, before he either got licked to death or they dashed past his legs, he quickly stepped back inside.

Once in the mudroom, he shucked off his boots to add to the collection of neat pairs beneath the low bench. On the wall above the boots hung a line of oilskins and hats. His gaze lingered on a long oilskin at the far end. No longer did his father's coat hang from its usual peg. Loss caused Rowan's chest to tighten, but the sensation soon passed. It felt right that Heath's coat should occupy his father's spot.

He turned to follow the wide hallway to the kitchen where he could smell the aroma of fresh coffee. The historic Ashcroft homestead was always going to be Clancy's. As much as he and Clancy both held fond childhood memories of where they'd grown up, he knew how much the house meant to her. When he'd been involved with Eloise, a time he referred to as his year of temporary insanity, he'd planned to build a stone home on the other side of the river. Not that Eloise had shared his dream.

Now he was content to live in the coach house and one day become a doting uncle to Clancy and Heath's future children. He ignored the tug inside that said how much he too would like to have a family and stopped to look at a photo on the wall. He smiled at the image that showed him and Clancy standing next to a snowman who had a crooked carrot for a nose. He had his hands behind his back and seconds after the picture was taken he'd thrown a snowball at his father. He couldn't wait to teach the next generation how to have a snowball fight.

His amusement died as he kept walking. Except teaching future nieces and nephews bad habits wasn't exactly being Captain Serious. Just like how yesterday after his house tour with Grace he'd given in to the impulse to comfort her. He still wasn't sure exactly what had gone on between them, only that when she'd stared out at the garden, her face impassive, she hadn't fooled him. She was worried and upset, or both. So he'd spoken without thinking, another trait he was supposed to be curbing.

At the time it made sense to say he was single to prove that the restoration work would have his undivided attention in case that had been her concern. Grace hadn't needed to put into words how much Crookwell Park meant to her. He'd seen it in the way her mouth had softened and her eyes had come alive as they'd walked through the rooms. Now all he felt was foolish. Instead of giving her a simple answer that he'd get the work done as soon as possible, he'd allowed his emotions to seep through his control.

He paused at the closed kitchen door. Just like every other morning when he dropped by, Clancy and Heath would be seated side by side at the kitchen island bench eating their breakfast. Even though he was done with relationships, a part of him still yearned for a bond as strong and as authentic as that between his sister and best mate. He squared his shoulders and pushed open the door.

Clancy greeted him with a smile before her attention went to the black stain on his stone-coloured work shirt. 'Please don't tell me you're off to Grace's place?'

He swiped a piece of bacon off Clancy's plate on his way over to turn on the kettle. 'No, it's Saturday. Why?'

'Just as well. Don't you even own an iron?'

He looked across at Heath who shrugged. No one ironed work clothes except Cynthia. Since she and Dan had become a couple, Dan had been looking as neat and clean as a day-old calf.

Clancy continued to stare at him, breakfast forgotten as she waited for an answer.

'No.'

'There's supposed to be one in the top of the laundry cupboard.' She looked between him and Heath.

Rowan pulled his no-idea face which Heath matched. Heath had stayed in the coach house during the spring and obviously hadn't ironed anything either.

'Men,' Clancy muttered loud enough for them to hear. 'At least the shirt you wore to Grace's yesterday was clean.'

Rowan looked down at the grease stain that had been the result of replacing a bearing in the tractor. 'And this one is too.' He held up the rolled sleeve that sported a new rip from Monet's puppy teeth. 'See ... it's been on the line.'

Heath grinned. 'Of course yesterday's shirt was clean; it's brand new.'

Rowan made himself a coffee. 'Don't remind me.'

His gruff tone conveyed exactly how excruciating it had been for Clancy to accompany him to the clothing store to restock his wardrobe.

Clancy laughed. 'For someone who can jump off a tower attached to nothing but a rubber band, I can't believe you hate trying on clothes.'

Rowan grunted as he sat at the island bench across from Heath and Clancy. Heath shot him a sympathetic look.

'Just as well,' Clancy continued, 'that extra pair of jeans and good shirt we bought won't need an iron. They'd still have their tags on.'

Rowan looked at Clancy from over the top of his mug. 'There was no *we* ... and why exactly would they need an iron?'

Clancy's smile was as sweet as the Anzac biscuits that now cooled on a rack on the side bench. 'For this afternoon's high tea.'

Coffee unfinished, he came to his feet. 'Sorry, I've got cattle to drench.'

'Rowan Parker,' Clancy said in a deceptively mild tone. 'I sent you an email with the flyer saying I bought tickets.'

'It must have gone to spam.'

'And your reminder text?'

He went to tip his coffee down the sink before he could incriminate himself any further. He was guilty of skimming his sister's texts and not always replying.

'Taite's going,' Clancy said, swinging around on the bar stool to watch him.

He folded his arms and leaned against the sink. 'What did Brenna bribe him with?'

'Nothing. She told him you were going.'

Rowan silenced a groan. Clancy on her own was a master negotiator and now with Brenna involved he was facing a stacked deck. 'I'm not.'

'Of course you are. As if you'd let Taite go by himself.'

Clancy knew that as the last single men standing, he and Taite would indeed have each other's backs.

Rowan flicked his attention to Heath. From his widening grin it was clear he'd managed to avoid going.

Before Rowan could speak, Clancy answered his unspoken question. 'Heath has to work on the design for the school mural.'

'I bet he does.'

Heath stood to collect his and Clancy's empty plates and clasped Rowan's shoulder on his way past to the dishwasher. 'There'll be cake.'

Rowan did his best to glower, which only made Heath chuckle.

Clancy gazed at him expectantly. They both knew he rarely refused her anything. Plus the afternoon tea was to raise money for the hospital's much-needed physio touch machine.

'I'll go for one hour and I'll need a list of all the ladies in the quilting club.'

'Two hours and I'll give you the list before we leave.'

'Take the deal,' Heath said, voice low. 'There's a fashion parade.'

Rowan sighed. He'd be there forever. 'Two hours and not a minute longer.'

Clancy left her seat. 'Wonderful.' She kissed his cheek. 'Of course ... you'll need to shave.'

He didn't reply as he scraped a hand across his stubble. His cows wouldn't care how scruffy he looked.

Clancy's focus shifted to his hair. When he'd been with Eloise she'd always expected him to have a short-back-and-sides style so when he'd gone overseas to sort himself out he'd allowed his hair to grow. He'd had it cut twice since he'd returned and didn't think he needed another trim. Except over the past few days Clancy had been giving him pointed hints he needed to see Julie at the hair salon. It wasn't his imagination that this timeframe coincided with when he'd met Grace.

'Clance ...' he said, tone firm.

'What?' Her eyes were round and innocent. 'Everyone's making an effort. A shave won't kill you. Brenna's already told Taite he has to brush his hair.'

Rowan didn't smile.

'I know what you're thinking,' Clancy added. 'And I know better than to push you and Grace together. If that was my plan I'd have organised for you to pick Grace up instead of Brenna.'

He knew he'd been too late to hide his reaction to the news that Grace would be at the high tea when Clancy swapped a quick look with Heath. Any damage control would be futile, both knew him almost better than he knew himself, so he just spoke the truth.

'Yes, I have noticed Grace, but that isn't going to lead to anything for either of us. She's only here for the summer and has personal things to work through. As for me ... I'm done. I'm not making a fool of myself a second time.'

'You never made a fool of yourself.' Clancy touched his arm. 'Half the males in the district, including the married ones, were in love with Eloise.'

Heath picked up an Anzac biscuit from the cooling rack and tossed it to him. 'Eat up. That sweet tooth of yours will get you into trouble. Stay away from the high tea table. Cream and scones equals mingling.'

Rowan caught the biscuit with one hand and took a bite. He then held up his other hand for Heath to throw him another one.

Clancy again muttered under her breath as she went to pack the rest of the biscuits away.

∝

By that afternoon Rowan's morning sugar rush had subsided. He'd drenched two mobs of cattle and sweltered in the shed fixing his broken boom spray. Dressed in dark denim jeans that felt new and stiff and a blue-and-white checked shirt that he was sure was a size too small across the shoulders, he parked at the far end of the main street. The high tea was to be held in the park adjacent to the library, so he and Taite had planned to meet as far away as possible. By his calculations his two hours started the minute he left his ute, so if there happened to be a leisurely ten-minute stroll to the event, the time still counted.

He'd already received a string of disgruntled texts from Taite about having to iron his shirt and brush his hair. Rowan passed a hand over his now clean-shaven jaw. In keeping with Clancy's side of the bargain she'd handed him a handwritten list of the quilting club members. To his dismay it filled the whole page. He'd committed the names to memory but there was one he didn't have to memorise. Grace Davenport. She'd been the last member listed and had been labelled with an asterisk.

When he'd glanced at Clancy, she'd explained that Grace was a potential member. While she'd said she'd be too busy to come regularly, when Brenna mentioned that she'd made a memory quilt for her mother, Grace had seemed more interested.

Rowan reached behind his driver's seat for his usual cap and then with a sigh grabbed his wide-brimmed hat instead. A tapping on his window had him turn. A tidy Taite scowled at him through the glass. Rowan couldn't help but smile. If Taite continued to wear such a glower no one would come near them. He was a man-mountain and already intimidating enough.

'You owe me,' Taite growled as Rowan left his ute.

'We owe each other. Our sisters played us both.'

'I might have known.' Taite's blue gaze scanned his clothes. 'Clance take you shopping?'

'Going for a run on Overflow Road would have been far less painful.'

Taite's laughter was a deep rumble in his chest.

They fell into step beside each other as they took their time to amble towards the park. From the variety of cars lined up and down the main street, half the town had to be at the high tea.

The closer they came, the louder the classical music lilting on the warm breeze and the slower they walked. Over near the park gazebo festooned with flowers was a series of long tables draped in white. Each chair sported a large fancy bow on the back. To the right stood a turquoise and white old-fashioned caravan decorated with bunting that already had a coffee queue.

'This is as bad as a wedding,' Taite grumbled.

Everywhere Rowan looked there seemed to be women, their dresses long and flowing or short and tight. Finally at the end of the furthest table he saw a small cluster of outnumbered men.

He glanced at his watch. 'Only one hour and forty-five minutes to go.'

Taite wasn't listening. He gave a low whistle. 'Who's that with our bossy sisters?'

Rowan turned. It was Grace. But not a Grace he recognised. He'd only ever seen her wearing dark-coloured tops and jeans. While she still wore black, this time it was a dress that clung to curves that were no longer hidden. As for her long hair, she'd twisted it into some sort of style that revealed the graceful line of her neck.

'My boss.' Even to his own ears his voice sounded taut.

'Let's say hi.'

Rowan grabbed his arm. 'To stay single we can't mingle, remember.' Already he and Taite were being cast hopeful smiles. 'Plus, if we go over we'll only draw attention to Grace. Trust me, it's the last thing she'd want.'

He weathered Taite's speculative look.

When Grace glanced their way, he gave her a casual wave. When she returned the gesture, even though she hadn't smiled, it made him feel glad he was there.

He and Taite made a beeline to where the majority of the local men had taken refuge. A collection of smaller tables were laden with silver trays filled with scones, cupcakes, pastries and finger sandwiches. Thankful they didn't have to leave their seats to eat, they settled back to talk about anything manly that didn't involve flowers, white linen or crystal.

While he joined in with the conversations, Rowan remained acutely aware of where Grace was at all times. At first she'd sat two tables over with Clancy and Brenna, where she'd been inundated with people stopping by to meet her. Then she'd stood over near the gazebo chatting with the sisters. Rowan risked another sideways glance. Now she was on her own in the coffee line. While she appeared relaxed, her shoulders were too rigid. Just like yesterday after their tour she was doing all that she could to hide how she really felt.

He caught Taite's eye and pushed back his chair. 'How about I make that introduction to Grace?'

The deer farmer didn't need to be asked twice.

Grace greeted them with a smile that didn't quite erase the strain pinching her expression. Just like the other times when around her, Rowan didn't stop to think before he spoke.

'Grace, this is Taite, Brenna's brother. He lives out your way and is heading home if you'd like a lift.'

Taite, who showed no surprise at Rowan's words, nodded. They often went along with each other's random ideas, which usually involved getting out of a social engagement.

Hesitation creased Grace's brow and her grip on her coffee tightened. Now he was close he could see the light application of makeup that made her large eyes appear more gold than green and turned her lips a glossy pale pink.

'I'll let Clancy know,' he added. 'I'm here for at least another half an hour.'

'It's no trouble,' Taite added with a grin.

'The truth is I am ready to go.' Grace lowered her voice. 'I am all talked out and don't want to leave Bundy for too long.'

Before she turned to walk away with Taite, her gaze met Rowan's. 'See you Monday.'

He only nodded. The three simple words had triggered a warning spike of adrenaline and anticipation through his veins. He didn't need to do a risk assessment to know that just when he was supposed to be Captain Serious, spending time with his new boss was fast shaping up to be one massive risk.

CHAPTER
5

'We really need to decide what to do today,' Grace said to Bundy as she shared her second piece of breakfast toast with the kelpie.

Midmorning sunshine streamed through the kitchen window, heating the small space. Usually by this time they'd be outside to see the last of the kangaroos and wallabies grazing on the green slope in front of the mansion. Now the only place any kangaroo or wallaby would be was in the shade. There was no excuse for being so indecisive. It wasn't as though she didn't have a hundred and one things to do.

Her bees needed to be moved to a new home, but that could wait. She liked hearing their busy hum and seeing them flit around the garden. A new skip had arrived ready to be filled with more rubbish and debris. She'd also taken delivery of compost bins for the wheelbarrow-loads of weeds she was yet to pull out. But as much as she didn't want to admit it, she'd taken to structuring her day according to whatever Rowan was doing.

She poured herself another mug of tea she didn't really want. Even though she'd discovered he was in fact single, which meant she should be limiting all contact, a stubborn and illogical part of her couldn't stay away. Each morning this week she'd taken him a coffee and discussed how his work was progressing. When he went to town for lunch, she had her own, and then she timed being in the garden in the evenings to wave him off. As today was Saturday and he wasn't there, she didn't quite know how to keep herself busy.

Bundy tilted his head at her sigh. She could go to town but after the high tea she was still recovering from a social overload. She'd spoken to more people that afternoon than she had in the past year. She thought she'd been hiding her exhaustion until the smile in Rowan's grey eyes had turned serious. Whenever he looked at her, he seemed to always know more than what she wanted him to see.

The high tea had also answered her question about whether or not it was her grief that was causing her to feel off kilter whenever around him. It wasn't. Taite too was good-looking, plus he had a gruff gentleness that put her at ease. But even though they'd been alone in his four-wheel drive, she had no idea what colour his eyes were, what his cologne smelt like, or what they'd talked about apart from his sculptures. Her reaction to the deer farmer was exactly the same as it had been to any other man: indifferent.

A word that couldn't be used to describe the way she responded to Rowan. If she'd thought him gorgeous when unshaven and work dusty, when he'd been cleanshaven, dressed in town clothes and smelling of fresh cedar, she'd found it difficult to look away.

She gave in to her restlessness and stood to collect her phone from off the bench. Until she worked out a way to combat her reaction, she had to keep her wits firmly in place. She already knew

Aubrey would agree, but needing to hear her say so, Grace returned to her chair to call her.

Aubrey's smile lit up the screen. 'I was starting to think you'd been whisked away by your resident ghost.'

Grace returned her smile. 'I'll have you know the figure I saw was human and Bundy saw it too.' She tipped the phone for Aubrey to see the kelpie, who wagged his tail.

'Aw, he's adorable, even if I'm not a dog person. How long will he be with you?'

'No idea. Apparently on Thursdays he has to be at school to be a story dog, but the holidays don't end for a few weeks so I hope he's in no rush to leave.'

She righted the phone to look at Aubrey properly. On the wall of her minimalist harbour-view flat was a large painting of a beach scene that she'd sourced for her. Even though it was the weekend and Aubrey was wearing a casual sleeveless white top, she had to be at her kitchen table working on her laptop.

'What's up?' her best friend asked, her tone no longer light. It seemed Aubrey had been studying her too.

'Nothing?'

'Grace Davenport ... even if you weren't the queen of understatements I wouldn't believe you. It's ten in the morning and you're still in your PJs.'

'In my defence, it is Saturday.'

'Are you missing your parents?'

'I am ... but apart from a bad moment at the start of the week it's a different type of missing, a less overwhelming missing. When I'm next door it's almost as though they're with me. When Mum was in hospital we spent hours discussing what we would do with the rooms. When I have a problem, I think about how Dad would have solved it.'

'By problems do you mean Rowan?'

Grace thought before answering. 'I wouldn't exactly call him a problem … more a dilemma. I also know what I need to do. I'm just not used to having my personal and professional lines blur.'

She expected Aubrey to make one of her witty quips. If she was the queen of understatements, Aubrey was the queen of boundaries. Instead she stared at her.

'Grace … it's not necessarily a bad thing if the lines have blurred. You've been through so much. If being around Rowan feels personal then if there was ever a time to take off your professional hat, it's now. This isn't some work project; this is your life.'

'Really?'

'I know I've teased you about Rowan, but even though now might not be the time for a relationship, what you do need is a friend. The fact we are even having this conversation tells me Rowan could be good for you.'

Grace silenced her words that there was zero chance of such a thing while she continued to feel so out of her depth when around him. 'Maybe I'll go easy on the overthinking?'

'Not that I can talk, but that might be sensible. How are those possums of yours? Moved back in?'

'No, it's safe to visit. The ants will be gone soon too.'

Aubrey's grimace was cut short by a loud beeping on her laptop. 'Sorry … I need to take this. I'll check in later to see what time you get out of your PJs.'

Grace ended the call and went to take a shower. Aubrey would worry if she wasn't properly dressed the next time they spoke. Overthinking also wasn't going to get the graffiti off the mansion walls.

But once outside, instead of heading into the old house, Grace strolled after Bundy as nose to the ground he followed the scent left by an animal visitor—probably the echidna they saw yesterday. Part of their usual morning routine was to take a walk before tackling the day's jobs. From the trees where the nesting boxes were installed came the hum of cicadas, while a faint honey fragrance carried on the breeze.

Grace stopped to snap a photo of Bundy against the mountain backdrop for Mabel then angled her phone to capture the wisps of clouds swirled through the blue sky. Her mobile was filled with almost as many scenic shots as images of Bundy. She slowly lowered her phone. While the foothill directly ahead of them was little more than a rocky outcrop, the ones to her left rolled in gentle waves. A small fenced area filled with the blocky shapes of headstones caught her attention. One place she hadn't yet visited was the Russell family burial plot. She'd avoided the site in case it triggered her grief. But this morning she felt strong enough to visit.

She whistled to Bundy. The kelpie raced to her side and together they went through the garden gate. Once at the elevated burial plot she paused beside the rusted fence to catch her breath. It wasn't a coincidence that the Russell family had been buried in this particular location. From where she stood, she directly overlooked the mansion.

To her surprise the old gate opened without a groan or creak. Unlike the other gates at Crookwell Park, there was also no thick grass growing around its base. While the weathered headstones were devoid of any vases or flowers, the more she gazed around the more she was certain that this place of remembrance hadn't been abandoned. Beyond the fence line the ground was covered in sticks, strips of bark and small branches while the area she stood in was tidy. Crookwell Park's trespassers hadn't only been vandals. Someone had visited to pay their respects.

She cleared away what few sticks lay scattered amongst the graves before walking along to read the names etched into the sandstone. Instead of the plots being laid out in neat lines, it was as though the family members had been buried in a random plan without any thought to design or order.

The first headstone was a large and very tall ornate cross set apart from the other graves, which after a large gap formed a row alongside it. The next line was indented so that it started directly below the second grave of the previous row. Grace slowly made her way along, reading the loving inscriptions that spoke of young lives lost far too soon to accidents and ill health.

To reach the final resting place, which had to be that of the eccentric bachelor Lawrence Junior, she walked down the hill to where there was a single grave. Unlike the other burial plots, this one was positioned in alignment with the first large headstone.

Sadness slipped through her. Whatever the cause of Lawrence's estrangement with his sisters, it must never have been resolved. Both of his siblings had been buried in the row that contained their parents. She bent to brush off the dust dulling the golden sandstone. After a moment of contemplative silence, she retraced her steps to the gate.

Instead of taking the path that she and Bundy had followed earlier, she took an alternative route. She hadn't yet explored the far-left garden corner that dipped behind the mansion and this new trail looked like it would lead them there.

When she reached the bottom of the hill, she found that so much grass had grown around the farm gate, it refused to open further than a hand span. Even if she climbed over, Bundy would be on the wrong side, so she set off along the fence line. It wouldn't be long until she'd come across a kangaroo-sized hole that she and Bundy could fit through.

Except the more they walked, the sharper the angle of the downward slope. When she saw what had to be a boundary fence blocking their way, she was about to turn around when she caught sight of a gate beyond the wire. Unlike the other Crookwell Park gates, this one was clearly used, and imprinted in the dirt were the tracks of a vehicle with a narrow wheelbase.

Grace looked over her shoulder to check where Bundy was. She hadn't forgotten about the figure she'd seen in the storm. City life had made her cautious but at the same time she wanted to know if anyone was loitering about. Instead of Bundy being near the tree where she'd last seen him, the kelpie had ducked through a hole in the boundary fence and was heading away from Crookwell Park and into the bush. He stopped and turned his black-and-tan head to look at her as if to say, *What's taking you so long?*

She checked she had phone coverage, in case they encountered trouble, before climbing through the gap in the wire. The further they walked the more certain Grace was that the kelpie knew where he was going. The narrow tyre tracks led to somewhere he must have visited before. Somewhere close by she could hear running water and through the thinning trees she caught glimpses of green. But whatever she'd expected when the trees opened into a clearing, it wasn't what she saw.

Nestled in a tiny valley cupped by the hills was a large bluestone cottage. Unlike her neglected home, this dwelling had been well-preserved and loved. A neat vegetable garden lay tucked by the side and a small garden shed was stocked with winter wood. Beside the cottage a second shed contained some sort of farm vehicle that resembled a golf buggy, its wheelbase a perfect match to the tyre prints.

She followed Bundy towards a chook pen filled with five white speckled hens. When the kelpie drew near, he gave a bark. At first there was only the cackle of the chickens and then a thin figure made his way out of the enclosed back section. Moving with the use of a cane, the old man carried two eggs in his other hand. He lifted his walking stick to shut the wooden door before slowly turning to face them.

'Bundy, how good to see you.' The stranger glanced across at Grace with a smile. 'And you brought a friend. I'd offer to shake hands but my balance isn't what it used to be. I'm Frank Williams.'

Even though she didn't trust easily—she was very careful about who she let in—Bundy having faith in this man eased her reservations.

She matched his smile. 'I'm Grace, your new neighbour.'

'It's a pleasure to meet you.' Frank's faded blue eyes twinkled. 'Hope those possums aren't bothering you? On a still night, I can hear them from here.'

'They've much nicer homes now than my draughty roof.' She looked around. 'I didn't know anyone lived nearby.'

'Not many people do.' Frank's well-modulated voice hardened. 'I don't go to town … I've dealt with enough people to last a lifetime.'

She fell into step beside him as they made their slow way to the cottage. It seemed as though she wasn't the only one to have come to the mountains to heal. 'If you ever need anything, please let me know.'

'That's very kind of you.' Frank halted to rest on his cane. 'I hope I didn't worry you the other day. I know you saw me.'

Grace nodded as relief unfurled inside. What she'd seen had been on her mind. While Frank's tall frame was now stooped, she could tell he'd once been a powerful man and in the poor visibility would have looked bigger than he was.

'I wasn't sure what I saw until I realised Bundy had seen you as well. To be honest, it did put my nerves a little on edge.'

'I apologise. I'd come to introduce myself and then the storm beat me over. The main house can be eerie but you don't have to worry about seeing or hearing anything unusual.' He winked. 'My arthritis might stop me from doing many things but I can still pass as a pretty respectable ghost when I need to. It doesn't take much to send those hooligans packing.'

Grace smiled, liking her new neighbour more and more. 'So that's why the back of the house has hardly been touched.'

Frank's grin was of a much younger man. 'Blame the ex-judge in me; I can't abide wanton damage. Now, would you like to come inside for a cup of tea?'

❧

It didn't matter how loud Rowan cranked up his country music in his Land Cruiser ute cabin, the volume wasn't enough to distract him from thoughts of Grace.

Saturday was technically a Grace-free day and he couldn't now spend his weekend wondering what she was doing. The only thing on his mind should be the latest project of the local historical hut volunteer group that he and Taite were members of.

As busy as he'd been all week stabilising and rebuilding the section of crumbling wall, he'd been just as busy listening out to see if Grace needed help with lifting things into the skip. He'd meant what he'd said to Clancy and Heath about not making a fool of himself a second time.

But that didn't stop him from looking forward every morning to chatting with Grace over a coffee. And now from thinking about her. He skipped a too slow song and took the turn that would take him into the mountains and to the high-country hamlet of Riley's Crossing.

Once a stopover for the herds of cattle heading south to the markets, now all that remained was an old schoolhouse and a riverside camping area. A fire ignited by a lightning strike had damaged the 1860s schoolhouse last summer. Since he'd returned from the Cotswolds, he'd repaired the stone foundations so that the wooden walls could go up. The plan for this weekend was to replace the roof shingles. Once the schoolhouse was completed, the volunteer group had an old miner's hut to restore so it could provide shelter to cross-country skiers.

It took several seconds to recognise the ring of his phone amongst his blaring music but the recognition of Grace's name was instant. He answered via Bluetooth, hoping his voice sounded far more casual than he felt.

'Hi, Grace.'

'Hi.' There was a slight pause as if she were processing that he either knew her number or had her in his contacts. 'Sorry to bother you but I was wondering if you were on your way to the schoolhouse yet.'

He slowed, ready to turn if she had a problem.

'I am but I'm not far away if you need any more Aubusson rugs or homes for deceptively cute possums?'

Her soft laughter, just like her smile, had the power to further weaken the hold he kept on his resolve. 'No, Frank just needs his car jump-started.'

Frank. It wasn't a name he knew. He kept his tone neutral as he did a U-turn. He'd soon find out if Grace had a city visitor. 'Flat battery?'

'That's what we're thinking. Neither of us have jumper leads and Frank has to leave for Canberra soon. His driveway is the first gate on the left when you drive into Crookwell Park. There's no mailbox.'

'Frank's a … local?' He was pretty sure he knew everyone in town, plus he'd never heard of any house out near Grace.

'Yes. I had no idea I had a neighbour.'

Rowan pressed harder on the accelerator. That made two of them. He hoped whoever this Frank was he was legit. 'Is Bundy with you?'

'He is.' Even without seeing her face he could hear the smile in her voice. 'Rowan, it's fine. Bundy took me to see him.'

Rowan's grip on the steering wheel loosened. 'Bundy knows Frank?'

'He's been to visit a few times.'

'Okay. I'll see you in about ten minutes.'

He ended the call and rang Taite.

'Let me guess …' Taite's deep voice rumbled. 'You're running late. Monet and Primrose bury your keys?'

'Ha, too funny. For the record I was late that one time because I was chased by Mrs Moore's goose. And, in my defence, I was on one crutch.'

Taite chuckled. 'So where are you?'

'Heading to Crookwell Park. Have you heard of a Frank who lives near there?'

'No. Why?'

'Grace is at some guy's place who has no mailbox.'

'Are you on your way? It sounds suss.'

'I am. Bundy's with her and she says he knows him.'

'Actually, I think there is a place at the back of Crookwell Park. Dad once went there to collect a butter churner.'

When Taite and Brenna's father passed away, he'd left numerous sheds filled with all sorts of collectibles, from meat safes to vintage cars. It was his extensive collection of old-fashioned tools that the historical hut group used to maintain the authenticity of the miner and grazier huts they restored.

'I'll let you know what I find. Tell the others I'll be there soon.'

'No rush. We'll save all the good jobs for you.'

'Gee, thanks.'

On the day he'd been late he'd ended up working on the stone chimney in the rain while the others had taken a long beer break under the tarpaulin. It wasn't always an advantage being the sole person with a specific set of skills.

The phone dropped out but not before he heard Taite's laughter.

It wasn't long until he turned onto Grace's road and there as described was a regular farm gate on the left. He'd always thought the entry was an access point for the section of the Smiths' farm that ran along this side of the road. Obviously not.

He opened the gate and drove through. Instead of an all-weather gravel road, the driveway was little more than a grassed track. Whoever this Frank was he'd have trouble getting out in wet weather let alone the snow.

The track wove through the gum trees as it climbed its way into the foothills. To his right he could see the distant rooflines and chimneys of Crookwell Park. The trees abruptly stopped and he found himself in a small green valley on the edge of which stood a large bluestone cottage. He'd been interested in stone since a child and over the years had become familiar with what he'd thought were all of the local bluestone buildings. He'd no idea this one existed.

As he drew near he registered the solar panels and a generator housed in its own shed at the back of the cottage. Frank most likely lived off-grid plus he was a stickler for order. The only sign of disrepair was that the left corner of the dry-stone wall surrounding the garden was missing some capstones.

Rowan parked near the open door of a garage which housed a fancy bronze four-wheel drive. There was no way Frank had ever driven this vehicle to town. Someone would have noticed.

Bundy raced out of the cottage doorway, closely followed by Grace. She gave him a wave which he returned. A smile relaxed her face, and it wasn't her usual gone-too-soon one. He left his ute as a figure leaning heavily on a cane approached. Rowan wasn't deceived by the stranger's age and apparent frailty. The shrewd look he shot him from beneath bushy grey brows was formidable. Even in his twilight years, Grace's mysterious new neighbour was a man to be reckoned with.

An impression confirmed by the steely strength of his handshake. 'Rowan, you making a detour is much appreciated.'

'Don't mention it.'

It wasn't just Frank's expensive car that would have caused a stir in Bundilla had he been a regular visitor but also the formal way he spoke. Frank definitely wasn't from around here, even if it looked as though he'd lived in the cottage for years.

Frank continued to study Rowan, his gaze sharp. 'I knew your father. He was a good man.'

'Thank you.' Rowan weathered a surge of loss that he fought to keep from showing in his expression. He didn't want the conversation, or his reaction, to trigger Grace's grief. 'He was.'

Rowan didn't ask how he knew his father. If Frank wanted to volunteer the information, he would.

Respect glinted in the older man's gaze. 'I had a flat tyre one winter and your father stopped to help. We shared a common interest in chess and a good red.'

Conscious of Grace's hazel gaze having never left his face, Rowan nodded before changing the subject. 'I take it your car hasn't been driven lately.'

Frank manoeuvred himself around on his cane so he could look at the four-wheel drive, which didn't sport a speck of dust. 'There's no need to go anywhere. I have everything I need.'

Rowan went to the toolbox on the back of his ute to collect his jumper leads.

When Grace passed him the four-wheel drive keys that she'd brought with her from the cottage, their fingers brushed. He didn't dare look at her even though the brief touch ricocheted through him. Frank watched the two of them closely and Rowan was sure he didn't miss a thing.

He lifted the bonnet on each vehicle and matched the jumper leads to the corresponding battery terminals. In Frank's car he attached the last clamp to the engine block to prevent an explosive spark. He turned on his ute and went to start the bronze four-wheel drive. After a moment, it spluttered and fired into life.

Grace beamed a smile so full of thanks that he forgot all about Frank and kept his attention on her for longer than he should have. Realising he was staring, he moved to remove the jumper leads.

Frank hobbled over as Rowan turned off his ute. 'Thank you.'

'I'm happy to help.'

Frank looked across at Grace. 'Could I offer you and Bundy a lift home?'

'We'd love one. After all those scones, I can hardly move, let alone walk.' Grace turned to Rowan and took a step closer. She half lifted a hand towards him. 'I hope we haven't held you up.'

He kept himself still, caught between moving forwards to feel her touch and the need to take a step back. The way Grace's gaze searched his warned him that he hadn't buried his earlier grief deep enough. 'It's all fine. I'll make it to the schoolhouse for morning smoko.'

Then, knowing that every second he stood with Grace an arm's length away increased the likelihood she'd discover his thoughts, he gave Frank a nod and climbed into his ute.

It was only when he'd made it back onto the bitumen road the tension in his jaw unlocked. So much for having a Grace-free weekend. The memory of how her smile lit up the gold in her eyes would distract him long after tonight's campfire flames had dulled to embers.

When his phone rang, this time the console screen displayed Clancy's name.

He cleared his throat to erase his lingering strain. 'Hey.'

'Hey yourself. I hear you've had an eventful morning.'

'Word travels fast.'

'It does when Brenna's involved. You know what she's like with her theories.' Brenna enjoyed people watching and often concocted outlandish and sometimes spot-on reasons behind why people acted as they did. 'Taite was a little light on details. What's this Frank like?'

'He speaks like he's a university professor and isn't someone I'd want to get on the wrong side of. He must have someone who collects his mail, brings him groceries and chops his wood. He also knew Dad.'

'I'm pretty sure he's the man Dad used to visit. He'd take a bottle of wine and Mum would send a cheese platter. When I asked where Dad was going, she said out to Summit Road to keep a friend company who'd lost his wife.'

'It's definitely Frank.'

'It has to be. So, Brenna's theory, and mine too, is that the rumours of Lawrence Russell Senior's arranged marriage to his society wife being a nightmare were true. He fell for someone else and this woman lived in Frank's cottage.' Clancy's voice turned dreamy. 'I think Lawrence Senior and the love of his life raised a family over there.'

Rowan frowned, hoping his scepticism wouldn't be obvious in his reply. 'Possibly.'

'Possibly? It makes perfect sense. Now you'd better hurry up or your sweet tooth is going to miss out. Brenna said Taite has already started on morning smoko.'

After their call ended, Rowan's frown deepened, food the last thing on his mind. Clancy's romantic faith in happily-ever-afters had sustained her for the decade Heath had been away. He wished he could share her optimism. Letting someone into your life came with risks, and even if he couldn't stop thinking about Grace, his risk-taking days were long gone.

CHAPTER
6

'Too much?' Grace asked Bundy, who lay sleeping on the rug in front of the fireplace.

Bundy lifted an eye to check out her wardrobe and then went back to his nap. No tail wag meant no tick of approval.

Grace smoothed her hands down her skirt before tugging at the top of her shirt. 'It is rather black.'

She went back into her bedroom. When she'd packed in a hurry to leave Sydney, she hadn't thought about what clothes she might need. To match her mood she'd thrown in any item that was dark coloured. She went to the tallboy Rowan had delivered and opened the middle drawer. The only clothes that weren't black or navy were a white T-shirt and a tan skirt. They'd have to do.

She changed into the outfit and then rummaged around in her suitcase where her shoes still lived. Just like the rest of the wardrobe, her choices were limited. She either had black flats, hiking boots, winter ugg boots, which she had no idea why she'd tossed in, and strappy gold sandals. Again, these had been an odd choice. It wasn't as if she had anything to wear them with let alone anywhere to wear them to. She slipped on the black flats. Surely a Monday morning quilting class in the community hall didn't require heels?

Bundy leaped to his feet as gravel crunched beneath car tyres. Rowan had arrived to start work.

After making two coffees, hands full, she manoeuvred her way through the cottage door. When the brisk breeze blew hair across her eyes, she remembered she hadn't straightened it let alone tied it back. Not that it really mattered how she looked. It might be week two of Rowan working at Crookwell Park but today was day one of re-establishing the ground rules between them.

As much as Aubrey had been right about her needing a friend, things had changed since their Saturday phone call. She'd now met Frank and as they'd shared a pot of tea they'd bonded over their fondness for history and having their own space. Since he'd stayed in Canberra for the weekend, she'd popped over yesterday to take his hens kitchen scraps and to collect their eggs.

But the most important thing to have changed since her conversation with Aubrey was that she'd again glimpsed the pain Rowan hid behind his smile. When Frank had mentioned Rowan's father, even though he hadn't appeared to react, she hadn't missed the hardening of his jaw. The urge to comfort him had been so strong it had made her forget about her own grief. When he'd gone to leave, she'd even taken a step towards him only for an unfamiliar brittleness in his eyes to stop her from going any further.

Whatever it was about him that pushed her off balance now also made her feel emotions that she wasn't equipped to handle. Instinct told her that even a simple friendship with Rowan would prove too intense. So this coffee run had to be all about ensuring their interactions remained on an impersonal and safe level. For both of them.

She rounded the corner and strove for calm, even though her heart quickened like it always did when she was about to see him.

'Morning,' she said, voice bright.

'Morning.' Rowan looked up from where he was using a chisel and mallet to shape a piece of bluestone. She wasn't sure but she thought he stilled as he stared at her before he straightened to peel off his gloves.

'How was the rest of your weekend?' she asked as she handed him his coffee.

Today stubble again roughened his jaw and the sun-bleached edges of his tawny hair stuck out from beneath his cap.

'Good. We replaced one side of the schoolhouse roof shingles.'

'Sounds like a big job.'

'It was made even bigger by some of the guys having a few beers around the campfire.' Rowan's grey gaze flicked over her. 'Off to town?'

'It's my first quilting group meeting.'

This time she was left in no doubt of his reaction. He'd gone to take a mouthful of coffee but instead his brow creased. 'Are Clancy and Brenna going?'

'I'm meeting them there.'

'I've known most of the quilting ladies all my life and they are lovely, but they like to *talk*.'

She nodded. She didn't think that was anything unusual.

'They like to talk about everyone's love lives or lack of.' Rowan paused to rub the back of his neck. 'If you have anyone waiting for you in the city, it would be a good time to mention him ... several times.'

'Seriously?'

Rowan seemed to be watching her extra closely. 'Yes.'

'And if I don't have anyone?'

An indefinable emotion flashed across his gaze. 'Then if you hear either my name or Taite's, or another guy called Trent, it would be wise to change the subject. Sandra just had a new grandson so that would be a safe topic … and when you meet Vernette, she may appear like a kind-hearted nanna who is hard of hearing, but she reads lips like a pro. So it's best if I don't come up in any conversation you have with my sister.'

Grace couldn't help smiling. Rowan's expression was intensely serious. 'I'll be too busy trying not to put the sewing machine needle through my finger to chat.'

Rowan didn't look convinced as he finished his coffee.

Sticking to her plan to keep their conversation to a minimum, unless it was about the mansion, she too drank the last of her coffee. Whereas the previous week she would have lingered, now it was time to go.

Rowan moved closer and she took hold of the mug he passed her. A gust of wind caught in her loose hair, blowing it towards his outstretched hand. The dark strands curled over his wrist and seemed to still before they slowly unravelled to slip through his fingers.

She reached up to restore order to her hair as Rowan stepped back and lowered his arm. The contact between them had only lasted seconds but it was enough to turn her breathing shallow.

Before she could get a sense of Rowan's reaction, he turned to pick up his gloves. 'Good luck with the sewing machine.'

His teasing tone didn't match the rigid set of his shoulders.

'Thanks.' Then, knowing her voice wasn't quite as steady as it should be, she added, 'I think you have a work buddy this morning.'

Rowan tugged on his gloves as he glanced over to where Bundy lay in the sun beside the bluestone wall.

'Wise decision. Bundy knows the quilting group is no place for any single male.'

∞

Rowan's words preoccupied her thoughts on the drive to town. It didn't take a genius to work out why she was still single but she couldn't fathom why Rowan was. Gorgeous, genuine and with a good heart, he could have any woman he wanted. For him to be on the quilting group's radar he must have been single for a while. She knew she hadn't imagined the rasp in his voice when he'd told her that his cattle were the only things in his life. His last relationship must have ended badly.

She followed her GPS to the corrugated iron community hall on the edge of town. Already the gravel car park out the front appeared almost full. As per Clancy's instructions, she texted to say she had arrived. By the time she'd collected her bag from the back seat, Clancy and Brenna had left the hall and were walking over.

'I'm so glad you could make it,' Clancy said after giving her a hug, her smile warm.

Brenna nodded. 'Now, before you have everyone talking to you at once, we'd better word you up.'

'Is that about the matchmaking? Rowan's already filled me in.'

Clancy and Brenna exchanged looks before Clancy said, 'I bet he did. He and Taite think nothing of riding down an almost vertical ridge yet they're petrified of being set up with anyone.'

Grace couldn't hide her amusement. 'He also mentioned someone called Trent.'

'He's the local vet,' Brenna explained. 'He lost his fiancée in a freak snowboarding accident a couple of years ago so he's usually left alone. Although he's happy to accept a few dinner invitations here and there on the proviso there's no expectations. If Rowan and Taite did the same, then they wouldn't be seen as such a challenge. Needless to say, neither of them will listen.'

Clancy's exasperated expression was almost identical to Brenna's. 'In Rowan's case, things are made worse by our mother having been a much-loved member of this quilting group. Many of the members think of him as family and will do anything to make sure he's happy … especially after the debacle with Eloise.'

Grace tried to not look curious. Her suspicions had been correct.

'Which means,' Brenna added, 'he's at the top of the matchmaking list. A crown he's not going to lose anytime soon seeing as Eloise's baby is due next month. Everyone believes the best way to get over her is to find someone else … someone like you.'

Grace blinked. No longer did she feel intrigued, just stunned and alarmed in equal measure. 'Me?'

Clancy squeezed her hand. 'Bear with us. Brenna and I have it all sorted. You see, it's not only single males the quilting group takes an extra special interest in.'

This was where Grace knew she had an opportunity to say she wasn't single, but she couldn't lie. 'I'm only here for the summer.'

'Speaking from experience,' Brenna said with a sigh, 'even a week is long enough for members to start getting ideas about your perfect match. There's a reason why Mabel says she has a deadline almost every meeting.'

Grace glanced between Clancy and Brenna. The last thing she wanted was extra attention and she wasn't getting over a messy breakup like it seemed Rowan was. He'd also gone out of his way to help her and so having his back seemed a small thing to do in return. 'What's your solution?'

'Well …' Clancy lowered her voice. 'It's really simple. With Rowan working at Crookwell Park, just go with the flow. There'll be lots of questions about him, so if you feel comfortable, answer them. The quilting ladies will interpret your answers in whatever way they want, and we know what assumptions they'll draw. Which means they won't feel the need to engineer cute meetings or give you a well-intentioned shove.'

Brenna nodded with something close to envy in her eyes. 'They will sit back and leave you both alone while they wait for Cupid to fire his arrow.'

'And when he doesn't?'

'Then you will have returned to Sydney and we would have bought Rowan more time to move on while out of the spotlight.' Clancy gave a pointed look over towards the hall where various quilting club members had congregated to peer out at them.

'One last thing,' Brenna whispered, her mouth barely moving. 'What happens in quilting club stays in quilting club. Rowan doesn't need to know Clancy and I are trying to help. He thinks we meddle enough.'

Clancy's quick grin reminded Grace of her brother. 'As if we'd do such a thing. Now we'd better go inside before Norma leans any further out of the door and falls down the steps.'

For the next hour Grace forgot all about their plan as she tried to learn everyone's names. Sandra she had no trouble remembering; the proud grandmother had shown her photos of her grandson within a minute of meeting her. Vernette was also exactly as Rowan described. Whenever Grace was chatting to someone she'd look up to see Vernette on the other side of the hall watching her with a sweet but intent expression.

She then became too busy planning her memory quilt in a checkerboard pattern to pay attention to what anyone else was doing. She chose green as a background colour, settled on a floral theme and texted Aubrey instructions on where to find her mother's suitcase of clothes. Thankfully she'd left a spare key to her storage unit with Aubrey, who would then package up what items Grace needed and send them to her.

Somewhere in the storage unit was a quilt that Grace's mother had made long ago from her own mother's clothes. Except she wouldn't be asking Aubrey to unpack it. She wasn't yet ready to see such a precious heirloom again. The quilt had protected and comforted her mother's frail body right until she'd slipped away on that starless winter night.

Realising she was staring into space instead of measuring squares, she checked to see if anyone had noticed. The lady who she thought was called Edith stopped sewing to give her a reassuring smile. Brenna waved from over at her table while Clancy sent her a questioning look as if to ask if everything was okay. Grace nodded and went back to work.

The fabric spread out before her blurred but then her sadness gave way to an uncertain sense of belonging. She'd spent so much of her childhood and teenage years feeling like she didn't fit in. As an English immigrant, sounding different and being unfamiliar with everyday Aussie words and customs had been isolating. Now, sitting in the community hall filled with the sound of sewing machines, laughter and camaraderie, it was as though she was surrounded by the warmth of the quilts the members were busy making.

She still had so much of her life to piece together and back at Crookwell Park was a stonemason who was always on her mind, but in that moment, this was exactly where she was meant to be.

Despite it being early morning on a Tuesday, Rowan already knew it was going to be a long day. It seemed as though the weather agreed.

A stiff breeze barrelled by him from where he stood on a scaffold platform, an assortment of stones and a bucket of specially prepared mortar beside him. Overhead the clouds hung heavy and low, and the tops of the high-country peaks were no longer in view. Raindrops splattered his cap and shirt, warning of the approaching deluge.

Instead of getting as much done as possible before the storm hit, Rowan kept stopping to see if Grace and Bundy were walking over. He'd made it clear on his first day when she'd brought him a coffee that she was under no obligation to make it a regular occurrence. He didn't want to impose on her kindness. But when she kept appearing, he'd grown used to starting his day talking through the things he'd be working on. He'd also enjoyed seeing how with every visit she grew more relaxed around him.

When there was still no sign of either Grace or Bundy, Rowan went back to work. It was just as well Grace had something else on this morning as there couldn't be any repeat of what had happened yesterday. When he'd looked up and seen her dressed in a colour other than black, with an unguarded smile, he'd forgotten what he was supposed to be doing. Then when he'd passed her his empty mug and the wind had blown her silken hair across his hand, it had taken all of his willpower to not close his fingers to savour the contact.

At least whatever had happened at the quilting group meeting hadn't resulted in any more matchmaking, especially with Grace. If anything he was being ignored. When he'd grabbed lunch at the café, no one had dropped by his table for a chat, which was a first. Then when he'd ducked into the post office, he'd been able to go in and out without being waylaid by any woman between the ages of eighteen and eighty.

Busy with his thoughts, he didn't realise Grace was standing at the bottom of the scaffolding until he saw Bundy climb the nearby pile of rocks. He looked over the guard rail to give her a wave before climbing down the inbuilt ladder. The aroma of coffee intensified as he reached the ground.

'Morning,' he said as he took hold of the mug she gave him.

'Sorry I'm late.' She offered him what looked like white chocolate and macadamia cookies. 'I had to wait until these were ready.'

Rowan took a still-warm cookie and tried not to stare. After the quilting club meeting Grace must have gone shopping as the cherry-red shirt she wore with her jeans was a half-button work design favoured by locals. On her feet, instead of her usual hiking boots, were brown cowgirl boots.

She too glanced at her outfit. 'No guesses where Clancy and Brenna took me after lunch.'

'As long as my beloved sister didn't make you try on almost every item in the store and then parade around like a catwalk model.'

Grace laughed softly. 'No, I suspect that's something a sister might do to her brother to wind him up.'

He took a swallow of coffee. He didn't know what surprised him more, that Grace was teasing him or that he hadn't realised by now that was indeed what Clancy had been doing.

Grace continued. 'But then again I'm no sibling expert and it might just be something Brenna does to Taite.'

Rowan made a mental note to call Taite asap. 'I can see Brenna doing exactly that ... but Clancy?'

Grace selected a cookie. 'I believe there was a certain trampoline incident.'

Rowan frowned as he thought back to all the high jinks of his couldn't-sit-still youth. There were a few trampoline pranks. He'd move Clancy's trampoline to the other side of the garden, or he'd cover it in shaving foam, or position it near a sprinkler. There also was the occasion when he'd tied it in the cedar tree. At the time he'd thought the act pure genius but his sister was the real mastermind if years later she was still exacting retribution.

Grace watched him with a smile. 'My money's on the tree one.'

'All these years ... Clancy's played me beautifully. Just as well I'm Captain Serious now.'

'Rowan ... Clancy was also quick to say how lucky she is to have you as her brother and she wouldn't have you any other way. Life can already be so serious sometimes, fun is what's needed.'

He only partially heard her words. He'd let down the people he loved by not keeping his head on straight and he wasn't doing so again.

The wind rattled the scaffolding beside them and Grace frowned at the interlaced steel and wood. 'Is it safe for you to be up there?'

'I'll call it quits once the rain arrives.'

At the rate the sky was darkening, the storm would be upon them soon.

'Before it does ...' She nodded across to where his ute was parked. 'Do you have anything in your toolbox to cut wire?'

'I do.' He sat his empty mug on top of a flat stone. 'Need a hand?'

Grace added her cup and the cookie container to the impromptu table before following him over to his Land Cruiser. 'Cutting a fence looks straightforward on the internet.'

At his raised brows she smiled. Even though it was something she was starting to do far more regularly, the sight of her face lighting up with warmth still scrambled his thoughts.

'Frank has one of those farm vehicle things and it won't fit through the gate so he's always had to walk in.'

'Always?'

'Yes, he's the spooky reason why the vandals rarely made it to the back of the house. Apparently a cape is the perfect way to hide his cane.'

Rowan's respect for Frank increased, along with his curiosity. 'No wonder there's been so many stories.' He opened his toolbox. 'How long exactly has Frank been Crookwell Park's ghost?'

'Frank said he and his wife used the cottage as a weekender before he retired and she's been gone over ten years.'

He passed Grace the wire cutters. 'That's a long time for none of us to know he lives there.'

'He has help, a husband and wife, so doesn't need to go to town. He said it holds bad memories. He was a judge and used to live in Canberra so still travels there for medical appointments.'

Rowan nodded. There would be far more to Frank's life story, but he'd already asked enough questions.

'Thanks for these.' Grace held up the wire cutters. 'I ordered a solar-powered gate but it won't be here for a few days.'

Rowan watched as Grace, with Bundy by her side, walked away. Even her gait seemed different. She moved quickly and with purpose and it wasn't just to cut the fence before the storm arrived. Her time at Crookwell Park appeared to be helping her.

He went to get back to work but before he'd reached the scaffolding, raindrops splattered across his gloves and shoulders. He turned to check where Grace and Bundy were. He'd learned long ago from his cattleman father to always respect the mountain weather.

Grace had trusted her own instincts and was on her way back.

The erratic raindrops turned into a steady patter and he scooped up the coffee mugs and cookie container. He waited for Grace and Bundy to reach him and together they headed for the side veranda. When the rain turned into a sudden onslaught, they raced up the steps.

'This feels like deja vu,' Grace said with a laugh.

Wisps of wet hair curled around her face and she stood close enough for him to breathe in her honeysuckle fragrance.

He bent to rub behind Bundy's ears. As much as this did feel familiar, he was determined it wasn't going to end the same way as last time when his need to help Grace short-circuited his common sense. He'd revealed far too much when he'd said he was single.

Grace sat the wire cutters beside where he'd put the mugs and cookies. 'Shall we finish our grand tour? This time I have lights.'

'Sounds like a plan.'

He followed her into the front reception room that while still dilapidated and in need of repair was now free from mould, rubbish and graffiti. His boots echoed on the hardwood floor as he crossed to where Grace had stopped to take a picture of a crack between two floorboards.

'I'm keeping a record of the trouble spots for the builder. I'm hoping it's only my imagination that this is getting wider.'

The concern in her voice and the worry in her eyes caused him to speak without thinking. 'Crookwell Park's lucky to have you.'

He regretted the low and quiet words as soon as they'd left his mouth. Grace stilled, her expression becoming unreadable. Just like in the café he'd overstepped some invisible line to make her feel wary.

He went to apologise but Grace spoke first. 'The truth is I'm lucky to have Crookwell Park. I bought it … in memory of my parents. They were English and this place reminded them of home.' Her chin lifted. 'I lost them last winter within a week of each other and this is my way back.'

'I'm sorry.' Rowan kept his hands by his side. It didn't matter how strong the impulse was to reach for Grace and hold her close, it would be madness to act upon it. 'When I lost my parents, they were together. England was where I went to find my way back.'

'I am so sorry too.' Grace searched his face. 'And did you?'

He chose his words carefully. 'I like to think I have. It's the poor choices I made that I'm still working on.'

She took her time to reply, as if processing his words. 'If Crookwell Park is lucky to have anyone, it's you.'

'And Frank.' Rowan lightened his tone as he felt his control disintegrating. It was getting harder and harder to keep Grace from slipping beneath his defences. She was as beautiful on the inside as she was on the outside.

Her lips curved. 'Of course. I'd hate to think how much damage would have been done without him.' She turned towards the hallway doorway. 'Not that this has anything to do with ghosts but you won't believe what I found in the library.'

Rowan let out a silent breath as he followed Grace across the room. So much for vowing this time he wouldn't say something he'd later regret.

Out in the hallway, Grace collected two camping lanterns that were sitting on the floor against the wall. Just like in the reception room, the hallway was spotless. Unlike last week, light streamed through the now clean glass of the courtyard windows.

'That's my next project.' Grace followed his gaze out to the weed-choked internal garden.

'What you need are a couple of goats.'

Determined to keep the mood upbeat, he'd meant the comment as a joke. When Grace's gaze snapped to him, he realised he'd made a serious miscalculation.

'What a great idea.'

'Actually, it's not … your fences are shocking and the goats would end up in Frank's vegetable garden. You'd also need a paddock to keep them away from the house when your builder starts. Then they'd need looking after when you're not here.'

Grace wasn't listening. She'd hooked the two lanterns over her arm and was using her phone to search on the internet. 'This one looks adorable.'

She held up a picture of an apparently angelic white goat with a curly fleece and twisting horns.

'That's a buck and even upwind you'd smell him a mile away.'

'What about these ones?'

This time the picture was of a mob of feral goats from out west who would be unused to humans.

'No.'

While she wasn't smiling, he had the distinct impression she wanted to. 'Don't you like goats?'

'I'm a cattleman.'

'Who does like goats? Trent?'

'Yes.'

'I'll talk to him. I'm sure whoever will put in the new gate could fix the fences and I was already going to need someone to look after everything when I'm not here.' She turned to look at the courtyard. 'My mum used to read me *Heidi* as a child.'

Even though he knew he shouldn't, the lost note in her voice had him glancing across at her sombre profile. And when he did, he also knew his most important job that day was now going to be finding her a pair of trouble-free goats.

They continued along the hallway. Bundy had already disappeared around the corner. When they arrived at the old library, Grace handed Rowan a lantern. He flipped the switch, and with Grace's also on, the room was flooded with light. As far as he could tell there was no sign of what she wanted to show him.

Grace moved to the middle of the wall that overlooked the back garden. Just like elsewhere in the room, the floor-to-ceiling bookcases were interspersed by thin wooden panels. Grace pressed the closest one to her and it opened to reveal a tall, narrow space. She reached in and took out what looked like a thick wooden pole dotted with brass studs and a cap on either end. The small latch halfway up the pole gave him a clue to what the item was.

'It's a fold-out ladder.'

Grace carefully lifted the latch and opened the ladder. 'There's another one in the middle panel between the windows.'

Rowan moved to touch the smooth wood of the ladder rungs. 'How did you find the panel?'

'Luck and overly energetic elbow grease.'

While Grace refolded the ladder and returned it to its hiding place, he went over to the marble fireplace to run his hand along the now dust-free mantle. 'This has come up well.'

'It has. I've cleaned five fireplaces, only two to go.'

Distracted by the way the lantern light threw a soft glow over her pale skin, it took a second for her words to register. 'Seven fireplaces? There's eight chimneys.'

She didn't ask if he was sure, just stared at him. As one they turned to retrace their steps outside. The rain was now a light drizzle and neither of them paid attention to the fine mist as they stood examining the roof line.

Grace pointed to the closest chimney and held up a picture of a fireplace on her phone. 'This chimney matches the reception room fireplace.'

They walked around the mansion, repeating the process until they came to a chimney at the back of the house.

Grace swiped through her phone images. 'This is odd. There's no fireplace to match this one.'

Rowan studied the chimney location, which put the associated fireplace to the left of the library. 'Perhaps it's been boarded up and is behind one of the bookcases?'

They took the quickest route inside through the original kitchen in which a cluster of servant bells still occupied a side wall. Bundy, sensing their urgency, ran alongside them. Once in the library, lanterns lifted, they surveyed the far wall which theoretically the fireplace should be behind.

Grace glanced at him. 'You said something didn't feel right in this room, remember?'

'It never has.'

As he spoke, Bundy came over and sniffed along the bottom of the bookcase in front of them.

Grace lowered her lantern to illuminate the section where the bookcase met the floor. 'Is it another rat? He always does that when he's in here.'

'Mice and rat holes are usually in a corner.' Rowan bent to run his hand along where Bundy had been interested. 'It's fresh air and there's a definite gap. The width of a … door.'

Grace's eyes widened.

Rowan straightened to feel the edge of the bookcase. When his fingers found a tiny lever on the far right hidden beneath the bookcase rim, he stopped. Grace met his gaze.

He pushed the lever. Nothing happened. Then the creak of old hinges filled the room and the heavy bookcase slowly moved away from them.

Without thought he placed a hand on the small of Grace's back. He wasn't sure what they'd find. If it wasn't something good, he wanted to be there for her.

Grace lifted her lantern. He felt rather than heard her gasp.

In the pool of light was the dull pale gleam of the missing marble fireplace. Far from being covered over, the space had been turned into a cast iron wood-burning stove, the centrepiece of what looked like an apartment frozen somewhere in time between the 1940s and 50s. Beneath the thick layers of dust and cobwebs, the room was neat and orderly, as though whoever had been living there had simply stepped out one day and never returned.

CHAPTER
7

Grace could only stare through the half open secret doorway. She didn't know what shocked her the most: the fact that there was a hidden apartment in her home or that Rowan's large hand was pressed against her lower back.

Through the cotton of her shirt she felt the warmth of his palm as well as the care and comfort in his touch. Even though his arm wasn't fully around her, the compulsion to step closer so that his heat and strength could enfold her was so overwhelming that her hand holding the lantern trembled.

'Grace?' The quiet rumble of his voice above her ear had her grasping for what little good sense she had left.

'What is this place?' She moved away to push the door open wider.

Rowan bent to collect his lantern and the room was soon fully illuminated. Bundy sat between them as they took in what they'd uncovered.

It was as though they were looking at a self-contained tiny house half a century before they'd become fashionable. Whoever had lived here would have needed minimal help from the outside world.

Below the boarded-up window was a kitchen sink, while an old-fashioned refrigerator occupied the corner closest to the library. Next to the fridge sat a cedar dresser, its upper shelves filled with dusty plates and bowls, and beside this stood a wooden chiffonier. A small table and four chairs occupied the middle of the apartment.

Halfway along the hallway wall was a door. From this angle it was easy to see that the wall had been stepped out to create a narrow space. Grace guessed it could be the bathroom. Despite the four chairs and the number of plates on the dresser, only a single-sized bed with a plain brown blanket was pushed up against the fireplace wall.

She spoke softly into the silence. 'It's odd ... the white linen on the dresser shelves and the china tea set on the chiffonier all suggest a woman's touch. Yet there aren't any photos or other personal knickknacks.'

'What's also strange is the attention to detail in the kitchen. Every need has been catered for, and yet the bed almost seems an afterthought.' Rowan moved forwards to take a closer look at the dusty blanket that was unpatterned except for two dark stripes. 'I can't be sure but this looks similar to a blanket of my grandfather's from the Second World War.'

Grace took a step back. 'It somehow feels like we're trespassing.'

'Whoever lived here took good care of their home, just like you're doing with Crookwell Park. They wouldn't feel like you were intruding.'

Grace only nodded. Rowan's words had started an ache in her throat. He had a depth and an empathy that touched her.

She tentatively walked into the room. 'It would have been pitch black in here without any natural light, not to mention cold.'

Rowan went over to take a look at the covered windows. 'Now this is clever.'

He put his lantern on the floor so he could unhook a clip in the centre of the wooden panels. A pair of bifold shutters opened. Rowan reached up to undo more clips in the middle of each section and the wood separated into two halves.

'When closed,' he said, examining each piece, 'the window from the garden would look like every other one.' He closed the bottom half of the left shutter. 'This half open option would then have allowed daylight in but also prevented anyone who was walking around inside from being seen.'

A magpie's warble carried in from outside and Grace experienced a sense of relief that whoever had been tucked away in here hadn't been totally isolated from the natural world.

She opened the second window's shutters and light flooded the room. Bundy's wagging tail sent dust motes dancing through the sunbeams that had been blocked for decades.

'Shall we try this?' Rowan asked from over at the side door.

She went to stand beside him and he edged open the door to reveal a compact but fully functional bathroom. She took in the vintage tapware and porcelain, which remained in perfect condition. As Rowan had said, everything had been planned and well thought out. The apartment didn't have the feel of being thrown together or being used as a temporary residence.

Rowan crossed over to the fireplace and then, taking even paces, walked towards the bookcase door to measure the room. Grace followed as he went through the library and into the hall. Rowan was checking something that had been on her mind too. Was this the only hidden room?

After Rowan paced out the equivalent space in the hallway, he ended up close to the corner. 'There's about a metre of extra space, but my pacing wouldn't be spot on. There's definitely no more rooms.'

Grace nodded as she touched the wall at about where she guessed the door to the original room would have been. No wonder Rowan had thought the symmetry was off. On every side of the courtyard there were the same number of doors, but on this library side there was one less. It would have been sealed and then covered in wallpaper to hide that there'd ever been an entryway.

She slid her fingers over the textured wallpaper and felt a subtle join where the plaster below was slightly uneven. 'This has been so well done.'

'It has.'

Rowan too smoothed his palm over the wall. 'Kathy at the library might know something about why the apartment's here.'

'Mabel could also run a story in the local paper. Everything in there belongs to someone.'

Even though at first glance there hadn't been any obvious personal items, something could still hold sentimental value to a family member. She'd just have to find out which family that was.

'Good idea.'

'While we're waiting for answers, I'll clean, catalogue and pack away anything of significance. The local museum might eventually like some of the pieces.'

'Brenna and Taite had to find homes for their father's many collections so they would be good to chat to as well.'

It wasn't her imagination that Rowan not only stood a little further away than he had when they'd been exploring the apartment but his voice had quietened. Now the rain had stopped he had to be busting to get back to work.

She gave him a bright smile. 'Thanks so much for all of your sleuthing help.'

'No thanks are needed.' He reached out to pluck something from her hair and when his arm lowered, cobwebs clung to his fingers. 'It's not every day you find a hidden door in an abandoned mansion.'

With a quick grin, he was gone.

Grace busied herself with taking photos of the apartment and not on revisiting the memory of how dark Rowan's eyes had turned when he'd touched her hair.

Bundy had followed Rowan outside but soon returned to flop on the library floor to watch her through the open bookcase door. Once she'd taken every possible photo of the room's items, she snapped one of Bundy, which she sent to Mabel along with a message to explain where he was.

Almost instantly her mobile rang.

'Hi, Grace, what did you find?'

Mabel's excitement was almost palpable.

'A hidden apartment. Would you like to come and see it? Maybe one of your readers will know something about it.'

'Would I ever. I'll grab you and Rowan a coffee on my way out.'

'Sounds great. See you soon.'

Now that she wasn't trying to capture everything on her phone, Grace surveyed the room, taking in all of its nuances. As an interior stylist she'd often been tasked with sourcing vintage items and collectibles and here she was surrounded by them. There was a dusty but distinctive fluted blue vase on the dresser that had to be Murano glass from the Italian island near Venice, while a floral Royal Doulton tea set had pride of place on the chiffonier.

But it was what she didn't see that piqued her curiosity. There were no photos, paintings or books. Then again, whoever had lived here would have access to the bookcases outside their door. Another thing missing was a wardrobe or somewhere to store clothes. Perhaps the occupant had lived out of a suitcase and only stayed for short periods of time.

She went to take a closer look at the dresser and chiffonier. Inside the first dresser drawer was silver cutlery and in the second were cooking utensils. In the cupboards below she found more kitchen items along with an old navy WW2 enamel water bottle that still had its cork stopper and khaki harness. She carefully took out the water bottle and after failing to find any date or other identifiers returned it to the shelf.

An investigation of the curved single front drawer of the chiffonier revealed an assortment of white linen. Grace went to close the drawer when a sliver of yellow caught her eye. She lifted a starched white tablecloth to find a cookbook published by the Bundilla branch of the CWA.

Holding her breath, she opened the fragile cover to see if there was any information about who may have owned it. At the top of the first page in neat loops was the date 1951 and the simple message:

Dearest Melly
Happy baking

Grace thought back to her visit to the Russell burial plot. She'd need to double-check but the name didn't match either of Lawrence Junior's sisters or his mother or grandmother.

She closed the cover and looked to see if anything was beneath the book, but there was nothing. A quick search of the cupboard below only turned up candles and other essential items. Apart from the cookbook, it was as though the apartment had been stripped of any personal knickknacks and mementos.

Her gaze went to the pretty Murano glass vase and then to the fine bone china tea set in front of her. Except intuition told her this was the home, at least at one time, of a woman who had made the most of her isolated life. Grace picked up a delicate teacup. The pretty pink pattern was called English Rose and had been a favourite of her mother's.

She turned the cup over. If there was a tiny number to the right of the stamped crown she'd just need to add the year 1927 and she'd have an idea about the china's age. Just as she'd hoped, a small green 23 told her that this set dated to 1950, a period that fit in with the cookbook, furniture and appliances. As she replaced the cup on the shelf, a swell of loss had her stare unseeingly at the teacups and saucers.

Just like her grandmother's quilt that was packed away in storage, so too was her mother's similar tea set which included a cup with a crack from when she'd dropped it as a child. She hoped there would come a day when she would be able to unpack the china without memories overwhelming her.

Feeling Bundy's nose push into her fingers, she ruffled his neck. 'I'm okay. I just need to keep busy.'

Her gaze strayed towards the doorway. Except occupying herself did not include going to chat with Rowan until Mabel arrived. Not only did he have his work to do, the way she'd responded to the light touch of his hand had been a red flag. She'd worked hard to pack away her heart so that she'd need as few people in her life as possible. Even though she was muddling her way through her grief, it was a journey she had to make on her own.

She took her phone out of her jeans pocket. As for her thoughts about how Rowan's calloused palm would feel on the bare skin of her lower back, keeping busy wouldn't be enough. She needed Aubrey to distract her.

After the third beep, Aubrey answered.

'What exciting thing's happened today?' Aubrey took off her glasses and stretched in her office chair with a yawn. 'See another wombat?'

'You know you would love it here.'

Aubrey's expression remained unconvinced.

'It just so happens an exciting thing did happen.' Grace turned the phone to film the secret room through the bookcase doorway. 'Check this out.'

'Whatever museum you're in, they need to fire their cleaners.'

'Aubrey, I'm in my house. The library ladders I showed you yesterday weren't the only things hidden. We found a door.'

'What? No way.'

The awe in her voice had Grace flicking the camera back so she could see Aubrey's face. 'I didn't believe it at first either.'

'Who exactly found this door?'

'Rowan, and don't look so smug. It was raining and we were finishing our grand tour.'

Aubrey's smile only grew. 'I take it the friends thing is going well.'

'I admit I do need a friend but Frank will fit the role perfectly.'

Aubrey's manicured dark brows shot upwards. 'Frank?'

'He's a widower, my new neighbour … and around eighty years old.'

'As friendly as he does sound, let's go back to chatting about Rowan.'

'Do we have to? Let's talk about the room.'

Before Aubrey could reply, Grace walked into the apartment and began summarising her search through the room's contents. 'So as you can see, apart from the name in the cookbook, there's nothing to identify who stayed here.'

'Have you checked under the mattress or looked for a loose floorboard?'

'Not yet.' The light tapping of a woman's heels sounded in the hallway. 'Mabel's here.' Grace blew Aubrey a kiss before she could get in one last comment about Rowan. 'I have to go.'

Before going to meet Mabel, Grace gave the room another once-over just in case she'd missed something. She could only hope there would be a clue hidden somewhere that would lead to answers. It was as though the apartment was still waiting for whoever once lived there to return.

'So … you and Grace found the secret door together?'

Rowan weathered the curious glance Clancy shot him from where she rode beside him. They were making the most of the mild summer morning to check his cattle. She'd asked him this exact question five minutes ago.

This time he answered. 'Seriously … is that all you got from Mabel's article?'

Ned had called around for a breakfast cuppa and had brought a copy of the *Bundilla Times* with him.

'Among other things.'

Her curious expression didn't make him any less suspicious. Clancy wouldn't be the only one whose main takeaway from the article was that his and Grace's name were mentioned in the same sentence. He had no doubt there was something strange going on in town.

When he'd briefly called in to the bookshop yesterday on his way home to pick up a novel Clancy had ordered, he'd again been left alone. Apart from a wave from Mrs Woods, who thanks to Clancy's list he now knew was a quilting group member, he hadn't had anyone approach to offer the usual dinner invitations. Instead of this lack of attention making him feel like less of a target, his senses were on high alert, especially when he learned Taite was being treated the same as always.

Clancy didn't seem to notice his silence. Instead she sat relaxed in the saddle as she kept a close eye on Primrose and Monet. While placid Iris was happy to stay beside the horses, the two younger dogs had the attention span of a goldfish. No sooner did they charge off to follow the scent of a rabbit or kangaroo than they were distracted by a galah or a rustle in the grass. Goliath gave a snort as first Primrose dashed in front of him and then Monet, his little kelpie legs working hard to keep up with the golden retriever. Rowan tightened his hold on the reins in case testy Goliath entertained any ideas about snapping his teeth at the puppy.

As they rode past a cluster of Herefords and their calves, the cattle lifted their heads to watch them.

'They're looking good,' Clancy said. 'If I do say so myself.'

Rowan smiled despite the lance of guilt inside.

It had been thanks to Clancy's daily rides during the spring calving season, and her quick actions in getting Trent out to treat a cow with mastitis, that the mothers and calves in his breeding herd were doing so well. Meanwhile he'd been over on the other side of the world getting his life back together.

He cast her a lingering sideways glance. 'Clance … I'm sorry about tying your trampoline in the tree and for anything else I did in the name of misguided brotherly love.'

'I take it you've been talking to Grace?'

He thought carefully before he answered. 'We had a brief discussion about shopping … I can't believe I didn't work out earlier what you were up to.'

'That's because, brother of mine, you have a good and open heart and wouldn't suspect your little sister of plotting anything underhand. And before you accuse Brenna of leading me astray, it was a joint mission to make sure you and Taite wore clothes that at least looked half respectable.'

He gave a mock frown. 'Is there anything else I need to know about?'

'No. You'd already apologised for the trampoline prank before you cut it down when you realised I wasn't laughing. It's just … I really do like playing mother hen. It reminds me of when Mum would drive us into town to get new school clothes and you'd be a grump until she bought us ice cream.'

'So, no more making me parade around as if I'm on a runway?'

Clancy nodded. 'Does that mean we can still go shopping?'

'Only if you buy me ice cream.'

'Deal.' She grinned. 'You know for someone who doesn't have siblings, Grace is very perceptive.'

Rowan loosened his reins so Goliath walked faster to edge ahead of Ash. He didn't want Clancy getting too close a look at his face.

Undeterred, Clancy nudged Ash so the gelding kept up with Goliath. 'How is it going finding her some goats?'

'It's not. Even Trent doesn't know of any that he'd call trouble-free.'

'Maybe Taite could lend her some deer? Brenna and I were wondering ... does Grace ride?'

Rowan grunted. It didn't matter if he'd had the same thought, he wasn't letting on to Clancy that he'd contemplated taking Grace up into the hills behind Crookwell Park to see the view.

'I'll find out,' Clancy continued. 'If she doesn't, Brenna said she has a lovely quiet mare she could use to learn. Taite could easily teach her as he isn't busy for the next two weeks.'

Before Rowan could throw his sister a what-are-you-up-to look, Goliath shied as a rabbit bolted from its grassy hiding place. Primrose and Monet set off after it. Once Rowan had calmed the blood bay, Clancy appeared too busy hiding her grin to continue the original conversation.

'You know,' she said, 'for a horse with a glare that would stop a bushranger in their tracks, he sure is scared of a tiny ball of fluff.'

Rowan didn't argue; he'd once come a cropper when Goliath had leaped sideways to avoid a feral kitten.

Primrose and Monet gave up on the rabbit and when they returned Monet's tongue was lolling and his sides were heaving. Rowan dismounted to pick up the pup. Once back in the saddle, he settled the kelpie in the crook of his left arm. Monet's little heart thumped against his forearm. The puppy was so tired that for once he didn't try to sink his needle-sharp teeth into Rowan's fingers.

Clancy flashed him a soft smile. 'And, brother of mine, that's why I love you.'

They turned Ash and Goliath for home.

After the horses were unsaddled and Monet had passed out on his dog bed, Rowan grabbed his ute keys and headed into town. As the

Saturday markets were being held in the park beside the library, he avoided the main street on his way to the grocery store. He ducked inside to put an advertisement on the community noticeboard for two sensible goats. He then made his way through the traffic to the rural store to load up Grace's solar-powered gate. He hadn't made it over the wooden bridge out of town before his thoughts returned to wondering about what his sister and Brenna were up to.

Clancy might have made it clear the day of the high tea that she wasn't pushing him and Grace together, but, call him suspicious, there was a purpose behind her words and actions whenever Grace was concerned. Even before the answer as to why materialised, he was frowning.

He hadn't been the only one who'd had to scrub up for the high tea; Taite had to as well. Then today it had been Taite who Clancy had mentioned could teach Grace how to ride if she needed to learn. Here he was thinking Clancy was making a big deal about him and Grace being in the paper because she wanted them to be together. Perhaps she'd just been making sure there wasn't anything between them so her matchmaking plan for Taite and Grace could go ahead. As much as Taite was a good man, and if Grace was to have anyone in her life he'd be perfect, the knowledge didn't quash a growing sense of restlessness.

Rowan's thoughts didn't slow as he drove through Crookwell Park's entryway. He'd messaged Grace earlier to say he'd collected the gate and that he and Taite would install it that afternoon. She'd sent him a quick reply thanking him and saying she was in town having coffee with Mabel and that Bundy was over at Frank's.

After a lingering look at Grace's bluestone cottage, Rowan continued around to the back of the mansion. Taite's black four-wheel drive was already parked near the corner gate. The deer farmer was talking on his phone and when he saw Rowan, he ended the call and slid his phone into his shirt pocket.

'What's with the doom-and-gloom face?' he said as Rowan exited his ute. 'You've been roped into dinner at Mrs Moore's?'

'I wish. I can't get used to going to town and being ignored. It's making me nervous. It's not like I've simply dropped off the quilting group's radar. There must be a plan afoot even though I'm yet to be pushed towards anyone in particular.'

'I haven't been in all week so with any luck I'll be left alone too. We'll be safe to go to the pub for more than an hour.'

'I'll drink to that. We might even be able to survive the long lunch.'

'Tell me about it. Clancy and Brenna bought tickets weeks ago.'

'Clancy put a big note on my fridge door. She said that way if I don't read her texts, I won't forget when it's on.'

Taite chuckled. 'I thought you got off lightly after trying to avoid the high tea.'

Rowan nodded as he surveyed their surroundings. Methodically he checked the nearby trees and the back corner of the mansion where Grace's bees buzzed.

Taite too gazed around. 'What are you looking for?'

'I'm not sure. Your sister isn't the only one to have a theory about things. Tell me, how does a man who lives with no line of sight to this place know when there are vandals around?'

'He's either here already or there's some surveillance cameras somewhere.'

'Exactly.' Rowan looked in the direction of the well-worn track that headed to Frank's cottage. 'I've only met Frank once but that was enough to know he's no rule breaker, so if he has installed CCTV cameras they won't be on Grace's property, they'll be on his.'

Taite's gaze followed the fence line beside them. 'Without knowing where the boundary is between their two places, it's difficult to know exactly where to look.' Taite turned his head slightly to listen as a faint engine noise sounded from the bush to their right. 'Is that Frank now?'

'It would be. See ... how would he know we're here?'

They walked over to Rowan's ute to unload the gate.

'I drove to the right past Grace's cottage,' Taite said, looking in the direction he'd driven.

'So did I.'

'Maybe the camera's near the front gate but on Frank's land. He simply sees who drives or parks there and walks in. He wouldn't need a power source with the solar ones.'

'That's what I thought too but when I left yesterday I couldn't see anything. I'll look again today.' Rowan glanced across at Taite as they lifted out the steel gate. 'I have another theory, one you mightn't like, which would explain why our sisters already have long lunch tickets ... they're playing matchmaker with you and Grace.'

Taite almost dropped his side of the gate. 'What? No way.'

The horror in his eyes proved strangely reassuring. A part of Rowan could actually see Taite and Grace being good for each other.

Taite held the gate with one hand while he rubbed at the back of his neck. 'Don't get me wrong, Grace is a sweetheart and I enjoy her company, but I'm far from ready to settle down. I honestly haven't given her a second thought.'

Rowan didn't say a word. Not only had he given Grace a second thought, he'd lost track of what number he was up to.

'What makes you think that's what they're planning?'

As Rowan went through the reasons behind his theory, Taite's frown deepened. 'I wondered why Brenna asked me what I was doing this week and then next week as well. I know she doesn't need help with her treks. We have to come up with a counter plan.'

'We do.' Not only for Taite's sake but for Grace's as well. She hadn't come here to start a relationship. 'I'll think of something.'

The noise of the gator intensified and around a bend in the track the side-by-side appeared with Frank driving and Bundy on the back.

Frank stopped in front of them and Bundy jumped to the ground to race over for his obligatory pats. It took several minutes for Frank to leave the gator and to hobble the short distance on his cane. Thanks to Grace's thoughtfulness, the solar-powered gate would only require a click from a remote control to swing open so Frank wouldn't have to leave his vehicle.

'Rowan.' Frank gave him a nod which he returned.

'Frank, this is Taite from Glenwood Station.'

Frank shook Taite's hand, his shrewd gaze assessing. 'I believe your father bought a butter churner off my wife.'

'He did.'

Taite didn't tolerate fools easily and from his mild tone Rowan knew that he had drawn the same conclusions he had. While Frank wasn't a man to be messed with, he also wasn't a threat.

In the sideways look Taite shot Rowan he also saw interest. Frank, with his polished speech and air of authority, wasn't someone who would easily blend in. The fact that he'd been living in the mountains for as long as he had with very few people knowing of his existence was a curiosity.

Frank looked between the two of them. 'I see Grace has put you to work.'

Rowan nodded. 'I wonder, Frank, just how did you *see* us?'

The older man's eyes turned a steely blue with such speed Rowan was reminded of how quickly the high-country weather could change.

'Your father was a quick thinker too.'

Rowan didn't let the reference to his father throw him. Instead he held Frank's stare and waited. He wasn't letting him dodge his question.

Frank's hard expression relaxed into a smile. 'Grace will be all right with you around, but an extra set of eyes never goes astray.' He tapped his nose. 'A good chess player never reveals his moves.'

CHAPTER
8

At first Grace thought the mournful wail that brought her half awake were her possums having returned. When the sound happened again, this time louder and somewhere outside to her left, her eyes flew open. It almost sounded like a ... sheep.

The strip of light between her narrow curtains let her know it was already daylight, while the empty space at the end of her bed had her looking towards her open bedroom door for Bundy.

A long, protracted bleat sounded again. Not stopping to pull anything over her navy top and mismatched black sleep shorts she slipped on her new cowgirl boots and clomped her way into the kitchen. Bundy wagged his tail from where he waited by the door.

She hesitated. With the fences being full of holes, maybe she'd had a sheep wander into the garden. Bundy might scare the animal so perhaps he should stay inside. But when the kelpie whined, she opened the door. He was a working dog. He'd know not to chase their visitor.

Even before the door was partway open, Bundy bolted outside and she followed. The airbrushed blue above gave her a more accurate estimate of the time. It was well past sunrise which meant Rowan wouldn't be far away to start his working day. She stifled a yawn as she tried to keep tabs on where Bundy was as he sped through the garden. She too had a busy morning as she was meeting the local studies historian to see if she could shed any light on the hidden apartment. Her sleep-fog brain had better be fully awake by then.

Without warning, two small dark shapes burst out of an overgrown garden bed near the side of the mansion. She blinked. Her four-legged trespassers weren't sheep at all—they were goats. By their size they didn't look very old. When they saw her and swerved to their right, she had visions of them running through the front gate that she'd left open for Rowan.

She turned to half run towards the entryway. If the goats did bolt down the driveway they'd end up on the busy road. Her steps slowed. Except the front gate was somehow shut and there was something white attached to the top. She glanced behind her but there was no sign of the goats or Bundy.

A breeze lifted what she could now see was a piece of paper taped to the steel. She removed the note and with her back against the wind attempted to decipher the scrawled writing.

Heard you were looking for goats. You can have these. I've too many.

Busy trying to work out what the next line said, she didn't hear Rowan's ute behind her until he was almost at the gate. She swung around, painfully conscious of what she was wearing and that her hair was a tangled mess.

No sooner had Rowan's ute stopped than he was out of the driver's seat. There was no sign of his usual easygoing charm, instead the fixed intensity of his stare matched the alert readiness of his stride. Just like on the day they'd met she sensed the power and restless energy that he carefully kept under wraps. Rowan was a man who would act quickly, love deeply and not hold any part of himself back.

'Grace, what's wrong?'

Even his voice sounded different, less a slow drawl and more a gravelly rasp that strummed across her senses.

She rubbed at the goosebumps on her bare arms, hoping he'd think she was cold. 'Nothing's wrong … it's just … this.'

She handed him the piece of paper.

While he read, she smoothed what she could of her windblown hair. She needn't have worried as Rowan seemed oblivious to the state she was in.

He passed her the note and scanned the gardens around the old mansion. 'Frank here yet?'

'No, why? He's never here this early.'

Rowan didn't answer as he unlatched the gate. 'How many are there? I take it Bundy's with them?'

'Two.'

Rowan looked at her, except his gaze didn't hold hers for very long. 'Hop in if you like.'

She nodded. It wasn't a long walk back but the goats were frightened and needed help. She waited until Rowan had driven through before closing the gate and climbing into his ute. To stop the passenger seat from beeping she slipped on her seatbelt.

Even though Rowan gave her a grin, there was something about his eyes that suggested he wasn't as relaxed as he appeared. They sat in silence as Rowan sped along the driveway.

'Okay,' he said as he parked near her car. 'I'll see what we're dealing with and then head into town for yards and hay. Have you a bucket for water?'

'I do.' Her hand rested on the seatbelt clip as she looked at him. 'Why would people dump goats here?'

'For lots of reasons. It would be a good idea to call Trent to look them over. He might even recognise them.'

'I'll call him now.'

She'd spoken to the personable vet about some goats only yesterday after Mabel, who was his flatmate, had passed on his number. Her parents had been right about news travelling fast in small towns.

'I'm going to need more hay,' Rowan said, his tone wry as he looked past her out the side window.

She turned to see what he was looking at. Not only had Frank arrived with Bundy on the back of the gator but there were now three small black and brown goats charging around her garden.

Disbelief held her still before she followed Rowan out of the ute. Frank gave them a smile as they approached.

'Quite the surprise seeing you here,' Rowan said to the older man.

'It is, isn't it. Sorry I'm late but it wasn't immediately obvious that you had visitors.'

Grace looked between the two of them as their gazes locked, unsure of what was going on. Frank's words made sense. No doubt he'd heard the goats like he had the possums. On a quiet morning sound would carry.

Rowan handed Frank the note the goats' owners had left. 'This was on the front gate.'

'That's ... unexpected.'

'Is it?'

Again something passed between Rowan and Frank that she didn't understand.

'What does that last line say?' she asked as a distraction. It wasn't animosity between the two men, more like a clash of stubborn wills.

Frank angled the white paper. 'It says *I know you'll give them a good home.*'

Grace looked off into the distance, her heart melting. She had no idea what she was in for, she didn't know anything about goats, but she'd been entrusted with their care by someone who had faith in her. It was a little thing but it made her feel as though she had been given a special purpose.

A bleat from somewhere behind the mansion pulled her focus back to Frank and Rowan.

'Frank, can you and Bundy please try to make sure they don't escape through the broken fence, and Rowan, that would be much appreciated if you could pick up some yards and hay. I'll find a bucket and call Trent.'

Not waiting for an answer, she headed towards her cottage, adding to get dressed to her list.

When she returned outside in what had become her usual everyday clothes—jeans, a cotton half-button shirt and a country cap the assistant in the rural store had given her—there was no sign of either Frank or the goats. It felt right to no longer be wearing dark colours. Her parents, her mother in particular, would have liked her new colourful work shirts.

In her hands she carried a container filled with blueberry muffins that she'd cooked last night for Frank. It also felt good doing something to brighten his day. As much as he hid his loneliness, she knew it existed. He had no children or living siblings and since his wife died had been on his own.

The chug of the gator engine had her head around to the front of the mansion. There she saw the three goats, their heads down eating, with Frank and Bundy keeping a close watch nearby.

She climbed into the spare gator seat. Bundy and Frank enjoyed the muffins while they waited for Rowan and Trent to arrive. The local vet had offered to call in on his way to the clinic to check the goats over.

She wasn't sure what made her glance sideways, maybe it was Bundy's sudden interest in something behind her, but when she did she stared straight into two amber eyes set below a pair of curving horns. Unlike the other three goats, this large and very fat one showed no nervousness at all. Instead she waddled out from the hedge that had hidden her, her attention on the remaining muffin Grace held.

Frank laughed quietly. 'This just keeps getting better. Wait until Rowan sees this one.'

Grace didn't reply, sitting intensely still as the goat came up to her. She broke off a tiny piece of muffin and the goat nibbled it from off her palm. When the goat was done she looked for more.

Grace tentatively lifted her hand and when the goat didn't move she scratched its nose. The goat leaned in closer and Grace couldn't help but smile as she rubbed the goat's neck.

'You're kidding,' Rowan said from somewhere on the side veranda. She looked up to see him and another tall man who had to be Trent.

Grace passed Frank the last muffin and, careful not to frighten the goat, slipped out of the seat. The goat accompanied her over to the veranda and when Grace reached the steps, stopped beside her.

'I think you've made a friend,' Trent said with a warm smile.

The vet in person was as approachable and friendly as she'd found him over the phone. 'Thanks so much for coming out on such short notice.'

'No worries.' Trent walked down the steps. He patted the goat before checking her over. 'I've never seen her or her friends before but her feet have been trimmed and her gums are a good colour so she's been wormed. She's come from a decent home.'

Grace only half heard Trent's words. Rowan had given her an indecipherable look before he'd left.

'Okay, I'm all done with this one,' Trent said. 'How about you head round to the old stables where Rowan has set up the portable yards. I'm sure your new friend will follow. Bundy and I will take care of the rest.'

Grace set off and the nanny goat didn't hesitate to walk behind her. Trent whistled to Bundy who ran to his side. Grace and the larger goat had just made it to the yards when the other three trotted around the mansion corner to join them. She led the small herd inside the circular pen and Rowan closed the gate.

When she went to exit she made the mistake of looking at Rowan as he held the narrow gate open for her. She was so close she could smell his sun-dried cotton and cedar scent, so close it would only take a lift of her hand to touch the cleft in his stubbled chin. She dipped her head, hoping that the brim of her cap concealed her expression. She still hadn't mastered staying composed whenever near him. As she stepped away to allow Trent to enter the yard, she made a point of standing as far away from Rowan as possible.

Once the younger goats had been given a clean bill of health and they all had hay and water, Grace found herself alone with her new pets. When she had more time she'd call Aubrey to tell her about her latest additions. While the two wethers remained skittish, the smaller doe was happy to stand beside the nanny goat while Grace patted her.

She scratched what she now knew was the soon-to-be mother's favourite spot on her nose. 'I have to go to town but Rowan and Bundy will look after you.'

With a last look at the goats, she went inside to grab her tote bag and car keys. By the time she had parked out the front of the historic library building she had names for the wethers. She'd call them Chester and Windsor after two English towns she remembered visiting as a child.

On the way to the local studies room at the back of the library where Kathy worked, Grace made a detour via the shelves that contained titles on raising goats.

Kathy gave her a smile as she opened the local studies room door and saw the pile of books in Grace's arms. 'Don't tell me you found some goats after all?'

'It's more like they found me.'

Grace placed the books on the floor beside a table on which a series of black-and-white photographs of Crookwell Park had been laid out. Even though she'd only briefly met Kathy in passing when Clancy and Brenna had taken her shopping, she felt at ease with the older woman. She didn't try to hide her interest or excitement as she bent to take a closer look at a photograph that featured a side view of the mansion. As well as white ducks she could see another animal.

'Is that a goat?'

'It is ...' Kathy motioned at her to take a seat. 'There's another one here.'

By the time Kathy had gone through the rest of the photographs, they'd found two more goats, plus a cat, dog and pony. Grace scanned the images on her phone. She had a lot of catching up to do animal-wise if she was to turn Crookwell Park into the home it once was. If possible she'd also replicate as much of the garden as she could. She ignored the whispers that reminded her she had no idea where she'd be once summer ended.

Kathy pointed to the grainy image of a leafy pergola that looked to be draped in a similar climber to what covered it now. 'This grapevine was apparently struck from a cutting brought from Wales and has to be over a century old.'

Grace took a photo of the vine, humbled by the tenacity of the place that she now was the custodian of. Her garden-loving mother would have been thrilled to know such a detail.

After they'd discussed the pictures of the various rooms, one of which was the ballroom with a stunning chandelier, Kathy sat back in her chair. 'As you can see, nothing in these photographs suggests there could be a hidden library door, let alone an apartment anywhere.'

Kathy reached for a nearby folder to take out the top piece of paper. 'I've also delved into the Russell family tree and there's no woman with a first or middle name of Melly, or even one that could have been abbreviated. There was a Millicent and a Mildred but these names would have most likely been shortened to Milly.'

'Mabel hasn't received any useful information either. She said the only people contacting her after the newspaper article were collectors.'

'That doesn't surprise me. I'll keep going through old newspapers as Melly might have been a family friend or someone who worked for the Russells. I'll also look into the local war records as the World War Two water bottle might prove to be a lead but to be honest it's a long shot. The CWA cookbook would still be our best bet to finding some answers.'

Grace swiped on her phone to find the picture she'd taken of the cookbook inscription and bit her lip as she examined the date and neat handwriting. Somehow they had to uncover another piece of the puzzle. She had to find a person connected to the apartment who she could pass the tea set and Murano vase on to just like their owner would have wished.

Kathy patted her hand. 'Edith would be a good person to chat to. You would have met her in the quilting club and, like her mother, she's a member of the CWA. Someone there might recognise the writing or the name. At least one thing is on our side: secrets in a small town don't often stay buried forever.'

'Any more goats turn up?' Heath asked as he wiped his oil-covered hands on the rag Rowan passed him.

Heath had come to help service the tractor and had replaced the oil filter. Next week he'd be starting on the mural at their old primary school so had wanted to catch up before he got too busy.

Rowan went back to checking the baler so it would be ready for when he cut the next paddock of lucerne for hay. 'No, just the four, but judging by the size of Olive's stomach Grace will need to choose at least two more names.'

Heath helped himself to a bottle of water from the beer fridge and sat in the closest camping chair that Rowan kept out for whenever he had company. 'Any idea on who the owners are?'

'None. There were no ear tattoos and no one has come forward, even after Mabel put a request on the local social media page.'

'Frank never saw a thing?'

Rowan tightened a bolt on the baler guards. 'He didn't, which means wherever he has a CCTV camera it's not at the front gate. I'm guessing he only saw the goats when they were running through the garden.'

'That has to narrow down where the camera might be.'

'It does but I'm pretty sure the only common boundary fence that would be within a camera's range is the side one and I've driven along there twice and found nothing.'

'I didn't see anything either when I was there.'

'Thanks for putting up a bigger goat yard and for fixing the garden fence, by the way.'

'No worries. There's still a section near the front that needs work. It was worth spending the day there just to see Grace smile. She already loves those goats.'

Rowan grabbed a water bottle from out of the fridge and pulled up a chair beside Heath. In the afternoon warmth of the steel shed a beer would send him to sleep. 'Tell me about it. She's found plans online for a tyre and wood climbing frame and Frank is helping her put it together this weekend.'

Heath surveyed Rowan over the top of his water bottle. 'Are you sure Grace is only here for the summer?'

'That's what she said.'

'What about once the mansion's finished?'

'I haven't got the impression that she bought the place to sell but I don't think she knows herself what she's doing. Not that my sister and Brenna are taking that into account with their matchmaking plans. What I want to know is why they think Taite would be Grace's best match.'

'Are you sure it's Taite?'

'It definitely isn't me and they've shown no interest in bringing Trent into the picture.'

Heath took a swig of water before answering. 'I'm only guessing it's not you because of Eloise.'

'Eloise? What has she got to do with anything?'

'The girls might be worried you're still beating yourself up about her and aren't ready to move on.'

Rowan frowned. He wouldn't use those exact words, but yes, he was still working through how to make sure that he didn't make a similar mistake again. 'I'm one hundred percent over her.'

Heath sent him a sympathetic look. 'If it gets out of hand, talk to Clance. She'll listen.'

Rowan drained his water bottle. As sweet as Clancy was, if the years of shopping payback were any indication, he'd discovered a new side to her. While her smile was the picture of serenity it also hid a will that could be as indomitable as the mountains beyond the shed door.

He left his seat to collect Heath's empty water bottle and then he and Heath finished up in the shed.

Once back in the coach house, Rowan took a shower. He was meeting Taite at the pub for an early dinner and would run errands beforehand. Even though he continued to be ignored whenever in Bundilla, neither of them wanted to chance eating too late on a busy Saturday night.

On the drive around the valley edge, Rowan's conversation with Heath replayed in his head. Now not only did he need a plan to save Taite and to shield Grace, he also had to prove that Eloise no longer mattered to him. His thumb tapped on the steering wheel. Not that Grace really needed his help. With every week he was at

Crookwell Park he saw more of the person she must have been before loss had dimmed her light.

When their paths had first crossed, she'd been reserved and he'd sensed a deep-seated wariness. Whereas when she'd met Trent last Wednesday, even though she had spoken to him by phone beforehand, her smile had been open and friendly. Over the past weeks it wasn't only her wardrobe that had changed; colour now painted her pale cheeks. It was as though he were watching the spring wildflowers that Clancy filled the Ashcroft homestead with blossom after winter.

The trouble was the more Grace came out of her shell, the harder he had to work to keep himself in check. It had been bad enough the morning he'd found her reading the note on the gate when she'd stood an arm's length away dressed in nothing but cowgirl boots, a fitted tank top and short shorts. But with every breath he'd taken, he'd breathed in the scent of honeysuckle that had clung to her long tousled hair.

When she'd then walked through the goat yard gate he'd held open for her and their bodies had all but brushed, even knowing Frank and Trent were watching, it had been a struggle to look away from the curve of her mouth. His sigh filled the ute cabin. If he wasn't careful, his attraction would undo everything he'd done to ensure that from now on he always thought before he acted.

Once he reached the town limits, instead of following the other dusty vehicles heading to the main street for a relaxing Saturday night, he turned right. Even though the afternoon heat had given way to a sullen sky, he'd have time before the storm hit to make a quick detour. His destination lay beyond a pair of iron gates and past a stone wall that encased weathered sandstone headstones. He continued through the Bundilla cemetery to where the headstones gleamed a granite black.

The slam of his car door echoed in the silence as he made his way over to where his parents had been laid to rest. Sometimes he came with Clancy but the fresh flowers told him she'd already visited this week. As Rowan stared at the names Isobel and Edward Parker, just like he had ever since he'd returned from overseas, he reaffirmed his promise to not lose his way a second time. He wouldn't again let them or Clancy down by acting in a selfish, reckless or foolish way.

A rumble of thunder followed by a flash of lightning had him turning to retrace his steps. By the time he reached town the hammering of rain on the ute roof had quietened to a dull murmur. He went to park out the front of the bakery so he would only be a few doors down from the pub in case he needed a fast getaway, but then continued on to stop outside the pharmacy. He still wasn't used to slipping in and out of town without being hailed down for a chat. But now he was being ignored he could park wherever he pleased.

He left his ute and strode towards the grocery store. He needed to take down the goat ad he'd pinned on the community noticeboard before any more animals turned up. He texted as he walked to see how far away Taite was.

When he looked up he saw Millicent and Beatrice leaving the grocery store, carting an assortment of bags. He increased his pace and caught them before they made it to the pedestrian crossing.

'Like a hand?' he asked.

Millicent gave him a brief smile. 'Thank you. That would be lovely.'

He took her bags and then the ones Beatrice passed him. Together they crossed the road on which small tendrils of steam rose now that the rain had stopped.

Millicent looked across at him. 'Crookwell Park's been keeping you busy.'

'It has. Grace has had quite a few things happen.'

He answered without hesitation. The sisters were about the only people in town who had never shown an interest in his love life.

'No answers yet on who the apartment belonged to?' Beatrice asked.

Rowan shook his head. He didn't add that they might never find out who had lived there or that he couldn't shake the feeling that the hidden rooms might still have more secrets to reveal. He'd revisited the apartment the day after he and Grace had found the bookcase door and something still didn't feel right.

'Tell Grace to let us know if we can help in any way,' Beatrice said as they reached their white sedan.

'I will.'

Rowan placed the grocery bags in the car boot and when he straightened he found himself pinned by identical blue eyes. While the sisters were above matchmaking, they were often involved with community projects and were always on the lookout for volunteers.

'So, Rowan,' Millicent said. 'I know the book festival is still a month away and last festival you were busy, but can we count on your help?'

'Of course.' He hoped his reply didn't sound like the rasp his own ears heard. He'd been so caught up with Eloise he'd let good people down as well as the town. Millicent and Beatrice were the powerhouses behind the festival that provided a huge economic boost to Bundilla's bush businesses. There'd been no excuse for skipping out last year, except Eloise had resented how much work he'd been doing on the farm so he hadn't felt free to spend time away from her. 'Taite and Heath would be happy to help as well. I'll make sure we're all available.'

'Thank you.' Beatrice gave him a rare full smile.

With a nod, he recrossed the road and hurried into the grocery store. A familiar charcoal grey car had driven along the main street. Eloise's mother was in town and he'd already heard her daughter's name enough today that he didn't now need a ten-minute pregnancy update. It wouldn't be long until he'd need to keep a watch out for any leggy blondes pushing a pram as Eloise would be sure to visit.

A text from Taite came through saying he'd just hit town and would meet Rowan in the pub in five minutes. Rowan tapped off a reply to say that he'd be there in three. He was long overdue for a drink.

The sliding doors shut behind him and he went over to where the community noticeboard hung on the back wall of the store entryway. He'd just unpinned the goat advertisement when the doors behind him opened. He glanced over his shoulder to check who it was. A prickle between his shoulder blades already told him it was someone he'd best avoid. An impression confirmed when he saw Mrs Moore's wide and delighted grin.

In the past Mrs Moore had been very forthright in wanting him to meet her unmarried granddaughter who was a lawyer in Tumut. Not to mention she had a gaggle of geese who didn't take kindly to visitors even if they were delivering a bucket of Clancy's spring peonies. But instead of bustling over to him, all Mrs Moore did was give him a cheery wave and continue into the store. Rowan stared after her.

He reached for his phone in his shirt pocket and dialled Taite's number.

The deer farmer answered after only a few rings. 'You're in a hurry for a beer.'

'You have no idea.' Rowan paused to check Mrs Moore wasn't watching him while she filled a bag with apples. 'Where are you?'

'About to walk into the pub.'

'Do me a favour ... come to the grocery store and buy a loaf of bread. Mrs Moore just walked past me without stopping.'

'Seriously?'

'If she leaves you alone, we'll know for sure you're safe.'

'And if I'm not?'

'Then we'll have a quick pub dinner and get out of town.'

Rowan ended the call and pretended to read the community notices on the board. He only got as far as the one advertising the upcoming long lunch before the sliding doors opened and Taite's boots rang on the floor. As Rowan turned, Taite gave him a wink before heading into the store.

Rowan stayed by the noticeboard so he could see what happened.

Within five seconds he had his answer.

Taite hadn't even made it to the bread section when Mrs Moore abandoned her bag of apples to sweep towards him. Arms outstretched, she air-kissed his cheeks. Taite threw a resigned look at Rowan over her shoulder.

Rowan scrubbed a hand across his jaw. Things were bad. Very bad. Not only was Taite still fair game, whatever was going on with the quilting ladies had to only involve him.

CHAPTER
9

Unlike the last time Grace parked outside the community hall for the weekly quilting club meeting, today she wasn't unsure about what she'd be walking into.

Just like how sharing her clothesline with a kookaburra and passing road signs with a wombat or kangaroo symbol no longer made her take a second glance, she was feeling more comfortable in her new life. There were still days when she missed her parents with a breath-stealing intensity, but there were now also days when she remembered them with more affection than sadness.

She reached for the large cloth bag on the passenger seat that held her work-in-progress memory quilt. The parcel Aubrey had sent of her mother's Liberty print floral shirts had arrived. Each evening she would lovingly iron one and could now cut the fine lawn fabric into neat squares without her vision misting. She'd decided to make several quilts and this first one would be in a green and pink colour scheme.

She closed her car door and checked her phone. It wasn't that she was expecting any messages, especially from Rowan, but he'd seemed preoccupied over their morning coffee. While she'd rambled on about how Windsor and Chester would eat carrots out of her hand and how much little Clover loved jumping off her tyre tower, Rowan had only nodded. She knew he was listening and was interested in what she was saying, it was just that for once she was the one steering their conversation.

The only time he'd really spoken was when she'd passed on Clancy's suggestion that Taite could finish fixing the fence so the goats could be let out into the garden. Rowan's comment that Taite had things to do in his workshop and wouldn't be leaving his farm all week had been a little hoarse. He'd then said he'd drop by on the weekend to fix the last of the holes himself.

She ignored the warmth that filled her at the thought she wouldn't now have to wait two days to see him. After finding the apartment together, it was getting harder to stick to her rules and to not label what they had as friendship. She'd be lying if she said that not seeing Rowan over the weekend didn't leave her feeling adrift. It was just the change in routine, that was all. She hooked her bag over her shoulder and headed for the hall door.

At least this quilting meeting she had a strategic diversion so it wouldn't be all about Rowan. While she hadn't been uncomfortable answering the questions about him at the last meeting when everyone had stopped for morning tea, this time she needed to be careful. Clancy and Brenna's plan was to have the quilting ladies draw their own conclusions, but she didn't want anyone to sense how much she really did enjoy his company, or how gorgeous she found him. Her grip tightened on the strap of her bag at the memory of how his worn blue shirt had moulded to his back and biceps that morning when he'd moved stones.

A dusty sedan pulled into the car park and she turned to wave at the woman behind the wheel who she remembered was called Lucinda. More names came back to her as she entered the hall and the ladies inside greeted her with cheerful hellos. Neither Clancy, Brenna, nor Edith, who Kathy had suggested she chat to about the cookbook, were there yet.

Grace went to her table and set her bag next to the sewing machine. The sense of belonging that she'd experienced last meeting again wrapped her in its embrace. She took out a plate of home-baked melting moments and went into the kitchen to add them to the other treats for morning tea.

When she returned, Clancy and Brenna had both arrived. They each gave her a hug, and Clancy whispered in her ear, 'Our plan's going really well. Rowan hasn't had a dinner invitation all week.'

Despite Clancy's reassuring words, Rowan's solemn expression that morning stayed with Grace as she settled into her seat. Edith gave her a smile, which Grace returned, as the older woman walked past to her table. Grace took out her colour-coded squares. Brenna would be over soon to check that she knew what to do next. But before she could take the cover off her sewing machine, someone clapped their hands. She looked over to see Sandra standing in the kitchen doorway.

'I know this is a little out of order,' said Sandra. 'But now we're all here, I wonder if anyone would like a cuppa? I believe we've all seen Mabel's article about Crookwell Park and I for one am dying to know more.'

Even before Sandra had finished, the scrape of steel on floorboards sounded as chairs were pushed back.

'I thought you'd never ask,' Vernette said, already halfway across the room. 'I've had some questions for Grace all week.'

From the twinkle in Vernette's eyes, Grace wasn't sure they were all about the hidden apartment.

She reached into her tote bag and took out the CWA cookbook that she'd carefully wrapped in tissue paper and placed in a plastic sleeve. Even though not all the quilting members were also CWA members like Edith, someone might still recognise the handwriting.

Teaspoons clinked on china and the aroma of fresh tea filled the kitchen alcove as everyone assembled around the large table. Covers were taken off the plates of home baking and Mabel's newspaper article with its colour photographs was spread across the far table end.

When faces turned towards her, Grace cleared her throat. 'What would people like to know?'

'Is it true,' Norma began, 'that our favourite young man Rowan was with you when the apartment was found?'

Grace didn't dare make eye contact with Clancy and Brenna, who she was sure had to be smiling. They had been spot on. The quilting ladies couldn't help but view any interaction she had with Rowan through a matchmaking lens.

'He was. It was raining so we were looking through the house with Bundy.'

Heads around the table nodded.

'Tell me about this CWA cookbook,' Edith said, leaning forwards in her chair. 'Kathy said it has an inscription inside.'

'It does.' Grace took out the cookbook and gently laid it on the table and opened the cover. For the first time she could have heard a pin drop in the small hall. She slowly turned the book around for everyone to clearly see the handwriting.

'Melly,' Gladys said, her forehead furrowed. 'That isn't a name I know.'

'Me either,' said Lucinda. 'I wish I did, though.'

Again there were multiple head nods.

'Can I take a photo?' Edith asked. 'I'll show my mother. She was only young in 1951 but my grandmother was a CWA member. I'll show the members at our next meeting too.'

'That would be great. Thank you.'

Grace stood so people could lean in close to snap a picture.

'In 1951 I would have been two,' Sandra said. 'The Second World War ended in 1945.'

Norma nodded. 'The Snowy Mountain Scheme started in 1949 and my father came out from Poland in 1950 to work.'

'Prince Charles was born in 1948,' Vernette piped up.

Everyone looked at her.

'What?' She took a sip of tea. 'My grandmother was English. I've still got a picture of the Queen somewhere.'

Grace returned to her seat and took a bite of a lamington as the conversation flowed around her. No longer was she the centre of the group's attention. However, her respite was short-lived.

'Grace,' Sandra said, 'a little birdie told me Rowan put a yard up for your goats.'

Across the table, Clancy took a gulp of tea to hide her grin.

'He did. Rowan, Trent and Frank were all very helpful in getting them settled.'

China clattered as teacups were suddenly placed on their saucers.

'*Frank?*' Vernette said. 'There's no Frank in town.'

'There is,' Brenna confirmed. 'Not that I've met him. He lives by himself in a cottage not far from Crookwell Park.'

Grace wasn't sure what interested everyone more: the hidden apartment or the name of an unknown single man. Speculation brightened the eyes of more than one quilting club member as pointed glances were swapped. Grace could almost hear the whirr of busy brains turning.

She spoke, voice firm. 'Frank is kind-hearted, keeps to himself and is old enough to be my father. As well-meaning and lovely as you all are … he is a widower and happy on his own.'

When silence settled over the hall, she thought she'd broken some unwritten quilting club rule, but then Sandra nodded. 'Well said, Grace. Sometimes when you lose someone, they can't be replaced.'

Chatter again filled the kitchen as Norma held up Mabel's article and people reminisced about the old-fashioned decor and furniture. Grace sat back and listened to the stories about family, friendship and a past way of life.

It was only when second cups of tea had been finished and the morning tea plates almost emptied that members began drifting back to their sewing tables.

Grace kept an eye on the time as she sewed the first of her squares together. She wasn't prone to acting on impulse. Spontaneity had only ever led to uncertainty and fun wasn't something she'd ever been relaxed enough to have. Even as a child she'd been conscious of the sacrifices her parents had made to give her a better life and had worked hard to make the most of every opportunity.

But this morning on the drive to town she'd made a split-second decision and called Julie at the hair salon who Mabel had recommended. Thanks to Julie having had a cancellation she was now due to have her hair cut at lunchtime.

She checked her phone again before packing up her quilting bag. After giving hugs to Clancy and Brenna and saying goodbye to the other group members who were still sewing, she headed to her car and then to the main street.

In less than ten minutes she found herself settled into a comfortable chair, a cape around her shoulders and a glass of chilled water in front of her. Soft music played and an air-conditioned breeze washed over her.

'So,' Julie said with a smile that had welcomed Grace as soon as she'd stepped inside the stylish salon, 'what are we doing today?'

'Just a trim … maybe this much off.' Grace made the largest possible space between her thumb and forefinger. 'I haven't had a haircut for at least twelve months.' She didn't add that it was ever since she'd moved home to help her father care for her mother.

Julie lifted a section of hair to examine the ends. 'You won't need that much off if you'd like to save the length.'

Grace studied her reflection, a furrow between her brows. She'd always kept her hair at a practical length that would be quick to twist and secure with a clip before she raced out the door to work. But somehow the words to cut it all off didn't form.

Instead she said, 'I don't really do much with it … any suggestions?'

'You have such a pretty natural curl, I'd recommend some long layers. Have you thought about highlights? Some subtle caramel tones would give you a summer glow.'

Grace ignored the whispers that said her hair was fine as it was and listened to the ones that reminded her she'd come to the mountains to rebuild her life. A new hairstyle would be symbolic of her taking a step forwards into the future, even if it was still unknown.

'Thank you, both of those sound great. Do you have time?'

'If you don't mind me eating my lunch, I've plenty.'

Two and a half hours later, Grace walked out of the hair salon feeling and looking like someone she didn't know. Her hair fell in shiny waves across her shoulders. She couldn't stop running her fingers through the sleek strands. On a day when acting on impulse seemed acceptable, she took a rare selfie and sent it to Aubrey.

When she arrived at the cottage, Bundy's exuberant tail wagging to welcome her home kept her smiling all the way inside. Once dressed in her work shirt, jeans and boots, she went over to the mansion. At the front door she hesitated before walking through onto the tessellated tiles. She didn't usually see Rowan twice a day and couldn't start doing so now, even if she wanted to check on him. Whatever the reason behind his preoccupation that morning, it hopefully had been resolved.

With Bundy beside her, she made her way to the hidden apartment. As per Aubrey's instructions she'd checked under the mattress and looked for any squeaky floorboards that might conceal a hidey-hole in case there were any further secrets. Her plan was to finish packing away the last of the items and then tackle the cobwebs.

Over in the corner, between the bathroom door and the bed, stood a folded ladder. Rowan had brought in a smaller double-sided one that he said would be easier to haul around than the type she'd bought to use for the nesting boxes. Even now when she thought about his thoughtfulness it made her feel warm inside.

Busy dusting glasses and wrapping them in bubble wrap, Grace didn't immediately register that she and Bundy weren't alone. But then the kelpie suddenly lunged to the right to chase a large rodent-shaped body around the room. A dull thud sounded as Bundy's shoulder clipped the ladder and it toppled sideways into the wall.

Grace grabbed the box of glasses to move it out of the way as the rat bolted across the floor and through the open bookcase door. Bundy followed and she could hear the pursuit continue through the library and into the hallway.

Heart racing, she sat the box on the floor and looked around to check if anything had been broken. The only damage seemed to be that when the ladder fell, the top corner had wedged into the plaster of the back wall.

She took hold of the ladder and gently pulled. Nothing happened. She tugged harder. This time the corner came free, along with a palm-sized portion of plaster. Grace laid the ladder on the floor and took out her phone. She'd inspect the damage then take a photo for the builder. Except as she shone the torchlight on the hole there was only darkness and no sign of the bluestone wall that she'd expected to be behind the plaster.

Confused, she moved closer to stick what she could of her hand into the small void. Her fingers brushed the wood of the internal wall frame but still no stone. The day they discovered the hidden door, Rowan had paced out the apartment and the hallway to check there wasn't another room behind this one. Apart from a narrow space, everything had matched up.

Knowing that the hole would have to be patched anyway, she looked around for something heavy. On the stove was a small but solid iron kettle. It only took a couple of hits to enlarge the plaster opening to the size of a plate. This time she changed position so she could look along the wall when she shone her phone torch inside.

Her breath stalled in a sharp inhale.

Within the cavity was a set of wooden stairs.

<hr />

It didn't matter how many times Rowan mulled over his and Taite's current predicament, there appeared to only be one solution. He stared unseeingly at the stone he'd placed on the almost finished side wall.

To ensure Taite wasn't bulldozed towards Grace by their well-meaning sisters, to make sure Grace was given the space she needed to heal and to prove to all and sundry that he was over Eloise, the answer was quite simple.

He needed to take Grace out on a very public and very fake date.

There was no other way to solve all three problems. That way Taite would be free, Grace would be left alone and the whole of Bundilla would know Eloise was the last woman on his mind.

There was just one catch. He had to convince Grace there was merit in such an off-the-wall plan. The wind carried away his sigh. There was a second catch, if he was being honest. He had to make it very clear to the part of him that hadn't thought it a bad idea to spend more time with Grace that it was in fact the last thing he should be doing.

This morning he'd already committed to seeing her on the weekend. When she'd brought him his coffee and mentioned that Taite might fix her fence, he hadn't hesitated to say he'd do it. While Taite really was hunkering down at Glenwood Station to avoid as many Bundilla females as possible, he still should have thought through his offer. It wasn't that he didn't want to help Grace, he had the time, it was just that it was getting harder to control the way she made him feel.

Even in his year of temporary insanity with Eloise he couldn't remember experiencing the same intensity of emotions. Instead of concentrating on his work at Crookwell Park, a job that previously would have fully occupied his mind, he was either listening for where Grace was inside the mansion or looking out for a glimpse of her. It would take him until winter to finish his part of the restoration at the rate he was going. So much for reassuring Grace that nothing would distract him.

Realising he was yet again staring into space, he went back to what he was doing. At least that morning at the quilting group the members would have been too busy discussing the hidden apartment to think about organising anyone's love life. Clancy had called on her way home to let him know that Grace had seemed to enjoy herself and that she did ride, even though she hadn't done so in a long time. He'd ended the call when his sister started talking about how Taite could bring Grace one of Brenna's quiet trekking horses next time he came to town.

Rowan hefted another stone into place, glad of the strain on his arms and back. It wasn't only his emotions that were feeling supercharged but his energy as well. It didn't matter how hard he worked, at the day's end when he drove past Grace's cottage he still felt wired. It didn't help that no matter how slow he drove down the driveway, or how many times he looked, he still didn't know where Frank had put his CCTV camera. He hated not having answers to a problem.

While he had no doubt Frank was an honourable man, the fact that he wouldn't reveal how he knew about the comings and goings of Crookwell Park only raised more questions. Frank had done Crookwell Park and Grace a great favour over the years by scaring away as many vandals as he could. But why would a man whose mobility was compromised make the trek from the corner gate where he'd have to leave his gator? He'd jeopardised his personal safety. If anyone had chased Frank, he wouldn't have been able to outrun them. His motivation couldn't simply be to protect a local historical landmark of a town he didn't want anything to do with.

When Rowan's phone rang in his shirt pocket, by the time he stripped off a glove the call had gone to voicemail. He slipped his mobile out to check who the caller had been. It was a fact of rural life that things did go wrong and he never wanted to be inaccessible in an emergency.

When he saw the caller was Grace and she hadn't left a message, he used his teeth to pull off his other glove so he could call her back.

She answered after a single ring, her voice breathless. 'Hi.'

Rowan was already two rungs down the scaffolding ladder when he replied. 'Everything okay?'

'Yes and no. The ladder fell …'

Rowan didn't bother with the last metal rungs or consider his bad leg before jumping to the ground. Even though he'd made sure Grace had a safe ladder, accidents still happened. She might be not so much breathless as winded after a fall. 'Are you still in the apartment?'

'Yes.'

'Hold tight.'

He took the side veranda steps two at a time and sped through the reception room and down the hallway to the library. His pulse kicking like brumby hooves, he raced inside and came to a sudden stop.

Grace wasn't lying crumpled on the floor. Apart from white flakes that covered her like a snowfall, she looked very much in one piece as she stood in the hidden doorway looking at him with wide eyes.

He slowed his breathing to switch his adrenaline off high alert and slid his hands in his jeans pockets to stop himself from reaching for her. He knew he should speak but all he could do was stare. The soft and styled waves of her dark hair fell across her shoulders and around her face, framing her high cheekbones and drawing attention to her mouth.

Before he could break the silence, Grace surged forwards to grab his bare forearm and pulled him into the apartment. 'You will *not* believe this.'

He didn't trust himself to reply. His words would only sound hoarse. What he couldn't believe was how strong the hit to his senses was from the simple clasp of Grace's hand.

A sizeable hole in the back wall where the bed had been finally caught his attention. No wonder Grace had flakes all over her; the floor was littered with pieces of plasterboard. A cast iron kettle covered in white dust sat on the table and had to be Grace's DIY tool of choice.

When they reached the now exposed wooden wall frame, Grace released his arm to pass him her phone to use as a torch. 'Look inside.'

Excitement flushed her face and turned her eyes a vibrant green-gold. Whatever Julie had used on her hair in the salon smelled like Clancy's flower shed at peony season. Even covered in plaster Grace was so beautiful he took a second to do as she'd asked.

When the torchlight illuminated a narrow cavity and then a staircase, he had no more trouble focusing. He gave a low whistle.

'I know,' Grace said. 'The apartment has to have two levels.'

He handed Grace her phone and looked up to study the ceiling. There would be plenty of space in the roof for another room. 'So ... what happened with the ladder?'

'Bundy was chasing a rat and knocked it over. The corner ended up stuck in the wall. When I pulled it out, a hole started.'

'Started?'

She matched his smile. 'Who knew bashing things with a kettle was so therapeutic? I just need to make it bigger so we can fit through.'

When she went to pick up the kettle from the table, he touched her shoulder. 'Hang on.' As she turned to look at him her hair slid over his fingers and he quickly lifted his hand. 'I've a plaster saw in my toolbox.'

'I love your toolbox.'

He gave what he hoped passed as a casual grin and left as fast as he could. This animated and sparkling Grace was making it impossible to remember that as Captain Serious he wasn't supposed to be thinking about tangling his hands in her hair and kissing her until they both forgot where they were.

When he returned, Grace had moved the bed further towards the window so the space between the bathroom wall and the fireplace would be fully accessible.

'Ready?' he asked before he set about removing a wide doorway-sized section of the wall.

Whenever he cut away a portion, Grace came over to take hold of the plasterboard. With each piece that was removed, he sensed her excitement building. He concentrated on what he was sawing and not on the way every smile she flashed him was full of life.

Once the opening was finished and he'd removed some non-essential pieces of the wall frame to give them room to climb through, they stood back. Grace turned on a lantern and shone the more powerful light into the wall cavity. The area had been sealed off for decades. Cobwebs clung to the stone wall and the wooden ceiling and dust lay thick on the stairs. While Grace could easily walk along the confined space, he'd have to angle his shoulders to fit. She must have shared his thoughts as when he glanced at her she'd been looking at his torso.

She bent to set the lantern inside to the right of the makeshift doorway. 'I'll go first ... but if it's okay can you please come with me so we have enough light?' She frowned over at the corner where he guessed the rat had been. 'I don't want to meet anything else that squeaks.'

He took out his mobile. While the lantern illuminated the bottom steps, the top ones would remain shrouded in darkness.

Grace rolled down the sleeves of her work shirt. Then with one sleeve pulled over her hand, she slipped through the hole in the wall.

Rowan climbed through more slowly. He needed to stand sideways on at least two stairs in order to have enough room in which to move. Every few steps Grace used her shirt-covered arm to brush away the cobwebs and he made sure he stopped so as not to crowd her. As the lantern light waned, he beamed the light of his phone torch ahead of where Grace needed to walk.

She spoke over her shoulder, her words quiet. 'Just as well Bundy's outside. Three would be a crowd in here.'

A musty smell tainted the thin air and every tap of Grace's boots on the wooden stairs seemed to echo.

She stopped again and took a couple of deep breaths. 'This … is a little claustrophobic.'

He climbed the steps that separated them to take hold of her hand. He didn't stop to examine his feeling of contentment when her fingers curved around his. 'Let's get some fresh air.'

Her chin lifted as she shook her head. 'We're almost there.'

With her hand still in his, they continued up the last steps to a tiny landing. Once through the doorway on their right they'd be standing directly over the apartment below.

Needing to get Grace out of the stairway, Rowan adjusted his hold on his phone and reached around her to twist the door handle. For a brief moment, with one hand in hers and his other outstretched, it was as though he embraced her. Not wanting to make her any more uncomfortable than she already was, he straightened to give her as much room as the snug space would allow.

It felt like the door took forever to slowly swing open. To his relief the high pitch of the attic roof created a large area in front of them and from the expanse of dusty floorboards it appeared empty.

He waited for Grace to let go of his hand. Instead she remained still. He half turned towards her.

Despite the light from his phone, her face remained in the shadows. As for the other parts of her he couldn't see, those he could feel. The warmth of her hip where it rested against him. The silkiness of her hair as it brushed his jaw. The depths of her uncertainty in the tight grip of her hand.

'Grace?'

She stiffened. 'Sorry, I was feeling light-headed.' Her fingers loosened their hold before they pulled free from his grasp. 'I've never been so happy to have a door open.'

He followed, feeling an unexpected sense of loss without her hand linked with his.

Grace stopped just inside the room and slid her mobile out of her shirt pocket. After shining her phone up at the ceiling as if to prove to herself that she had space around her, she directed her torch straight ahead. Her gasp filled the silence.

Rowan went to stand beside her to add his beam of light to hers. His assumption that the room was empty had been wrong.

CHAPTER
10

Grace swallowed, hoping the sound wasn't audible in the quiet of the attic room. Rowan was probably already thinking she was a nervous wreck.

She didn't blame him. She had no idea what had happened in the enclosed stairwell. All she knew was that when Rowan had enfolded her hand in his, instead of easing her tension it had made her chest tighten with longing. She didn't want his touch to just be a one-off. Then when he'd reached past her to open the door and she'd been surrounded by his strength, her yearning had collided with a loneliness so deep she'd been unable to think straight.

'Grace?'

Just like on the stairs, his husky voice saying her name brought her back to her senses. His calloused fingers traced along her jaw. 'Are you okay?'

It was all she could do to stop herself from turning her face into his palm. The item in front of them gave her a heartbreaking clue as to what the hidden apartment had been for. 'I'm just … stunned.'

Realising she'd lowered her arm, she raised her phone so its light again shone on the wrought iron baby cot.

'It was a family who lived here,' she said, voice hushed as she took in the dappled grey wooden rocking horse whose pale mane and tail had come off second best against the rats. Next to the horse stood an iron double bedframe that matched the cot. 'There was a baby and possibly another child who perhaps had never known life outside these walls.'

Rowan aimed his torchlight to their right where there was another door. 'That second room would be a bedroom too. No wonder the bed in the kitchen seemed out of place. It was never meant to go there.'

'That's also why there was nowhere downstairs to store clothes.'

Against the wall she counted two wooden trunks but no other furniture or toys. Unlike the rooms below, this one seemed to have been packed away and the bare basics left.

'These have to be some sort of windows.' She bent to examine what appeared to be a section of panels where the roof slope ended and the wall straightened.

Rowan joined her and walked along to flick a series of small latches that opened tiny doors. Natural light shone into the room.

'Again, this is very clever,' he said, examining the construction of a panel. 'The roof eaves are decorative and so the uniform pattern would help hide that when these are open there's glass behind them instead of the usual wood.'

Grace bent to look through the closest window. As well as seeing the eave brackets that needed a fresh coat of paint, she also saw how high up they were. She could see right to the corner of the back garden where she'd installed Frank's new gate.

She turned to glance behind her at the closed door before crossing the room. While she still felt unsettled, she needed to prove to Rowan, and herself, that her emotions were not going to get the better of her again. She opened the door and stepped inside.

This bedroom had a damp and mildewy smell and appeared to have been left as though the owner had rushed out intending to be back soon. There was a mattress on the double bed as well as greying linen. Against the adjacent wall was both a cedar wardrobe and a dressing table.

While Rowan went to let daylight in through the windows that again lined the far side, she opened the wardrobe. A heavy moth-eaten wool coat and a collection of dresses with tiny waists hung there just as they had for more than half a century.

When Rowan came to look into the wardrobe, she glanced at him. 'In the fifties a woman would only hide her children if they were in danger or born out of wedlock. There are no men's clothes here.'

'The number of kitchen chairs and plates, plus the World War Two water bottle, suggests that the father, whoever he was, could have visited.'

Grace went to examine the dressing table, which held crystal bowls filled with jewellery and trinkets. 'If so, the woman wasn't hiding out of fear from the father of her children.'

Rowan nodded as he walked to the other side of the bed. As he shone his mobile on the marble-topped corner table Grace saw streaks of what looked like water damage running down the wall.

'Please don't tell me there's been possums in here too?'

'No, this time those stains are from water ingress where the roof has leaked. See?' Rowan altered the angle of his phone light. 'There's mould on the ceiling. Rats would have knocked off all the pictures.'

A collection of tarnished and broken silver frames lay on the floor. Water had seeped through the cracked glass, ruining the photographs below. When she got the chance, she'd take a closer look. While the actual pictures might now be of little use, perhaps there was a name or some other identifier on the back.

She turned to head into the other room. With any luck they mightn't need the photos for answers anyway; maybe the two trunks contained the information they were after.

Already covered in plaster and cobwebs, she knelt in the thick dust that coated the hardwood floor. She wouldn't be sending Aubrey a follow-up picture to show what had happened to her clean and styled hair.

Grace unclipped the two metal latches and opened the wooden lid. The inside of the trunk was lined with a cream and green floral wallpaper. There seemed to be some sort of insert that divided the trunk in half to help keep what looked like folded clothes tidy. From the glimpse of tiny smocked stitches she already knew the items had been made for a baby.

Rowan came to crouch beside her. Glad of his company, she took out the insert, below which there was cot linen. A small bump had her carefully lifting the handmade pink and white quilt to reveal an old-fashioned plastic doll with dark hair dressed in a white nightdress. Grace's hand shook. The mint condition of the children's toy confirmed that the items in the trunk had never been used. The precious baby girl they had been meant for had never lived long enough.

Throat aching, she settled the covers back over the doll and returned the top layer before closing the lid. She had no words.

Rowan spoke quietly. 'Maybe we should take a break before we look in the other trunk.'

She rubbed at the goosebumps on her arms. 'I have a bad feeling too but we need to look inside.'

They moved along to the second trunk.

Grace took a moment before she unlatched the two clips. Just like the first trunk, it was again lined in the same wallpaper, but this time there wasn't a wooden insert. Instead of reaching inside to examine the contents, she sat back and folded her hands in her lap. She'd seen all that she needed to. This time she not only had no words but no defences against the tide of emotion that swamped her.

On the top of a pile of neatly folded shirts and shorts that would have belonged to a young boy were three items. Two were a pair of chipped and well-loved tin toy trains, one in blue and another in red. The other item was a pair of metal and leather polio callipers.

'I need some air.'

Not waiting to see Rowan's reaction to the way her voice had cracked, she dashed down the narrow stairs.

She'd only made it to the apartment kitchen when Rowan's arm caught her waist.

'Grace, it's okay.'

She didn't know if it was the concern in his gentle words or the solid wall of his chest that had offered her solace earlier but instead of pulling away, she turned. His arms wrapped around her to hold her close as tears wet her cheeks.

Since she'd lost her parents, she'd never indulged her sadness. They wouldn't have wanted her loss to mire her in despair. While she was the first to admit she was still navigating her way through the stages of her grief, she could also count on one hand the amount of times she'd let her sorrow overwhelm her.

Between the moment on the staircase and now the loss symbolised by the pair of lovingly packed trunks, her emotions proved too unwieldy. Whoever had put up the wall, their grief had become too much to bear and they hadn't been able to face going upstairs to the empty rooms. The single bed pushed up against the wall suggested they'd then slept as close as they could to the ones they'd loved.

Grace didn't realise how many tears were flowing until she felt the damp cotton of Rowan's shirt beneath the clutch of her fingers. For a delusional moment she thought his lips touched her temple. But even knowing how out of control she was didn't stem the flood of her sorrow. As comforted as she felt in Rowan's arms, it was as though his support unleashed all the anguish she'd been withholding since her parents' ashes had drifted across the pale winter sand.

When the storm finally subsided, it only took two shuddering breaths before embarrassment kicked in. She edged away and Rowan eased his hold just enough so their torsos no longer touched. She knew she should put more distance between them, but his gentle embrace felt right.

She met his gaze, head high. 'I'm so sorry.'

'There's nothing to be sorry about.' His low voice matched the seriousness that turned his eyes a smoky grey. 'Take it from me … nothing good comes from holding in your grief.'

'After that marathon effort I can't have much left.'

A trace of a smile shaped his mouth. 'It was hard finding the trunks.'

'It was.' She paused to keep her voice steady. 'Somebody loved those children so much they couldn't face losing them.'

'It was the father.'

'How do you know?'

He lifted his hands from her waist to place a palm over his heart. 'Here. Plus the blanket on the downstairs bed. I checked and it was identical to the one my grandfather brought back from the war.'

Grace didn't immediately answer. Now that Rowan was no longer touching her, she didn't feel as anchored. It was all that she could do to stop herself from taking a step towards him. 'Do you think the mother could have died too? Maybe it was in childbirth and both mother and daughter couldn't be saved.'

'It makes sense. The mother's things are still upstairs just as she would have left them.' Rowan looked over at the large hole in the wall. 'The father sealed up the rooms to block out his pain. I … didn't use a wall, I just lost myself in the temporary insanity of someone else's world.'

From the strain in his words Grace suspected he was talking about Eloise.

'Rowan, grief is messy. We all do what we need to in order to get through.'

'Yeah, well.' He dragged a hand through his hair. 'Not all the things we do, and the choices we make, are good.'

She gave in to the urge to offer him the comfort that he'd given her and took hold of his hand. 'Not all the things we do, and the choices we make, are bad.'

He didn't reply, just looked down to where their hands touched before turning his over and lacing her fingers with his.

'Grace … I've said this before … Crookwell Park is lucky to have you. I hope when the summer ends you've found the peace you came here for.'

She only nodded. Her volatile emotions hadn't heeded the memo that they'd caused enough havoc for one day. Rowan gazed at her with such gravity and held her hand with such care, she had no hope of hiding the longings that surfaced whenever she was around him.

'Is there anything you want out of the upstairs rooms?' he asked, his gaze not leaving hers.

She cleared her throat before slipping her hand free. 'Not at the moment, thanks. I think a hot shower and a pot of tea are in order.'

He nodded, his attention lingering on her face before he turned to leave through the bookcase door.

Grace released an uneven breath and when she could no longer hear his footsteps, left to return to her cottage.

After the plaster and cobwebs had been washed from her hair, she sat the tea pot covered in her mother's tea cosy and a china mug on the table beside the lounge. Bundy had popped in to see her and then disappeared outside again. He'd taken to sitting beside the goat yard as if to keep watch over Crookwell Park's newest inhabitants.

Grace curled up in the corner of the lounge. She'd left a message for Mabel about the new rooms and was now officially giving herself the rest of the afternoon off. She'd finish her book, which was by one of the medieval historical authors who would be attending the book festival.

As she reached for the novel, her phone rang. Aubrey would be calling about her earlier selfie taken outside the hair salon.

Aubrey's shocked face stared at her. 'That's not quite the look I was expecting.'

Grace lifted a hand to her still shower-damp hair. 'Trust me, this is an improvement on how it looked an hour ago.'

'Have you had a bad day?'

Grace sighed. No doubt her eyes were still puffy. 'Rowan and I found two new rooms, bedrooms, behind a fake wall. There were some trunks, one filled with things for a baby girl and the other for a little boy. We think the mother could have died in childbirth.'

'That's so sad.'

'It is. I basically lost the plot in what couldn't be called one of my finest moments.'

Aubrey's gaze sharpened. 'With Rowan?'

'Yes. I sobbed all over his shirt.'

'What did he do?'

'He didn't seem to mind ... he just held me.'

Aubrey looked away from the camera as if to check something on her laptop screen. 'Right ... I have a breakfast meeting Sunday morning but can leave after then.'

'Leave? Aubrey ... I'm fine.'

Aubrey's unsmiling brown eyes met hers. 'You never let anyone get close enough to touch you, let alone hold you.'

'I hug you and have sobbed all over you.'

'That's different.'

'You're busy ... I really do feel better. I think I just had to let everything go.'

Aubrey's fixed stare didn't waver. 'I've just blocked out five days in my calendar. It's locked in. I'm coming. And no more getting up close and personal with this stonemason of yours until he has my tick of approval.'

It didn't matter that the croak of a frog from the depths of a hollow wooden fence post warned Rowan of rain when he fed Goliath his morning biscuit of hay. It didn't matter that when he drove out Ashcroft's front gate raindrops pelted his windscreen. And it didn't matter that when he turned off the bitumen to drive to Crookwell Park the downpour was so heavy he couldn't see the gravel road.

Even though it was a Thursday and a workday, he wasn't going to finish off the final stones in the side wall. He was going to see Grace.

Rowan parked beside her car. Ever since she'd cried her heart out yesterday, he couldn't relax. His body still remembered the feel of her in his arms. His lips still remembered the softness of her hair. And he still remembered how powerless he'd felt at not being able to ease her pain. Her sadness hadn't only been from finding the heartbreaking contents of the trunks.

Grace's strength humbled him. Her dignity awed him. She'd dealt with her grief head-on. There was no running away from her emotions like he had done. He scraped a hand over his face. There was so much he'd do differently if he had his time again.

He stared at the water streaming over the glass in front of him. After yesterday it was even more important that Grace be left in peace to continue to work through what she needed to. And for that to happen, after he'd made sure she was okay, he had to talk to her about putting to rest all the rumours and matchmaking agendas.

A break in the rain had him leave his ute and jog towards Grace's cottage. She'd earlier texted to make sure he wasn't coming to work in the bad weather. She still wasn't a fan of his scaffolding even if he kept reassuring her it was safe. In his reply he said he needed to come to town so could pop over for a morning coffee. He hadn't wanted to turn up unannounced. A smiley face emoji had communicated she'd be expecting him.

He went to knock on the door but it opened before his knuckles rapped on the wood.

Grace smiled as she moved away to let him in. 'Bundy's been waiting for you.'

Rowan bent to ruffle the kelpie's neck. This morning, instead of wearing jeans with her pink work shirt, Grace wore black leggings that showcased every toned curve. Her feet were bare and her dark glossy hair fell down her back.

'Coffee?' she asked as if him coming to pay her a social call was a common occurrence.

'That would be great.'

He patted Bundy for a few seconds more. When the kelpie tilted his head, Rowan knew he'd seen through his ruse to buy time to collect himself. Whereas from Grace's perspective things wouldn't have appeared to have changed between them after yesterday, they had for him. Being around Grace was a definite risk, but it was one he couldn't stop himself from taking. Her wellbeing trumped any calls of his self-preservation to stay away.

Unlike when he'd visited the day she arrived, the cottage now had little touches of home. Colourful summer flowers perfumed the kitchen while through the living room doorway he could see sage-green cushions on the lounge. He only knew the name of that particular green as in their coach house renovation days Clancy had sent him to Tumut armed with a colour swatch and instructions to find a throw rug that matched.

Grace too glanced at the lounge. 'I think I'm already the vintage charity shop's best customer. I only ever plan to duck into town … but I'm forever finding all these gorgeous things.'

When her gaze lingered on his face he thought a tinge of colour dusted her cheeks but then she turned to pour water into their coffee mugs. 'Take a seat,' she said over her shoulder.

He pulled out a chair at the small table on which Grace had already placed a plate of neenish slice.

He snuck a small piece and gave it to Bundy under the table.

'I saw that,' Grace said, laughter in her voice as she brought over their mugs.

'Is this another of Frank's favourite things for morning smoko?'

'Not this time.' Grace too sat. 'The recipe is from the apartment cookbook.'

The sudden shadows in her eyes made him glad he'd come to visit. What they'd found still affected her.

'Grace … do you want me to put the wall back up?'

'No. As sad as it all is, I can't help feeling we were meant to find the extra rooms.' She cupped her hands around her mug. 'I'd really like to keep looking for answers. Mabel's coming this afternoon to take more photos. Those trunks and that rocking horse belong to someone.'

'I don't think you've met Ned but he's a friend of Heath's and he restores rocking horses. I could give him a call?'

'That would be wonderful.'

'Speaking of horses, Clancy said you ride.'

'I do, but it's been a while.'

'The weather should clear by the weekend. After I fix the fence on Saturday, maybe we could go for a ride into the hills. Brenna has a quiet trekking horse I could bring over.'

The light returned to Grace's eyes. 'I'd love that. I've been meaning to find out where the boundary fences are.'

Rowan nodded. The rain on the tin roof had quietened enough to hear the unmistakable sound of Frank's side-by-side. Bundy looked up from where he'd been asleep beside Rowan's chair before padding over to the front door. His conversation about a fake date was going to have to wait a little longer.

'I hope Frank isn't too wet,' Grace said as she left to switch on the kettle.

Rowan went to open the cottage door. Bundy bounded over as Frank took his time to climb out of the gator. For a moment Rowan caught a glimpse of Frank's unguarded expression. The creases etched in the older man's face conveyed physical discomfort while the haunted look in his eyes spoke of a deep emotional pain. Whatever Frank's full story was, Rowan had no doubt that parts of his life hadn't been easy.

When Frank saw Rowan, his shoulders straightened. 'Not even the rain can keep you away.'

'That makes two of us,' Rowan said with a grin.

It was fleeting but a twinkle softened Frank's gaze as he hobbled through the doorway.

When they were seated at the table and Frank had a pot of tea in front of him, talk turned from the wet summer to when Olive's baby kids would arrive and places in the United Kingdom they'd each visited. Rowan took his time to drink his coffee and managed to slip half his neenish slice to Bundy without being caught.

Comfortable and at ease, Grace chatted more than Frank and Rowan combined and at times her English accent was quite pronounced. No longer was there any sign of the reserve that she'd shown when she'd first arrived or any sense that she chose her words with care before she replied.

It was when the conversation switched to the trunks in the hidden bedroom that Rowan registered a shift in Frank's mood. When Frank rubbed at his left leg, Rowan knew the action was because the older man had been sitting too long in the same position. He also was feeling twitchy and his once-broken leg ached. But when Frank's gnarled fingers tightened around his teacup at the mention of the doll in the baby girl's trunk, he wasn't so certain of the answer.

The only explanation that possibly fit was that Frank could have lost a daughter.

Grace glanced across at him. She too had noticed Frank's reaction. Rowan changed the topic to what goat climbing masterpiece Frank and Grace were going to build next before Grace offered Frank the final piece of slice.

Once Frank's plate was empty, he slowly pushed back his chair. 'Grace, that was as delightful as always.' He turned to Rowan. 'I see that side wall is almost done. What are you working on next?'

Frank's use of the word *see* was no accident. They both knew Rowan still didn't understand how Frank was across what was going on at Crookwell Park.

'That would be telling. I believe a good chess player never reveals his moves.'

Frank chuckled. 'Your father was an expert at that.'

Rowan went to hold open the front door. When Frank walked by, he said so only Rowan could hear, 'Another thing your father was good at was putting the past behind him.'

Rowan caught his frown before it formed. Grace was watching them. Not only did his father have very little past to put behind him, his parents had married young and enjoyed a happy marriage. How did Frank know what past Rowan needed to let go of? For someone who didn't visit Bundilla or know who he was before now, he sure kept track of what was happening in town.

Not waiting for a reply, Frank continued outside. Rowan, Grace and Bundy followed. The rain had stopped and the breeze carried a fresh clean scent tinged with lemon from the lemon-scented gum behind the cottage. Once in the gator Frank gave a wave before driving away.

'He's such a lovely man,' Grace said from where she stood beside Rowan.

'He's not someone I'd want to cross.'

Grace gave him a curious look. 'Before you go, is it okay if you moved something for me?'

'Sure.' He rubbed the back of his neck. 'There's also something I need to talk to you about.'

Grace stilled. 'You can't keep working here?'

'No ... nothing like that.' He tried to find the right words and failed. Asking Grace out on a fake date wasn't as easy as it had been in his head. He'd never had any trouble socialising with the opposite sex before, but for some reason this just seemed more important. 'I'll move whatever you need moved and then we can talk.'

'Okay.' While her expression had cleared, the wariness he'd associated with her when they'd first met had returned.

'What do you need help with?' he asked in a casual tone to keep things light as they turned to walk inside the cottage.

'The furniture in my spare room. Aubrey's coming Sunday night.'

From previous conversations he'd worked out that Aubrey was her best friend and a diehard city girl. 'Just as well your possums have moved out.'

Grace's smile gave him hope he might get two minutes into his date pitch before she said no.

In the second bedroom he repositioned the heavy bed so it faced the window and then took out a green velvet chair to the living room. Once he'd placed it in the correct corner, Grace plonked herself on the sofa. Bundy jumped up to lie next to her, leaving Rowan with no choice but to sit in the velvet chair that was about as comfortable as a bag of oats.

'So,' Grace said, her face carefully blank in what he now recognised as her default expression whenever uncertain.

'So ... there's actually three things to chat about.'

She nodded and waited for him to continue.

'It turns out it isn't just the quilting ladies who love to matchmake; Clancy and Brenna do as well. They think that Taite and ... you ... would make a perfect couple.'

Whatever response he was expecting, it wasn't for Grace to calmly say, 'They've told you this?'

'Not exactly. It's obvious. They always mention your names together.'

'Okay. So what's the second thing?'

'No one thinks I've moved on from Eloise.'

This time there was silence. Grace searched his face. 'Have you?'

'Yes. I already doubted my feelings when we were together.'

'And the third?'

'While you're believed to be single you won't ever be left alone to do what you came here for.'

Her expression appeared thoughtful. 'So how do we deal with these three ... things?'

He cleared his throat. 'I have a plan.'

'Just one?'

He slowly nodded. 'For us to have a ... fake date.'

She studied him as if all he'd asked was whether she preferred her pizza with or without pineapple.

'That would cover me appearing to be unattached and you not moving on from Eloise, but how does that help with Taite and I being seen as a match? You'd never lie to your sister and from what I know about Taite he wouldn't either.'

'You're right. I'd never lie to Clancy and Taite wouldn't lie to Brenna.' He stopped to organise his thoughts. The logical and unemotional Grace who quietly sat on the lounge, her attention never leaving him, would be a formidable opponent in any negotiation. 'My thinking was that Clancy and Brenna would abandon their matchmaking plan, because if they kept pushing you and Taite together, then that could compromise us being seen around town as a fake item. And they wouldn't want that to happen for both of our sakes.'

'I agree. So, how many fake dates?'

'One ... the sooner the better ... like on Sunday at the long lunch.'

'That would be enough?'

He pushed aside the thought that if he was asking Grace out on a real date, one would never be enough. 'Yes.'

'True, it would be ... we're already alone together out here all week anyway.'

Rowan stilled. Suddenly him being ignored in town made perfect sense. He should have fully thought through the implications of him working out at Crookwell Park earlier. No wonder he hadn't been steered towards any particular women. The merry matchmakers knew he saw the person they had in mind every day. The question was how did Grace, even though she was whip-smart, manage to be one step ahead? Being matched with him wouldn't have even been on her mind.

Gaze steady, she held his stare. She knew he'd picked up on something.

'Grace?'

'I'm not saying a word. What happens in quilting club stays in quilting club.'

He briefly closed his eyes. That was a Clancy and Brenna saying. Wait until he saw his sister next.

'I take it,' he said, voice weary, 'there's no need for a fake date because everyone in town already thinks we're on the way to being a couple. Clancy was just doing reverse psychology on me by making me think she was shoehorning you and Taite together.'

Grace touched a finger to her mouth as if to say her lips were sealed.

It was enough of an answer. He went to push himself out of his seat, which had become even more uncomfortable.

Grace held up a hand, her eyes serious. 'Wait.'

He settled back in the small chair and folded his arms.

'Rowan … you're always looking out for me and I want to repay the favour. As I see it, the main thing we have to deal with is people not believing you're over Eloise, so we need to prove you are. I like your plan. I think it's a good idea to go to the long lunch on Sunday together. I'd love to be your fake date.'

CHAPTER
11

Just as the weather forecast had predicted, by the weekend the mountain peaks were no longer eclipsed by cloud and the summer sky was as blue as the small Wedgwood vase Grace had placed in Aubrey's room.

Grace parked near the clock tower, happy to walk to where she needed to go. As she strolled along the main street, the sun burned through the thin grey T-shirt she wore with denim shorts. At least Bundy was somewhere cool as he'd stayed with Frank after they'd visited the burial plot to check the dates on the Russell spinster sisters' headstones.

As she'd hoped, the years each Russell sister had passed away roughly fit within the apartment timeframe and the scenario that the mother had died in childbirth. While neither of the spinsters' names could be linked to the name in the cookbook, it was possible that Melly might have been a nickname. There also was a chance that the cookbook didn't belong to the woman who'd lived in the hidden rooms and had nothing to do with anything. So, until Kathy could dig a little deeper and prove otherwise, both Russell sisters were still very much in the picture as being the mother of the secret family.

Grace stopped to take her water bottle from out of her tote bag. She'd better add a pedestal fan to her shopping list as she wasn't sure how well the air conditioner worked in the guest room. She still couldn't believe Aubrey would be here tomorrow evening. Just as well she hadn't told her about the fake date or about her ride with Rowan that afternoon, otherwise she would have arrived earlier.

Grace continued walking. Despite already knowing what Aubrey would say, she had no doubt that she'd done the right thing offering to accompany Rowan to the long lunch. While she'd believed him when he said he was over Eloise, she hadn't forgotten the grim bleakness that she'd glimpsed in his eyes several times now. There would be a reason behind why he seemed to be so hard on himself about the way he'd coped after losing his parents.

A car horn tooted and she waved at Sandra as she drove by. It only seemed fair that as Rowan had been prepared to make sure she had the space she needed that she too had his back. She ignored the murmurs that said what she had with Rowan was now personal and that she'd been right to worry about even such a simple connection. Just the thought of being with him tomorrow on a fake date made her stomach swirl.

She turned to enter the air-conditioned pharmacy to replenish her limited makeup supply. Then next on her list was to find a long lunch outfit and that might take a while. She couldn't remember the last time she went dress shopping.

Once she'd finally found everything she needed, it was well after midday when she made it back to Crookwell Park. Not wanting to hold Rowan up when he arrived with the horses, she printed out the computer-generated map of Crookwell Park's boundaries that the solicitor had passed on to the real estate agent.

Dressed in jeans and a blue work shirt, she was cutting up apples for the goats when the rattle of metal sounded from the driveway. Bundy was already outside and she could hear his excited barks. She went to the front door as Rowan's ute pulling a horse float drove by. In the back she glimpsed the rumps of a large glossy brown-red horse and a smaller buckskin one. She slid the folded boundary map into her jeans pocket, collected the container of goat treats and tugged on her boots.

As soon as Olive realised what was in Grace's hand, she bleated and waddled towards the yard gate. The three younger goats, who had been startled by the horse float and were running around the yard, also came over. Grace smiled as the four goats gobbled up their apple. She was learning it was the simple things that layered joy into a day.

Rowan waved from where he'd parked nearby before he went to unload the horses. She quashed a further rush of happiness at knowing they would be spending the afternoon together. After her meltdown the other day, she had to keep the wits that kept deserting her firmly in place. And that included not revealing how much she'd missed not seeing him yesterday because of the rain.

She gave each goat a last pat and went to help. While the buckskin mare had been tied up near the stables on a low rail, the gelding was secured to the float by blue baling twine. As she approached, the blood bay swung around to glare, his ears pinned back.

'Ignore Goliath,' Rowan said, walking to meet her. 'He's harmless.'

Grace raised her brows. 'Harmless?' She recognised a bad temper when she saw it.

Rowan grinned as this time Goliath bared his teeth. 'He's just not happy. My normally antisocial stockhorse has a crush on little Miss Jindy over there.'

Goliath turned his head to whinny at the mare, who ignored him.

Grace laughed softly. 'I think Goliath may need to rethink his wooing strategy.'

'I never even knew he had one until an hour ago. It was a first he loaded onto the float without any trouble. But if anyone could put up with him it's Jindy. She's a brumby and a gentle soul.'

It wasn't long until both horses were saddled. Whereas Jindy had stood still, Goliath surged and fussed so much that Grace, as well as Bundy, stayed away.

She'd saved some of the apple slices she'd given to the goats and she offered them to Jindy on her flattened palm. The buckskin sniffed and then nibbled at them. 'You're a sweetheart. No wonder Goliath's head over heels.'

Once the treats were gone, she ran her hand down the buckskin's neck and breathed in the horse scent that she remembered from her childhood. Whatever the future held for her, she had to make more time to do the things she enjoyed. It had been far too long since she'd been around horses.

When Rowan came over to pass her a black riding helmet, she hoped her expression didn't reveal how much the sight of him with his cantankerous gelding moved her. As uncooperative as Goliath had been, Rowan had remained calm, gentle and patient. One day he'd treat his children the same way.

Realising that she was staring at the helmet she held, she slipped it on and clipped the buckle of the chin strap into place. Instead of the strap touching her skin, a loose loop hung below her jaw.

Rowan stepped closer, his eyes a soft grey as he smiled. 'Here …
I'll fix that.'

His fingers briefly brushed her cheek as he unclipped the strap. After he'd adjusted the length, he resecured the buckle. Grace barely noticed that the strap now sat beneath her chin. The feel of his fingers on her skin and the view she had of his tanned throat above the open collar of his green shirt were making her feel too warm. As for how near his mouth was … She took a quick step away on the pretext of tipping her head forwards to make sure her helmet wouldn't move.

'Okay, we're good to go,' Rowan said, his voice sounding slightly husky before he moved to untie Jindy.

Grace took a quick calming breath while his back was turned.

'Like a leg-up?' Rowan asked as he handed her Jindy's reins.

She shook her head even before he'd finished speaking. After the way she'd just reacted, she wasn't tempting fate a second time by having Rowan stand close to her. 'It won't be pretty but I'll be right to get on.'

Hoping she didn't startle Jindy or mess everything up, she passed the reins over the buckskin's head. She gathered them in her left hand, put the toe of her boot in the stirrup and swung into the saddle. While it was a far from elegant move, at least she made it. Her grin must have said how relieved she was as Rowan gave her a thumbs up before he went to his ute to collect a wide-brimmed hat.

Once he too was in the saddle and Goliath was walking forwards and not sideways, they set off along the track that led to the hills. Bundy ran between them, nose to the ground.

As they drew near to the rocky hillside behind the right corner of the mansion, Rowan halted Goliath and pointed to a staggered section of rock.

'This is where some of your bluestone comes from. You can still see the drill marks in the square cut stones.'

Grace took out her phone to take a photograph.

Pebbles clattered under the horses' hooves as they followed the trail that wound upwards. Beside them, the eastern boundary fence ran in a ribbon-straight line. Kangaroos watched from where they rested in the shade of a tree and when the horses drew near, they bounded away. Somewhere overhead a plover called.

Grace relaxed in the saddle. Jindy was a pleasure to ride. Sweet and responsive, the mare didn't seem to mind that Grace didn't always know what she was doing. The higher they climbed the more the temperature cooled. All too soon they reached the back boundary fence that cut across the hilltop. Beyond the wire, foothills continued to undulate until they steepened into timber-covered slopes and granite peaks.

Rowan rode along the fence line to where the trees separated to reveal a grassed clearing. He dismounted and tied Goliath to a fallen tree. Grace too left the saddle, her legs feeling as boneless as jelly. She led Jindy over to Rowan who tethered the mare near Goliath. For once, Goliath stood quietly and the two horses dropped their heads to graze.

Grace made her way to where a smooth slab of granite provided a perfect vantage point to rest her riding muscles and absorb the view. From this height she could see that Crookwell Park had been built at the edge of the valley carved by the river that was now a meandering line of distant trees. A flock of cockatoos dipped over the mansion, their wings flashing white.

Rowan sat and passed her a water bottle he'd taken out of his saddle bag. Bundy joined them and flopped onto the ground, his tongue lolling. Rowan took off his felt hat and poured water from his bottle into the crown for the kelpie.

'It's so gorgeous up here,' Grace said into the quiet after Bundy had finished drinking.

'It is.' Even before Rowan picked up a small rock and tossed it, Grace sensed his restlessness. As relaxed as he appeared, his muscles were coiled as if ready for instant action. 'There's nowhere else I'd rather be.'

She watched as he threw a second small stone. 'Let me guess, you were the kid who never sat still in class?'

'That was me.' The corner of his mouth lifted in a grin. 'Whereas I bet you were the one who always sat still.'

Grace thought before she answered. 'I was but I always wished I could be the ones who were fidgeting, who were told to stop laughing and who got into trouble for dancing in the rain.'

'You could do all of those things now.'

She picked up her own rock to throw. 'I suppose.'

She felt rather than saw Rowan search her face. 'Grace … I feel like I need to explain about Eloise.'

'Need or want?' She pitched her rock down the hill. 'You don't owe me any explanation.'

He gave her a half smile. 'I'd like to.'

'Okay then.' She returned his smile. 'I'd like to hear it.'

Rowan threw a rock in the same direction hers had flown. 'I've always had certainty in my life. I was always going to be a cattleman, like my father, and work with stone. I did an ag degree, then a stonemasonry apprenticeship, before going to the United Kingdom to further my skills. When Dad had a health scare I returned home to help run Ashcroft.'

Rowan paused while he threw another rock. 'By now Eloise had moved to town. She was a beautician and a model. If I saw her I'd say hi, but that was about it. Then … Mum and Dad took that cruise in Budapest and never came home. The truth is I felt like I had drowned too.'

Grace passed him another stone to toss.

He stared at it before throwing it after the others. 'Life became a blur of jumping, diving and basically throwing myself off whatever I could to get an adrenaline rush because if I stopped, my grief would hit me. I don't even know how it really started with Eloise. One night we had a drink in the pub and before I knew it I'd moved in with her. I bought an engagement ring on impulse and before I could blink a wedding date had been locked in.'

Grace stayed quiet. She hadn't known he and Eloise had been engaged.

'Then I caught Eloise being unkind to Clancy and it was as though I could breathe again. I put the wedding on hold and moved back to Ashcroft. But Eloise didn't understand I needed things to slow down. Even though we were technically still engaged, by the end we had no relationship. Eloise met someone else and, as they say, the rest is history.'

Instead of passing Rowan another rock she reached out to touch his arm. Beneath the cotton of his green shirt, tension rendered his bicep as hard as the granite around them. 'Everyone will soon know you're over her.'

His eyes met hers. No longer light, they were a slate grey. 'Are you sure about tomorrow?'

'Yes. It's been so long since I've been on a real date, a fake one will remind me what I'm supposed to do.'

As she'd hoped, a smile curved his mouth. 'Those city boys don't know what they're missing.'

Instead of replying, she dusted her hands on her jeans and came to her feet. She had about five seconds before the certainty showed on her face that it wasn't any city boy she wanted.

'Time to head back?' he asked as he stood and settled his hat on his head.

'We'd better. Aubrey wants a virtual tour of the cottage to see what things she can't live without that she needs to bring. Maybe we could ride along the other side boundary another day?'

'Sounds great.'

She took her time to follow Rowan over to the horses. She hadn't missed the flex of muscle in his jaw when he'd turned. His body language and tone confirmed that he was telling the truth about being over Eloise. But something dark still weighed on his mind.

She stroked Jindy's nose. It didn't matter if their date tomorrow was fake, she'd still enjoy every minute. It also didn't matter that she didn't do relationships and she kept telling herself she was only here to deal with her grief; she was fast becoming a lost cause. Aubrey was right to come to Bundilla on an emergency mission. For when it came to the man before her who swung into the saddle with such ease, she couldn't get enough of him.

❧

'Knock, knock.'

'You do know,' Rowan said, buttoning the cuffs on his best shirt as he walked down the coach house stairs to where Clancy already waited in the living room, 'you're supposed to say that at the door.'

'Pfft. It was open anyway.' She moved in close to tug at his navy tie that must have been off centre. 'You do scrub up well when you make the effort.' She paused to frown at his hair. 'But you do really need to see Julie or you'll end up looking like Fergus.'

'I'll take that as a compliment. Shaggy-haired highland cattle are a photographer's dream.'

Clancy's only reply was a roll of her eyes.

'You look nice too,' he said, taking in her simple white sundress.

'Thank you.' She curtsied. 'I bought it in Lucerne.'

'Listen to you … you world traveller.'

She swatted his arm. 'Stop avoiding the subject.'

He flicked his cuff to check he'd buttoned everything he needed to. 'I'm not. I'm making conversation.'

'As much as I'd like you to compliment me on what I wear every day, we both know you wouldn't notice if I was wearing chaff bags.'

He crossed his arms. 'There's nothing to talk about.'

'I know you've worked out why you've been left alone in town. Grace also mentioned your fake date. Why did it take you so long to realise what was going on and, more importantly, why didn't you tell me about taking her to the long lunch?'

He knew his grunt wasn't going to pass as a reply but it would buy him time until he had another coffee. He strode into the kitchen. A strong coffee.

Clancy followed him and pulled up a chair at the bench. She shook her head when he took two mugs out of the cupboard.

With the water boiling behind him, he finally spoke. 'I was going to tell you but not until we got there because I didn't want our fake date being made into a bigger deal than it is. And I took so long to work things out because … I've been a little distracted.'

'I'm not making it into a big deal.'

He simply looked at her.

'Okay, I am. It's your first date since Eloise.'

'It's *fake*.'

Her lips twitched. 'Do you want to say that with any more of a frown?'

He relaxed his face.

'Rowan … I never once said I was setting Taite and Grace up … you filled in the dots yourself. You would only do that if you were interested in Grace.'

'I'm not—' He paused at Clancy's raised brow to slow his words. 'Yes, we are friends and yes, as I've already said, I've noticed her but nothing is going to happen between us. It can't.'

'That first afternoon you met Grace, I could tell she left an impression. You've been spinning ever since.'

The kettle had boiled but he made no move to make his coffee. 'That's the problem, spinning is bad. It's what I did with Eloise.'

'No, it wasn't.' Clancy's soft voice was firm. 'Eloise and her mother saw you coming a mile off. Eloise made you spin on purpose. What you have with Grace is a real type of spinning, a spinning that will stop and then all you will feel is peace.'

'I don't trust myself to know the difference.'

'Then trust me. Grace is not Eloise. They couldn't be any more different. Go on your fake date and then ask Grace for another one … a real one that only the two of you know about.'

When he didn't answer, just stared over Clancy's shoulder at the view of the back garden, she stood. 'Think about what I've said.' She reached out to squeeze his arm. 'I have to go. Brenna has messaged three times to say she hasn't got anything to wear, which would be the truth because she doesn't own a dress. I need to find her a shirt to go with her best jeans.'

Clancy's words about how different Grace and Eloise were refused to fade on the drive out to Crookwell Park. The conversations he'd had with Grace were nothing like the superficial ones he'd had with Eloise, and they weren't even a couple. While he and his ex-fiancée had been compatible on a physical level, it was their emotional connection that had been lacking. He now knew what it truly felt like to enjoy someone's company and to be comfortable being himself when around them.

He chuckled as he stopped at the closed Crookwell Park gate that sported a new and humorous sign that warned to beware of goats with attitude. Once through, he continued to the cottage where Olive and Clover came to greet him just like any dog would. By the time he'd patted them, Chester and Windsor had arrived. All four goats followed him along the path.

He rapped on the front door and heard a faint, 'Come in. I'll be ready soon.'

'It's all good. I'm early.'

'Make yourself at home,' Grace called out, the creak of the floorboards in her bedroom telling him where she was.

Feeling strangely nervous, as if this was a real first date, he loosened his tie that suddenly seemed too tight and walked into the kitchen. Grace had prepared for Aubrey's arrival. Bottles of wine stood on the bench while over on the table sat a pile of glossy tourist brochures that Grace must have collected from the shelves in the library entrance. Beside the pamphlets was an unfolded piece of paper that appeared to be a map of Crookwell Park. He took a step closer. Something didn't look right about the boundary fence.

Before he could take a closer look, Grace walked into the kitchen and all thoughts emptied from his head.

She had already affected him on so many levels and in so many ways he believed he'd never be caught unawares again. He was wrong.

His heart pounded and his mouth dried.

Dressed in a floral dress with thin straps and a fitted waist, Grace was all smooth pale skin, delicate hollows and feminine curves. Her usual light honeysuckle scent had been replaced by a sensual fragrance that awoke every hormone he owned. But it was her mouth that slayed him. He was used to seeing her with no makeup, or sometimes a light gloss, but today whatever shade of deep pink lipstick she wore made it impossible to look at her without wanting to press his thumb to the full softness of her bottom lip.

'Is this outfit okay? Bundy approved.'

Her quiet words had him dragging his attention from her mouth to her long-lashed eyes.

He cleared his throat. 'You look ... beautiful.'

His compliment didn't clear the crease between her fine brows. 'Thank you but I wouldn't go that far. Wait until you meet Aubrey ... she really is.'

Grace lifted the hem of the dress that swirled around her bare legs to show him her gold strappy shoes. 'Will these be okay? I sent a photo to Clancy and she said the heels should be right for the riverbank. But do you think I should take my boots?'

He slipped his hands into his chino pockets. This fake date was going to be the death of him. If it was real there was no way they'd still be standing so far apart and he'd already have the answer as to whether or not her lipstick was smudge-proof. 'They'll be fine.'

She dropped the dress hem and it floated into place. 'Bundy's with Frank and the goats have been let out of their yard, so we're right to go.'

Rowan had already turned to open the front door. Even though Grace's smile was now a regular occurrence, it hadn't lost any of its power.

Once in his Land Cruiser he didn't bother with his seatbelt. He'd be getting out to open the gate. His mother had raised him to be a gentleman, plus he'd need the chance to clear his head. His ute cabin was already filled with Grace's perfume and all he could think about was discovering just what parts of her smelled so good.

Once the gate was closed behind them and he returned to his seat, Grace turned to him. 'We need to talk about Aubrey.'

Glad of the distraction, he focused on the gravel road. The trick to surviving the next few hours would be to look at Grace, and particularly her mouth, as little as possible. 'What do I need to know?'

'You have not seen bossy and blunt until you've met Aubrey. But under all her snark and sass she is all mush. Oh … and do not say we look like sisters or mention her height … or lack of it.'

'What can I say?'

'Just be yourself. If you're not she'll see straight through you and be merciless.'

'Do I need to wear body armour?'

'Only if she takes a dislike to you.'

When he risked a sideways look, Grace wasn't smiling. 'Is she single? I'd like to see the quilting group wrangle her love life.'

'She is.' Grace paused. 'But she has her reasons for being on her own. It's not from any lack of male attention. I think some guys actually like being rejected as they keep going back for more.'

Rowan shook his head. 'City boys.'

He slowed as they joined a string of cars travelling to the long lunch. The charity event was being held this side of town on the river flats beneath the largest of the historic wooden bridges. Amongst the red river gums that shaded the Tumut River, five food stations had been set up with the concept being that guests strolled from one to the other enjoying the lunch on offer.

In the past he and Taite had only ever made it to the first station before they hightailed it to the pub where they'd enjoy an uninterrupted game of pool. Today the last thing he'd be doing was leaving early and cutting his time with Grace short, even if every minute of this fake date was going to test his willpower.

He glanced at her. 'Any second thoughts?'

'Not at all. The sooner we do this the sooner the quilting club can get back to quilting.'

He parked at the end of a row of cars that were either covered in dust or sported a bullbar and aerials. He left his seat to open Grace's door, except she was already out and running her hands through her hair to keep the loose waves off her face. When the breeze moulded her dress against her, he knew it was time to join the other locals walking towards the first food station. The secret to getting through the next few hours wasn't only to not look at Grace but also for the two of them to not be alone.

He went to move when she closed the distance between them and reached up to fix his tie. Left with no time to hide how her nearness affected him, he tensed.

She stilled before meeting his gaze. 'Relax. Fake date, remember? Norma and Sandra are coming up behind you.'

He gave a small nod and forced his shoulders to lower as she finished straightening the knot of his tie.

Norma and Sandra gave them a wave as they passed, their heads bending together as they lowered their voices.

'This is almost too easy,' Grace said, a smile in her voice. 'As they say in Aubrey's favourite Regency show, shall we promenade?'

When Grace curled her hand around his arm, Rowan didn't trust himself to speak. He did the only thing he could: he walked.

Their visit to the first two food stations passed in a haze of much-needed beer, curious looks and listening to the carefree sound of Grace's laughter. While she might not have been the student who laughed in class, she was making up for it now.

At the third food station he found himself hanging back with Heath in the shade of an ancient gum while the girls went to fill their plates and Taite did another beer run. He watched Grace as she listened to something Clancy said. When she looked across at him and smiled, he couldn't help but return it.

'Fake date, huh,' Heath said beside him.

'No comment.'

Taite strode towards them. His fast pace had nothing to do with wanting their company but a means to escape the two young women heading his way, their champagne spilling from their glasses in their haste to talk to him.

'Ten more minutes and I'm out of here,' he growled as he handed Heath and Rowan their beers.

Rowan gave the girls a nod to soften the blow of Taite having his back towards them as they hovered nearby. They giggled and sashayed away to rejoin their group.

Taite threw him a desperate look. 'They gone yet?'

'Yep.'

The deer farmer sighed as he turned around and looked across to where Clancy, Brenna and Grace laughed at something Brenna said. 'So it was you who our meddlesome sisters had in their sights all along.'

When Rowan nodded, Taite touched his beer to his in silent sympathy.

'Don't look now,' Heath said, voice low, 'but, Rowan, your day's about to get worse. Janice has spotted you.'

Rowan followed Heath's gaze to where an elegant older woman was making her way on high heels over to him. It wasn't until she drew near that the lines on her face and the purse of her tight lips showed both her age as well as her character.

'Rowan,' Janice gushed, after she'd barely acknowledged Heath and Taite. 'I was hoping to see you. I thought you might like an update about Eloise. This *baby* will be here before we know it.'

The way she said *baby* was as though they shared a secret. They didn't. It was a fact Eloise was not carrying his child. He'd moved out to slow things down well before she'd fallen pregnant.

'I'm sure it will be.'

The conversation paused as Clancy, Brenna and Grace came over to join them. He breathed in Grace's perfume as she again took hold of his arm.

Janice's blue eyes sharpened as she looked between them before her gaze zeroed in on Grace. 'So you're the city girl who bought that pile of rubble keeping Rowan away from his farm.'

He opened his mouth to put Janice in her place, but when Grace squeezed his arm in a silent request to let her handle this, he settled for a glower.

'Yes, I am,' Grace said, tone smooth. 'Nice to meet you.' She offered the older woman her hand. 'And you are?'

Janice had no choice in the face of Grace's politeness but to clasp her fingers. 'Janice. *Eloise's* mother.'

'I haven't met any Eloise yet, but I'll be sure to keep an eye out for her. Everyone's been so friendly since I arrived.'

Janice had no chance to reply as Heath and Clancy moved to stand beside her.

'Now, Janice,' Clancy said, taking hold of her elbow to steer her away. 'It would be a crime to let this delicious food go to waste. Have you tried the bruschetta?'

Rowan slipped an arm around Grace's waist and turned so they could walk through the red gums away from the crowd and to where the river flowed beneath the historic bridge. They both remained silent until they stopped out of sight behind a towering gum.

He faced her. 'I'm so sorry.'

'No apology needed. That was nothing. I've been treated far worse.'

His intention had been to lower his hand from where it rested against the indent of her waist but at her quiet words his other arm lifted to encircle her. It was what was missing from her revelation that spoke of how much hurt she'd once suffered. There'd been no sadness, just a dignified resignation.

He didn't know if she realised that she took a step closer before she again spoke. 'My parents emigrated when I was four. It didn't matter what school I went to, I spent my childhood and most of my teenage years, until I met Aubrey, as an outlier because I sounded different and didn't fit in.'

Everything fell into place. Her initial reserve and her measured speech when she made sure that her accent wouldn't be noticeable and that the words she used were the correct ones. 'That's why you don't easily trust people when you first meet them.'

'Old habits are hard to break.' Her hands settled on his chest like they had when he'd held her when she'd been upset in the hidden apartment. 'I trusted you.'

Now had to be the time when he spoke or did something, anything, to put physical space between them. He was a heartbeat away from lowering his head and seeking her mouth.

'Grace.' His rough whisper didn't have her step away, only caused her to lift her hand and touch a finger to the cleft in his chin.

'Is it selfish to want our fake date to last a bit longer?'

Her words were soft and husky and spoken with the lilt of her English accent. Even before her attention focused on his mouth, he knew he had no more defences left to salvage.

He wasn't sure who moved first. When her lips met his, all he could process was that kissing Grace was like freefalling without a safety net, like going from zero to one hundred in seconds. Beneath all her sweetness and self-possession lay a spirit as restless and intense as his own. Hands in her hair, he angled her head to deepen their kiss as her fingers unbuttoned his shirt to seek access to his skin.

As if from a long distance away, he heard voices.

'Oh, don't mind them,' someone said. 'They're on their first date.'

'That doesn't look like any first date I ever went on.'

Rowan lifted his head to drag in air and to claw back some common sense. He'd never meant to let their kiss get so out of control. He wasn't sure who'd seen them, but a quick scan of the riverbank confirmed whoever they were they were gone.

Her breathing unsteady, Grace stared at him and then she smiled. A smile so brilliant he kissed her again. But this time he kept a rein on his need. The real world might again intrude at any moment.

When they broke apart, he knew from the solemnity in her eyes she shared the same thought.

'We'd better get back to reality,' she said with a sigh before she ran her fingertips over his jaw.

He laced her hand with his and kissed the inside of her wrist, inhaling her perfume.

Neither needed to say the words that this was only ever meant to be a fake date. Once back in the real world, there could be no more heady kisses beneath the majestic branches of an old gum beside a slow-flowing mountain river.

CHAPTER
12

'When am I going to meet this stonemason of yours?'

Instead of answering Aubrey, Grace opened one eye to check if there was any morning light shining through the gap in her curtains. The silence outside her window confirmed the birds weren't even awake yet.

She rolled over. 'Go back to bed. It's not like the city ... there's no street lights. When it's dark it's night and no one is awake.'

'I am.' Grace felt her pillow being pulled away. 'It's five thirty. I thought people in the country got up early. I would have already done one workout and cleared my inbox by now.'

Grace went to grab the pillow from where Aubrey stood holding it and then realised she'd wake Bundy who was somehow sleeping through Aubrey's early morning wake-up call. She instead sat up. 'Rowan won't be here for two hours. There's no rush.'

Aubrey took a seat on the side of the bed, staying a careful distance away from where Bundy slept on the end. 'I can't believe you let him sleep there.'

'I can't believe you're awake. I thought you were taking a break and relaxing.'

'That's the pot calling the kettle black.'

'Hey, I took the afternoon off last week and read a book. I've also been working on my memory quilt.'

'I suppose there was that one video call where you were in your pyjamas at ten o'clock in the morning.'

'Exactly.' Grace dragged hair out of her eyes to see Aubrey better. Even at five thirty she wore black lycra activewear and her mid-length dark hair had been straightened. 'How come you never look like you just got out of bed?'

She grinned. 'Sleep is for the weak.'

Grace flopped back on her mattress. 'In that case I'm definitely weak.' She sat up again in case Aubrey did leave her to rest and she slept through Rowan and Aubrey's first meeting. Her best friend wouldn't hesitate to introduce herself. 'You need to be nice to Rowan. He's my friend.'

'I thought you said Frank had filled that vacancy.'

'He has … now I have two.'

She did her best to not think about the kiss she'd shared with Rowan yesterday. The heat between them definitely did not come under any friendship banner.

Aubrey's eyes narrowed. 'You're smiling.'

'I'm not.'

'Yes, you are, a cat-got-the-cream smile. You were smiling last night too.'

'We opened a bottle of wine.' Grace paused as with a sigh Bundy came to his feet and jumped down from the bed to find somewhere quieter to sleep. She didn't blame him. 'You smiled as well.'

Aubrey stared at her, brown eyes speculative. 'Grace … you didn't.'

'Didn't what?'

'Get up close and personal again with your stonemason.'

She didn't have to say anything. The heat that flushed her cheeks provided enough of an answer.

'I *knew* I should have left earlier.'

'It's no big deal … we just went on a fake date and … then had a sort-of fake kiss.'

Concern pulled Aubrey's dark brows together. '*Sort of.*'

'Well, it was in the context of having a fake date but the kiss was real. Fireworks type real. But it was a one-off.'

Aubrey simply stared at her. 'What type of fireworks? Sparklers?'

Grace used her hands to show fireworks going sky high.

'Right.' Aubrey got off the bed and marched to the door. 'I'm officially worried. That wasn't your usual understatement. I'm making breakfast and then we're going to meet Rowan as soon as he arrives.'

'I'm not having any of those green smoothie things,' Grace called out. 'Bundy and I have peanut butter toast.'

Aubrey's only answer was the loud buzz of the fancy blender she'd brought with her. Bundy reappeared and jumped onto the end of Grace's bed and closed his eyes.

Grace reached for her pillow that Aubrey had left on the bedroom chair. 'I'm with you. I'm having another hour of sleep.'

As it turned out, she only managed to stay in bed for another thirty minutes and not a minute was spent sleeping. Aubrey had taken what had to be an overseas work call on her laptop and was soon arguing with some guy with a London accent. Grace gave up trying to catch any more shut-eye and went for a shower.

It hadn't solely been Aubrey keeping her awake; thoughts of Rowan kept making her stomach knot and her senses hum. If she'd known just how mind-blowing a kiss could be she would have kissed a whole lot more frogs. She just hoped whoever had seen them behind the old gum hadn't been too eloquent in their description of where her hands had been. Even now her fingers remembered the feel of the corded muscle beneath the hot skin of his chest.

She wiped the steam off the bathroom mirror to reveal her serious expression. As much as she wouldn't be able to look at Rowan and not want to repeat the experience, there could be no more heart-stopping kisses.

Apart from the satisfied looks that had greeted them when they'd returned arm in arm from the river, by the time the long lunch had ended hardly anyone had paid them any attention. It was as though the box of turning them into a couple had been ticked. As for their own plan, it too could be considered a success. The town had proof Rowan had moved on and she would no longer be on any single Bundilla ladies list.

The reflection that stared back at her was now more sad than serious. But the main reason why she couldn't again experience such magic with Rowan was that neither of them were in the right place for anything more than friendship. She needed to concentrate on coming to terms with her loss while Rowan had things to work through too. She suspected he believed he'd let his sister down with the bad choices he said he'd made.

After meeting Eloise's mother, she now had an idea about the nature of his relationship with Eloise. It would be a miracle if a mother like Janice had raised a kind and understanding daughter.

As for her and Rowan's fake date, it had started her thinking. What was her real world? Was it in Bundilla? Or was it back in the city? At the moment, she had no idea.

'Rowan will be here in one hour,' Aubrey's voice shouted through the bathroom door. 'And you're right, Bundy doesn't like green smoothies.'

Grace dressed in her jeans and a pink work shirt and went out to the kitchen to rescue the kelpie.

'You know,' Aubrey said, looking up from her laptop. 'A dog is actually good company. Bundy just sits there and doesn't say a thing. Is there a dog breed that doesn't have hair?'

Knowing Aubrey didn't expect an answer—she was already typing on her keyboard—Grace set about making two pieces of peanut butter toast. The conversation didn't again return to Rowan but when Grace sat at the table and shared her breakfast with Bundy, Aubrey kept checking the time on her computer screen. At twenty past seven, she disappeared into the guest bedroom.

Five minutes later, Aubrey reappeared in the doorway wearing a fitted white shirt that failed to conceal her cleavage, sprayed-on jeans and luminous white lace-up shoes. Aubrey really didn't realise how stunning she was. It wasn't just her cutting repartee that rendered male work colleagues tongue-tied.

'No and no again,' Grace said.

'What's wrong? The sales assistant said this was a perfect outfit for escaping to the country.'

'That would be a city sales assistant.'

Grace went into her bedroom to collect a large box that when she lifted the lid filled the small room with the scent of leather.

She returned to the kitchen and handed Aubrey the new boots. 'I bought you a present. Your white shoes would last about five minutes … especially if you don't pay attention to what you're stepping in when around the goats.'

The horror on Aubrey's face kept Grace smiling while she finished her toast.

Even though she tried not to, she watched the kitchen clock. Rowan was usually punctual. The clock hands had just settled on seven thirty when Bundy's ears pricked and he padded over to the front door.

Aubrey noticed the kelpie's reaction. She pulled her hair back into a ponytail as if getting battle ready.

Grace took her plate to the sink and flicked on the kettle. 'Aubrey, remember to play nice.'

'Of course.'

Grace didn't buy Aubrey's mild tone or serene smile. 'Stop crossing your fingers behind your back.'

Aubrey's reply was lost beneath Bundy's barking as gravel crunched on the driveway.

Grace went to open the front door to let Bundy out. The kelpie could have a few minutes with Rowan before she and Aubrey followed.

But Aubrey wasn't waiting. She was through the doorway even before Grace called out, 'Wait. We need to make Rowan a coffee.' Grace moved to quickly pull on her boots. 'He's going to need one,' she muttered under her breath as she dashed outside.

Even at a jog it took until midway across the front lawn of the mansion to match Aubrey's power walk.

Grace caught Aubrey's arm to stop her and to catch her breath. 'At least give Rowan time to get out of his ute before you ambush him.'

She then looped her arm through Aubrey's so they'd proceed at a slower pace. They rounded the corner to the sight of Rowan loading bluestone onto the back of his ute. He wore his usual faded jeans and a cap and today his shirt was royal blue. Just like always, he moved with masculine grace, lifting the heavy stones seemingly without any effort.

Aubrey stopped to fan her face. 'His pictures don't do him justice.'

'I thought you were here to give him the third degree,' Grace said, tone wry as she let go of Aubrey's arm.

'I am but, call me shallow, I just need a minute. Please tell me he has single friends.'

'Yes, Taite and Trent. Taite would run a mile if you even looked at him and as for Trent, I don't know him very well.'

Rowan waved before tugging off his work gloves and walking over.

Grace bit the inside of her cheek. She didn't know why it was so important that the next five minutes went well.

Rowan gave her a relaxed grin before he offered Aubrey his hand. 'Hi, I'm Rowan.'

'I know who you are,' Aubrey said, stepping forward.

Aubrey's forthright stare had been known to make seasoned CEOs sweat but when she gripped Rowan's hand his easygoing expression didn't change.

'So, Aubrey of the killer handshake,' Rowan said when she finally released his fingers. 'I don't have a criminal record. My worst habit according to my sister is skimming over her texts. And I give you my word your best friend will always have my utmost respect.'

Aubrey didn't skip a beat in her reply. 'I don't have a criminal record but it's an option if you disrespect Grace in any way. I'm too busy for bad habits. And I know that when someone looks too good to be true, they usually are.'

Rowan nodded, expression thoughtful. 'I agree.' He glanced pointedly at Grace. 'But I think you'd also agree that there are exceptions to that rule.'

Grace was too busy tracking Aubrey's reaction to say that she was far from perfect. If she didn't know better she would have said that Aubrey almost appeared confused.

Aubrey gave a little nod. Grace wasn't sure if it was in agreement or an acknowledgement that this round was a tie.

A flurry of raindrops swept over them, causing Rowan to glance at the mountain peaks etched against the storm-grey sky. 'I'd better get these stones moved. Enjoy your first day in Bundilla, Aubrey.'

Grace hoped it wasn't her imagination that his gaze held hers for longer than necessary before he turned and, with Bundy by his side, strode to his ute.

Aubrey stared over her shoulder at Rowan as they walked away. This time there was no missing the confusion that drew her brows together in a fierce line. 'He can't be the real deal?'

'He threw me too when I first met him, and he still throws me every single day.' Grace met Aubrey's quick look. 'That's why you don't have to worry about me doing anything that won't be good for me. You know I always play it safe. Especially when the only words to describe my life at the moment are emotional instability.'

Aubrey gave her a hug.

'Now,' Grace said when they pulled apart, 'let me show you the house and the apartment. You'll love the cedar chiffonier. There was also a beautifully carved rocking horse but Rowan has taken it to town to be restored.'

They continued to the front of the mansion. At the bottom of the veranda steps Grace stopped when she heard the approach of Frank's gator. He too was up early. He didn't usually pop around until morning teatime.

Frank drove around the corner to park in front of them. 'Good morning, Grace, and to you too, Aubrey. I hope, Aubrey, that you had an enjoyable drive from Sydney. I must say, you're wearing a very stylish pair of boots.'

To Grace's surprise, Aubrey laughed instead of firing off a sassy quip. 'Why, thank you.' She moved closer to hold out her hand. 'You must be Frank?'

'It's a pleasure to meet you.'

Aubrey shook his gnarled hand with care.

Frank studied her. 'I have a feeling you might know your way around a chessboard?'

'It just so happens I do.'

'In that case, may I offer you both a dinner invitation for tonight?'

'You may,' Aubrey said, as if she were the Queen.

Grace simply stared. She knew she'd bonded with Frank on their first meeting, but prickly Aubrey rarely warmed to anyone even after a year.

'That sounds lovely,' Grace said. 'We'll bring dessert. For the record I play chess very badly.'

Aubrey looped her arm around Grace's shoulders. 'You do but for the very best of reasons … you're too generous and kind-hearted.'

Frank sent Grace a warm smile that said there was nothing wrong with being that way. He chuckled as Aubrey rubbed her hands together to indicate she wasn't at all generous and kind-hearted and was looking forward to annihilating him on the chessboard.

'Frank,' Grace said, inclining her head towards the mansion behind them. 'We're having a look inside if you'd like to join us. We could meet you at the kitchen door where there aren't as many steps?'

The bleakness in his eyes was so fleeting Grace wasn't sure she'd seen it. He rubbed his knee. 'Sorry, my gammy leg isn't the best this morning. Besides, I don't want the real Crookwell Park ghosts being unhappy to see me.'

Even though he winked and gave them a cheery wave before driving away, Grace wasn't so sure he'd been joking.

'This is all your fault,' Rowan said to Taite as he sat slouched on a bench in the deer farmer's workshop, every muscle protesting. Just as well Grace had sent him a text to say to have the day off, which he took as code for she wanted to keep him and Aubrey apart. He wouldn't have been able to lift or climb anything.

Taite looked up from the box of rusty horseshoes he was rummaging through. 'You've gone soft. That was only a little jog.'

'*Little?*' Rowan groaned as he made the mistake of trying to move on the seat welded out of old farm tools. 'We went up Overflow Road *twice*.'

'Yeah. As I said, little.'

Rowan shook his head. That was about the only thing he could do without grimacing with pain. 'I needed to get rid of some energy, not sentence myself to a week of lying on the lounge.'

'You won't feel it so much tomorrow.'

'There is no way I'm doing that again tomorrow. Actually … I'm not doing that again. Ever.'

Taite shot him a grin. 'Until the next time you think it's a good idea to go on a fake date with Grace.'

This time Rowan's groan wasn't from his aching limbs. 'Blame Captain Serious. The old me would never have thought through the plan so many times that it ended up making sense. I just would have gone … yeah, nah.'

'Look on the upside, your not-so-private moment by the river has now gone around town at least three times, each version crazier than the last. I even had Mrs Moore come up and ask me if it's true you're eloping next week.'

Rowan didn't immediately reply. Any reminder of what had happened with Grace by the old gum and his testosterone went into overdrive. The aftermath of their kiss and the deep need to kiss her again had been the reason why he'd gone for a jog after work last night. It had been hard enough seeing her briefly with Aubrey and then catching glimpses of her throughout the day. He would be in real trouble when Aubrey left and he and Grace were alone together. 'It's only a temporary reprieve … Grace will be gone at the end of summer.'

'Is she really leaving?' Taite's teasing tone turned serious.

'She hasn't said that she isn't. She would have a city life to return to and if it's anything like the one Aubrey has come from, it's vastly different to here.' He carefully sat forward on the bench. 'Once I'm done with the stonework there's still a truckload of work to be completed so she'll be back but it's more likely it will just be for the weekend to check on the progress.'

'I thought for sure Grace would want to live at Crookwell Park.'

Rowan went to shrug and then stopped himself. 'To be honest I've never asked what her plans are.'

All he knew was that she was restoring the house in memory of her parents. And while she now had her goats, she had mentioned needing someone to look after the place when she wasn't there. Whether or not this was when the building was still being worked on or after it had been completed was anyone's guess.

'So, this Aubrey that you said was single … are you sure she's not here to find anyone?'

'Relax. You're safe. Grace said she's happy on her own. If she wasn't, whoever she took an interest in would have no hope of resisting or avoiding her.'

Taite went over to a large work table to add the horseshoes to the other rusty metal objects that he'd laid out in a pattern. It didn't matter what project Taite was working on, whether it be an animal sculpture or a farm entryway, Taite had a talent for creating beauty out of discarded steel. Clancy's birthday was coming up and he'd asked Taite to make her a gate for the paddock that housed her precious peony beds.

While Taite concentrated on his design, Rowan sat back to rub his leg to ease the ache of his old skiing injury. As much as the run last night had tortured his body, his mind wasn't in any better shape.

From day one Grace had affected him and now after their riverbank moment it was impossible to get any respite from thinking about her. She was the ultimate risk he simply couldn't take. He knew firsthand how it felt to grieve and at the same time try to find the energy to sustain a relationship. He wasn't putting Grace through such a thing by drawing her focus away from what she came here to do.

As for him, after their kiss he was under no illusion that being with her wouldn't be like flying too close to the sun. He was already well down the road to being consumed by her, and he wasn't making the same mistake he did with Eloise. He wouldn't have Clancy pay any more of a price for his inability to stay in control or in touch with reality. He'd also promised his parents he'd never again let them or his sister down. As unforgettable as his and Grace's fake date had been, from now on they had to stay on either side of the friendship line.

'Was this something like what you were thinking of?' Taite's question interrupted his thoughts.

He took his time to hobble over. 'It's spot on. Clancy will love it.'

The horseshoes had been combined with other circular metal shapes, such as small bike tyres, old bike chains and rusted saw blades, to form loops and swirls that resembled flowers. From the other gates Taite had made, Rowan knew he would then use rounded strips of metal to weld all the pieces together into a flowing pattern.

'I have to finish Waldo over there.' Taite nodded towards a life-sized stallion sculpture made from recycled machinery. 'Then I'll get this done.'

'There's no rush. When do you want me to take a look at the hut?'

In exchange for the gate, Rowan had offered to fix the stone chimney of Glenwood Station's high-country hut, which had been damaged by a wombat hole.

'We could go now except you're moving slower than a hibernating turtle.'

Rowan eased himself away from the table he'd been leaning on. A trip to the hut was exactly what he needed to keep his mind off Grace. 'I've got beer in the back of my ute.'

Taite chuckled. 'Thanks to all this rain there's no total fire ban so we can light a campfire.'

'Which means,' Rowan said, turning to the door that he was sure was further away than on his last visit, 'a road trip in The Beast.'

The Beast was Taite's tricked-up four-wheel drive and his pride and joy. A little like how Taite called every sculpture Waldo, he'd previously had at least two other four-wheel drives named The Beast.

Soon Rowan's beer had been added to the sausages, bread, onions, sauce and bottled water in Taite's camping fridge. Chairs were loaded and then all that was left to do was for Rowan and Taite to take their seats.

Rowan opened the passenger-side door but didn't immediately climb in. Thanks to Taite's vehicle having every four-wheel drive modification possible, both on the outside and under the bonnet, at least the side steps would technically make it less painful for him to get in. He reached for the hand grip, hoisted himself up and landed with a grunt. His theory had been wrong.

Taite grinned as he fired up the engine, which was noisy enough to wake the hibernating turtle he'd compared Rowan to. 'As I said, you'll feel much better after tomorrow's run.'

Taite's stone cottage and the nearby main Glenwood Station homestead soon disappeared behind them as they climbed into the hills. There were several ways to the hut, by road and horseback, and Taite took what Rowan knew to be the most direct route. The deer farmer must have taken pity on him after the first wince when they'd hit a road rut. Black cockatoos flittered amongst the alpine branches while kangaroos disappeared into the dense undergrowth as The Beast roared by.

Rowan settled back to enjoy the view. Like he'd said to Grace on their afternoon ride, there was no other place he'd rather be. He'd travelled and worked in many majestic places but his heart belonged to the Snowy Mountains in which he'd grown up.

Near the top of a steep ridge that required Taite to go back to second gear, the trees gave way to a clearing in which a rustic hut stood as a centrepiece. Constructed of timber and stone, the historic structure continued to provide a welcome haven for both horses and riders. Unlike the last time Rowan had been there when he'd rolled out a swag with Heath and Taite before Heath had left to paint his overseas mural, the chimney now leaned like it had consumed too many beers. A cavernous hole at the base explained why.

Taite pulled up alongside the post-and-rail wooden yards and they left The Beast to take a closer look. A magpie settled on the yard gate to watch them.

'There's still no scratch marks or freshly dug dirt,' Taite said as he examined the wombat burrow. 'Mr or Mrs Wombat isn't living here now.'

Rowan looked around to check there wasn't a second entrance. Wombats usually had more than one home to cater for differing weather conditions so for whatever reason this new one had been abandoned. Just to be sure, he arranged a row of narrow sticks at the entrance. If they were undisturbed when he returned, he'd know for certain that the burrow was unused and safe to be filled in.

He assessed the leaning chimney. Stones had fallen out of the bottom and middle section, but it was stable enough to be left for a little longer. He'd need to find a few days to dismantle the structure and then reassemble the stones into their earlier positions. 'Too easy. I'll put it on my to-do list.'

Taite gave him a lighter than usual slap on the back. They headed around to where the coal remnants of a past campfire filled a fireplace surrounded by tree stumps cut as seats. It wasn't long until flames crackled and the aroma of fried onions and cooking sausages wafted through the clearing.

They were each onto their third sausage sandwich when Rowan brought up the subject of what he'd seen on the boundary fence map in Clancy's cottage. Thanks to his year of temporary insanity over Eloise, as well as travelling and working away, there was a large chunk of local news that he'd missed.

'Do you know who bought the Crookwell Park land that was sold off?'

Taite shook his head. 'Why?'

'I haven't asked Grace about it yet but she had a map of the Crookwell Park boundaries and the western one steps in and out as though half a paddock has been cut out of her share.'

'That sounds odd.'

'It does.'

'I just assumed Frank owns all the land on that side. You haven't found any cameras yet?'

'Nope. There's also a tonne of land behind Grace's back boundary that would have been part of the original Crookwell Park estate. Maybe whoever owns that owns the half of the paddock.'

Taite was silent for a moment. 'You know … we've found homes for most of Dad's things that he stored in the sheds but we haven't gone through his boxes of old newspapers, photographs and maps.'

'It's likely he would have been at the Crookwell Park clearing sale.'

'There's no way he'd have stayed away.' Taite finished his sausage sandwich. 'If those high-maintenance muscles of yours can climb the steps to the main house we can take a look in the storeroom. Brenna's away trekking but she won't mind if we visit.'

After they'd made sure the fire was out and collected wood for whoever used the hut next, they drove home along the track they'd arrived on.

Even though every muscle complained when they climbed the numerous steps to the main house where Brenna lived, Rowan didn't say a word.

Once inside, he did however say what he always said whenever he went there. 'It's so pink.'

Tomboy Brenna refused to wear a dress let alone heels and would never be caught doing anything remotely girly, yet her favourite colour was pink. While the house had a minimalist and no-frills style, the kettle and toaster were a pale pink. The three paintings on the walls were of pink-and-grey galahs and the cushions covering the cream lounge were fuchsia.

Taite shuddered. 'You should see her bedroom.'

Rowan followed Taite to a side room, which emitted a musty aroma when they opened the door. Taite switched on the light to reveal shelves on every wall filled with boxes.

'That's a lot of … stuff,' Rowan said.

'Tell me about it. That's why they're still here.'

Taite walked along reading the labels. 'This one has maps.' He plonked it into Rowan's arms. 'And this one.' He loaded another two boxes on top of the one Rowan held.

At his grimace, Taite grinned. 'So, those stonemason muscles of yours are just for show?'

'They worked just fine,' Rowan said over his shoulder as he left the storeroom, 'until I followed you up a death hill. Twice.'

They soon had the contents of the boxes spread across the dining room table.

'Your father sure did like maps.' Rowan added another wad to the pile beside him.

'He was obsessed with them.'

Rowan didn't miss the edge in Taite's voice. As passionate and invested as Taite's father had been in the things that interested him, this hadn't always extended to include his children. There was far more to why Taite held on to his single status with such determination than his simple explanation that he wasn't ready to settle down.

'But,' Taite added, 'for once his being a hoarder has its uses. Check this out.'

He smoothed a faded map out onto the table. The words *Crookwell Park* were at the top in neat copperplate writing.

Rowan ran his eyes around the arrow-straight boundary fences of the original land holding. 'Crookwell Park was huge, maybe three times the size of what Grace has bought. Where has all the land gone? No local has bought it as that would be common knowledge.'

'Frank must have some, and I guess Lawrence Junior would have sold the rest so he had money to live on.'

Rowan continued to study the map before taking a photo.

'Speaking of Frank … does this look familiar?' Taite laid two black-and-white photographs over the top of the map.

'That's his cottage.' Rowan leaned forwards to see the blurred figures in the first image. 'It looks like a woman standing with a baby in her arms and a small girl is holding onto her skirts.'

'Same in this photo too.'

Rowan nodded. The second photo was more formally posed. This time the woman was seated with the baby on her knee and the small girl sat on a tiny chair beside her. The mother's deep love for her children was clear by the way she cradled the baby and held her other daughter's hand. 'Clancy's convinced the cottage was built for Lawrence Senior's secret family.'

'There isn't any father in these pictures so she might very well be right.'

Rowan turned both images over but there was no date or any other writing. He held the second photograph to the light to see it better.

'What are you looking for?' Taite asked.

'Any family resemblance to Frank.' He lowered the picture when he found none. 'His surname might be Williams and while he told Grace he'd originally used the cottage as a weekender, my gut tells me there is far more to why Frank retired to live near a town he never visits.'

CHAPTER
13

'Why didn't you tell me Bundilla had so many things to buy?'

Grace hid her smile as she and Aubrey walked along the main street. Multiple bags dangled from Aubrey's hands and they'd already left another three in Grace's car. A quick trip to town was going to take all morning at the pace they were going. A non-shopping Aubrey had become a shopaholic. In The Craft Cottage alone she'd bought at least six months' worth of handmade relish and jams.

'Because you wouldn't have believed me.'

'True. Look, a candle shop. We must go in and buy local.'

This time Grace couldn't hide her smile. A blackboard outside the gift shop had reminded everyone about buying local for the good of bush businesses. Aubrey had embraced the suggestion with enthusiasm.

By the time they'd left Rosie's candle shop, Aubrey had added another bag to her collection.

Grace turned to make sure Bundy was following. The kelpie had been waylaid by several tourists who'd wanted a selfie and he was now having his photo taken with a group of grey nomads.

'Who knew,' Aubrey said, also looking back at Bundy, 'that we had such a celebrity in our midst?'

Grace was tempted to say that Aubrey too was proving to be a celebrity. She seemed oblivious to the second glances and double takes as she strolled along in her black lycra, her hair in a sleek ponytail, and wearing power red lipstick.

'Didn't you click on the links I sent you about Bundy's social media page and the water tower mural?'

'No.'

'I thought you told Rowan you didn't have any bad habits?'

'I said I was too *busy* for any bad habits. And wasting time on social media is a bad habit.'

Grace had no logical reply. Her brain was still recovering from two late nights over at Frank's and the epic chess battle raging between him and Aubrey. So far they'd won a game apiece.

Aubrey spoke again. 'Speaking of a certain stonemason ... he started early this morning.'

'He did.' Grace kept her voice casual as she stopped at the bookshelf that housed the local street library. She didn't want Aubrey to sense how close she'd come to sneaking outside to see Rowan while her best friend had been in the shower. Today was the second day she hadn't had her usual chat over a coffee with Rowan. 'He'd just be wanting to get things done as he didn't work yesterday.'

Aubrey's gaze didn't leave Grace's face. 'You do know I lost count this morning of the number of times you looked out the window and sighed while we were cleaning the back room.'

'It wasn't that many times.' Grace pretended to concentrate on where to place the book she was donating to the street library. 'I could have been sighing over anything.'

Aubrey smirked. 'Like why you bought a mattress in a box? I'd be sighing over that too; it's going to be so uncomfortable.'

'No, it won't.' Grace chose a title from the bookshelf that she hadn't read. 'It was so easy to have it delivered. Wait until you see the gorgeous iron bed that's coming next week. Then you'll be happy I bought a very comfy mattress in a box.'

They continued along the street.

'You should have asked Rowan to get you a proper mattress from a proper shop.'

'I thought you wanted me to avoid him?'

Aubrey shrugged. 'He's growing on me.'

'You've only met him once.'

'I didn't say that he wasn't growing on me like a fungus.'

Grace shook her head with a laugh.

She hadn't realised Aubrey had stopped and was no longer beside her until she turned to remind her they had to meet Kathy at the library in five minutes. Kathy had called to say she had found pictures of the spinster Russell sisters. Expecting Aubrey to be peering into another shop window, Grace was surprised to see her standing in the middle of the footpath frowning at something, or someone, across the street.

'Who is *that*?' Aubrey asked.

Grace stared at the people occupying the outside tables and chairs across at The Book Nook Café. She had no idea who Aubrey meant. Then she saw Trent at a table by himself. He wore dark sunglasses, a white shirt and chino shorts and lounged in his chair, his arm over the back, as if he were in a Parisian café.

When he turned to look at them, she waved. 'It's Trent, the local vet.'

Trent waved in return.

'Single Trent?' Aubrey's voice was strangely quiet.

'Yes, but sadly he lost his fiancée two years ago so perhaps single isn't the right way to describe him.'

Grace kept walking and Aubrey fell into step beside her. No longer did she appear to find the nearby shops so interesting. Grace also didn't miss when, as they turned into the library, Aubrey snuck a last look at the café.

Kathy greeted Grace with a hug and Aubrey with a welcoming smile as they joined her in the local studies room. After introductions were made and Kathy placed a grainy picture of a woman on the table at which they sat, Grace forgot all about Aubrey's reaction to Trent.

'This is Bernice Russell, the older sister,' Kathy explained. 'As you already know from her headstone, she died in 1953, which fits the window for the mother who was living in the apartment to possibly die by childbirth. Her death was listed as natural causes.'

'Which could mean anything,' Aubrey said, expression interested. She too seemed to have forgotten all about Trent.

'It could,' Kathy said with a nod. 'I've also searched the birth certificate and marriage certificate records and at face value it doesn't appear that either Russell sister married or had a child.'

Grace examined the austere profile of Bernice's unsmiling image. The woman wore no jewellery and her dark hair had been scraped back into a severe bun. She knew she shouldn't make a judgement on one photo but Bernice didn't seem to be the type to like dainty floral china or the trinkets left behind in the crystal bowls on the dressing table.

Aubrey shared her thoughts. 'That is one lady I would not want for a mother.'

Kathy placed a second photo on the table. 'Now, this is Evelyn.'

Grace studied the younger Russell sister. While her picture showed a more rounded face and less harsh expression, again her sombre clothes and tight bun didn't hint at any softness. Evelyn had passed away in 1956, which was perhaps too late to fit in with what they knew about the apartment.

Grace's gaze lingered. But the date did fit in with the leather polio callipers in the trunk. While Frank and Aubrey had been embroiled in their chess battle, she'd used her phone to research polio in the 1950s. The final epidemic had ended with the introduction of the first vaccine in 1956. Perhaps Evelyn's death date could still fit if any hypothetical baby girl had been born after her brother had passed away.

She glanced across at Kathy. 'I was hoping Mabel might have had some leads, but she hasn't had any luck with newspaper readers recognising anything from the apartment photos or coming forward with information.'

'That's a shame. I've spoken to Edith who will ask around at the next CWA meeting but as they are only held monthly, it won't be until after the book festival.' Kathy reached into a folder to produce a final photograph. 'Now I also found this, which is interesting. The sisters are younger here and with two other girls.'

'A picture tells a thousand words.' Aubrey pointed to the pair of figures on the right. 'Look at that body language. The expressions of the Russell sisters couldn't be any icier if they tried, and there's no mistaking the way their bodies are turned away from the other two.'

Grace's attention focused on the girls on the left who stood close together and who also had to be siblings. While one was taller than the other, they both had wavy hair tied back with ribbons and pretty, friendly faces. But it was their expressions that captivated Grace. Their eyes were smiling. 'Who are they?'

'That I don't know,' Kathy said. 'But I will keep searching. I've also organised to go through the local church's cemetery records to see if there are any unmarked graves of children, or a woman, that could match our timeframe.'

'Thank you,' Grace said. 'Let me know if you need any help.'

She again looked at the girls and their open expressions, her head filled with more questions than answers. Both of them were a much better fit than either Russell sister with the mental picture she had of the apartment mother. The problem was their age; they were perhaps too young. She could only hope that what Kathy had said at their first meeting would prove true, that secrets in a small town had a way of coming to the surface.

After they'd said their goodbyes, Grace followed Aubrey out into the summer heat. She automatically looked along the street for Bundy. There would come a time when the kelpie would move on and stay with someone else. Until then she'd enjoy every day that she had left with him.

She spied him outside the florist shop where he was being fussed over by a group of children. School holidays ended this week and she had a note on her calendar to make sure he would be at the local school every Thursday. Clancy had explained he'd been trained as a story dog and went into the classroom to listen to students read. Bundy saw her and wagged his tail.

Grace smiled and turned to Aubrey. 'What shop would you like to go to now?'

Except Aubrey wasn't looking at the businesses around them or even appeared to have heard her. Instead she stared across at the café.

After all the matchmaking shenanigans Grace had been privy to since arriving in small-town Bundilla, the last thing she'd do would be to meddle in anyone's love life. But there was a hint of vulnerability in Aubrey's expression that Grace had never seen before. She looked over at the café to see if Trent was still there. Not only had he not moved from his table, he was gazing straight at Aubrey.

'Let's have a coffee,' Grace said, taking a step in the direction of the pedestrian crossing.

Aubrey didn't move. 'You only have one coffee a day and you already had one before we left.'

'Okay, so I'll have a tea. It's thirsty weather.'

Aubrey's brows drew together as she glanced over at the café and then back at Grace. 'Don't even think about it.'

'Too late. Blame the quilting group; they're a bad influence.'

Without waiting for a reply, Grace headed across the road.

'Grace,' Aubrey said when she caught up to her, but there was no anger in her voice, only an unfamiliar uncertainty.

Grace tucked Aubrey's arm in hers as they stepped onto the footpath. 'A wise person once told me nothing ventured, nothing gained.'

'That was a slip of my tongue and was in reference to you buying a new pair of jeans. Grace ... just let me enjoy my brief moment of bliss. No one is ever as good as they seem. Trent will just be another egotistical jerk.'

'I promise you he isn't, and I'd never be doing this if he was.'

There was no more chance for any further talk as they approached The Book Nook. To reach the doorway, they had to walk past Trent.

He lifted a hand in greeting. 'Hi, Grace. How's that rapidly expanding goat of yours?'

She changed direction and stopped in front of his table. Beside her she could hear Aubrey mutter under her breath.

'Hi. Trent, this is Aubrey.' She paused to wave between them. 'Aubrey, Trent.' Then, as if the two of them weren't staring at each other as though they'd never seen another human before, she continued, 'Olive's good, thanks. She has an udder full of milk so Frank said she's getting very close.'

Trent's gaze returned to Grace. 'If there's any problems let me know.'

The sincerity in his voice spoke volumes about how much he cared for his animal patients.

'I will.' She sought for something to say to fill the gap. Normally Aubrey handled the social chitchat.

But then Trent nodded at the bags hanging from Aubrey's wrists. 'Christmas looks like it's come early.'

At Aubrey's narrowing eyes, he smiled. 'Sorry, I didn't mean any offence ... I have three sisters ... my comment was a poor attempt at humour.'

Aubrey's expression didn't thaw but her voice was mild when she replied, 'I'd advise you to not give up your day job then.'

Grace jumped in. She couldn't tell yet if Aubrey was going to be on her best or worst behaviour. 'So, Trent, it's your day off?'

'It is. I delivered a foal late last night so must confess I've been half asleep sitting in the sun.'

Bundy came to join them and flopped onto the ground at the vet's feet. Trent stretched so that the toe of his shoe would reach Bundy's stomach. 'I see my favourite patient still likes his belly rubs.'

The line of Aubrey's red mouth softened.

Grace's phone rang in her tote bag. She checked the caller ID and when she saw Rowan's name, she caught Aubrey's eye. 'I have to take this.'

'Everything okay?' she asked as she walked to stand in the shade of the newsagency awning.

'Yes, I'm just calling to let you know that you'll have a surprise when you and Aubrey get back. Olive has had her kids.'

'Kids? Plural?'

'Two little does. I'll send you a photo.'

Grace couldn't stop grinning as an image appeared of two tiny black kids peering around Olive's legs. 'They are too adorable.'

'They are.'

Grace looked across to where Aubrey appeared to be listening intently to something that Trent said. 'Wait until I tell Aubrey. She threatened if Olive had twins to call them Check and Mate.'

The sound of Rowan's deep laughter had her gripping her phone tighter. For someone she'd seen only two days ago, how was it possible that she could miss him so much?

She held her mobile slightly away from her ear to dilute the effect of his voice. 'While I have you on the phone, I feel bad not bringing anything this afternoon. There has to be something Clancy needs from town.'

There was a beat of silence before Rowan's wry reply sounded. 'I take it I should have paid more attention to another of my sister's texts?'

'Clancy's invited us for a picnic at the river.'

'Ahh ... so that's why she gave me a shopping list and said see you at three. I thought she had something on and just needed me to get back to dog-sit.'

'Aubrey wondered why you started work so early this morning.'

'I bet she did.' Amusement tinged his words.

Grace was glad this wasn't a video call so he couldn't see the flush in her cheeks. The truth was she'd also been listening out for him. She again glanced over at Aubrey who was using her hands to emphasise whatever she was saying to Trent. Their conversation already appeared to have moved past small talk.

'While I can't guarantee Aubrey will be all sweetness and light the next time you meet, I've a feeling she'll have more on her mind than she did the other day.'

'Grace … Aubrey was fine. The truth is I admired how protective she was of you. She only has your best interests at heart.'

Feeling her emotions unravel, Grace worked hard to keep her voice casual. Even though their date had been fake and they were back in the real world, Rowan's empathy and perceptiveness still had a way of tapping straight into her heart. 'I'm glad you didn't find her too much. She really would do anything for anybody. I'd better go. We've bumped into Trent at the café and Aubrey has just sat at his table.'

Rowan chuckled again. 'Enough said. See you this afternoon.'

Two days might have passed since Rowan's ill-advised run with Taite, but his body still complained every chance it could.

Instead of lifting multiple grocery bags from his ute, Rowan tested the weight of three before adding another. The list Clancy had given him that morning contained enough food for twenty picnics. After checking that the path from the coach house to the main Ashcroft homestead was clear of any puppy obstacles, he headed into the back garden.

His peaceful walk was short-lived. Wherever Monet and Primrose had been hiding it allowed them to execute the perfect stealth attack. One moment he was enjoying the silence and the next he had a growling kelpie body attached to the bottom of his jeans. Meanwhile, an excited Primrose thought the grocery bags were for her and she was determined to see what was inside. He lifted the bags to shoulder height, an action that made his biceps burn, and walked with his left leg straight so as not to hurt Monet who still had his teeth anchored into the denim.

The back door opened to reveal Clancy standing in the doorway. Her smile couldn't have been any bigger. Monet finally released his jeans and Rowan strode through the open door.

Clancy quickly closed it, making no attempt to hide her laughter. 'You should have seen your face. Whatever cat tricks Orien has been teaching them, they've mastered the art of pouncing.'

Rowan grinned. 'That and how to fit through the cat flap.' He accompanied Clancy into the large kitchen. 'I found Monet in the laundry yesterday wolfing down Orien's cat food. At least Primrose is now too big to fit.'

He sat the bags onto the marble island bench. 'Do I need to confess I missed your picnic text or did you assume I had no idea why you asked me to be home by three?'

Instead of shooting him an exasperated glance, Clancy continued to take items out of the closest grocery bag. 'I never sent you a text. It's time for Brenna and me to stop meddling, even if we see how perfect you and Grace would be together. It's only fair the two of you are in control of what happens next.'

Rowan frowned. He wasn't sure how he felt about suddenly not being pushed towards Grace. Instead of relief, he felt almost uneasy. As for what would happen next with Grace, nothing could. 'I don't have to go to the picnic?'

'Heath's going, but if you don't want to, you don't have to.'

Clancy went to put the milk into the fridge. When she turned to look at him, he realised he was still holding the bread rolls he'd removed from the bag beside him. 'I'd like to go.'

'Great,' was all she said.

After he'd helped unpack the rest of the groceries and Clancy had rearranged everything he'd put on the pantry shelves, he went to take a shower. Now that the side wall was finished, he'd been working inside the mansion to plaster the bare stone and his shirt was more white than blue.

Hair still damp, feet bare and wearing jeans, he grabbed a black T-shirt before heading downstairs. He padded into the kitchen to switch on the kettle. As he slipped his shirt over his head he heard a muffled 'knock, knock' that was almost drowned out by the kettle noise. He headed for the door, putting his left arm through his sleeve as he went. Clancy's sense of humour would now have her say 'knock, knock' from the actual door instead of waltzing inside like she usually did. He shoved his right arm through the other sleeve before reaching for the door handle.

Except it wasn't Clancy standing on the small front porch, but Grace.

He registered two things. The warm breeze across the bare skin above his jeans meant his T-shirt was hiked up on one side. And that he had two seconds before a wet and dirt-covered Primrose and Monet launched themselves at an unsuspecting and very clean Grace.

He wrapped his hand around her upper arm, pulled her inside and shut the front screen door. The once adequately sized entryway suddenly seemed too small. All he could breathe in was Grace's honeysuckle scent. All he could feel was the softness of her skin beneath his fingers. All he could think about was how perfectly she'd fit against him on the riverbank.

Their eyes met. Grace's lips parted and he swayed forwards. Then the loud rattle of the screen door as Primrose battered it with her front paw brought reality back in a rush. Rowan uncurled his fingers from around Grace's arm, took a step back and pulled down his bunched T-shirt.

Before he could gauge her expression, Grace turned to where Primrose and Monet pressed against the gauze. 'No wonder Clancy said Aubrey and I had timed our arrival perfectly as we only had Iris to welcome us.' Grace bent closer to the door, causing both dogs to wag their tails so much their muddy bodies wriggled. 'Yes, you're both gorgeous and have been having fun wherever you were.' She glanced over her shoulder. 'What are their names?'

'Monet and Primrose.'

'Very nice. Aubrey and I compromised on what to call Olive's twins. The smaller one is Lavender and then Aubrey called the bigger one Rebel.'

Rowan held back his laughter; he didn't want Grace to think he was disrespecting her best friend.

But when Grace straightened and turned with a smile, he gave in to his amusement. The distraction of the dogs had worked to defuse the intensity between them. 'All I will say is that I hope Rebel doesn't live up to her name.'

'If she does, I'm changing it to Daisy.' Grace looked past him into the kitchen. 'I came to see if you have any hickory barbeque sauce. Clancy thought you might. Not mentioning any names, but it's the only type a certain person likes on her hamburgers.'

'Should I be concerned that a certain person and I seem to have another thing in common?'

Grace followed him into the living room that was separated from the kitchen by an island bench. 'Only if a certain person finds out. She likes to be an individual.' Grace paused as she looked around. 'This is a fabulous space.'

Rowan took a bottle of hickory barbeque sauce from out of the fridge and sat it on the bench. 'Clancy and I spent a summer putting this old place back together. I now know there is more than one shade of white paint and that when Clancy says this won't take long, she really means there will be five problems to fix before we get to the easy part.'

Grace laughed softly as she moved to the oversized window that overlooked the back garden with its mature trees and green lawn. Two little doggy faces appeared at the glass sliding door, their expressions hopeful they'd be allowed inside. 'They really are just too cute.'

'They are when they're asleep.'

Grace nodded towards the dry-stone garden wall. 'I might have known you'd have stone here somewhere.'

Rowan came to stand beside her, making sure he kept a careful distance away. The light from the window picked out the gold in the hazel medley of Grace's eyes and made him all too aware her lips were as soft as they looked.

'That wall is why I like working with stone. As a child I'd spend hours putting it back together. The corner that overlooks the mountains was my favourite place to sit so I could watch when Dad brought cattle in from the hills.'

'Your childhood sounds wonderful.'

'It was. There was plenty to keep me busy besides moving my sister's trampoline.'

When Grace glanced at him, instead of seeing a smile, concern indented her brow. 'What Janice said at the long lunch … is

Crookwell Park keeping you away from what you need to do here?'

He slid his hands into his jeans pockets. It was either that or touch Grace's smooth cheek to reassure her. 'Not at all. If anything, working at Crookwell Park provides the perfect balance between doing my stonework and running my cattle. I'm sorry again Janice had her claws out.'

Grace nodded. Then, as if they both acknowledged that the conversation was getting too close to their one at the long lunch, they looked out the window to where Bundy now wrestled Monet and Primrose.

Rowan turned towards the door. He didn't need to do a risk assessment to know that every second they remained alone in the coach house the likelihood increased that he would kiss Grace again. 'If we're quick, we can make it to the house while Bundy distracts the terrible twosome.'

Except when they walked into the Ashcroft kitchen and Aubrey pinned him with her take-no-prisoners stare, being licked to death by Monet and Primrose suddenly didn't seem so bad.

'Aubrey.' He gave her a nod.

'Rowan. Nice of you to finally join us.'

The way she eyed his tousled hair and unironed T-shirt, it was as though he hadn't showered in a week.

He held up the hickory barbeque sauce. 'I believe the ball ... or should I say bottle ... is in my court.'

Aubrey gave an exaggerated sigh. 'In that case, you and your hickory sauce can accompany me in the gator. Grace can ride in style with Clancy in Heath's four-wheel drive.'

He silenced his groan. It was a fifteen-minute drive to the waterhole where they always picnicked. In that time Aubrey would have more than enough time to hit him with a barrage of curly questions. 'What a good idea. That means we get to take all the dogs.'

Aubrey's eyes widened before they narrowed. '*All* the dogs?'

'Yep. Bundy, Iris and the two very wet and muddy ones you didn't see on your way in.'

By now Clancy and Heath seemed to have found something very interesting to do over at the kitchen sink, except from the movement of his sister's shoulders it looked like she couldn't stop laughing. Grace too seemed to be having trouble keeping a straight face.

'Hmmm,' was all Aubrey said with a look that promised retribution should she get even a speck of mud or a single dog hair on her white shirt and shorts.

The conversation switched to general chitchat as they loaded Heath's four-wheel drive with the food and items they'd need for their swim and early barbecue.

Rowan soon found himself sitting beside Aubrey in the gator with the four dogs breathing down their necks from where they stood in the trayback. If possible, Monet and Primrose were even muddier and in their excitement were rarely still. Aubrey perched as far forward on her seat as possible.

'Don't say a word,' she warned, as Rowan started the engine.

After everyone stopped at Jindy and Ash's paddock to see the horses, the convoy continued on to visit Fergus and Fenella and then Goliath. While the two highland cows were happy to come over to have their noses scratched, Goliath merely lifted his head from where he grazed. He shot them such a snarky look that Aubrey smiled. 'I like this one.'

They then followed the track along the creek that fed into the Tumut River. Thanks to the wet summer, both the creek and river levels were high and the waterhole would be a cool and inviting place. Not that Aubrey would be keen to swim once she realised who would be in the water with her. Primrose particularly liked the river.

Rowan snuck a sideways glance at Aubrey as she again sat on the end of her seat to avoid the dogs. She'd surprised him by so far not asking a single question or even talking much at all. A curving line of trees ahead indicated the point at which the creek met the river. Their destination, a flat grassy area that gently sloped down to the water, would be around the bend.

Aubrey suddenly turned to him. 'I leave tomorrow.'

There was a seriousness to her tone that had him only nod. This was the caring side of Aubrey that lived beneath her brusque exterior.

'Promise me,' Aubrey continued, 'that you'll keep an eye on Grace. I worry about her.'

'I will.'

'You'd better. I still think some people seem too good to be true, but Grace trusts you and that's enough for me.'

He didn't reply. Just like on the riverbank when Grace had said that she trusted him, uncertainty uncoiled inside. But unlike last time, he didn't have Grace in his arms to silence his doubts. How could Grace, and now Aubrey, trust him when he couldn't even trust himself to never again lose his way?

Aubrey shot him a searching look. 'Hey, country boy who hefts stone and has gone quiet, you're not going to renege on your promise, are you?'

'No, city girl with a handshake that would crush stones, I was just thinking.'

'And ...'

'And ... Grace is lucky to have you as a friend.'

His reply kept Aubrey silent until they reached the river.

After they arrived, the tranquillity and peace of the idyllic picnic spot was short-lived. Cockatoos screeched at no longer having exclusive use, while Primrose and Monet yipped in high-pitched exuberance as they raced each other to splash in the shallows. Iris and Bundy followed at a more sedate pace.

When Clancy and Heath had stripped down to swimmers and board shorts and Aubrey to skimpy activewear that wouldn't ever be practical in a gym, human shrieks followed. Once in the water, and well away from the swimming dogs, Aubrey made the tactical error of splashing Heath, who returned the favour.

The only person who was still and quiet was Grace. She sat on the picnic rug spread beneath the shade of an old gum, her arms around her knees. Before they'd left, Rowan had returned to the coach house to change into his Bundilla rugby shorts so he would be right to swim. The more he looked at Grace the more he doubted that she had on anything beneath her denim sundress suitable to wear into the river.

After he'd checked there was enough wood in the metal fire pit that Taite had welded out of plough discs for their favourite summer meeting place, he joined Grace on the rug.

She tightened her grip on her knees. 'Before you ask, I'm not swimming.'

'There's no rule to say you have to. At the rate Aubrey's been splashing Heath, I'm happy to sit this one out as well.'

Grace briefly smiled. 'It's not that I don't want to, it's just there weren't a lot of opportunities to learn to swim in England and once we came here money was tight.' From the defensiveness in her words, this was another reason why she'd been different from her peers as a child. 'I mean, I like the water ... I just never go in past my knees.'

Longing flickered in her eyes as she gazed over to where Clancy drifted serenely on an inflatable tractor innertube.

Rowan came to his feet. Even though they were in the shade, they weren't spared from the hot afternoon breeze.

'See that log on the edge?' He held out his hand. 'It would be the perfect place to cool off.'

For a moment he thought Grace wasn't going to move, but then she took hold of his hand and allowed him to pull her to her feet. Once standing, she slipped her fingers free.

Together they strolled over to the fallen tree which had been a casualty of a long-ago spring storm. Rowan walked along the log first before sitting in the middle. The cool river water reached halfway to his knees. Grace took her time to follow. When her balance teetered, he lifted his arm, which she grabbed to steady herself. She sat, her sigh saying how good the water felt on her warm skin.

Rowan shifted a little to his left so a space opened up between them. Aubrey now floated on a tractor innertube and without the distraction of drenching Heath, they would have her undivided attention. The dogs were no longer in the water and instead ran up and down the riverbank searching for new scents. Clancy and Heath had moved over near the rocks worn smooth by snow melt and were having a private PDA moment, their arms around each other.

'Do you think Aubrey's asleep?' he said so only Grace could hear.

'Plotting more likely. You're not the only one who isn't a fan of sitting still.'

'Yet another thing we have in common. I've enjoyed meeting Aubrey. It's just as you said—she isn't as tough as she looks.'

'I'm glad you can see it too.' Grace's soft tone whispered over his skin like a touch.

A dragonfly flittered past while the low moo of a cow calling to her calf carried on the breeze. He glanced sideways at the woman sitting beside him. Being with Grace by the river on his family farm, with the mountains keeping watch over them, felt natural and right.

'I've missed you.'

His admission slipped out. Even before the words died in his ears, his fingers dug into the weathered wood of the log. What had he been thinking?

Without looking his way, Grace slid her hand across the space between them until her little finger touched his.

'I know we're back in the real world,' she said, looking straight ahead at the river. 'But I've missed you too.'

As their hands stayed connected, there seemed to be no more need for words. Just like Clancy had said, a sense of peace replaced the feeling of his world spinning. But the realisation didn't bring any relief. As much as the stillness and simplicity of that moment with Grace centred him, his pulses hammered in a silent warning.

CHAPTER
14

'Don't think I didn't see you and Rowan getting all cosy on that log yesterday,' Aubrey said as she twisted on the lid to her blender.

Grace was saved from replying by the almost deafening sound of kale being pulverised.

'And,' Aubrey continued as she sat at the table to drink her seaweed-green breakfast, 'as for the way the two of you kept looking at each other around the fire pit, it was enough to put me off my hamburger, even if it did have hickory sauce.'

Grace took a sip of her tea. Aubrey was on a roll and wasn't expecting an answer.

'And then,' Aubrey said, scowling into her smoothie, 'Rowan had to give me a hug goodbye. Me. A hug. I'm so not a hugging person.'

'For the record, you hugged him back.'

'He did share his hickory sauce.'

Grace looked at her over the rim of her mug. They both knew that Aubrey not only hugged Rowan back, she'd given him her best and most genuine smile.

'Oh, okay,' Aubrey grumbled. 'He has won me over and gets a tick of approval. But …' She held up a hand. 'You are still settling into your new normal so are in no position to make any serious relationship decisions, so please go slow. I don't want to have to come back here until I've worked out a new chess strategy to beat Frank.'

Grace searched Aubrey's face. There was a note of wistfulness in Aubrey's words that led Grace to think Frank wasn't the only person Aubrey might see if she returned. When she'd joined Aubrey and Trent at the café table, she'd been hard-pressed to get a word in. Aubrey and Trent had been debating the merits of city and country living and each appeared oblivious to her being there. Before they'd left, Trent had offered to show Aubrey the best high-country spots next time she was in town.

'You know you're welcome to stay anytime.'

'I know.' Aubrey drained her smoothie cup. 'But right now I've got money to make, deals to broker and people to bluff.'

After her bags were loaded, Aubrey visited the yards to take some last-minute photos of little Lavender and Rebel. Grace smiled as even though Aubrey made sure she stayed behind the steel fence, she gingerly scratched Olive's nose.

Once back at her car, Aubrey gave Grace a tight hug. When she pulled away, her brown eyes were over-bright.

Grace blinked to control her own sadness at having to say goodbye. 'Drive safe.'

'Always do.' Aubrey hesitated before bending to give Bundy a careful pat.

When Grace waved Aubrey off, Bundy's solid warmth came to rest against her legs. She lowered her hand to touch the kelpie's head, glad of his steady presence.

When she could no longer see the dust kicked up by Aubrey's car, Grace walked along the driveway to shut the front gate. Rowan hadn't arrived yet but she needed to let the goats out early. Bundy had to get to town to be a story dog and she had a grocery shop to do, but most of all she had to reinstate some space between her and Rowan.

Yesterday had been a wake-up call. Twice she'd come close to disregarding Aubrey's advice to go slow as well as her own rule to always play it safe. When Rowan had opened the coach house door with his T-shirt half on and tugged her inside, she'd had to stop herself from winding her arms around his neck and picking up from where they'd left off at the riverbank. She'd never thought her hormones would ever override her common sense. As it turned out, they could and did, and all it had taken was a glimpse of Rowan's tanned abs.

Then when they'd sat on the log together, even though something had come to life inside her when Rowan had said he'd missed her and she'd spoken the truth about missing him, the complexities of the real world seemed closer than they had beside the idyllic river. While there was no denying they had a connection, they both had things to work through. In order for this to happen it wouldn't be wise for things to progress any further between them.

Once back at the cottage, as if Bundy knew the school holidays had finished, he waited by her car while Grace went inside to get ready. Soon they were on their way into town. As a familiar dark-red ute drew close, she lifted her hand to give Rowan a wave. He grinned and waved in return. Despite her earlier pep talk, she couldn't stop herself from looking in the rear-view mirror. She now wouldn't see him until that afternoon.

When his ute was no longer visible she focused on the road ahead and the jobs she had to do in town. Her early start would be wasted if all she did was think about how much she missed Rowan.

After driving over the historic wooden bridge, Grace switched on her GPS. She wasn't surprised to find nerves tightening in her stomach now they'd reached the town limits. The thought of dropping Bundy off at a school ushered in memories of feeling trapped and having nowhere to hide. While she'd never been physically bullied, cruel words and being ostracised had left their own scars. Her parents had moved around to find work and with each new school she'd always hoped things would be different. They never were until the day she'd met Aubrey who'd had her own reasons for hiding out in the high school library.

When the street sign indicated Grace was entering a school zone, she slowed. A stream of children in light and dark blue uniforms left a minibus, while other children exited vehicles stopped in the drop-off area. Grace drove to the far end where there were no cars. As she let Bundy out she made a point of not looking at the playground or the buildings. Heath had almost finished the mural he'd been painting for the school and Clancy had invited her for a sneak preview on Saturday. She was yet to decide if she'd go.

She waited until Bundy jumped the wire fence to race across the empty oval before returning to her driver's seat. She rolled her shoulders to disperse her tension. Thankfully she didn't need to pick Bundy up as Clancy mentioned that if she parked in the main street he would find her there when he was done. She pulled away from the kerb and, without looking back, drove to the centre of town.

Even if there hadn't been multiple flyers in shop windows reminding everyone the book festival would soon be on, Grace would have known by the bunting that was strung across the main street. She parked outside the second-hand bookshop and glanced at the clock tower. Once her errands were done she should have enough time, if she felt strong enough, to visit the Bundilla cemetery.

Last night Kathy had sent through an email update about her hidden apartment research. Her search of the local church records had revealed multiple unmarked graves. While there hadn't been any associated with the name Melly, there had been two baby girls and three young boys whose lost-too-soon lives fit in with the apartment timeframe. One of the babies and one of the young boys also shared a surname, though it wasn't Russell.

Kathy had explained that while children who had been born out of wedlock would often be buried with their mother's surname, just because the Russell name hadn't popped up didn't mean the graves could be discounted. If one of the spinster sisters was the mother of the children, then they simply could have their father's name. Kathy was doing further investigation into who the baby girl and young boy were who shared the same surname.

Grace left her car. Across the road Dr Davis waved to her as he led his small white dog along the street. She returned the gesture. Despite the heat, and even while out walking his dog, the older man always seemed to wear formal trousers, brown boots and a dress shirt. Mabel had introduced her to the former town mayor the afternoon they'd had coffee. Dr Davis had let Mabel know, twice, that he was available for an interview about his role in the book festival.

The vintage charity store appeared on Grace's right and she pushed open the glass door to enter the air-conditioned interior.

'Hi, Grace,' the grey-haired lady behind the counter said with a smile.

'Hi, Tina. It's busy today.'

'It is. Wait until next weekend, you'll barely be able to move with all the crowds.' Tina nodded towards the cabinet at the back of the store. 'We've some new things I think you'd like.'

Steps light, Grace walked through the shop filled with collectibles, bric-a-brac and small items of furniture. She didn't just enjoy visiting this store because she loved old things, it was also because she knew the names of the ladies who volunteered. She regularly heard about their families, the latest trips they'd taken and who had been unwell. If her mother were still here, she would have been a volunteer.

Grace stopped to collect a large crystal vase and then peered into the cabinet which held a collection of sterling silver teaspoons. She looked towards the front of the shop. Tina was already walking towards her with the cabinet keys. When Grace had added a small blue-and-white jug to her purchases and had chatted to Tina about her two little granddaughters, she again went outside into the heat.

Her next stop was the gift shop. She wanted to find Kathy something special to say thank you for her help. On her way over to the display of colourful handmade bags, a strange sound from a pram parked near the counter had her steps slow. Not quite sure what she'd heard, she stared at the pink blanket covering the pram.

The young shop assistant who looked to be Fiona, the owner's daughter, grinned. 'It's okay. You're not hearing things.'

She took off the blanket to reveal two half-feathered magpies with their beaks open. The largest one squawked.

'They fell out of their nest in the wind storm the other night,' the girl explained. 'They want their meal worms.'

Grace smiled. Only in Bundilla.

'Can I take a photo?'

'Of course.'

Grace sent a picture to Aubrey to show her what she was missing.

After selecting a bag, Grace left to let the baby magpies have their lunch in peace. Even if she stopped for a pot of tea in the café, she still had an hour until Bundy was due to be finished. Biting her lip, she hesitated and returned to her car. A cuppa could wait. If she was going to go where she needed to, she had to leave now before she could overthink things.

She entered the local cemetery's address into the GPS. Her first test to gauge how well she was coping with her grief had been when she'd visited the Russell family burial plot. It hadn't unnerved her because there'd been no new graves or flowers. The second test would be to visit somewhere where there were visible signs of loss. The third test would be to deal with the small urn that sat on the mantlepiece in her bedroom. While she'd chosen her parents' favourite beach as the perfect spot to scatter a portion of their ashes, she was yet to work out where to finally put them to rest.

When she arrived at the cemetery, she turned past the iron gates, and not feeling brave enough to drive into the more modern area where stark black granite was softened by the vibrancy of flowers, she parked in the shade near the pioneer section. While she knew she wouldn't be able to see the unmarked graves Kathy had mentioned, she'd just felt the need to pay tribute to those whose lives had never been commemorated by even a simple cross.

Once out of her car, she walked along the rows of weathered sandstone, noting any grassed areas or narrow gaps where a possible hidden grave could be. Engrossed in her exploration, she didn't realise she wasn't alone until a male voice said, 'Need a hand finding someone?'

She looked up to see a tall man with a shock of snow-white hair and kindly eyes. Behind him, a battered white Hilux was parked further in the cemetery.

'Not at the moment but thank you.'

'I'm Ned. It's my wife's birthday today and I always take her flowers.'

'I'm Grace. I'm sorry your wife isn't here to share her birthday with you.'

Ned slowly nodded. The older man didn't appear to be in a hurry. If he had, she wouldn't have intruded on his grief by keeping their conversation going. But he'd sought her out and now seemed content to stay and chat. From the curious way he looked at her, she also suspected he'd known who she was.

'Are you who Rowan took my rocking horse to?' she asked.

'Yes, I am. He's a beauty. I should be close to finishing him by next weekend.' Ned rubbed at his chin. 'Restoring rocking horses has been a passion of mine for years ... one of the early ones I did was almost identical to yours.'

'Is that common?'

'Not around here. Rocking horses don't have maker marks but from the quality of the workmanship and materials I'm certain the two rocking horses were made by the same hand.'

'You don't know who owned the first one, do you?'

'If this old memory of mine is correct, it was a friend of my wife's. I've photographs of every horse I worked on and always keep the paperwork ... except this would have been twenty years ago and I might not go back that far. I'm out at Heath's farm for the week but if you're in town for the festival and have time, pop around and I can show you the pictures.'

'Thank you. I will.'

'Don't mention it.' Ned's blue eyes twinkled and again she got a sense he knew far more about her than she did about him. 'Any friend of Rowan's is a friend of mine.'

It was a Saturday and yet again Rowan found himself driving through the front gate of Crookwell Park. Just like last weekend he had a horse float on the back, and just like last time the usually surly Goliath had given him no trouble to load. Rowan passed a hand over his face. As if he could talk. When it came to the woman he was about to see, he was proving to be as smitten as Goliath was with Jindy.

Just as well Grace was being sensible. With Aubrey no longer there, it was as though she had taken over the role of making sure clear limits again existed between them. In the past week their conversations had either been about the animals, the apartment or the mansion. There'd also been no further situations where they'd been in close proximity.

He shared her unspoken message that all it would take was an accidental touch for chemistry to again flare between them. Yes, they'd both missed each other, but they were both of the belief that a relationship wasn't the best thing at the moment for either of them. Such a status quo had allowed him to relax and not dwell on his suspicion that his world no longer spinning wasn't a good thing. Now whenever at Crookwell Park his self-preservation didn't remind him every five minutes what a bad idea it was being around Grace.

As he drove past her cottage, Grace gave him a wave from the goat yard where she was playing with Lavender and Rebel. Yesterday when she'd been gardening in the courtyard it was as though she was a goat whisperer as her small herd followed her everywhere. Whoever had gifted Grace the goats had been right in believing she would give them a good home.

'Morning,' she said as she came over to help unload Jindy. The cherry-red of her shirt highlighted the darkness of her glossy hair, which she'd tied into a low ponytail.

'Morning.'

His greeting was interrupted by a sharp kick by Goliath to the back of the float.

'He's all yours,' Grace said with a smile.

The horses were unloaded and saddled and it wasn't long until they were following Bundy around the back of the mansion. Today's ride would take them along the left boundary fence line that had caught his attention on the Crookwell Park map.

Grace threw him a grin. 'Last one to the gate has to open it.'

The spontaneous challenge was something he'd have never expected from the solemn and cautious person Grace had been when she'd arrived. For once he and Goliath were on the same page; neither wanted to outdo the woman and mare in front of them. They stuck to a sedate canter.

When they arrived at the farm gate below the family burial plot, he didn't need to dismount to open it. Last Saturday when he'd fixed the front fence, he'd brought his brush cutter to clear away the grass choking the gates and fence line. He waited until Grace and Bundy went through before swinging the gate closed behind him and Goliath.

Grace reached into her shirt pocket for a small square piece of paper which she passed across to him. He unfolded the map and looked up to track the fence line beside him. He and Grace didn't need to ride any further for it to be obvious that the physical boundary fence didn't match the legal one. The one beside them was arrow straight, while the one on the map stepped in and out.

'You can see why I wanted to check the boundaries,' Grace said.

He pointed to the map lines that divided a paddock in the middle of Crookwell Park in half. 'It's hard to know exactly where these are but we can make a rough estimate.'

Together they rode up the hill. Rowan kept an eye on the ground in case there were any old fenceposts to indicate where an alternative fence had once been. He halted Goliath midway up the hillside and checked the map again. The back boundary fence at the top of the hill matched the position on the map and gave him a reference point. He looked across the paddock to where the horizontal boundary fence should run. It then appeared as though the vertical boundary went right through the Russell family graves.

Grace followed his gaze. 'That can't be right.'

'It could be if the boundary went this side of the burial plot.' He leaned over to hand Grace the map for her to take a closer look. 'The question is who owns this land that we're on, as technically it isn't yours.'

He turned in the saddle to stare in the direction of where Frank lived. The treetops hid his bluestone cottage but from their position on the hill he could see a large steel shed tucked at the back of the valley. Whoever owned the cottage before Frank must have had the shed constructed as he wouldn't have any need for a building usually associated with a working farm.

A familiar gator noise caused Bundy to wriggle beneath the bottom wire of the fence beside them to dash into the bush.

'Frank's here.' Her smile delighted, Grace headed Jindy down the hill towards the corner where Rowan and Taite had installed the solar-powered gate.

Rowan didn't say anything as he and Goliath followed. He still had no idea how the older man knew so much about the comings and goings of Crookwell Park. If he was serious about finding the concealed CCTV camera, he needed to borrow Heath's drone for an aerial view.

Both horses were used to farm vehicles and didn't shy when Frank stopped close to the fence that separated them.

'Impeccable timing as always, Frank,' Rowan said with a nod.

The older man's smile could only be described as smug.

'How's Aubrey?' Frank asked Grace as he turned off the gator engine.

'Never better. She says hello.' Grace slid from the saddle to walk closer to the fence. She leaned over the top wire to pass Frank the map. 'We're trying to work out this side boundary. You don't happen to own this paddock that's cut in half, do you?'

Frank stared at the computer-generated drawing. 'As a matter of fact, I do.' He waved towards the high country behind Grace's back boundary fence. 'That's all mine as well, not that I've been up there in years. My wife was the bush walker.'

Rowan studied Frank. There'd been an odd note in his voice. Perhaps with his arthritis he hadn't been able to join his wife on her hikes. Now that he knew what land Frank's was, Rowan was certain from the map he'd seen at Taite's that Frank owned all the parts of the original Crookwell Park that had been sold off.

'Do you know then where the boundary goes through the paddock?' Grace asked as Frank handed her back the map.

'Somewhere in the middle. The only map I've seen, and it was a long time ago, was hand-drawn.'

Grace nodded. 'I'll organise for a surveyor to come in so we know exactly where the legal boundary runs.'

'Why go to the trouble? I don't use the land so you're welcome to use it.' Frank winked at Grace. 'Now you have your goats, a horse might be next.'

She gave a dreamy smile as she stroked Jindy's neck. 'I like your thinking.'

Rowan didn't take his attention away from Frank. He could understand why Frank loved chess; he gave very little away in either his expression or body language. But something wasn't right. He didn't know how he knew, but he trusted his instincts.

'Frank, do you still have the map that you saw?' he asked.

'I would. It's in the filing cabinet.'

It was only fleeting but Rowan saw his gnarled fingers twitch. 'So, all this land you own, and you've never used it?'

'I don't know the first thing about agriculture. I also don't need the money. Besides, I value my privacy too much to lease it out.'

'Fair enough.' Frank had an answer for everything. Rowan reached for his phone and slid from the saddle. 'You might be interested in these … Taite found them amongst his father's collections.'

He swiped to the first picture of the women holding the baby with the child outside Frank's cottage and handed the phone over the fence to him.

When the older man looked down at the images, Rowan lost sight of his expression. 'How interesting,' Frank said, in his usual well-modulated tone. 'I don't have many pictures of the cottage in its original state. Are there any more?'

'Just one. Taite's looking through the rest of the boxes for any others.'

Frank flicked to the next more formal picture of the woman and children. 'Do you know who they are?'

Rowan shook his head as Frank returned his phone to him. He showed Grace the images and, after she'd taken a quick look, swung into the saddle.

Frank switched on the gator. 'Enjoy the rest of your ride. I'll go and see how our new additions are today.'

With a wave he continued towards the solar-powered gate that he opened with the remote-control clicker before driving off to visit Olive's twins.

This time Rowan and Grace rode all the way up to the top of the hill before turning Goliath and Jindy for home. The gentle sun had strengthened to a glare and Bundy's lolling tongue had become a pant. After Grace helped Rowan unsaddle the horses, he washed the gelding and mare down. Bundy took a swim in the concrete trough that had been recommissioned for the goats and then rolled in a patch of bare dirt.

'If only Aubrey could see you now,' Grace said, taking a photo of the kelpie covered in mud and looking very pleased with himself.

Rowan loaded the horses and when he closed the back of the horse float, he glanced across at Grace. Their morning ride felt like it had ended too soon. 'Are you coming to see Heath's mural at the school this afternoon?'

'Sorry ... no. I told Clancy I couldn't make it.'

Rowan turned to face Grace. Her stilted tone was unlike the Grace he now knew.

She'd taken off her riding helmet and pulled out her ponytail, and her dark hair fell around her face, making it difficult to read her expression. Her gaze slid away to focus on Bundy.

'Grace, is everything okay?'

She folded her arms. 'Everything's fine. I'm just … busy.'

Rowan filled in the blanks. Even when Grace had first arrived, reserved and wary, she'd never avoided facing anything head-on. From attending the high tea in the park to going on a fake date, she'd never shied away from anything. Until now.

'Is it because the mural's at a school?'

He thought she wasn't going to answer and then her chin angled. 'Yes.'

He slid his hands into his jeans pockets to stop himself from reaching for her. While they had previously offered comfort to each other, since the river picnic the lines keeping them both in the real world had been firmly drawn.

'I'm sorry you don't have better memories of a place where you should have felt safe and accepted. I'm also sorry that they still have a hold over you.'

'It's all okay. Really.'

The strain in her voice contradicted her words.

'Grace … I've always had a thing about bullies. Standing up to them was never about taking a risk, just about doing the right thing. I could pick you up and we go together? Or I could distract you with my very long list of schoolyard injuries, starting with when I jumped off the monkey bars in kindy and broke my arm.'

Grace stared at him for a silent moment. Then a small smile shaped her lips. 'I'll go. I really would like to see the mural. But you don't have to come and get me, I'll drive. What time will you be there?'

'Four.'

'I'll see you then. And Rowan … thank you.'

'You're welcome,' was all he said before he turned to walk past the horse float to his ute. Another second longer and he'd be saying a whole lot more, like how much it meant that she trusted him enough to have changed her mind.

After he'd taken the horses to Ashcroft and moved a paddock of cattle, he made sure he was in town by four o'clock. Just to be on the safe side he arrived at his old primary school ten minutes early. Instead of joining the others who were over at the original honey-coloured stone schoolhouse, he stayed in his ute to wait for Grace. Her car soon parked behind him.

He left his ute to join her on the footpath. Apart from a pinched expression around her eyes, she appeared composed.

'Okay.' She took a calming breath. 'Let's do this.'

Once through the gate, Rowan matched his steps to hers and began a schoolyard commentary. 'Over behind that tree is where Taite had his first kiss. He says he was seven but he was really nine. Then over there were the infamous monkey bars …'

By the time they were a third of the way over to the school buildings, Grace's pace was no longer dragging and her shoulders not quite as braced. When Clancy waved to them from where everyone stood beneath a large pitched-roof assembly area, Grace lifted a hand in return.

They'd only taken a few more steps when she suddenly stopped. 'The mural, it's beautiful. Heath's so talented.'

Rowan had been too focused on Grace to notice Heath's work. The once blank wall of the undercover area was now a high-country scene that appeared so realistic Rowan could almost hear the sound of the brumby hooves and the calls of the black cockatoos.

Grace began walking again, her pace quickening as Brenna motioned at her to come over to where she stood looking at the mural. To the left of the artwork appeared to be a small legend that listed the wildlife Heath had concealed within his painting. Grace gave him a smile before going to help Brenna find whatever it was she was searching for.

Clancy produced a bottle of champagne and they all made a toast to Heath. Grace's laughter as she and Brenna returned to look for more animals was a sound Rowan would never get tired of hearing. Once everyone's glasses were empty and Heath had revealed where the final corrobboree frog had been hidden, they drifted back to their cars. The plan was to head to the pub for an early dinner.

Grace came to walk by his side. 'You were right,' she said softly when it was just the two of them. 'My fears did still have a hold over me. I'd like to come back and hear some more stories … we only got up to when you were in year two.'

'Anytime.'

He hoped his reply sounded casual as the emotions filling his chest were far from relaxed. It shouldn't mean as much as it did that he had been able to help her.

Heath's Land Cruiser drove by and they both turned to give Heath and Clancy a smile. When he looked back at Grace, her attention was on the phone in his shirt pocket.

'Can I please see those photos you showed Frank again?' she asked.

'Sure.'

As he took out his phone, Grace rummaged in her bag to produce hers. After he found the formal photo of the woman, baby and child, Grace held up a photo of four girls.

'Kathy tracked down this picture of the Russell sisters but we don't know who the other two are.' She held her mobile next to Rowan's. 'Do you think either of the girls on the left resemble the woman in your photo?'

Rowan didn't need to take a closer look to answer. 'Definitely. The older girl in your photo has the same shaped face and nose as the mother in mine.'

'I think so too. I also think perhaps Clancy was right, that Lawrence Senior did have a second family. This is possibly a picture of all his daughters; the spinster sisters and then these two girls who lived in the cottage.'

Grace swiped through the pictures on her phone. 'Which means that the mother in the apartment could also have been one of Lawrence Senior's other two daughters. But, even though the apartment bedroom photos were water-damaged, neither girl would perhaps have been the right age let alone height.' She found the picture she'd been searching for. 'See ... you can't see the face of the mother holding the baby wrapped in a shawl in this one, but she was very tall and slender.'

Rowan stared at the ruined photo Grace showed him, except it wasn't the woman he noticed. The man was all but obliterated except for his left side where Rowan could make out the detail of an old-fashioned tweed coat and the wheel spokes of a bicycle behind him.

He took a moment to reply. 'Grace, we've been looking in the wrong place. The mother wasn't either of the spinster sisters or the daughters in the cottage. I've seen someone wearing that same coat, someone who always rode a bicycle ... except he was supposed to be an eccentric bachelor. The father who had loved and lost his family has to be Lawrence Russell Junior.'

CHAPTER
15

The weekend of the Bundilla book festival delivered on its blue-sky promise of bright sunshine. The rain that had fallen over the past week had cleared, leaving the rural landscape around the small town green and vibrant with a proliferation of yellow and purple colour beside the roadside.

Grace slowed to appreciate the scenery. Today the mountain peaks were in full view, their granite outcrops glinting in the sun. She wasn't the only one to be enjoying the scenery. She'd already passed two cars of tourists en route to the festival who had pulled over to take photographs. As pretty as the purple blooms of the Paterson's curse were, especially when they blanketed an entire paddock, no local would stop to take pictures of the noxious weed.

Even though she knew Rowan wasn't heading to Crookwell Park and would be setting up for the stall holders in the main street, she still checked every ute she saw. Over the past week since their visit to the local school to see Heath's mural, she'd barely seen him.

Between the rain and being needed to help out at the festival, he'd only been to Crookwell Park for a day. It was the least contact they'd ever had.

Instead of using the time apart to sort through the tangled thoughts in her head, all she'd done was miss him. So much so she'd taken to texting him and sending photos of the goats. On the night he'd called to see if Kathy's research into Lawrence Junior had yet uncovered any proof that he'd fathered two children, they'd talked for hours.

After their school visit it was as though a heavy layer of darkness had lifted and now all she felt was light. It shouldn't have taken so long to face the past, but perhaps she hadn't been ready to deal with her fears until now. Coming to Bundilla, where she wasn't consumed by work and had time and space to work through things, had proved healing on more than one level. She wasn't naive enough to think that grief no longer held her hostage, but for now she was at peace. All she needed was to see Rowan for more than five minutes and her day would be complete.

Grateful for Clancy's advice to park two blocks over from the main street at the dance studio, Grace left the throng of festival traffic. It was only early Saturday morning and yet the town was the busiest she'd ever seen it. Bundy had made a wise choice to stay with Frank. She nabbed a parking spot and then walked towards where she could hear the live music of a bush band.

The aroma of something delicious from a food stall made her stomach grumble at having to wait for breakfast. It wouldn't be long until she was at the café with Clancy, Brenna and Mabel. But, as she walked through the cobblestone alleyway she'd taken as a shortcut, she revised her breakfast estimate.

Now shut to cars and only open to foot traffic, a sea of people filled the main street. Tina from the vintage charity shop had been right. It would be difficult to move amongst the festivalgoers let alone cross the road. Grace stepped into the throng. Apart from being momentarily distracted by a stall that had a book about goats and one on growing a cottage garden, she managed to find a path through the crowd. She pushed open the café door and when she saw Brenna wave, navigated her way through the full tables towards the back corner.

She sat in the last empty seat with a sigh. 'That was an experience.'

'It's only early; wait until lunch,' Brenna said with a grin.

Mabel peeked in the bag draped over Grace's arm. 'Okay, what books did you buy?'

Grace showed them her purchases while the young waitress took their order. Grace settled for the big breakfast and a large coffee; she was going to need both to face the crowds again.

Once the waitress had left, Grace found herself the centre of attention.

'Any more news on the apartment?' Clancy asked, leaning forwards. 'I've been flat out trying to see Rowan all week and when I do he says about two words.'

Grace gazed around at the three expectant faces and her earlier sense of peace returned. She knew she could still sound English and different and that she was sometimes reserved, but the three women around her had accepted her from the start. She even felt she could call them friends.

'Well ...' She smiled. 'Thanks to Rowan and his perfect plot twist I do think we are getting closer, even though Kathy has confirmed Lawrence's name isn't on any marriage or birth certificate.' Grace paused as she searched for a photo on her phone. 'Kathy also found this newspaper photo of Lawrence and, just as Rowan remembered, he's wearing the same tweed jacket.'

'It's such a tragedy,' Mabel commented. 'It's like when he lost everyone, time stopped.'

'It is sad,' agreed Brenna. 'I wonder if his sisters knew about his family and that's why they fell out. They could have done so much to help him through his grief.'

'Perhaps they tried?' Grace showed everyone the picture of Bernice and then Evelyn.

'I doubt it,' said Mabel. 'I always like to give people the benefit of the doubt, but they both look cold and unfeeling.'

'So, if we assume that they did know,' Clancy said, looking around, 'they mustn't have approved of who Lawrence loved. If this is true, the reason why they didn't approve might also be why Lawrence had to hide his family.'

They all nodded.

'What I don't get,' said Mabel, 'is how this has all stayed secret. Someone in town has to know something. From the builder who worked on the apartment to the doctor who treated the little boy for polio, someone knows something.'

Grace opened the photo of the cookbook inscription. 'So now we are back to thinking that this Melly has to be the mother.'

'There definitely wasn't a name similar to Melly in the cemetery records of the unmarked graves?' Clancy asked.

Grace shook her head. 'Without her surname, it's impossible to know whether any of the unmarked graves could be her children. Kathy has ruled out the two that shared a surname. Kathy also suggested, to explain why none of the remaining unmarked graves share a surname, that perhaps Lawrence is only the father of the baby. If the mother had been married, then her older son would have her husband's last name.'

'This is making my head hurt, but maybe that was why the family had to be hidden?' Brenna said as the waitress came to deliver their orders. 'The mother was a married woman?'

Their discussion lapsed as they tucked into their breakfast.

Mabel appeared thoughtful. 'Here's another idea … the mother didn't die in childbirth. Maybe just the baby girl did. The mother couldn't cope so she left, or if she was married, she went back to her husband.'

Clancy took a sip of her tea. 'If the mother did survive and then go, that would leave Lawrence Junior heartbroken just as if she had died.'

'Like Miss Havisham from *Great Expectations*,' Brenna said.

When everyone looked at her in surprise—tomboy Brenna would rather be on horseback than reading—she shrugged. 'What? I listen at book club … sometimes.'

Once the laughter had subsided, Clancy said to Grace, 'Show everyone the photo you showed me at the pub of the Russell sisters and the other two girls who we suspect are Lawrence Senior's secret family.'

When Grace held up the photo, Mabel stared at the picture. 'I can't help but think the two secret families are connected. Maybe that's how Lawrence Junior got the idea to hide his own family. If so, it's heartbreaking that both generations couldn't live with the ones they loved.'

'No wonder the mansion is said to be cursed,' Brenna said, her solemn expression matching the others around the table.

'What's the next step?' Clancy asked. She didn't need to say what they all were thinking, that they needed to right the wrongs of the past. Two families had already suffered enough.

'Edith's very kindly asking around at the CWA meeting this week,' Grace replied. 'I have everything crossed someone will recognise the cookbook handwriting or the name.'

The waitress returned and after they'd made a second coffee and tea order, the conversation changed to what festival events everyone was going to.

When they'd finished their hot drinks, they readied themselves to leave the sanctuary of the café. While Grace and Clancy headed off to a talk by Allison Butler, a medieval historical author, Mabel and Brenna went to listen to a panel of crime writers.

As Grace and Clancy made their way to the library where the talk was being held, they passed Dr Davis speaking at a podium in the adjacent park. His introduction for the writer standing beside him must have been going for a while as Grace saw an elderly man's head bob as he briefly nodded off.

Once their own author talk was over and in Grace's bag were several signed books, Grace and Clancy went out to wander through the book stalls. By now the live music was provided by a brass band playing old-time favourites. Brenna soon joined them.

Grace had just added another book to the pile in her arms when she heard her name. She turned to see Millicent and Beatrice. The identical twin sisters each gave her a small smile which she knew by now was their version of a real one.

'How lovely to see you, Grace,' said Millicent. 'Apparently Bundy's still with you?'

'He is. Somehow he's lasted all this time.'

Beatrice's attention went to the books in her arms and the bag hanging off her shoulder. 'You look like you're having fun. You must enjoy reading?'

Grace didn't immediately answer. Clancy and Brenna stood behind the sisters and Brenna was shaking her blonde head.

'I … do.'

'I said to Beatrice you were a reader,' said Millicent. 'Now the festival won't be taking up so much of our time, book club will be on again. We'd be delighted if you'd join us.'

This time Brenna's headshake was both fervent and rapid.

'Ah … thank you. I'm not sure how long I'll be in town but I'll keep book club in mind. I always love to talk about books.'

'Wonderful,' Beatrice said with a nod before both women continued on their way.

Brenna came to Grace's side. 'That was close. Next time I have to get out of something I'm asking you what to say. That was very smooth.'

Grace looked between Clancy and Brenna. 'What's wrong with book club?'

'Nothing really,' answered Clancy. 'It's fun, it's just that missing book club is a serious offence; once you're in it's basically for life. If you do join, don't be surprised if you're expected to attend meetings via your laptop when you go back to Sydney.'

'And when it comes to saying what you think of a book,' added Brenna, '*sucked* isn't exactly on the approved word list.'

Grace resisted a smile. She could see Brenna saying such a thing much to Millicent and Beatrice's disapproval.

As they moved on to the next stall, Brenna drifted away to talk to two teenagers who had to be sisters with their yellow-blonde hair. Thrilled with finding a 1916 copy of Jane Austen's *Sense and Sensibility*, Grace lost track of what Clancy was doing. When she looked around to see where she was, she found her standing stock still. Her attention seemed to be on a willowy blonde wearing a short cream shift dress with a tan designer handbag draped over an elegant shoulder. The woman was talking into her phone and when she turned she revealed a classically beautiful profile.

Even before Grace registered her compact but definite baby bump, she knew who the stranger was. Eloise.

'Clance?'

Clancy seemed to come to life. She grabbed Grace's arm. 'I have to find Rowan. Eloise being here isn't good. She never does anything without a reason.'

'Go. I'll take my books to the car and meet you later.'

Clancy nodded before pulling out her phone and dashing away.

Grace couldn't help but stare as Eloise continued to talk into her mobile. She was breathtaking. There was no other word to describe her. No wonder Rowan had lost his heart.

She turned to make the trek back to her car. She had no doubt Rowan was over Eloise but between her mother's attitude at the long lunch and now Clancy's worry, unease made the bags she carried feel extra heavy. Seeing a pregnant Eloise would have to have an effect on Rowan. He'd once wanted to spend his life with this woman.

After she'd offloaded her books, Grace wasn't in any rush to leave the quiet of the car park. As much as she was enjoying the festival, she needed some time out. She scrolled through her texts to find the message where Rowan had sent her Ned's address. A quick check on her phone map revealed that Ned wasn't far away. Instead of driving and losing her car spot, she set off for the short walk.

The battered white Hilux parked out the front of a weatherboard house let her know she'd arrived even before her phone GPS announced she'd reached her destination. The sound of hammering led her up the driveway towards a large shed.

She stopped at the garden gate. 'Hi, Ned. It's Grace.'

Ned appeared at the shed doorway, his smile welcoming. 'I was hoping you'd call round. Come in out of the sun.'

Grace let herself through the gate. Even though she wore a sleeveless white dress the cool of the air-conditioned shed provided a welcome respite from the summer warmth. She gazed around at the interior, which was as neat as Ned's garden outside. Dismantled rocking horses hung on the walls, while stacked containers of smaller parts and what looked like paints were clearly labelled on the shelves.

A dappled grey rocking horse that she barely recognised stood in the middle of the shed. No longer did the apartment horse appear bedraggled and unloved. Instead it was the proud owner of a flowing pale grey mane and tail, its polished wooden coat gleamed and the leather of its bridle and saddle had been oiled.

'Ned ...' Grace touched the soft mane. 'This looks like a different horse.'

'There's nothing better than discovering what's under the dust.' He motioned towards a chair. 'Take a seat and I'll find my photo album.'

He went to the filing cabinet before settling himself in the chair beside Grace. After opening the album of the horses he'd restored, Ned flipped over two pages. 'See, this one is almost identical; the only difference is the paint colour.'

Grace glanced from the photograph of a golden horse with dark dapples to the grey horse in front of her. 'They are.'

'I checked but I haven't kept my paperwork from twenty years ago, and for the life of me I can't remember the owner's name.'

Grace banished a pang of disappointment. 'It's a long shot that both of the rocking horses would have been connected to the apartment.'

'This one wasn't in as good shape as yours. I had to replace this.' Ned pointed to the blue saddlecloth that didn't match the picture.

'The woman was adamant that she wanted it blue and not its original olive green because the horse had belonged to her nephew.'

Grace's gaze flew to Ned's twinkling eyes. 'They could have been bought by the same person … the dapple grey could have been for the baby girl and the golden one for the older boy.'

'If they were, since the woman was a friend of Pen's and we've lived in Bundilla all our lives, whoever you're looking for has to be a local and could still be here.'

Rowan carried a box of books over to a trestle table that had been labelled with the author's name. He'd spent the majority of the morning setting up the street stalls and since the crowds had arrived was now helping in an empty store that formed the epicentre of the book festival. Authors could come for a quiet cuppa or to leave their books while festival volunteers could use the private space to recharge.

At the moment it was just him and Heath on duty as Taite had disappeared to do a food run. It felt like they'd eaten their breakfast burritos hours ago. As Taite was making the most of being able to go out without being recognised in the crowd, he was yet to return.

Rowan looked through the front window. The festival was proving as popular as ever. People relaxed in camp chairs in front of the makeshift stage enjoying the live music, lines had formed outside the food venues and the book stalls were barely visible amongst the crowds milling around them. An author talk must have just finished as a large group of visitors streamed from the library. He scanned their faces. If he'd thought he'd missed Grace over the days Aubrey had been here, it was nothing compared to this past week when he'd hardly seen her.

Heath sat a box of books on the table beside Rowan. 'Grace is with Clancy looking at the book stalls.'

Rowan didn't attempt to deny that it was Grace who he'd been searching for. 'I've only been out to Crookwell Park for a day this week.'

Heath clasped his shoulder. 'I know that feeling.'

Heath had seen Clancy once in ten long years.

Rowan's nod turned into a frown as he leaned back against the table. 'I never missed Eloise like this.'

'That's because she made sure you were never apart. When you moved out and had time away from her was when you were able to see things for what they really were.'

'I wish I'd come to my senses sooner.'

'If you hadn't been with Eloise, you wouldn't have gone overseas and we never would have had our conversation in London that brought me back to Clancy. We can't change the past, but the future is something we can shape.'

Rowan stayed silent. If anyone knew the truth of such a statement it was Heath. His complex family life had darkened his past and now he was making the most of his future with Clancy.

'Rowan … as I've said before, we're all human. Hardly anything scares you but getting close to Grace does. Being Captain Serious isn't going to protect you, it's just going to get in the way of going after who and what you really want.'

The door opened as an author entered carrying a box of books. Heath gave Rowan a think-about-what-I-said look before he went to help. Rowan remained where he was to process Heath's advice. When his phone vibrated in his jeans pocket, he ignored it.

As much as he'd tried to hide the way he responded to Grace, Heath and Clancy knew him too well. Both would know he'd

fallen and fallen hard, even if he wasn't in a position to do anything
about it. He didn't think it was fear holding him back. Grace had
lost her parents and his conscience simply wouldn't allow him to
start anything with her unless she was in the right place. He wasn't
taking advantage of her grief like it increasingly appeared as though
Eloise had done with him. His phone vibrated again and after a
long moment he straightened to reach for his mobile.

As he did, he realised that the author had left and Heath was
walking towards him with his phone pressed against his ear. 'Yes,
Rowan's here. I'll put you on speaker.'

Heath tapped on his mobile before laying it on the table.

'Rowan Liam Parker.' Clancy's voice was breathless but loud.
'Why do you never answer your phone?'

He rubbed the back of his neck. 'I was about to look at my
messages. What's up?'

'Eloise is up, that's what. She's here and we all know she never
does anything without a reason. She also looks to be by herself.'

Heath's gaze met his.

'Clance … it's okay,' Rowan said, voice calm. 'I'll handle this.
Where is she?'

'Wait. No. You're not going to see her?'

'Why?'

'Because …' Clancy seemed uncharacteristically lost for words.
'Because she's trouble.'

'She might just be here for the festival.'

'Rowan, she doesn't read books. She also has the bag you gave her.'

When Rowan glanced across at Heath, he shrugged. They had
no idea what that meant.

As if she knew what they were doing, Clancy spoke again. 'Which
means she's feeling sentimental, and feeling sentimental means she

has regrets and that she's here for only one thing ... and that's to *bump* into you so she can reel you in again.'

Rowan's lips twitched. 'I'm not some brown trout.'

Clancy muttered something he couldn't decipher before she said with clearly enunciated tones, 'Heath, please talk sense into him.'

'I will,' he said, expression serious. 'Leave it with me.'

'Okay.' Relief softened her tone.

'I still need to know where she is,' Rowan said, holding Heath's gaze.

Clancy sighed. 'Outside the stall in front of the bakery, talking on her phone while she watches who walks by. And before you race off—and, Heath, you better be going with him to talk that sense—Grace saw her.'

Tension ticked in Rowan's jaw. 'Did Eloise see her?'

'No. Grace went back to her car.'

Rowan picked up Heath's phone so he could continue the conversation on the way to the door. 'To leave?'

Rowan knew Clancy had registered the edge in his words when she replied, 'Rowan ... relax. Give Heath back his phone. Grace messaged me. She's at Ned's.'

Heath took hold of his mobile and said something to Clancy before ending the call. He looked at Rowan. 'Do I need to come? Taite's crossing the street so can take over in here.'

'You would if Eloise had seen Grace. No doubt Janice has passed on the town gossip. I know Grace can stand up for herself ... it's more you'd keep a cool head. I know I wouldn't if either of them disrespected Grace again.'

Heath returned his phone to his shirt pocket, a smile in his eyes. 'My words of sense are: see Eloise, then don't waste another minute of what's left of your summer with Grace.'

Rowan gave him a nod before he strode out the door and into the crowd.

Eloise was right where Clancy had said she would be. It was impossible to miss her. Just like always, she looked like she'd stepped out of a fashion magazine. If he didn't know her baby was due soon, he'd have thought she still had months to go. It was also impossible to not miss his reaction. He felt nothing, just a sadness that while Eloise looked like she had everything, her life was so empty that she and her mother had needed to trade on other people's vulnerabilities.

Whoever Eloise had been on the phone to—he suspected it was Janice—she hung up the second she saw him. He walked straight up to her. He didn't wish her any ill will and for the sake of her baby didn't want to cause her any stress. When she feigned surprise, he kissed her cheek, catching a waft of her strong perfume. Once the scent would have distracted him from whatever he'd been doing, but now it only smelt cloying.

'Rowan. How fabulous to see you.'

Time hadn't changed the sensual and seductive tone of her voice.

He arched a brow.

For the first time he caught a flicker of uncertainty in her blue eyes. He also noted fine lines of strain beneath the perfection of her makeup.

'Enjoying the festival?' he asked, full well knowing the answer.

'It's all right, if you like this sort of thing.' She touched his arm, her fingers lingering. 'Maybe we could go somewhere quiet and have a coffee for old times' sake.'

'I'll pass on the coffee, but a catch-up is definitely in order. I know the perfect place.'

Conscious she was in heels, he kept his pace slow as he led the way through the crowd to another empty shop where they would not be disturbed. Millicent had given him the keys in case they'd needed a second space for author books.

Once they were inside and the door was shut, the noise of the festival receded.

He rested his hip on what had been the store counter and got straight to the point. 'Why are you here?'

When her lashes fluttered and her crimson lips pushed into a playful pout, he held up his hand. He had no time for games. 'You have three minutes to tell me the truth and then I'm walking.'

She blinked.

'Eloise?'

She slipped the tan bag he'd once given her off her shoulder and with a thump sat it on a nearby table. 'Geoff left me.'

'Why?'

Her laugh was brittle. 'I wanted emotional intimacy. He didn't.'

The irony wasn't lost on him. He'd been the one to want to talk through things and she hadn't.

'I'm sorry to hear things didn't work out but that doesn't really explain what this visit's about. We both know, despite your mother wanting to believe otherwise, your baby isn't mine.'

'She knows it isn't, even though she's always wished it was. She thinks you're far higher up the social ladder than a travelling salesman, even if he is loaded.' Bitterness turned her mouth hard. 'The first thing my mother said when I told her I was on my own is that you'd take me back. That we could use the baby to appeal to your good heart.'

'Is that what you came here to do?'

'I saw her ... Grace. She was with Clancy looking at books.'

His eyes narrowed as he waited for Eloise to answer his question.

She studied him and then sighed. 'No. I wanted to see if the rumours about you were true. A little girl beside Grace dropped her book and Grace picked it up. She has a smile a camera would love. She's also a decent person.' Eloise paused. 'That look on your face. You'd do anything for her. You never looked at me that way.'

'Eloise … what we had wasn't based on anything real.'

She slowly nodded. 'I owe you an apology. That night in the pub you were lost and just looking for a friend and I used that to get close to you. I truly did think we could have a fulfilling life.' She rested her hand on her stomach. 'I'd like to think I'm a little wiser now. I can see how much my mother's needs influenced what I thought I wanted.'

'It's definitely over with Geoff?'

'My baby comes first. I'm not staying with a man who won't be an invested father.'

'Will you move back here?'

'I've bought a small place in the southern highlands. I'm opening a beauty salon with an old work colleague. And no, my mother isn't coming.'

'If there's ever anything you need, let me know.'

A sheen of tears intensified the blue of her eyes. 'Thank you. Grace is a lucky woman.'

He didn't answer as he moved to give her a hug. 'You'll be a great mother, Eloise.'

When they separated, she touched a finger to the corner of her eye. 'Please apologise to Grace for what happened at the long lunch. I'll make sure it won't happen again.'

He followed Eloise out the door and then accompanied her to where she was parked near the newspaper office. Before he waved goodbye, he made sure she still had his number.

Instead of returning to the festival, he stayed beneath the shade of the historic newspaper building. He sent a quick text to Clancy and another to Heath to let them know Eloise had left. Needing to think through what he said to Grace, he stared at her name on his phone.

There was now no doubt that Eloise had used his grief as a means to further her and her mother's own ends. She'd also acknowledged that their relationship hadn't been based on any true emotional foundation. Such admissions helped to put his year of temporary insanity into perspective. But at the same time today he'd seen in Eloise an integrity that he'd never glimpsed before. The part of him that had believed her capable of such a trait had been vindicated. His judgement hadn't been completely wrong.

Except none of this changed the way he'd dealt with his grief. He shoved a hand through his hair. He had to take responsibility for the choices he alone had made. He'd been looking for a distraction and a way to run away from his pain, which Eloise had provided. Heath thought that he was too hard on himself, but until he knew he could trust himself to act responsibly at a time when strength and courage were needed, he still had work to do.

He typed a message to Grace to see how her morning was going and to ask if she'd like to catch up for coffee. Eloise was a topic best kept for a proper conversation. An almost instant reply whooshed in. Instead of words, Grace's message consisted of an emoji of a sun, a stack of books, a red heart and a thumbs up.

He smiled. Even though the festival noise surrounded him and people walked by, just like when sitting on the log at the river, he experienced a sense of stillness and peace. This time he didn't fight the sensation or label it as dangerous. His talk with Eloise had provided confirmation, and proof, that his feelings for Grace were different to what he'd believed he'd felt for her. Clancy had been right. What he felt for Grace was real, and as real as it could get.

Still smiling, he left the shade and headed for the main street. But before he could act on how he felt, let alone think about a future with Grace, she needed to heal. He hoped that between the goats and her talk about getting a horse, and Crookwell Park still having a long restoration road ahead, she would be in Bundilla on and off for quite a while. Once she was in a better emotional place, he'd ask her out on a proper date.

Until then he had to stop being Captain Serious and, as difficult as it would be, become Captain Patient.

CHAPTER
16

'We'll leave in a minute to take Rowan his coffee, I promise,' Grace said to Bundy as she switched on the kettle for the third time. The kelpie tilted his head from where he sat at the front door.

She'd been too busy putting her hair up into a ponytail and then taking it down again to have yet made any morning coffee. She'd also changed her jeans. She wasn't going to admit that was because she wanted to wear her best ones for when she saw Rowan; it was just because the original pair had been covered in mud from playing with the goats.

She spooned coffee into two mugs and took a breath to quieten the anticipation that whirled through her. It was no big deal that finally she could have a morning chat with Rowan like she'd done before Aubrey had visited and last week's wet weather had set in. While she had seen Rowan over the weekend at the festival and they'd grabbed a quick coffee, they'd been surrounded by people.

Clancy had sent a brief text when Grace was on her way back from Ned's to say Eloise was no longer in town but otherwise Grace hadn't heard any further details. Rowan had appeared his usual easygoing self, but after seeing Eloise, he might need to talk through his ex-fiancée reappearing in his life.

With a container of jam drops tucked under her arm and carrying two mugs of steaming coffee, she followed Bundy over to the mansion. Now Rowan had finished reassembling and replastering the ballroom wall he was repointing any sections where the mortar was missing or unsound. He could be anywhere.

Olive bleated another good morning from where she munched in a garden bed, a willie wagtail perched on her back. Lavender and Rebel were curled up asleep nearby while the three younger goats grazed on the corner lawn. Grace had already been outside to let them out and to watch the sunrise seep across the mountain sky. She didn't know if it had been remnants of grief that had disturbed her sleep or if seeing Rowan had been on her mind, but she'd awakened early.

Bundy trotted past the front of the house. Rowan must be again working on the left wing. But when she walked around the veranda corner there was no sign of him or the kelpie, which meant Rowan had to be in the courtyard. She continued past the side veranda and where Rowan had fixed the wall before turning left into the cobblestone walkway. Draped over the rusted pergola was the old grapevine Kathy had mentioned had come from Wales. Grace couldn't wait until autumn when the leaves would turn a deep russet red.

She stepped into the sun-drenched courtyard and Rowan gave her a grin from high up on his scaffolding. She returned his smile, hoping her happiness that he'd been looking out for her wouldn't show in her expression. She'd worked hard to keep things simple between them this past fortnight, but it was becoming more and more difficult to do so.

He climbed down and tugged off his gloves as he came over to join her. The grey of his eyes was a pure pewter today.

She passed him his coffee, making sure her voice would sound as normal as possible. 'Morning.'

'Morning. This all looks a bit different.'

'It does.' She offered him a jam drop. He took one for himself and one for Bundy. 'The courtyard seems so much bigger now the weeds are gone. I've ordered an espalier apple and pear tree for the far walls.'

She didn't need to say the trees were in memory of her parents. The way Rowan's gaze searched hers told her he'd already guessed.

'Maybe Taite could make you a double gate for the walkway so the goats won't waltz in every apple and pear season.'

'Good thinking.' Even though Rowan appeared relaxed, she sensed a familiar coiled restlessness. But before she could broach the subject of Eloise, Rowan turned to collect a brown paper gift bag resting against the pergola post.

'I thought you might like this.'

From the shape and feel of the gift she could tell it was a book. 'I like it already.'

When she pulled out a vintage hardcover copy of *Heidi*, her breath caught. She didn't just like it, she loved it. Rowan had remembered that her mother used to read this story to her as a child.

She cleared her throat. 'Thank you so much.'

'I was hoping you hadn't found a copy.'

'I was looking … so you were the person the lady in the red dress said she'd sold her one to.'

He smiled.

She looked down at the book to hide how much his kind gesture had touched her and returned it to the safety of its bag.

When she glanced up, Rowan wore an indefinable expression. 'Sorry we didn't get much of a chance to chat at the festival. Clancy said you saw Eloise?'

'Only briefly. No wonder she's a model. She's stunning.'

'Pregnancy suits her. We had a talk that was beneficial to both of us. She said to pass on her apologies about the way her mother treated you.'

Grace nodded. While she was pleasantly surprised that somehow Janice had raised a daughter capable of empathy, she was also uncertain about where the conversation was heading. A beneficial talk could mean two things. One, Rowan and Eloise had provided each other with closure, or two, they had resolved an issue that had pushed them apart.

Rowan took a mouthful of coffee before he continued. 'Eloise is on her own now.'

Grace ignored the dip in her stomach and chose her next words carefully. 'That must be difficult.'

'It would be, but she's moving to a new town and getting on with her life. I said I'm here if she needs me, but I'm getting on with my life too.'

His eyes met hers and in his clear gaze she saw nothing to suggest he still wasn't over his ex. The nerves in her midriff settled.

Rowan chose another jam drop for himself and Bundy. 'So, what time is the CWA meeting this morning?'

'Nine thirty. Edith said she'd call if there was any news.'

'Here's hoping.'

'Yes, we're running out of leads. Even though thanks to Ned we now have the possibility that an aunt was a local. He's also talking to some other rocking horse enthusiasts to try and track down who made the horses in case they kept any sale records.'

By now both their coffees were finished and there were no more excuses to stay, even if she was reluctant to leave. She reached for his mug, which he handed her.

When their fingers touched, she pretended not to notice even though her cheeks warmed. 'I'll let you know if Edith calls.'

Grace made it to the end of the pergola and out of sight before she stopped to look at her new book. She ran a hand over the cover. She usually was the one sourcing items for people's houses or personal collections; she'd rarely been on the receiving end. To now have Rowan gift her such a meaningful treasure moved her in a way she wasn't expecting.

Deep in thought, she returned to the cottage alone. Bundy had remained with Rowan and would already be asleep in the shade. She made her way over to the mansion and headed for the far-right corner rooms that Aubrey had helped her clean. The end room was now home to the furniture and collectibles that she'd been buying from the local online marketplace.

Her muse had returned and she couldn't wait to get creative with interior concepts. The ballroom particularly called to her to be brought back to life. Instead of bothering Rowan with picking up her large and heavy purchases, she'd taken to using Steve, Frank's workman. She'd also met Steve's wife, Kate, who helped Frank around the cottage.

The room next door to her storage room she'd turned into a personal haven. Despite Aubrey's scepticism, the mattress she'd bought in a box proved to be very comfortable. When she couldn't sleep and there was a breeze so the mansion wasn't too hot and stuffy, she'd come over to use the wrought-iron bed that Steve had picked up last week. With a candle providing flickering light, the high ceiling above her and Bundy at the end of the bed, she'd drift off to sleep.

Busy in the end room moving a pile of wooden chairs that she planned to upcycle, she didn't immediately realise her phone was ringing. She took the call, hoping the unfamiliar number would be Edith.

'Grace speaking.'

'Hi, Grace, it's Edith. Are you busy?'

Grace kept her voice calm as she tried not to get her hopes up. 'Not at all. Why?'

'There's an old CWA member called Lorraine who has a story to tell you. Her daughter, Ruth, says she is better in the morning than the afternoon, and they're happy for you to come in to see them now if it suits. I'll send through their address in a text.'

Grace was already walking along the hallway. 'That's so wonderful. Thank you.'

By the time she reached the courtyard she was out of breath. Finally, there might be some answers as to who had lived in the apartment and why. As soon as Rowan saw her, he stripped off his gloves and left his scaffolding platform. Just like he always did, he'd read how she was feeling.

'Edith's called?' he said, striding over.

'She has. There's an old CWA lady who knows something.' Grace curled her hands into her palms to stop herself from throwing her arms around him in excitement. 'I'm going to see them now.'

'Grace ...' Rowan's tone turned serious as he reached out to tuck loose hair behind her ear. 'There might be things that will be difficult to hear.'

She nodded, wishing the slow sweep of his fingers over her skin hadn't ended so soon. 'But we still need to hear them. I have to return the apartment belongings to the rightful owners. Especially the rocking horse. It needs to be loved by children again.' She turned. 'I'll call as soon as I know something.'

After a brief stop at the cottage to collect jam drops and her car keys, Grace zoomed down the driveway. Her anticipation only built on the journey into town. When she parked outside a neat brick house, she stayed in her car a moment to collect herself. Always used to hiding her emotions, now that she had relaxed her tight grip, it was harder to make sure she had them under control. She didn't want to rush in and ask too many questions; she was there to listen.

She left her driver's seat. A slight woman with grey hair waved at her from the doorway. Grace made her way through the small garden gate and along the path to her.

'You must be Grace. I'm Ruth.'

'It's lovely to meet you.'

'Likewise. My mother's very excited to talk to you. Come inside.'

Grace walked into an uncluttered home in which the polished timber floorboards had been left bare. Any potential hazards for elderly Lorraine had been removed.

'Mum's this way. She will be ninety-five next month. She can at times forget what she's saying and will tire easily, but I hope I'm doing as well as she is when I'm her age.'

Grace followed Ruth into a sun-filled room in which a frail, white-haired lady with bright eyes sat in a comfortable chair, a light quilt over her knees.

Lorraine gestured for Grace to come closer and to sit on the chair beside her. 'I love having visitors and you brought me jam drops. My favourite.'

Grace gave the jam drops to Ruth who accepted them with a smile.

Lorraine reached out to take Grace's hand. 'You're a pretty one with a kind soul. Carmella would have liked you.'

'Carmella … Is that what Melly is short for?'

Lorraine nodded.

Ruth returned to sit in a nearby chair. 'As soon as I saw the photograph of the handwriting in the cookbook I knew it was Mum's. I came straight home to check.' Ruth looked across at her mother. 'You gave the book to Melly, didn't you?'

'I did. She was such a darling. See that vase over there, it was a gift from her. Brought it all the way from Italy on the boat, Melly did.'

Grace looked to where she pointed and saw a small green Murano vase. No wonder the apartment also had a genuine Murano vase.

Lorraine smiled as she stared straight ahead as if in another time and place. 'Melly came out to be with her sister whose husband worked on the Snowy Mountains Scheme. The CWA ran English classes and that's where I met Melly. I knew she was special. When she couldn't find work I organised for her to come to Bundilla as a cook at Crookwell Park. She was very nervous, so I gave her the cookbook.'

Lorraine stopped and Ruth moved to give her a glass of water, which she held in shaking hands.

The older woman again clasped Grace's fingers in hers. 'Lawrence loved Melly from the start. He'd been injured in the war so would sit in the garden and they'd talk when she brought him his tea. But those dreadful sisters of his were just like their cold-hearted mother. They made fun of Melly's accent, thought she was beneath them, and did everything they could to keep her and Lawrence apart. But he sorted them out. He gave them an ultimatum: accept Melly or leave. So they moved into their town house.' Lorraine sighed. 'But it wasn't just his sisters who didn't accept poor Melly. Many locals couldn't see past her not being from around here. Even before she fell pregnant Lawrence planned to have their apartment built. Only a few of us ever knew that they'd had a family together.'

'You've been to their apartment?'

'Many times. It was always a happy place.'

Lorraine's eyes clouded and her expression crumpled.

Grace rubbed her hand. 'We can stop there.'

Lorraine didn't seem to hear her. 'I thought with the war over I wouldn't lose anyone else I cared about. First, that beautiful baby girl failed to take a breath, and then that night Lawrence and the children lost their dear sweet Melly.'

Grace swallowed past the lump in her throat, not sure if she'd heard Lorraine correctly.

'Children?'

She and Rowan had believed that there had only been a baby and one child, a boy, born to the couple in the apartment. Now it sounded like there were more.

'Yes. Two of them. A boy and a girl.' Lorraine paused, looking momentarily bewildered. 'They both died. Melly's son, Eduardo, fell sick with the illness that left children crippled.' Lorraine again appeared confused.

'Polio?'

'That's it. He went to some city hospital that had an iron lung and even though he came home it wasn't for long. I remember the day Lawrence told me he'd lost him too. It was as though he'd died as well.'

Grace went to ask about what had happened to Eduardo's sister but when tears slipped over Lorraine's thin cheeks and her mouth trembled, she decided to stay silent.

She glanced at Ruth who had come to her feet.

Grace gently squeezed Lorraine's hand. 'Can I come and see you again?'

'I'd like that. We can talk about Melly again. I've never laughed as much as when I was with her. Will you bring jam drops?'

'I will.'

Grace stood to let Ruth take care of her mother.

Once she was back in her car, Grace didn't call Rowan or start the engine. She stared unseeingly through the windscreen. While they now had more pieces of the puzzle, there were still some missing and without them the picture remained incomplete.

She didn't know Carmella's last name to cross-reference with the unmarked graves. There had been no mention of Carmella's sister or where Carmella and what she now knew were a baby and two children had been buried. But, most of all, Lorraine hadn't given any details about the little girl who had died. There had been no third trunk in the apartment. Had Lorraine got this detail wrong? If the child hadn't died, Lawrence couldn't have raised her, so where did she go?

Still Grace didn't move. What had shone through Lorraine's story was the love Lawrence and Carmella shared. No matter what hurdle had been placed in their path, they'd found a way over. For them there had been no cultural or social differences and they'd done everything possible to have a life together.

A realisation slipped through her, followed by an acknowledge-ment and an acceptance of the deep emotion she hadn't yet named.

She would do the same thing if it meant she could be with Rowan.

'You sound like you're in the tractor,' Taite said as Rowan answered his mid-morning call. 'It's a weekday. Aren't you supposed to be out smashing rocks?'

'They're called stones, not rocks, and I never smash, I chisel with purpose. The hay needs baling before this next lot of rain arrives.'

'You'd better be quick. The front's supposed to move through tonight.'

Rowan glanced over his shoulder to where large rectangular bales dotted half of his paddock while the rest was nothing but green strips of mown lucerne. 'I'll be here for a while yet.'

'Let me know if you need a hand. I'll do a shift on the tractor and can bring Clancy's gate over.'

'Thanks. Clancy and Heath have offered to move the bales once I'm done.'

'No worries. I'll bring the gate next time I'm in town.'

Rowan chuckled. 'Which will be when?' After the anonymity afforded by the book festival crowds, Taite had returned to being a hermit.

'Don't get too smug,' Taite said, laughter in his voice, 'you may be a free man now the quilting group believes you and Grace are an item, but just you wait until all the wedding and baby talk starts.'

'That cottage of yours had better be big enough for two.'

Rowan hoped his tone reflected mock horror and not the truth that he wouldn't find wedding and baby talk about him and Grace at all abhorrent.

'Only if you bring the beer.'

'Deal.'

'Brenna told me the latest Lawrence update.'

'I bet she did.' Since Grace returned from visiting Lorraine two days ago, it was all Clancy had talked about. 'Does she have a theory about the little girl and if she could still be alive? Clancy has at least three.'

'Brenna too. By the time Grace goes to see Lorraine again it will be up to ten. She's been through every box in the storeroom looking for more photographs.'

'Did she find anything?'

'Only more pictures of Frank's cottage.'

'I still have no idea where his CCTV camera is.'

'My bet is that it's been in plain sight the whole time.'

'Mine too. I should also get to the hut soon to fix the chimney.'

'No rush. It's not going anywhere. Besides, you're going to be busy answering questions about what type of ring you've chosen for Grace.'

'Very funny.'

'It will be next time you go to town. See you at the schoolhouse if we don't get washed away by this rain.'

Their local historical hut volunteer group hoped to finish replacing the shingles on the schoolhouse at Riley's Crossing this weekend.

'This time I won't be late so you'd better leave me some smoko.'

Taite's laughter rumbled before he ended the call.

Even though the sky ahead had been a cheerful blue, when Rowan turned the tractor, he saw that clouds had now gathered on the horizon. He'd texted Grace to let her know he'd be late and she'd replied saying not to come in at all if he ran out of time getting the hay baled. So while technically there was no hurry, apart from beating the bad weather, he still wanted the paddock done asap. He wasn't going a day without seeing Grace. Before he knew it summer would be over.

As he'd suspected, being Captain Patient wasn't proving easy. He hoped he hadn't overstepped the mark when he'd tucked Grace's hair behind her ear on Monday morning. She hadn't seemed to mind or notice; she'd been too excited about Edith's call. Still, such a lapse couldn't happen again. He had to abide by the ground rules Grace had implemented, rules that he hoped she'd one day be ready to do away with. Until then he needed to double-down on making sure he acted as normal as possible whenever around her.

By the time the sun was almost directly overhead, the paddock was filled with hay bales. He returned to the machinery shed to leave the baler so the tractor would be ready for when Clancy and Heath arrived. Clancy would use the hay forks on the tractor front to lift the bales onto the truck that Heath would unload in the hay shed.

After a quick shower and a late lunch, he travelled the familiar route around the valley to Crookwell Park. As he drove up the gravel, his attention went to the high-country backdrop. Cattle would have once grazed on the foothills and spent the summer on the higher subalpine pastures. But for at least the past ten years, especially if the fences were in the same condition as the ones around the mansion, the land would have become home to wildlife as well as deer and brumbies. He'd have a talk to Frank about taking him into the mountains by four-wheel drive to enjoy the views that his wife would have loved.

Once through the front gate, Rowan slowed. No longer did the pall of decay and neglect hang over the house and its gardens. Sunlight reflected off clean windowpanes in the right-side wing and the veranda floorboards were swept clean. Grace's goats had chewed their way through the weeds and taken over from the kangaroos in keeping the grass lawn smooth. There would come a time when Grace would want to reclaim her garden but for the moment the goats were free to roam.

He parked in his usual spot beside Grace's car. While it still sported its city dealership sticker, it was now perpetually covered in country dust. But as much as Grace, and her car, appeared to fit into her new life here, he wasn't under any illusion she didn't have another world to return to.

He left his ute and headed for the mansion. Bundy had poked his head out of the front door as if to let him know that he and Grace were inside. The closer Rowan walked, the louder the old-fashioned music coming from inside. He followed the sound to the ballroom where he found Grace tapping her foot as she bent over large black-and-white photographs spread across a trestle table. She must have been to town as she wore the sleeveless white dress she'd worn to the first day of the festival that hugged every gentle curve. Her dark silken hair was twisted into a loose knot and crystal earrings sparkled on her ears.

Bundy raced over to greet him, causing Grace to turn with a smile. When she looked away to turn off the music coming from her phone, Rowan forced his jaw to relax. If he wasn't careful, what he felt for Grace would be broadcast all over his face. Silence fell across the ballroom, only broken by the faint buzz of bees through the French doors that opened out to the grapevine-covered pergola.

'Hay all done?' she asked.

'Yes and on its way into the shed.'

He showed her a selfie Clancy had sent of her in the tractor cabin with Primrose and Monet running amuck.

Grace laughed. 'Poor Clancy.'

'They only lasted a minute before they were back outside with Heath.'

'I'm surprised it was that long.'

He went over to the table to look at the photos to put physical distance between them. Some of Grace's hair had fallen to brush her cheek and he was having trouble resisting the urge to smooth it off her face.

'Are these from Kathy?'

Grace nodded as she came to stand beside him. 'I took her out to lunch to say thank you for all her help. She had these enlarged and copied.'

'I'm guessing she had nothing to add to what Lorraine said?'

'Unfortunately no. Kathy needs Carmella's last name before she can run some more database searches.' Grace leaned over to trace a line of pine trees that ran along the driveway in a photograph. 'I'd like to plant some more trees. These were all apparently cut down to make bullet boxes during the war.'

'The same happened at Ashcroft so my parents planted poplars when they were married.'

'I think I would have liked your mum and dad,' Grace said softly.

'They would have liked you too.'

Their eyes held before they both looked back at the pictures.

After a moment, Grace pointed to the chandelier in the picture of the old ballroom. 'It's a shame the original was either stolen or sold. At least I have a photo so I know what the replacement should look like.' She glanced across to the replastered far wall. 'It's thanks to you I have a ballroom at all.'

'I'm just doing my job.'

The way her words reached inside to touch him told him from the day he'd met Grace this had always been more than just a job.

As she gazed around the light-filled room with its large windows and ornate ceiling, her expression sobered. 'Do you think Lawrence and Carmella would have been free to enjoy such a beautiful room?'

'Once Lawrence's sisters left he and Carmella would have had the house to themselves, except for perhaps some trustworthy staff. Maybe they only used the apartment when Crookwell Park had visitors.'

Grace stared at the ballroom photo. 'I hope they did dance together. I also hope their children were able to see the chandelier shine like a thousand stars.'

'I'm sure they would have. Was that a 1950s playlist you were playing?'

'Yes, 1951. By the mid-fifties rock and roll was king but in those earlier years they still would have been waltzing in here.'

Just like at the river when the others had been swimming, a wistful yearning washed across her face.

'Grace ... did you ever learn to dance?'

'No, but hardly anyone did.'

'I did ... or rather had to.'

Her brows lifted. 'Really?'

'It's just our secret, otherwise the next thing I'll know is that the quilting ladies have organised a town ball.' He paused while Grace smiled. 'My father might have liked chess but my mother liked to dance. It seemed to be her life's mission to make sure I knew my way around a dancefloor. That way I could partner Clancy when she made her debut and could also waltz at my wedding.'

For the briefest of moments Grace's gaze brushed across his mouth before she bent to examine the closest photograph.

Rowan didn't think to stop himself when he tapped Grace's phone to turn the playlist she'd been listening to back on. An older version of a song he recognised as 'Mockin' Bird Hill' filled the ballroom. He offered Grace his arm.

At first her brow furrowed and then the spontaneity he'd glimpsed when she'd challenged him to a horse race sparkled in her eyes. 'Okay, but I take no responsibility for the damage I'll inflict to your toes.'

The instant she stepped in close to slide one hand into his and place the other on his shoulder, he realised what a risk it was to act on the impulse to give her a moment of frivolity. Her honeysuckle fragrance filled his lungs and when he grasped her waist and settled his hand around hers, he had to fight to keep a sensible distance between them.

He focused on guiding her to at first do simple side steps before stepping forwards and back until they'd mastered the box step. He felt her relax and they were soon travelling around the ballroom to the slower tempo song. By the time the music ended her cheeks were flushed.

Instead of letting go of his hand and moving away, she waited for the next song. 'I can't believe you don't like dancing. That was such fun.'

Rowan smiled before he carefully swept her around the room to a song appropriately titled 'Tennessee Waltz'. Having Grace in his arms more than compensated for every dance lesson he'd ever grumbled about.

When a stream of sunshine broke through the heavy cloud cover to shine through the light rain, Grace's words returned from the afternoon of their ride. The French doors to the pergola were open and it seemed logical, not reckless, to catch her hand and lead her outside so she could dance in the sun shower.

She didn't hesitate to follow or ask what he was doing as they walked beneath the dappled shade of the leafy grapevine into the garden. When he again took her in a dance hold, she laughed as they waltzed.

His own enjoyment lasted less than five seconds. He'd underestimated the effect of the raindrops sliding over the delicate hollows of her collarbones. He'd misjudged the need to keep their bodies apart. His hand no longer rested above Grace's hip but now splayed around the indent of her waist. But most of all he'd miscalculated the point at which his self-control would break.

Not content with showering them with gentle rain, the clouds opened to deliver a sudden deluge. Grace gasped at the onslaught of cold water and closed the gap between them as if seeking warmth. He enfolded her in his arms, savouring the feel of her pressed against him before shifting his weight to turn them towards the pergola.

But when Grace stood on tiptoes to press her mouth to his, all thought of moving to shelter fled. There was no more rain, no more distant music, just an intense heat and a need that consumed them both. Grace's hands slid into his hair and he anchored her to him as though he'd never let her go. Just like on the riverbank, it was as though every adrenaline rush he'd ever felt faded into insignificance. Having Grace fill his arms was like nothing he'd ever experienced or ever would again.

When lightning arced overhead, he edged far enough away to link her fingers with his. They headed for the pergola but before they made it through the French doors and into the ballroom, Grace was kissing him again. As if from a long distance away he heard the faint voice of reason.

He lifted his head to speak, not caring that his words would be hoarse. Grace already had to know how much she undid him. He caressed her warm cheek. 'Real world, remember?'

She placed her hand over his heart and took his hand to place over hers. Beneath the almost transparent white cotton of her dress he could feel the steady pulse of her heartbeat.

'This is our real world. It's also the only one I'm certain of. I don't want to keep pretending there isn't something between us ... I hope you feel the same.'

Rowan's only answer was to frame her face with his hands and kiss her to show her how much he shared her thoughts. This time she was the one who drew away. Her fingers wrapped around his and she led him not into the ballroom but to the French doors on the opposite side of the pergola. She followed the hallway to the far-right corner where she opened the door to reveal a room containing a large antique iron bed and a bedside table covered in candles. 'I come here when I can't sleep.'

When she shivered, he pulled her close to rest his forehead against hers. He had so much to say he didn't want to overwhelm her. There was also a trace of fear inside him that he didn't want to examine. He kept his question simple. 'Are you sure?'

'I am. This has nothing to do with my grief. Even before I lost my parents I can see now that I was living a half life ... I don't want to anymore.' Her beautiful smile flashed as she unbuttoned his wet shirt. 'I want a summer of dancing in the rain.'

He dipped his head to kiss her and silence his words that a single season of doing such a thing would never be enough. He wanted a lifetime.

CHAPTER
17

Just like on so many other mornings when Grace came awake in her bed in the cottage bedroom, she heard the warble of a magpie, the croak of the frog in the water tank pipe and the splatter of rain on the tin roof. The familiar sounds soothed and grounded her. Against her ankle she could feel Bundy's warm weight and if she opened her eyes light would shine through the gap in the curtains that she could never fully close.

She kept her eyelids shut. So much was the same and yet after yesterday afternoon with Rowan so much was different too. Good different. Hopeful different. Life-affirming different.

She hadn't come to the mountains looking for anyone to heal her. She'd been determined to travel through her grief on her own and it was a journey she was still on. But from day one, Rowan with his easy grin, empathy and restless intensity had thrown her. She'd had to leave her comfort zone and in the process she'd found a part of her that had been lost beneath the weight of her childhood and her own expectations.

It hadn't been her parents who had been the drive behind her workaholic lifestyle. They'd only ever wanted her to be happy. Instead it had been her tunnel-vision sense of duty that had cut all the fun from her life. The suspicion grew that while her parents had been genuine in their desire to spend their twilight years in a small close-knit community, their plans to move to Bundilla had also been for her. They could see what her life would have ended up like if she'd continued on the path she'd been on.

But she now knew what was truly important. Yesterday, she'd lied when she'd said to Rowan that she just wanted a summer of dancing in the rain. She didn't. She wanted the whole kit and caboodle. She wanted rocking horses, dolls and toy trains, she wanted a wedding waltz, but most of all she wanted to grow old with the man she loved.

Her eyes opened and she slid out of bed so as not to wake Bundy. But now wasn't the time to jump headfirst into anything, even if she was embracing her spontaneous side. Rowan still had things he was working through about the past choices he'd made. As relaxed and at peace as he'd seemed when she'd lain beside him and his fingers had drifted through her hair, she'd sensed his underlying tension. At least they now had the rest of the summer to navigate through what exactly their relationship was and where she hoped it might lead.

Smiling, she went to check her phone that was charging in the kitchen. It had run flat when she'd talked to Rowan until after midnight. He'd already sent a text to see how she'd slept and a photo of Monet and Primrose playing tug of war with a gardening glove. As it was a Saturday, he was helping Clancy rearrange her flower packing shed. Grace began tapping out a reply when her phone rang.

'So you are in the land of the living,' Aubrey said, her too-awake face filling the screen. 'Even if you are in your PJs.'

'It's the weekend, and besides, it's not that late. Even Bundy only just woke up.' Grace stifled a yawn.

Aubrey didn't immediately answer. 'You're smiling again.'

'I'm yawning.'

'That's the smuggest yawn I've ever seen. When are you seeing that stonemason of yours next?'

She left it too late to ignore the memory of Rowan exploring the sensitive skin of her neck before he said he'd see her after lunch today. Heat fired in her cheeks.

Aubrey's gaze sharpened. 'Grace? You didn't.'

She couldn't help but again smile.

Aubrey groaned. 'There obviously were even more fireworks … and no, I don't want to know any specifics as you'll just make me jealous.' She paused as concern shadowed her expression. 'Do I need to explain what going slow means?'

'Despite how it looks, we're not rushing into anything. I suggested a summer fling just to keep things light between us.'

'Did Rowan agree?'

'Well, he didn't disagree.'

Aubrey laughed, her face relaxing. 'Of course he didn't. What happens after the summer ends?'

'I'm hoping what's between us doesn't have a time limit.'

'What about your life here?'

'I haven't really thought beyond next month, but I'll need to come back to decide what parts of my city life could work here.'

'You're welcome to couch surf anytime.' Aubrey's tone grew teasing. 'Not that I'll be expecting you soon. Nothing is going to separate you from that stonemason of yours now.' Aubrey paused as beeping sounded in the background. She blew Grace a kiss. 'Work calls. We'll chat later.'

Grace returned her phone to the bench. After she let Bundy outside for a run, she propped the door open with a gumboot so he could come back in whenever he was ready. Already counting down the hours until she'd see Rowan again, she needed to keep busy so she didn't spend the morning watching the clock. She'd make jam drops for when she visited Lorraine tomorrow and take some to Frank. He'd expressed an interest in seeing the photos Kathy had given her as some had been of his cottage.

Once she'd had breakfast and a shower and the jam drops had cooled, she readied herself to go outside. It was on rainy days like this that she needed a farm gator. She took her oilskin from off the peg behind the front door and slipped the jam drops container into the deep pocket. After putting on the wide-brimmed hat Clancy and Brenna had helped her choose, she pulled on her gumboots. Bundy was going to get soaked, but he didn't seem to mind as they splashed their way along the garden path.

Their first stop was to check that the goats had fresh hay and were dry in the old stables. Grace lingered to watch little Lavender and Rebel as they jumped and pirouetted over any obstacles they could find while the others munched. Then, pulling her hat brim low, she continued around the back of the mansion.

Behind the foothills the granite peaks were invisible due to the low and moody cloud.

'If this rain keeps up,' Grace said, glancing at a very wet Bundy as he walked beside her, 'we're going to need a boat to get home.'

The rocky hillside to their right was now awash with rivulets that ran over the exposed veins of bluestone, while on either side of the family burial plot temporary streams coursed down usually dry gullies.

Unlike the first time she'd followed the track to Frank's cottage, this trip she knew where she was going. It wasn't long until the trees thinned and Frank's home came into view. She increased her pace as much as she could in the heavy gumboots as she and Bundy squelched their way to the front door.

Somehow Frank always knew when they were coming and would greet them at the door. But this time it remained closed. She stepped beneath the small awning and knocked.

'Come in,' Frank's voice called out.

'We're a bit wet,' Grace said, opening the door. Already puddles of water were collecting on the stone steps.

'There's a peg on the wall to hang your coat.' Frank's voice sounded like it was coming from the kitchen. 'And towels in the laundry.'

After she'd mopped up after herself and the kelpie, they went in search of Frank. It was unusual for him to not be bustling around the cottage. He gave her a smile from where he sat at the kitchen table, a crossword in front of him and his left leg elevated by a cushion on a small stool.

'I'm fine,' Frank said to her unspoken question. 'I slipped in the rain and my gammy knee didn't like having to keep me upright.'

'That doesn't sound good.'

'It's my own fault. I should have known better than to go out in this weather.'

She searched his face before she sat the jam drops and photographs on the table. Frank's expression appeared relaxed and there was no obvious sign he was in pain.

He took the pictures out of their plastic folder. 'I've been looking forward to seeing these.'

While Frank sorted through the photographs, Grace went to make a pot of tea. As she placed two mugs on the table she caught him squinting at an image that he held up as if to take a closer look.

With a sigh he glanced at the doorway. 'Sorry, Grace ... could you please get my glasses? They're on the small round table in the living room.'

The living room was a part of the cottage she hadn't yet visited and it proved to be a cosy space. The dark sombre leather of the lounge was offset by a red patterned floor rug as well as touches of bright colour around the room. On a dark wooden bookcase stood a collection of vintage books with faded crimson covers beside which sat a pair of wooden Pinocchios dressed in red coats and hats. Frank's glasses were where he said they'd be, sitting next to a cherry-red enamel box.

With his reading glasses now on, they discussed the photographs and enjoyed the jam drops while outside the rain continued to pour.

Grace pointed to the picture of the ballroom chandelier. 'This is my new obsession. I'm determined to find one exactly the same.'

Frank gazed at her over the top of his glasses. 'Why not look for the original?'

'I've tried. It wasn't listed in the online auction house catalogue so must have either been sold beforehand or stolen.'

'Let's hope a private collector made the old owner an offer they couldn't refuse. Those vandals already did enough damage.' Frank looked up, a smile in his faded gaze. 'Tell Rowan I haven't forgotten about looking for the boundary fence map. It's just not where I thought it was.'

Before Grace could dwell on why Frank was smiling at her in such a way, his attention refocused on the billiards room picture. He seemed to be examining it very closely.

'Are you looking for something?' she asked.

'I'm just trying to see what the pieces are on the chessboard.'

Grace leaned over to see the blurred image of a chessboard sitting on a table in the corner of the room. 'I didn't even know that was there.'

'It was the first thing I saw.'

Once they'd finished their tea and Grace was sure Frank was right for lunch and had anything else he might need within reach, she put their mugs in the dishwasher. 'Let me know if your leg isn't feeling better by this afternoon.'

'Don't you worry; it does this every now and then.' Frank inclined his head towards the kitchen dresser. 'In that blue bowl is the gator key. You can bring it back over when the rain stops.'

Grace kissed his cheek. 'Thank you.'

By the time Grace reached the front door of her cottage she had no doubt she was getting a side-by-side. Not only was it fun to drive, it was practical and would save her pushing a wheelbarrow full of weeds around the massive garden.

Despite her and Bundy taking their time to eat lunch, when they were done there was still an hour until Rowan was due to arrive. Not bothering with her oilskin, Grace threw on the only warm top she had, a fine woollen pink jumper she'd found in the charity shop, and grabbed an umbrella for the short walk to the mansion.

Bundy had fallen asleep on the lounge in the living room, so she let herself outside. As she needed her gumboots, she propped the door open with her cowgirl boot in case Bundy later decided to follow.

She left the umbrella at the front entrance of the mansion and headed for the far back right corner. As she passed the room where she'd taken Rowan yesterday afternoon, a warm contentment flowed through her. While the part of her that would always miss her parents mourned that they would never meet him, her heart knew that they would approve.

Once in the end storage room filled with the items that she'd bought off the local online marketplace, she set about rearranging the area to accommodate a kitchen hutch that would arrive tomorrow. She dragged the oak dresser that she was planning to turn into a bespoke bathroom vanity against the wall and turned her attention to the large table that would be perfect for quilting. She managed to push it a little to the left. She just needed more space between the table and door to get the hutch in.

Above the loud drum of rain on the tin roof she thought she heard a crack. When she stopped to listen, she also thought she heard a rumble. Then, not sure if she'd really heard anything at all, she went to move the table again. This time she lifted it instead of pushing, but the solid wood and heavy steel proved too cumbersome. When she dropped the end, she didn't think the force would have been strong enough to shake the wall behind her but it was as though it had moved.

When a loud and definite cracking sound came from over her head and chunks of ceiling plaster plummeted to the ground, she had no doubt that what she'd seen was real. It was as though some great force had been exerted on the corner outside walls, pushing them inwards.

At a conference in Auckland, she'd been told in the event of an earthquake to drop, cover and hold. While this couldn't be an earthquake, she'd need to do something to protect herself if she couldn't reach the doorway in the next few seconds. But before she could move, the ceiling in front of her gave way to block her exit. With pieces of plaster falling on her head and shoulders, she had no choice but to spin and dive under the nearby table.

The roof tore apart with a metallic screech and it was as though it were raining stones. The wood covering her shuddered beneath the onslaught as she held on to the table legs. Icy water flooded the floor and soaked into her jeans. All she could breathe was the cloying smell of wet earth as she curled into a ball. As much as she loved her parents, she refused to even think about joining them. She had a life to live with Rowan and she wasn't having their future stolen like it had been from Lawrence and Carmella. She'd wait until the roof stopped falling and find a way to get free. Then, something hard hit the side of her head and the world went dark.

∝

Rowan took the familiar turn-off from the road that skirted the valley to the one that would take him to Crookwell Park. His wipers worked continuously to keep the windscreen clear. Usually he'd have country music blaring but today his ute cabin was quiet except for the sound of water sloshing beneath his tyres. It was just him and his thoughts about Grace. Thoughts that he was very careful to keep controlled and measured. He was not freefalling into the emotional insanity of what he experienced with Eloise, even if he now knew those feelings hadn't been based on anything of substance.

As much as what happened between him and Grace yesterday filled him with happiness, there was still a residual unease he couldn't shake. It was nothing to do with the way he felt about her. From the afternoon they'd met, she'd been the only woman he'd ever want.

His disquiet was to do with how he felt about himself. A niggle of doubt remained about his ability to cope with deep emotion. Instead of handling his grief with a maturity and sensibility like Clancy had, he'd run, first to Eloise and then overseas. He couldn't again let down anyone he loved, especially Grace.

He didn't know what he'd done that morning with Clancy in the shed to let on that things had changed between him and Grace, but they'd only been working together for a brief while when his sister had stopped sweeping the floor to grin at him.

'Finally. It's about time you and Grace became the real deal. I was beginning to think you had more rocks in your head than what's outside in the garden wall.'

'Is it that obvious?'

'Only to me and Heath … it has been since day one. That's the only reason why I meddled. You and Grace are magic together.'

'There is together and *together* and we are still feeling our way.'

Clancy had sent him another smile as she resumed sweeping. 'Mum and Dad would be so pleased.'

Clancy's comment had made him smile too.

Rowan slowed as he caught up to a battered Hilux travelling under the speed limit. He was just about to overtake when his phone rang. He didn't recognise the number but answered by Bluetooth as he settled back behind the slower car.

'Rowan, it's Frank. Aubrey gave me your number.'

Frank's voice was almost unrecognisable. Not in a stressed or unsteady way, but grim and determined.

'Everything okay?'

'We have a situation.' Rowan's blood chilled. Frank would only call if Grace was involved. 'I'm sending you CCTV photos. You need to get to Crookwell Park. The back right corner has collapsed.

Grace took my gator and my car battery's flat again. Steve's coming to get me, the SES are on their way. I'm hoping …' Frank paused as if to swallow. 'I'm hoping Grace isn't inside, as Bundy's in sight. Her phone just might be flat and that's why I can't reach her.'

Rowan overtook the old-model Hilux. 'I'm five minutes away.'

'Great.' Relief deepened Frank's voice. 'You'll know how to read the old house. Keep me updated.'

'I will.'

Rowan ended the call. Despite the cold fear sweeping through him, between the slick road conditions and his speed, he couldn't waste time stopping to look at Frank's photos. The main thing to focus on was that Frank had seen there was a problem and help was on the way. Rowan had never been more thankful that Frank had a camera concealed on his land somewhere.

His grip tightened on the steering wheel. The structural integrity of the back-right corner had somehow become compromised. It was the area where he and Grace had spent yesterday afternoon. Today she could very well have been pottering in the same room or next door. He had no doubt that the walls were sound so they shouldn't have randomly collapsed. What perhaps wasn't stable was the rocky outcrop behind the mansion. If the torrential rain had weakened the hillside's stability and caused a landslip, the affected corner would have been in the path of any mudslide.

He left the bitumen for Grace's gravel road. Stones flicked up beneath his ute. He had to hold on to the hope that if Bundy was visible then Grace was safe. They rarely were apart. To his relief the front gate was open as the goats were in their yard and the stables out of the rain.

As he sped up to the cottage, through the frantic windscreen wipers he could make out the shape of the gator parked outside the front door. His mouth dried. The rocky hillside had given way. There was no mistaking the mound of dirt and debris banked up against what was left of the right back corner.

He stopped beside Grace's car and reefed on the parking brake so he could scan the photos Frank had sent to his phone. Wherever Frank's camera was it provided an elevated view. In one image he could see the collapsed roof of the end room while in another Bundy was running across the driveway towards the mansion. Uncaring that he'd soon be soaked, he left his seat. Even though the hollow feeling in his gut told him he already knew the answer, before he went to check the mansion he needed to confirm Grace wasn't in the cottage.

But as he dashed out into the storm, he changed direction. There was no doubt Grace was where he'd prayed she wasn't. Bundy had appeared at the mansion front door, his bark agitated and loud. As Rowan raced up the steps, he registered Grace's umbrella propped up by the entryway. He sent a quick text to Frank and one to Clancy as he followed Bundy around the hallway corner.

He slowed to look where he was going and dragged in a deep breath. He'd be no help to Grace if he didn't do a risk assessment. As he went he checked for cracks and any other signs of movement but somehow the old stones had held together to confine the landslide damage to the far corner.

At the end of the right-side hallway Bundy paced outside a door whining. When he reached the kelpie, he placed a hand on Bundy's head to reassure him and dialled Grace's number. A faint ringing made his jaw ache that only intensified when she didn't pick up. At least he knew she had her phone. If he could hear the ring it meant there was enough space in between the mud and rocks for sound to carry as well as air for Grace to breathe.

Before he could do anything to get to her, he needed to finish assessing the potential for any further structural collapse. He checked the hallway around the end door and while there were cracks, they weren't significant. He then looked in the adjacent room where he and Grace had been together, making sure he didn't glance at the bed. The control keeping his emotions in check felt like it was fraying with every second that Grace remained trapped. Again, while the wall this room shared with the one next door had sustained cracks, there was no danger of it giving way.

With Bundy running by his side, he returned to his ute. After getting what he needed from his toolbox to remove the door, plus his heavy leather gloves, he raced inside. His phone in his pocket vibrated almost continuously. He kept tabs on who had rung or left a message. If Grace had been knocked out and regained consciousness she might call. Clancy had texted that she and Heath would be there soon. He replied with a structural status update to pass on to the SES.

Once outside the door, he dialled Grace again. The faint ringing stopped before Grace's dazed but steady voice said, 'Rowan.'

He briefly closed his eyes. There were so many words in his head and his heart fighting to be said, but he managed to settle for a calm and simple, 'Are you okay?'

'My head's sore and I'm cold. I've been asleep under the table.' His clamped hold on his phone eased fractionally at the news she'd found a pocket of safety. 'My phone's also going flat.'

'Have you enough battery to send me a photo of what's around you and what's between you and the door, if you know where it is?'

Grace ended the call and he resisted the urgent need to dial straight back.

Photos whooshed through to his phone. Shoulders locked, he studied them. The table had given Grace a cavity beyond which there was a mass of bluestone and mud that looked like it was being held back by another piece of furniture that had toppled over. The next image showed a similar picture of debris but at the top there was a gap and he could see the door.

He called her.

She answered after the first ring. 'Were the photos any good?'

'Perfect. I'm taking off the door.'

'Rowan ... thank you.'

He kept his voice light as emotion threatened to swamp him. 'You're welcome. I'll call you soon.'

From the corner of his eye he saw Bundy run along the hallway. Somebody else had arrived. Not wasting any time, he used a hammer, nail punch and plyers to pop the door pins out of the hinges. He then unlatched the door handle. Moving carefully, he removed the door to provide access to the room. A pile of rocks fell out into the hallway to hit his steel-capped work boots.

Through the rubble he could make out the corner of a large sturdy table and the thin gap below the rim. He assessed the roof, which hung in precarious angles along the room sides, but over Grace and the area between her and the door was a massive hole through which the rain fell. While this was a positive from an SES safety perspective, a path would still have to be cleared and this would take time. He sent some quick photos to Clancy to show whoever was outside and then called Grace.

'Hi.' Her voice sounded brighter. 'I can see you.'

He blew her a kiss and the sound of her soft laughter caused the fear he'd been keeping a tight grip on to uncoil. His hold on his phone became white-knuckled. He'd come so close to losing her.

Footsteps sounded in the hallway behind him but he didn't look away from the gap in the debris below the table edge. He mightn't be able to see Grace but she could see him and he wasn't breaking their connection until he had to. 'The calvary's about to arrive.'

'You know this is going to take months to rebuild. Just as well I happen to know a stonemason.'

He took a moment to answer. The humour in her words and her dignified strength was almost his undoing. All he wanted to do was rip through the rubble. But getting her out had to be done properly and it would take more than him to remove the debris.

'It is,' he said, his jaw feeling as hard as the stones that separated him from the woman he loved. 'We'll get you out of there as soon as we can.'

Time seemed to lose all meaning as the SES volunteers worked inside the mansion to free Grace and outside to stabilise the mudslide and to put a tarpaulin over the missing roof. To everyone's relief the rain soon stopped.

Clancy brought him a dry jacket and a constant supply of coffee while he helped remove the internal rubble and Frank kept him in the loop as to when Aubrey would arrive from Sydney. She'd jumped in her car as soon as Frank had called.

When the last of the wreckage in front of the table was finally removed, Heath took hold of Rowan's arm to stop him from rushing forwards. 'Let the ambos do their job,' he said quietly.

After a muddy and dazed Grace was assessed, she was moved from beneath the table onto a stretcher.

Heath again spoke, voice low. 'Rowan, breathe. Have a shower then go to the hospital. Clance will pack Grace a bag of her things from the cottage.'

He only nodded. He didn't trust himself to speak. Grace's eyes had been closed as they carried her past and out to the ambulance.

Rowan made the trip to Ashcroft and then back to town in record time. Even though Grace had texted from the hospital to say that while she was concussed she was feeling better, he needed to see for himself she was okay. She'd messaged again to let him know that later that day she would be transferred to the larger Tumut hospital for a CT scan to check for head fractures and bleeding. Since then she'd been silent and he hoped she'd be sleeping.

Except when he walked through the Bundilla hospital doors, he not only knew she wasn't resting but also what room she was in. Aubrey's distinctive voice directed him along the corridor.

At the half-closed door, he hesitated. His world had gone back to spinning. The adrenaline that coursed through him was only matched by the emotions that thrashed inside. The more he tried to control them, the more they rioted. He rolled his rigid shoulders but before he could walk through the doorway, as if she'd had a sense he was there, Aubrey slipped from Grace's room. Dressed in a black suit with a crisp white blouse, she looked like she'd literally stepped out of a board meeting. She gestured at him to follow and they walked to a quiet corner.

She spoke first. 'I could almost hug you right now. Thank you for all that you did.'

'It was a joint effort.'

It was no surprise when she searched his face. His voice had been little more than a hoarse whisper. He folded his arms and held her gaze.

Aubrey lifted a brow. 'Your manly steely silence doesn't work with me. I know you're hurting, which is why we need to be on the same page to do the best thing for Grace. After she's been checked out at Tumut, I'm taking her to Sydney to recover.'

He frowned.

'I know you don't want to let her out of your sight, but you also know it's the best place for her. I'm the boss queen. I'll make sure she rests. She'll just smile and sweet-talk you into letting her do whatever she wants.'

His frown eased. Aubrey was right.

She spoke again, her tone surprisingly gentle. 'She's happy to go and this is probably the only time she will be. While she's with me she can sort out the loose ends of her city life.'

'How long?'

'However long she needs.'

He unfolded his arms. 'I'll bring her home.'

'That depends ...' Aubrey pinned him with her usual narrow-eyed stare. 'Is this just a summer thing for you?'

'The short answer is no.' Even though this was how Grace had framed things yesterday, he couldn't lie about how he felt. 'The long answer is Grace is still grieving and I will wait however many summers it takes to be with her.'

Aubrey's expression didn't change. 'It doesn't matter if you're an exception to the rule that if someone looks too good to be true, they are ... if you ever hurt Grace I'm still willing to get that criminal record.'

'Copy.'

Aubrey's expression softened into a genuine smile. 'We'd better get back before she decides she's well enough to check herself out and go home.'

Rowan followed Aubrey into the room and went straight to Grace's side. Her skin had always been pale but now without the covering of mud her face was ashen white. A bruise marred her cheek and an angry scrape over her jaw left the corner of her mouth swollen. He wasn't surprised to find his hand shake as he brushed back her hair and pressed a kiss to her forehead.

Her fingers gripped his. 'I won't be gone for long.'

He squeezed her hand. 'I'll look after Bundy and the goats until you get back.'

'Rowan …'

The arrival of a nurse and a doctor he didn't recognise had Grace stop. Rowan again kissed her forehead before he reluctantly let go of her hand.

Aubrey gave him a nod as he walked to the door. She would stay to make sure Grace would be okay here and in Tumut hospital. At the doorway he turned to take a last look at Grace but all he could see was the doctor's back.

Rowan quit the room.

He didn't again look over his shoulder or slow even if the feeling grew that he'd just taken the biggest risk of his life. Once Grace returned to the city and a familiar world where she hadn't experienced the trauma of what she'd just endured, she might choose to not come back.

As for him … as much as he loved her and as resolute as he was to not lose his way a second time, the chaos tightening his chest and making it difficult to breathe reminded him that even the strongest of stones could break.

CHAPTER
18

Nothing felt right. Grace plumped up her pillow in Aubrey's guest room and stared at the same spot on the ceiling she'd stared at for the past three days.

The noise outside the window was not magpies, frogs or goats. Instead traffic hummed, sirens blared and whatever the construction workers were doing across the busy road it involved lots of clanging. The night sky never really got dark and the air didn't feel fresh as it circulated through the air-conditioning vents. As for not having Bundy by her side ... She just wanted to go home to Crookwell Park.

She pushed off the bedcovers. Along with the headaches, dizziness, the noise and light sensitivity, she'd been warned she might feel more emotional thanks to her concussion. Well, she sure ticked that box. She couldn't think about Rowan without feeling an overwhelming need to talk to him or see him. Then when they did chat, she missed him so much she had to keep their conversations casual as otherwise she would burst into tears. There was so much she needed to say to him but it would have to wait until she saw him again.

She sighed as she swapped the oversized T-shirt she slept in for the black activewear Aubrey had lent her. What she wouldn't give for jeans and a loose cotton work shirt. At least today she had plans to leave Aubrey's unit. Even though her CT scan had been clear, Aubrey had taken her nurse duties very seriously. Nothing Grace had said could convince her to relax her rest-and-recuperation rules. No wonder Aubrey always emerged triumphant in any work negotiation or merger.

'Did you want cinnamon in your banana smoothie?' Aubrey called out.

Grace had drawn the line at seaweed-green smoothies but had conceded to having one that at least looked a drinkable colour. 'Yes, please.'

She walked into the small kitchen in Aubrey's chic flat with a water view that no longer impressed her. It was mountains, not waves, that Grace yearned to see.

Aubrey cast a quick eye over her. 'You're looking better … marginally. If you have no more neck pain in two days we can go out for lunch.'

Grace sat at the small kitchen table. 'So … what's your itinerary for today?'

Aubrey paused in adding a banana to her blender. 'Why?'

'No reason.'

'Grace Davenport, don't give me that innocent look. You're going to skip out when I'm in an online meeting, aren't you?'

Aubrey had been working from home this week.

'If the roles were reversed you would have snuck out days ago.'

Aubrey's frown was fierce, but Grace had never been intimidated even on that first day when they'd met in the school library.

'I'm going stir crazy cooped up in here. I've got a to-do list and I'm doing it today. I'm feeling heaps better and I won't drive, I'll catch the train.'

Aubrey remained silent, then she sighed. 'No trains. They'll be too loud. I've had a client cancel so can have a two-hour lunch. We could go to the storage unit then.'

Grace nodded. She hadn't needed to explain that on the top of her list was to look through the things she'd saved from her parents' house. She wanted to find her mother's tea set to match with the one in the apartment plus she wanted the quilt her mother had passed down from her own mother. It was time to use it again. She also wanted the box of her father's favourite books for the Crookwell Park library.

'Thank you.'

Aubrey still didn't resume making Grace's smoothie. 'Cross your heart you won't sneak out because I know once you make your mind up to do something nothing will stop you.'

Grace drew a cross over her heart.

Aubrey smiled. 'Now you might want to cover your ears.'

Grace did so as the blender annihilated the banana and whatever else Aubrey had snuck in there.

While Aubrey went to make a work call, Grace made some calls as well. She left a message for Ruth to apologise for not seeing Lorraine and that she would be in touch again as soon as she was back. She also called her colleague who was managing her interior styling business to see if they could meet for a catch-up. Then she left a message for the real estate agent renting out her inner-city apartment. Finally, to silence a persistent niggle in her brain, she went through the pictures on her phone that she'd taken of the hidden rooms and when she was certain that her new theory made sense, she sent Kathy an email.

She was just sharing a mid-morning cup of tea with Aubrey when a call came in on Grace's tablet. Quilting club was on.

She waved to all the faces gathered around Clancy who held her phone high to make sure Grace could see everyone. 'Hello.'

Voices all sounded at once before she heard Sandra say, 'One at a time, please, ladies.'

Vernette spoke first. 'We miss seeing your smiling face, Grace. Hope you're back soon.'

'I hope so too.'

Aubrey leaned over to see who Grace was talking to and in the process she too appeared on the screen.

Clancy smiled. 'Hi, Aubrey.'

Aubrey waved but before she could sit back in her seat, Norma spoke. 'Aubrey, you must come to Bundilla again. You looked like you were having such a nice time in the café with our lovely young vet Trent.'

'Yes,' Lucinda said. 'We're such a friendly small town and we love introducing new people around.'

'You mean matchmaking,' Aubrey said, expression deadpan.

Grace went to speak in case anyone took offence but before she could, the group laughed.

'My, my,' Vernette said, still chuckling. 'You're a feisty one and also a non-believer.' The older lady winked. 'We do like a challenge.'

'Did that sweet old lady just sass me?' Aubrey muttered so only Grace could hear.

Grace nodded, trying not to smile. 'She also lip-reads,' she said from the corner of her mouth as Vernette chuckled.

Aubrey gave the group a nod. 'Ladies ... as much as I'd love to chat, I've work to do. Enjoy the rest of your day.'

As soon as she was off screen, Aubrey pulled her I-would-rather-have-my-wisdom-teeth-out face that she usually reserved for when she went on a date. She disappeared into her bedroom to work on her laptop.

After Grace talked to the quilting ladies for a little longer, Clancy turned to the women beside her. 'Okay, everyone, I'm going outside to talk to Grace *alone*. Brenna is on guard at the door to make sure there will be no eavesdropping.'

The camera bobbed as Clancy left the corrugated tin hall and went to stand in the shade beside the mottled trunk of a gum tree.

'How are you?' Clancy asked as the camera steadied.

'Feeling better every day.' Grace paused to check Clancy's face. Her eyes were serious. 'I'm hoping to be back on the weekend.'

'Wonderful ... Has Rowan been in touch today?'

'This morning. He sent photos of Lavender and Rebel. Why?'

'Did he say he was going anywhere?'

'Only to Taite and Brenna's hut to fix the chimney. He has Bundy with him. Instead of doing day trips he's camping out so he said he won't have phone service for a few days.'

Clancy seemed to relax. 'The time to himself will be helpful.'

She'd never talked to Clancy about her and Rowan but she knew how close they were so she hoped Clancy approved.

'Clancy, why did you ask if I knew where he was? What's wrong?'

'Nothing really ... Rowan's been a little quiet and subdued since you left. But if he's told you where he's going, it's all good. I worry too much. Now I'd better get inside before Brenna loses her patience. Make sure you keep resting. Concussion was the only thing to keep Rowan on the lounge as broken bones certainly didn't slow him down.'

Clancy gave her a wave before disappearing from the screen.

Grace's first instinct was to return to Bundilla and find Rowan. Despite Clancy's reassurance, she was clearly worried about her brother. It was also apparent that she suspected he'd gone to the isolated hut to do more than fix the chimney.

But another instinct urged caution. Grace had always known Rowan had things to work through. Something about what had happened to her could have proved triggering. Or he could be having second thoughts about them being together, even for the summer. The question was, did she stay away to give him space, even though she knew he was hurting, or did she go to help him talk through things knowing that he'd gone somewhere to be by himself? Maybe he wouldn't want her there.

She stared unseeingly at the now blank tablet. Just like on the day that seemed so long ago when she'd left the city and reached the crest in the road, she only had two choices. Both had the potential to break her heart.

∞

'Thanks so much for your help, mate.' Rowan patted Bundy's side as the kelpie leaned against his leg while they inspected the now straight hut chimney. 'Job well done.'

When they'd arrived three days ago, the neat rows of sticks that he'd placed at the entrance of the wombat burrow last visit hadn't been disturbed. So with the abandoned hole right to be filled in he'd restabilised the ground so the chimney would again be supported. The stones had then been numbered, dismantled and reassembled.

He rubbed at a new ache in his lower back that matched the dull pain in his once-broken leg. It wasn't the work that had punished his body but the speed at which he'd toiled.

Rowan again patted Bundy. 'Let's hit the road.'

He and the kelpie had finished breakfast and his tools and swag were already loaded. He went inside to tidy the hut and replenish the wood pile for the next visitor. Once everything was how he'd found it and there was no trace of him having been there, he glanced around the clearing.

The two magpies who had kept him and Bundy company were perched on the wooden horse yards as if ready to watch the latest instalment of the strange things humans did. He took a last look at the blue-tinged ridges through the gap in the trees behind the rustic hut. At sunset he'd stop whatever he was doing to watch crimson light fire across the sky before the sun slowly lowered.

Bundy jumped onto the back of his ute and Rowan smiled. The kelpie was ready to go as much as he was. While he loved sleeping in a swag under the stars that up here seemed so close he could touch them, he too had somewhere else he needed to be. He slid behind the wheel and fired up the Land Cruiser engine to head for home. He just hoped that what seemed so clear in his head still made sense when he reached there. He also had to hold on to the belief that his trust in himself hadn't been misplaced.

In the days after Grace had left for Sydney, he'd done nothing but think. He'd followed her cue to keep things light and breezy whenever they spoke, but on his own he allowed his feelings free rein. It hadn't worked suppressing them when he'd lost his parents; they'd only intensified to such a point that they controlled him. So, to deal with the stress of almost losing the woman he loved, he didn't try to fight them. He already knew if he did, they'd break him.

Instead, just like an adrenaline rush, he harnessed the energy of his emotions and rode the wave through his fear. Now on the other side all he felt was calm and in control. He hadn't run to the hut to escape; he'd simply come to fix the chimney. He slowed as kangaroos jumped across the bush track to disappear into the trees. He'd also needed to give Grace time to recover.

It had now been almost a week and whether Aubrey approved or not he had a long drive to make once he dropped Bundy off at Ashcroft. If Grace's city life was going to pull her back, he'd remind her of all the things her new Bundilla world offered.

Once he reached the valley floor, he continued past Taite's cottage and the Glenwood Station homestead. Even if Taite and Brenna hadn't been away on a trek, he wouldn't have stopped. As soon as he reached the bitumen road and his phone showed a consistent signal, he called Grace. When she didn't pick up he left a voice message asking what she was doing that afternoon.

He then called Aubrey who answered after two rings. 'So, rock boy, you're back in civilisation?'

'I never left.'

'Anywhere that doesn't have three-phase power is not civilisation.'

He chuckled. 'How's our patient?'

There was a subtle pause. 'Much better. So much so, she's out.'

'What time will she be back?'

'No idea. Why? Don't even think about driving up here.'

He frowned as the thought formed that maybe Grace had slotted back into her old life and wasn't ready to come home. It had been a few days since they'd been in contact. If she was out and about, it wasn't her concussion keeping her in Sydney. 'Too late.'

'Rowan.' Aubrey's voice was serious. 'You need to talk to her first. Where are you now?'

'Almost home.'

'Stay there until Grace calls. That's an order, which I strongly advise you not to ignore. I've got to go, my laptop's having a hissy fit.'

Before he could reply, Aubrey ended the call.

After trying Grace again and getting her voicemail, he called Clancy. When she also didn't pick up, he left a message to say he would be home soon. Once he arrived, Primrose and Monet greeted him and Bundy with such exuberance it was as though they'd been gone for years.

He scratched Iris's special spot on her neck as the two younger dogs, their yips high-pitched, tore off after Bundy as they raced each other away from the coach house. 'I know,' he said to the gentle golden retriever. 'We all need ear plugs.'

Clancy walked through the back garden to give him a hug. 'Chimney all fixed?'

'It is.'

He studied her face. Before he'd left he hadn't missed the worried looks she'd been sending him when she didn't think he was watching. Now she just appeared her relaxed and usual cheerful self.

'Cuppa?'

He shook his head. 'I'm going to have a hot shower and throw some things into a bag.'

He didn't need to say where he was going. Clancy would know.

She smiled. 'Even in summer that bucket shower at the hut is freezing. I'll pack you some blueberry muffins for Grace and for you to eat on the way.' She half turned. 'Before you go, do you have time to find Jindy? She's off somewhere and Goliath's going nuts. She'll probably be in the snow gum paddock as all the other gates are closed.'

'I'll take Goliath to get rid of some of his energy. Ash still there?'

Clancy nodded. 'He is. Thanks.'

If it wasn't cattle rubbing on gates to open them, it was the horses. Whereas Clancy's quiet gelding Ash would stay in his paddock, Jindy's brumby instincts would encourage her to go exploring. As for Goliath, he would be missing the buckskin mare and proving a handful. The ride would do him good. It would also give Grace a chance to call. If she didn't, he was still driving to Sydney. The things he needed to say had to be said face to face. The risk of letting Grace slip away far outweighed Aubrey being mad at him.

Showered and caffeinated—he'd need the extra edge for anything Goliath threw at him—he saddled the agitated blood-bay gelding. They hadn't even made it to where Fergus stood chewing his cud when Goliath put his head down and turned into a buckjumper.

Once the stockhorse finally settled, he and Bundy seemed united in their mission to find Jindy. The kelpie ran ahead, nose to the ground, as he tracked a scent along the trail that led from the river flats up to the clusters of smooth-trunked snow gums. For once Goliath was happy to follow.

When they'd passed through the paddock gate, Rowan checked his phone for the fifth time since leaving the coach house. Even though the signal was weak, Grace would still be able to call; the phone would just drop out before they would have much of a chance to talk. He looked down to slip his phone in his pocket when a bark from Bundy had him glance up. He was lucky Goliath was distracted as in that moment the last thing Rowan was focused on was staying in the saddle.

They'd found Jindy.

But the mare wasn't all they'd found.

Grace was riding her.

All he could do was stare as Grace gave him a smile and a wave. No wonder Aubrey had been so bossy about him staying. No wonder Clancy had asked him to find Jindy and not done so herself. They'd been in on the whole thing. Grace being at Ashcroft could only mean one thing. Bundilla, not the bright city lights, was where she wanted to be. The tension that had been brewing since his phone call with Aubrey dissolved. He didn't have to be captain of anything anymore. He could just be himself.

Goliath needed no encouragement to close the distance between him and Jindy. As they drew near, Rowan was glad to see Grace wore a riding helmet to protect her head. She also had on black jodhpurs that fitted like a second skin and a loose pink work shirt. When he reached her side, he didn't waste time with words, just leaned over to cup her face and kiss her. She melted into him.

An impatient stomp of Goliath's hard front hoof had Rowan lifting his head to search Grace's face for all the answers he was hoping for. He'd never seen her smile so joyful or her eyes such a soft green-gold. He slid from the saddle to reach for her. Her hands settled on his shoulders and before her feet touched the ground her mouth had found his.

This time it was Goliath's forceful nudge to Rowan's back that ended their kiss. Hand in hand, they led the horses over to a low snow gum branch to secure their reins. Rowan wanted no further interruptions. Bundy flopped in the shade as if to say he wasn't in any rush to go anywhere.

Rowan turned to Grace. She'd taken off her helmet and her dark hair fell loose down her back. He was again surrounded by the fragrance of honeysuckle.

He slipped his arms around her waist and pulled her close. 'I was coming to Sydney.'

'Aubrey told me … she always keeps such a cool head but she said she was panicking as she knew you wouldn't listen to anything she said. Clancy's plan if I got caught in traffic was to take your keys and blame them being missing on Monet and Primrose. Asking you to find Jindy was all her idea. Mine was to wait in the coach house.'

'Clancy and her romantic heart.'

Grace's lips curved before she lifted a hand to trace the line of his jaw. 'Rowan … I couldn't stay away any longer. Not talking to you, not seeing you, I felt so far away. I was also worried … especially when you went to the hut alone.'

'I'm sorry if I gave the impression that I needed time out. I just went to fix the chimney. My running from my feelings days are over.' He wrapped her fingers that toyed with the collar of his shirt in his and touched his mouth to the back of her hand. 'I love you, Grace. I have from that first afternoon. It's never been fake dates or a summer fling for me.'

'It never has been for me either.' Her palm pressed against his heart. 'This is where I belong, with you. I love you too, Rowan. You are my real world.'

He kissed her again to let her know she wasn't just his real world but his whole world too.

When they drew apart, she took his phone from out of his front pocket and checked the time with a sigh. 'As much as I'd love to stay exactly where we are, we have to get back. It's going to be a day for revelations. We have somewhere to be and someone to see. The final clue about the apartment has been there all along.'

CHAPTER
19

'You're not going to give me any hints?' Rowan asked with a grin as they drove through the front gate of Crookwell Park.

Grace's only answer was to smile and slide her fingers into the back of his tawny sun-bleached hair. She breathed in his fresh cedar scent. It had only been an hour since they'd spoken the truth to each other surrounded by the snow gums and mountains and she couldn't get enough of him.

As if privy to her thoughts, when they parked beside her car—she'd left Aubrey's at Ashcroft—Rowan turned to give her a tender kiss that stole her breath and promised a lifetime of such moments.

A loud bleat caused them both to smile and sit back in their seats. She'd said she needed to see the goats before they went where they had to go.

'I won't be long,' she said as she left to see how much Lavender and Rebel had grown.

On the way to the old stables, she looked over to where a blue tarpaulin covered the right corner of the mansion. Apart from the crumbled wall and the scarred hillside there was no sign of any landslip. Rowan had organised for the mud and debris to be removed and for an engineer to inspect the site. Once his report arrived she'd implement the recommendations to ensure the hillside never gave way again.

Her attention lingered on the end room where she'd been trapped. As for her, she felt no anxiety or residual trauma. She'd only just regained consciousness when Rowan had called so hadn't been lying there buried and alone with her fear for too long. When he'd taken the door off and she could see him through the gap between the table and the rubble, any feelings of claustrophobia had vanished. While they'd physically been separated, his care and concern and the way his focus had never wavered from her had given her the strength to stay calm and to wait until she was freed.

A chorus of goat bleats had her smile and walk faster. It was good to be home. Once she'd given all six goats enough pats and cuddles to make up for being away for a week, she returned to Rowan's ute.

'Okay, where to now?' he asked after she slid into her seat and he laced his fingers with hers.

'Our rendezvous point is where the boundary fence cuts the paddock in half.'

At Rowan's intrigued look, she laughed. 'No clues. There's still a chance I'm wrong about all of this.'

As they drove up the hill to where the paddock had been legally divided, she bit her lip until she was certain that the person they were supposed to meet was there.

A familiar gator was parked beside the burial plot.

'*Frank.*' Rowan glanced at her. 'I knew there was more to his story.'

They pulled up beside the small gate and walked into the cemetery to where Frank sat in a camp chair looking out over Crookwell Park. He'd brought somewhere to sit to take the weight off his bad leg as they were in for a long chat.

She kissed his lined cheek.

'I'm glad you're back,' he said, voice low and solemn.

'I am too.'

He nodded at Rowan who stood close by her side. 'And I'm glad you've finally put the past behind you.'

The warm weight of Rowan's arm settled around her waist.

Frank's attention returned to Grace. 'Before we start ... how did you put it all together?'

'Toy trains, rocking horses and the Pinocchios on the bookshelf in your living room.'

'You have the perfect brain for chess. It's our little secret that you only let Aubrey win because you know how much it means to her to always be in control.' He paused to wave his cane around the Russell family cemetery. 'Right, Rowan ... what do you see?'

Rowan barely turned his head. 'I finally see what I've been looking for. Over behind the closest headstone is a metal pole to which is attached a solar-powered CCTV camera that sits just above the top of the cross ... which means, Frank, this is your land and the boundary line goes straight through this burial plot.'

Grace turned to look at the cross. Sure enough, there was a camera where Rowan said it was. It was so small and well hidden she'd never noticed it. She'd just thought the rusted pole had been to support the aged sandstone.

'I can't wait to teach your little ones chess.' Frank dug into the front pocket of his shirt and took out a folded piece of paper. 'The camera only picks up from the bend in the driveway so that's why I never saw who left the goats.'

Frank handed the paper to Grace and she carefully opened the yellowed and fragile folds. She showed Rowan what appeared to be a hand-drawn map, except the faded drawing didn't only depict the boundary fence. She glanced at Frank who watched her, expression sombre.

She looked back at the map but it wasn't the off-centre boundary line drawn through the plot that carved off Lawrence Senior and Lawrence Junior's graves from the others that drew her focus. Instead it was the small neat squares, some labelled with ink and others in pencil, that showed where each grave was. There were more plots on the map than there were headstones on the hillside.

She glanced sideways to count the gravestones in the staggered rows beside her. Seven more to be exact. According to the hand-drawn plan, there were three graves on Frank's land on this side of Lawrence Senior's cross. Then down the hill, again on Frank's land, there were four graves next to Lawrence Russell Junior's final resting place. He hadn't been buried alone after all.

'The missing graves,' she whispered.

Frank slowly nodded. 'The two secret families were buried here but on the land that Lawrence Senior gave to the woman he loved who lived in my cottage. Even in death he and Lawrence Junior wanted to protect their own.'

Grace looked down and then up from the map. 'But ...'

Frank's face seemed to age. 'I know ... there are four graves beside Lawrence Junior and there only should be three. One is empty.'

When Rowan spoke, his quiet words told Grace he too had put most of the pieces together. 'Which means the missing child from the apartment didn't die and also that Lorraine was a little confused. Eduardo didn't have another sister, did he? He had a brother.'

Frank's gnarled hands clenched where they rested on his thighs as he stared at the mansion below.

Grace knelt beside him. 'I thought you may have once had a baby girl as you reacted to the photograph of the doll in the trunk, so when I saw the Pinocchios in your living room I wondered why you also had boys' toys. Then I remembered that Pinocchio was an Italian story and that there had been two toy trains in the trunk along with clothes that could have belonged to two boys if they had been the same size. Ned had been right; the rocking horses had been bought together. Frank … Eduardo wasn't just your brother, he was your twin, wasn't he?'

Frank took a moment to speak. 'He was. He and I chose the doll in the trunk from a catalogue for Helena. Except when she was born she never cried.'

Grace moved to take Frank's hand in hers.

Rowan clasped the older man's shoulder. 'Your name? Do you have an Italian one too?'

'Francesco. They shortened our names in hospital.'

'You and Eduardo both had polio?' She'd always thought Frank limped from his arthritis.

'Yes. Eduardo was able to go home but I wasn't. I don't know the whole story, I never will, but somehow my father believed I died. I can only guess that someone thought this had been the right thing to tell him, as for a long time they thought I wouldn't survive, let alone walk.' Frank rubbed at his brow. 'As I didn't have any proper paperwork to identify me, when I was moved to a new hospital it was assumed I'd been abandoned. There was a boy in the bed near mine. His father, a lawyer, would play chess with me and his mother read me books. When my friend died, they formally adopted me. I had a happy life even though I never forgot my real family.'

'Did you look for them?' Grace asked. Despite how hard it had been for Kathy to find any information, somehow Frank had discovered his origins.

'I did, but as you know there's no paper trail. About fifteen years ago a woman contacted me calling me by my birth name. She was my half-aunt, the baby in the pictures Taite found. My grandfather's second family, who lived in the cottage, would come to visit us in the apartment so I remembered her. As my body had never been returned to them, she never gave up hope I was still alive. I think she searched every hospital and every adoption record she could find.'

Grace smiled. 'She was the aunt who Ned restored the rocking horse for?'

Frank's expression softened. 'The golden one was mine and the grey one Eduardo's. I was always trying to ride the fastest.'

'Why didn't you come forward when Crookwell Park was for sale?' Rowan asked.

'I don't have any paperwork to prove who I am, even though a DNA test would, but there's no one really left to compare it to. Besides, I wouldn't ever want to live in the mansion again. It's like going to town. I still associate Bundilla with the people we needed to hide from.'

'Yet you kept watch over the house all these years,' Grace said gently.

'I did. While I can't face going inside, it's the only thing linking me to who I really am. Over the years I purchased whatever land had been sold off. Then when my half-aunt Clara passed away in the care residence we found near us in Canberra, she left me the cottage.' Frank smiled at Grace. 'I held on to the hope that one day someone would give this place another chance. Which is why I have a shed full of things you might like ... including the golden rocking horse and the ballroom chandelier.'

'So, *you* were the collector who made the previous owner an offer they couldn't refuse.'

Frank gave a chuckle.

She met Rowan's gaze and in his eyes she could read her own thoughts. Crookwell Park would have its second chance and the curse it had laboured under for generations would be lifted. No longer would couples be kept apart and their families be separated and hidden. The mansion would be a true home where children's laughter would echo, along with their footsteps, down the many hallways.

Frank looked between the two of them. 'Everything I've done has been worth it. You both are the future of Crookwell Park.'

Grace squeezed his hand and reached for Rowan's. 'No, Frank. We all are.'

EPILOGUE

A velvet darkness blanketed Crookwell Park's ballroom. Grace stood still and silent in the expectant hush.

Even though she couldn't see anyone, all around her were people she was lucky enough to call friends. She'd come to small-town Bundilla alone and grieving, only to be enfolded in the warm embrace of a tight-knit community. Close beside her she felt the brush of Rowan's arm against hers. The summer might be drawing to a close but the man she loved was never far from her side.

In this moment it also was as though her parents were with her, just as they had been on long-ago Christmases when the living room had been dark while she and her mother had waited until her father switched on the Christmas tree decorations.

In about another five seconds the ballroom too would be filled with light. She'd only had power connected to one part of the mansion but for now that was all she needed. The original chandelier

Frank had preserved in his shed had been reinstalled and tonight it would again shine like a thousand stars.

She took hold of Rowan's hand and his strength and love wrapped around her.

In true Aubrey style, her best friend started the countdown in a clear and strident voice before she pulled the cord to turn on the chandelier.

'Five, four, three, two, one!'

Brilliance flooded the room, followed by gasps.

Grace stared at the delicate prisms of glass that chased away every shadow in the room. The crystal chandelier was more beautiful than she could have imagined. It was as though Crookwell Park's soul had been returned. She glanced at Rowan and found him looking at her instead of the ceiling. He pressed a kiss to her temple.

Aubrey crossed the ballroom to where Frank sat in a comfortable wingback chair that he'd also had stashed in his shed. As he touched a handkerchief to his eyes, Aubrey put her arm around him. Grace's own eyes misted.

Frank now felt comfortable coming inside and his visits often unlocked precious memories such as of his father and grandfather playing chess in the billiards room and of his mother and father laughing and waltzing in the empty ballroom. The unmarked graves in the Russell burial plot would soon have headstones. On one of their now regular trips to town, she'd introduced Frank to Kathy and the three of them were looking into what could be done to put crosses on the other unmarked graves in the Bundilla cemetery.

Grace's attention lingered on Aubrey. For a city girl who liked her comforts, she was becoming a regular visitor. After seeing Rowan on Goliath mustering cattle, she'd now taken to calling him Grace's cattleman. Even though Aubrey had never taken up Trent's offer of a local tour, Grace hoped one day she would.

She hid a smile as she glanced at the quilting ladies who were standing near the long table laden with an array of desserts. Every so often they'd look across at Aubrey and then bend their heads to whisper together. Millicent and Beatrice were also over near the table where they were talking to Mabel. Grace was yet to attend book club but when she did she'd made a mental note to take Brenna's advice to never say that any story sucked.

From the corner of her eye, she glimpsed Taite make a hasty retreat through the French doors. Earlier everyone had congregated on the side veranda for a barbeque and he'd be either getting another beer from the esky or heading for his ute to make a getaway. Rowan exchanged a look with Heath before Heath followed the deer farmer outside. Grace had her fingers crossed that Taite, like Brenna, who stood on the far side of the room laughing with Clancy, would one day be off the quilting group's matchmaking hit list.

Rowan's thumb brushed across her hand in a silent message before he too left via the French doors. On his way past the dessert table he swiped a slice of vanilla cake. Bundy trotted behind him, knowing full well the treat would be for him. She'd moved out of Possum Cottage and into the coach house and Bundy so far had stayed with them. But the time would come when he'd leave to bring joy to someone else's lives. When he did there'd be a Bundy-sized hole left to fill. Frank had offered Rowan the use of his land for his cattle which provided even more of a reason for Rowan to look for a kelpie of his own.

While Rowan would be busy with his Herefords and rebuilding the damaged mansion corner, she would continue to restore Crookwell Park. The plan was for them to move in by next summer.

She'd sold her inner-city apartment and her colleague who was running her interior styling business had made an offer to buy it, which she would accept. Once Crookwell Park no longer consumed all her time, she'd start a new styling business. This one would be online and involve sourcing bespoke and special items so she would be able to stay in the mountains as much as possible.

She swapped smiles with Aubrey before she walked out to the grapevine-covered pergola. Her best friend knew what she and Rowan were doing. After she collected a small patchwork bag she'd left on an outdoor chair in the cobblestone walkway, she joined Rowan in the courtyard. He'd run an extension cord from the ballroom and fairy lights lit up the rectangular space that was the heart of Crookwell Park.

Thanks to Taite's ornate walkway gates, the espalier pear and apple that she'd planted in memory of her parents were safe from any plundering goats. Rebel was fast living up to her name. Around each tree, Rowan had used bluestone to make two large beds in which colour would bloom all year round.

Heart full, Grace walked to stand in front of the first garden bed and from the cloth bag took out a small urn that held the last of her parents' ashes. Rowan came over to tuck her by his side. Her journey to find peace had led her here, to this small mountain town, to this house and to this man. She looked up at the night sky and the stars that were as bright as the chandelier inside. She was home and it was time her parents were as well.

ACKNOWLEDGEMENTS

In a year of lockdowns and limited contact I am ever more grateful for the hardworking and lovely HarperCollins team of Rachael Donovan, Julia Knapman and Annabel Adair for keeping the publishing wheels turning. A heartfelt thanks to my wonderful writing buddies who were always at the end of an email. Thank you to my four not-so-little children for all the things you continue to do to inspire me and as always thank you to my rock, Luke.

Special thanks to each and every one of my readers as your year too would have been far from normal. Thank you for reading my books, for revisiting my small Snowy Mountains town and for asking for more stories. Taite's book will be the next Bundilla story published and until we catch up again, take care and stay safe and well.

Other books by

ALISSA CALLEN

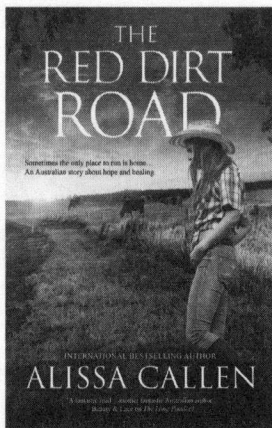

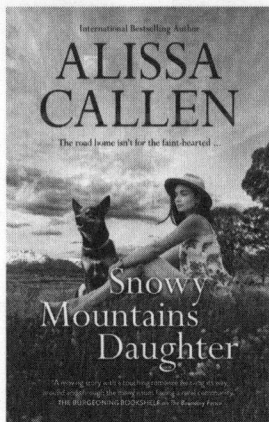

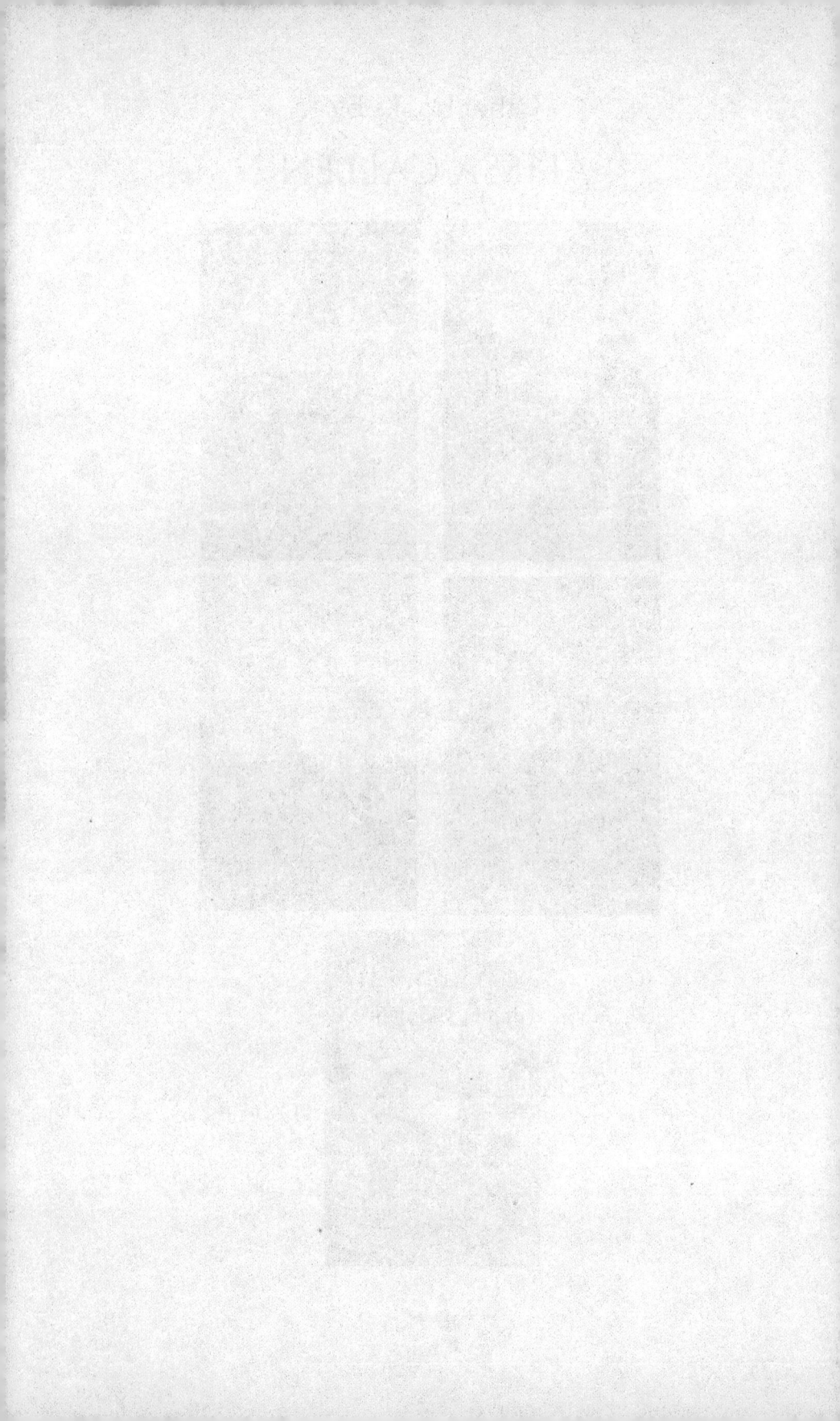

talk about it

Let's talk about books.

Join the conversation:

facebook.com/romanceanz

@romanceanz

romance.com.au

If you love reading and want to know about our
authors and titles, then let's talk about it.